Thandi's Love

By.

Angel Strong

D1520872

This is a work of fiction. All names, characters, places, and events are the work of the author's imagination. Any resemblance to real person, places, or events is coincidental.

Thandi's Love
Copyright © Angel Strong 2012
Publisher: Angel Strong
ISBN-10: 1542693772
ISBN-13: 978-1542693776

DEDICATION

For my mother Tommie Lee Strong, and in loving memory of my aunts and uncles, Cora Lee, Odessa, Daisy, Eddie, Johnny, and Vincent.

Also, a special dedication to my children, Joyous, Raymond, Ray'var, Jordan, Jamaria, and Jade.

And to my siblings, Jean (Kissey), Oshun (Nicole), Victor, Merranda, Karimah, and Star (the baby) – love you Berkys!

And finally, to all of my family within The Eastern Pequot Tribal Nation- may the Creator continue to bestow upon us his many blessings – Aho.

"True love is wild. It is boundless. It screams with a silent voice that can't be quelled." – Haiti Boran

CONTENTS

Chapter 1

Newport, South Carolina – 1838

Tom Lexington smiled at the luminous morning sun as it slowly rose above a cloak of parting clouds. He had waited for this day with great anticipation. Today was the day he'd begun the harvest and, more importantly, today was the day he would see his dear childhood friends again. He smiled widely at the thought of Isaac and Thandi.

The two were like siblings to him as a child, and he had never forgotten them. The years they shared together were forever etched in his mind and heart, and even now, they remained the happiest of his life.

He looked on as the field hands went out to the cotton fields. *Today will be a bright day!* He thought to himself. His eyes sparkled with enthusiasm he hadn't felt in a very long time.

Shoving his hands into his work trousers, he leaned in the doorway and proudly marveled at the vast sea of white. This year's crops were certainly the best he'd seen in many years.

After suffering three brutal dry seasons, Tom had nearly forgotten how gratifying it felt to reap such a bountiful harvest. Now, after much suffering, it appeared that God had finally begun to smile upon the Lexington plantation again. A sudden morning breeze swept through the gardens, filling the still warm autumn air with its sweet perfume. Tom shut his eyes and inhaled deeply.

"Morning, boss!" Ben chimed as he walked down the winding pathway alongside the house. Tom opened his eyes and grinned at him.

"Yes, it is, my friend," He said.

"We're sure goanna need that help you sent for," Ben added with a strong, matter-of-fact tone. He shook his head disbelievingly as he looked out at the thick, white fields. Like Tom, he too was astonished by the year's yield. He hadn't once seen a crop of this magnitude in his time there. Or ever, in fact.

Tom turned his gaze back to the cotton. "Yes indeed."

Ben adjusted the burlap bags and the swing blade he carried on his arm. "Well, see you out there, boss," He said. With a tip of his hat and

1

a departing smile, he started out for the fields when, all of a sudden, the sound of oncoming wagons stopped him mid-stride.

Tom shielded his eyes from the blinding sun and peered out into the hazy distance. Before long, two wagons appeared far off on the trail. Soon after, he could see a third and then a fourth!

He raised a puzzled brow. *Could it be?* He wondered, hope causing him to smile. He stepped outside onto the open veranda to get a better look.

"Is that them, boss?" Ben asked, his gaze locked on the wagons.

Tom nodded, his smile growing bigger by the second. "I do believe so," He said with a note of zeal in his voice.

He hadn't expected his old friends and the extra laborers until later that evening, or even nightfall. If this was really the extra help coming towards them, their early arrival would be most welcome.

Like many of the other cotton farmers in Charleston, Tom had sold off many of his slaves in the devastating aftermath of the past three years of droughts. Now, the cotton crop was very large and he desperately needed the harvest help that his aunt promised she would provide.

Stepping forward, Tom strained his eyes as he struggled to make out the distant figures in the first approaching wagon.

"That's got to be them," Ben insisted. "You want me to wait a bit, boss?"

Tom set a hand on the porch's banister and looked out at the wagon intensely. The wagons had now reached the path leading to the plantation.

"Yes, I suppose I'll need your help, Big Ben," He said, smiling down at him.

Ben grinned widely, showing off his toothy, white smile and deep dimples. Tom had given him that nickname years earlier, and rightfully so. The large Negro appeared almost menacing at six-foot-seven and he was as strong and solid as an ox.

Tom had purchased him for a very reasonable price just two years earlier at a trader's market in Glen. The seller had boasted that Ben could do the work of five men, and that he was a skilled craftsman. He also claimed that, despite his foreboding exterior, Ben was as gentle as a lamb. He strongly conveyed his reluctance to sell such a fine worker, but like most farmers at that time, he had been forced to sell off slaves as a result of the merciless droughts.

All that the seller had said about Ben proved true and made the gentle giant a fast favorite of Tom's. He became a much loved counterpart to Tom's other field hands. In no time, Tom had appointed him overseer.

Initially, Ben had expected Tom would be like his masters before him, wicked and malicious men who regarded their slaves as soulless stock. But to his surprise, Tom had proven to be far different. Though he was stern and meticulous about business matters, he treated his slaves with dignity and respect. As the droughts prolonged, there came the time when Tom himself had been forced to sell slaves. He refused to even consider selling away his right-hand man. Ben had even accompanied him at market. Ben often reflected on Tom's solemn state after each auction; it was like Tom was selling members of his large family.

In truth, Tom had felt as though he'd betrayed his slaves by handing them over to the wolves in his temporary moment of crisis. But with little cotton to yield and so many slaves to house, he found it increasingly difficult to keep them all properly fed.

It had taken some time for him to get over it, and even now, he hadn't fully.

"Your people here early?" His wife, Anna, asked in a smooth, but condescending, southern belle tone.

Tom turned to face her as she stood inside, looking out at him from behind the door screen. After nodding in acknowledgment of her presence, he focused his attention again to the oncoming wagons.

Anna glanced up at the bright sun. The day had only just begun and already the sun was blaring. She shielded her eyes with both hands and stepped out onto the grand porch.

"By God! Can't believe it's fall at all!" She complained, fanning herself with a cream colored glove. Tom wore gloves, too, but his were for working. She, his darling wife, never even got close to the dirt in the fields.

Ben tipped his hat and nodded immediately in polite recognition of his master's wife. "Morning, Missus." He smiled nervously.

Anna returned his greeting with her usual cold, dismissive look. She tossed a batch of wayward, fiery red curls behind her back and joined Tom on the veranda.

His immediate reaction to her company appeared less than pleasant. He sighed heavily as if her company was unwanted, and the dismal look

3

he gave her was far from inviting. She smiled back at him coyly with piercing gray eyes, capturing his gaze for a lingering moment. Without question, she was a very beautiful woman, but the foulness within her profoundly diminished her outward beauty.

Tom's joy returned, along with his smile, as the first wagon thundered through the plantation's open gates.

Ben removed his blade and satchels from his shoulders with haste. "Hold!" He yelled as he threw up a yielding hand and walked towards the oncoming carriage. The wagon slowed at Ben's command, then came to a halt on the cobblestone path facing the mansion. Almost immediately, Tom recognized the passenger sitting alongside the carriage driver.

"Isaac!" He called out to him.

A light skinned Negro peered back at him curiously for a moment, then smiled.

"Tom!" He shouted back in delight. With arms wide open, Tom descended the porch's stairs.

Isaac jumped down from the carriage and the two men embraced like long-lost brothers. After a hearty hug and several pats on the back, they stood marveling at one another.

"By God, it's been too long!" Tom beamed. He looked Isaac over again. "You've shot up like a bean stalk!"

Isaac chuckled. He could hardly believe his eyes, either. Tom was no longer as he remembered. The scrawny, baby faced boy of yesteryear had transformed into a fine, full grown man. "No, look at you!" Isaac replied in a surprising and unfamiliar baritone.

Tom laughed heartily at the deep, manly bass in his voice. The young Isaac he remembered sounded far different. Though he still resembled his past self, Isaac had transformed dramatically. The once short and stubby, smooth faced boy was now colossal in height and structure with a mustache and beard to boot!

The second wagon pulled in behind, and the others soon followed suit. Both Tom and Isaac turned their attention to the settling wagons. Tom's blue eyes widened. Two open wagons were chocked full of manpower from his aunt's plantation. He and his aunt had discussed her lending him a few hands, but this was far more than he had expected. He looked on as the slaves began to disembark at Ben's instruction. His chest swelled with pure elation at the glorious sight of so many.

Aunt Lacy has sent a bloody cavalry, he thought, impressed.

"More than you expected, huh?" Isaac said, reading Tom's expression.

"More indeed!" Tom affirmed with a laugh.

Suddenly, the coverings of the second wagon lifted and a stunningly beautiful young woman emerged. For a moment, the day stood still and all else faded for Tom but her. He stood numb as the captivating vision walked right up to him.

"Tom." She smiled.

For a few minutes, he stood speechless, mesmerized by the green-eyed beauty before him. There was a certain familiarity about her eyes. Even if nothing else had been the same, he would know her anywhere by her eyes.

"Tom, you *do* remember Thandi, don't you?" Isaac teased.

Thandi smirked at Tom's shocked expression.

He gave Isaac an embarrassed, bug-eyed look, then turned to Thandi again. He shook his head in amazement and smiled.

"No way!" He said, half jesting, half serious.

Isaac's transformation had taken him by surprise, but Thandi's completely blew him away.

The former tomboy, pig-tailed girl from his childhood had surprisingly morphed into a beautiful goddess. Tom reached in for a hug and she embraced him warmly.

As he held her, she noticed the glaring expression of a white woman standing on the porch behind them. The bright smile on Thandi's face quickly fell away and she instinctively released herself from Tom's embrace.

Following her sudden sober gaze, Tom looked over his shoulder.

Anna forced a phony smile at them, but not before he noticed the stony glare she had been giving Thandi. Picking up her skirts, she stepped down from the porch and went to her husband's side. He shot her a scathing look, which she casually pretended not to notice. Instead, she kept her eyes and attention on the fetching young girl before him. Finally, forcing her eyes from Thandi after a few cold moments, she glanced at all the others who'd accompanied her.

"My, oh, my!" She exclaimed breathily. Touching a gloved hand to her breast, she looked around at the many strange, dark faces. "My husband said we'd get a few extra slaves, but I didn't expect a small nigger army!" She declared with a smile as her gaze fell upon Thandi.

Tom's jawline clenched with anger at the use of that demeaning word, but he quickly decided to keep his head. He knew that getting a rise out of him was just what his wife had wanted, and he wouldn't give her the pleasure of spoiling his joyous moment.

"Please forgive my wife's severe lack of manners," He said. "She has a frightful sense of humor.

Thandi, Isaac, this is my wife, Anna. Anna, these are my dear friends I told you of, Thandi and Isaac." Thandi took note of the slight flare of his wife's nostrils and the evil look she gave him. She looked down her little nose at them as though they were ants that needed to be squashed.

As Thandi's eyes again met with Anna's, she gave the Madame of the house a respectful half curtsy and smile, despite the obvious shot she'd taken at them.

"Nice to meet you, Ma'am," Isaac said politely with a courteous nod and tilt of his straw hat.

Like with Ben, their warm regard was unreturned. Instead, Anna twisted her ruby red lips and looked back at the pair as if they were lepers. The obvious disdain in her expression made it grossly clear that she had no desire to make their acquaintance.

An awkward silence filled the air.

Feeling the tension, Ben thought that it was a good time to intersect with his questions. He stepped up from alongside the wagon and spoke. "Boss, you want me to show them to their quarters now?" He asked. He glanced around at the groups of slaves standing about the wagons, then at Tom again.

"Yes, Ben," Tom answered. "But not before I've introduced you." He gestured a hand for him to join them.

Ben hesitated for a breath, then walked over. He'd always felt uneasy in close company of the Missus. Unlike Tom, she didn't care for his kind, and she made sure they knew it any and every way she could.

Tom gestured a hand towards his childhood friends. "Ben, these are my friends, Isaac and Thandi. Thandi, Isaac, this is my overseer and right- hand man, Big Ben."

The two men locked eyes and shook hands. Ben then turned his attention to the smiling beauty standing at Isaac's side. Thoroughly entranced, he stared at her for a long moment before speaking.

"Nice... nice to meet you, Miss," He finally stammered.

Thandi took his extended hand and gave it a hearty shake. "And you," She replied, gently pulling her hand from his lingering grip.

"These are the two I've talked so much about," Tom continued.

His words fell on deaf ears as Ben stood in some sort of momentary fog. Never in the big man's life had he seen a woman so beautiful, colored *or* white and he wasn't altogether sure which one of the two she was.

Seeing a repeat of his own earlier dilemma, Tom grinned. Placing a guiding hand on Ben's shoulder, he brought him down from the stars and back to Earth again. Cured from his daze, Ben turned at his touch.

"You two will stay in the house," Tom continued. "I believe Esther's prepared your rooms by now."

Anna's porcelain face grew pink at the notion. She sucked in a deep calming breath of air, then she put on another pretentious smile. "Darling, we never discussed them staying in the house," She said.

The thick tension and subtle prejudice of before quickly filled the air again.

Isaac and Thandi looked at each other as if it suddenly became crystal clear to them that their presence wasn't entirely welcomed there.

Tom looked Anna hard in her steely gray eyes. "There was no need to discuss it," He said flatly. The harsh tone of his voice and piercing glare he gave Anna made her flush white again in anger. She flexed her long fingers and then balled both of her hands into little fists.

Thandi swallowed back the developing knot in her throat. Tom must have seen her expression, for he smiled at her reassuringly, and placed his hand on her shoulder. "Just lead me to your luggage. I'll help you two get settled in," He calmly told her.

Thandi hesitated for a beat. After what she'd just witnessed, she didn't exactly feel comfortable with the idea of lodging in the manor during their stay. She gave Isaac a quick, concerned glance and then showed Tom to her things.

Anna stood silent and clearly livid. Happy to be free of the awkward moment, Ben tilted his hat's brim to Isaac and the new miss, then hastily resumed his previous task.

Isaac quickly followed their lead, leaving Anna standing all alone and thoroughly incensed. She watched for a while as Tom gaily went about his business, as if she and what she wanted or didn't want mattered not in the slightest to him.

This isn't over… not by far, she thought, un balling and balling her fists. She quickly turned on a proud heel and stormed back up the stairs and into the house.

Esther could tell by her mistress's furious expression and haste that something was seriously wrong. Something had gotten her infuriated. The house slave's big eyes followed the fiery, fuming trail as Anna stalked through the room.

Something to do with Master Lexington, no doubt, she quickly surmised.

The inquiring maid quickly walked to the open door and looked out its screen. She was surprised to see the wagons and the many unknown Negro men and women. They were unloading bags and what looked like tools of some kind.

One of the porch's marble columns obstructed her view of Tom. She caught a glimpse of him here and there as he poked in and out of view. She could see he was smiling, then bending over; down and up again.

Her looming curiosity willed her outside for a better look. As she reached the porch's front, her short, round frame slowed and then froze at the sight of the awfully pretty, young woman in her master's company.

She peered closer at the mysterious girl, stepping forward to get a better look. As she did so, the sound of the old creaking porch grabbed Tom's attention and he looked up.

"There you are!" He called out to Esther. He said something to the girl and she smiled delightedly. The two gathered a few bags and headed towards the porch.

Tom flashed Esther his brilliant white smile as he breezed right past her and into the house. The beautiful young girl followed close behind him.

Esther quickly stepped inside as well, anxious to see more of her.

Tom dropped the large burlap bag he carried onto the floor of the entryway and the girl carefully did the same. He took a swipe at the forming sweat on his brows, then looked into the stunned face of his head maid.

"Esther, this is Thandi," He said in a slightly winded voice. "Thandi, this is Esther, the *true* lady of this house." His eyes sparkled along with the joke.

Esther grinned and Thandi smiled at the hearty woman's blushing face, then extended her dainty hand.

Esther giggled. It always tickled her when he said that.

"Nice to meet you," Thandi said.

Esther paused for a breath before taking Thandi's hand. The odd color of the girl's eyes temporarily distracted her. "Nice to meet you, too," She said, nodding slowly.

Suddenly, the bustling sound of Isaac coming inside shifted the room's attention.

Esther quickly straightened her skirts and kerchief at the sight of the handsome young Negro. He walked up and stood next to the pretty young girl.

"Esther, this is Isaac, Thandi's brother and my dear old friend," Tom introduced.

Isaac looked into the large brown eyes of the woman before him. "Hello," He nodded and smiled, revealing a perfect set of straight white teeth.

The plump maid bashfully blushed at his polite greeting, then smiled up into Isaac's deep brown eyes. "Nice to meet you. I've heard a lot about you," She sputtered shyly.

Thandi's lips quirked into a little smile. The school girl reaction Esther had toward her brother was unsurprising. Her brother's good looks and gentlemanly ways had always had that effect on women. Thandi never got tired of the reactions to him, though.

"All good, I hope," Isaac teased. His voice was a smooth bass and seemed to make Esther even more likely to swoon if he wasn't careful.

Esther nodded repetitively as she spoke. "Yes. All good."

Isaac adjusted the bags on his shoulder and turned to Tom. "Where should I put this?" He asked.

Tom looked at Esther. "Have you finished their rooms?" He asked.

"Yes, Sir …I've had them fixed up since yesterday; just have to put in some clean towels, is all."

"And *that's* why she's the operator of this place," Tom said. He gave Esther a little smirk and she smiled wide. Grabbing both bags from the floor, he looked to her to lead the way as he stepped aside, making way for her, then he and the others followed her down the long hall.

Surprisingly, Thandi could hardly keep up with the plump woman's pace. Both Tom and Ben struggled some distance behind with the heavy bags. Flashes of various oil paintings that adorned either side of the pale blue walls flickered by as they walked.

From what she had seen thus far, much had changed about the old plantation since her stay there. She'd first noticed the astonishing change in the manor's former façade. It had once been an awful shade of dull, weathered white, but now it boasted a most brilliant shade of dark gray. And then there were the missing slave quarters. They had once sat just opposite the manor. She made a mental note to take a look at the paintings later.

Esther slowed her stride, then stopped at a door near the hall's end. She paused for a breath before entering, allowing Thandi a brief moment to catch up. Thandi remembered the room almost immediately.

The rich, red sandalwood door boasted a silver lion's head handle and was the only like of its kind in the whole mansion. She remembered it particularly because of its story, told to her by Tom himself when they were children.

He told her that when his father, Tom Lexington, Sr., was just a boy, he and his family suffered a tragic house fire. Many slaves perished in the fire, along with Tom's grandparents. He never had the chance to meet them. His father and aunt were saved by some of their slaves. This door, and few family heirlooms, were said to be the only things that remained of his family's old mansion. Tom's father told him that he'd kept the door until he had acquired his own plantation.

Esther turned the handle and Thandi followed her inside the room, leaving the door ajar for the oncoming men.

"This will be your room, I suppose," Esther stated.

Thandi smiled with satisfaction as her eyes examined the quaint space around her. New furnishings and décor had changed the room dramatically since she had last seen it as a child.

A large mahogany four poster bed centered the spacious chamber. It had crimson and gold bedding. Long gold velvet drapes covered the tall windows. Like the hall, several oil paintings hung alongside each other on either side of the wall; portraits of family ancestors, no doubt.

The old mustard-hued walls were newly papered in a lively floral print. A beautiful tapestry of the Lexington coat-of-arms hung above the room's fireplace. Thandi was so enthralled with the room's décor that she hardly noticed Tom and Isaac's entrance.

Her eyes lit up with further curiosity when they fell on a door she didn't remember. There didn't used to be another door in the room except for the closet. She was fairly certain of that.

She turned around to question Esther about it, and found the maid's probing eyes already on her, as if she had been staring at her from behind the whole time. She swiftly dismissed the vague feeling of unease it gave her. "Where does that door lead to?" She asked, pointing a finger at the unfamiliar entry.

"That's the bath," Esther answered at once. She promptly walked over and opened the door, looking back over her shoulder at Thandi. "It's..."

"Which room is Isaac's?" Tom asked, interrupting Esther's words. Thandi had briefly forgotten he and Isaac were there.

She turned her attention to them. She could tell the bags Tom carried were particularly heavy by the way he struggled to keep them up on his shoulder. She now regretted bringing all the extra dresses she had packed. But, with the prospect of possibly staying on for a full harvest, she hadn't been certain of how much attire she should bring.

Without surprise, her burly brother handled his load with ease.

"The room down the hall from the sewing room, Sir," Esther answered. "The one with the painting of your aunt."

Tom nodded knowingly, then set the bags on the bench at the foot of Thandi's bed. He shot the two women a smile, then both he and Isaac headed out the door towards the other bedroom.

Esther picked up where she had left off. "It's new. Master's father had this addition put on years ago," She explained.

Thandi briskly walked across the room's hardwood floor. Her ruffled skirt swayed and swooshed side to side in her eager rush. Though she'd been more than comfortable with her quaint maid's quarters back at home, it paled in comparison to this elegant apartment. She walked through the open door to the bath, then stopped abruptly in her tracks. Her eyes widened with astonishment. Slowly, she took in all the bathroom's charms.

The large bath's posh interior consisted of a sizable porcelain tub, marble vanity, wash basin, plush towels, and shelving containing various toiletries.

"It sure is stuffy in here," Esther complained.

If it was, Thandi hadn't noticed. Everything about the room seemed perfect to her.

As Esther opened the large bay windows, the dim room filled with light and a lovely warm breeze. Along with it came the intoxicating scents of the garden.

Thandi inhaled the pleasant aroma deeply. "What is that delightful smell?" She asked. Her sleek brows furrowed inquisitively above her wide eyes.

"That's the garden," Esther replied. She turned her large frame inside the window and stared out.

Thandi's eyes lifted up and over Esther's broad shoulders. Her face widened with a grin. The sight was absolutely breathtaking. Thoroughly intrigued, she stepped up and stood at Esther's side.

Hundreds of colorful rows of flowers, trees and plants circled in intricate designs over what used to be two acres of wild flowers and barren land. Her eyes then darted to what appeared to be a white gazebo standing off in the hazy distance near the garden's end. She looked past the vivid garden and the short line of oaks that followed to six or more ambiguous white structures.

"And that there, what is it?" She asked, pointing a finger at the obscure buildings.

"That is the slaves' quarters. Master Lexington's father built it shortly after I came on. Did this bathroom, too. And even put a closet in my room in the attic," Esther said with pride.

Her ending statement reminded Thandi of something.

Only one of the four servants' rooms in the attic lacked a closet. It had once been the room of her late mother. Three other quarters occupied the attic; two of which had once been hers and Isaac's. Master Lexington, Sr. had given her mother exclusive use of the attic's apartments so she could keep her children close while seeing to the operations of the house without distraction or worry.

Thandi stopped her thoughts as she felt an oncoming case of melancholy. "This place has changed so much," She said, smiling thinly.

Esther nodded agreeably, for many of the renovations had been made during her time there. "Master Lexington told me lots of stories about you and your brother," She said.

Thandi's smile returned and her eyes lit again. She wondered exactly what stories he'd told. "We were such misfits back then," She replied.

She shook her head from side to side in remembrance. Hollis Creek had been the primary site of all their wrong doings. She suddenly wondered if it still existed. She turned to Esther. "Do you know of Hollis Creek?"

Esther nodded. "We ride by it all the time when we go into town, Master and me... or me and Ben."

Thandi felt a small measure of relief. With so many changes, she was pleased to hear that the place of which she had so many fond memories was still present. She had thought of Hollis Creek and all the memories created there more than anything else over the past years. So had Isaac.

She could see Esther staring again from the corner of her eye and she smiled inwardly. The curious maid's staring didn't make her feel uncomfortable anymore; by now she had gotten used to it. She imagined there must not be many Negro's that looked like her, because people always gave her a second glance, whites and blacks alike.

Esther informed her about when breakfast would be ready, then left her alone to get settled.

Chapter 2

After a soothing warm bath, Thandi felt refreshed. The trip from Dawson had been long and particularly grueling. She smiled at her reflection in the vanity's mirror. Though her skin was lighter, her eyes colored, and her hair "different," She still strongly resembled her beautiful mother. And even more so now as she stood at the mirror in her mother's old servant gown.

Instinctively, she lifted the skirts of the modest blue frock in search of her mother's initials. Haiti had marked all of her clothing with her personal monogram. Almost instantly, Thandi found it on the dress's hem.

She traced a loving finger across the small, white, stitched letters ...H. B. "Haiti Boran," She whispered. A slight smile creased the corners of her mouth as she envisioned her mother's face smiling back at her.

"Ms. Thandi?" Esther called from outside the bathroom door.

Thandi looked up at the sound of her voice. She dropped her skirts and straightened herself in the mirror. "Come in."

Esther entered, stopping just inside the doorway. "Master Lexington wants you to know that you'll be having breakfast with him and your brother in the kitchen," She told Thandi. "And, uh, the Missus won't be joining you. She's got a headache."

The last part of her statement sounded unconvincing. Thandi's thoughts went to Tom's wife. After just witnessing the woman's horrid behavior, Thandi seriously doubted that it was a headache that ailed her. Still, not having to sit at breakfast with Mrs. Lexington was a good thing.

"I need only to braid my hair," Thandi replied with a smile. She turned to the mirror and pulled the mass of lengthy, wet tresses behind her shoulders. Oddly, Esther lingered in the doorway, peering back at her.

"I can help you with it," She offered.

Thandi turned to graciously decline, but after seeing Esther's big anxious eyes and earnest smile, she accepted. The eager maid quickly shut the door, then hurried over and stood behind her. Thandi gave her a caring smile as their eyes met in the mirror as Thandi passed her the hair brush over her shoulder.

Esther readily began to brush the long wavy locks from root to end. The flowing mass felt like satin to her rough hands. She parted the hair into three sections with her fingertips, then slowly began to fashion a single braid.

For a while, there was silence. Then, suddenly, Esther paused her braiding and looked at Thandi in the mirror.

"You've sure got some pretty hair, Ms. Thandi," She said. "And pretty eyes, too."

Thandi looked up at the curious woman's reflection and returned her compliment with a warm smile and a "thank you."

Esther cleared her throat and Thandi knew that more would follow.

"You must have some white folk up in you," Esther blurted with a slight chuckle.

Though she wasn't at all surprised, Thandi hadn't expected this line of inquisition so early. She hadn't been back at the manor an hour and already her lineage was being questioned.

She let out a small sigh, then said what she always said when asked. "I was fathered by a white laborer."

Her eyes met Esther's again in the mirror. The maid swallowed back the nervous lump in her throat and smiled thinly. She hoped she hadn't offended the young girl by letting her curiosity get the best of her. It was just that she had never seen anyone like her before, and she had seen more than her share of mulatto's over her forty-two years.

Reaching over, she took a blue ribbon from the vanity stand, then wrapped it tightly around the tip of the completed plait. "All done," She said, smiling into the mirror.

Thandi turned her head from side to side, examining the finished braid. "Thank you, it's perfect," She said, smiling up at Esther's reflection.

Esther grinned back at her, stepping away from the vanity. "Well, you remember where the kitchen is, don't you?" She asked.

Thandi pondered for a second, recalling its whereabouts. "Yes, I believe so."

"Good," Esther said. "I'll be serving in just a few minutes."

"I'll be right behind you," Thandi replied, smiling and continuing

15

to preen herself a bit. It had been a long time since she had sat down for a meal with Tom, and she wanted to look her best.

The smell of sizzling ham filled the halls as Thandi made her way to the kitchen. She stopped for a moment and eyed the oil paintings she had seen earlier. There were at least a dozen self portraits in various sizes, colors, and poses, none of which she remembered seeing before. Her eyes slowly roamed the faces of portrait after portrait. Suddenly, her gaze froze on a depiction hanging at the center of the long wall. She remembered this painting so well.

It was a likeness of Tom's father, and it once hung in the parlor above the fireplace. She could not forget this painting. A similar one currently hung in the hall of her Missus' mansion. Pleased to at last see something from her childhood, she walked up to it.

The portrait was four feet tall and three feet wide, and it showed the regal face of Thomas Lexington, Sr. standing with one elbow leaning against his office chair, his expression stoic and green eyes stern. The skilled artist had captured his likeness in marvelous detail. Even the long scar Lexington, Sr. received from a riding accident was clearly depicted beneath his left eye.

Thandi's thoughts went to that time. Though she had been no more than ten or eleven years old at the time, she could still remember the events of that tragic day as if they had happened just yesterday. The house was all a fuss after Master Lexington, Sr. suffered a fall from his horse, which left him with several broken ribs, a broken leg, and that awful scar. *It was also the day Tom went away*, she recalled.

"Here you are," Tom said from behind her.

Thandi turned in surprise and smiled. "Forgive me, I just had to see this," She apologized, slightly embarrassed for lingering so long. She glanced at the portrait then looked to Tom again.

His eyes went to his father's painting. "Do you remember it?" He asked.

"Why, yes, of course!" Thandi beamed up at him. "If I recall correctly, it used to hang in the parlor above that huge fireplace."

Tom's face lit up with delight at her accurate memory. He suddenly wondered what other memories she held, and what Isaac could remember, too. "Come along, we can catch up over breakfast," He said, extending an arm for her.

She accompanied him through the hall and into the blinding bright-ness of the sunny kitchen. Instantly, she shielded her eyes from the sun's rays with her hand. As they slowly adjusted, she peered around the room. The large kitchen had always been full of light due to its line of eight windows facing the sun, and the wall's luminous yellow paint. Other than the furnishings and a long hanging pot rack, nothing had changed.

She wasn't at all surprised, for Tom's father had loved the sun-ny space more than any other room in the mansion. He had given the former Mrs. full reign over the manor's décor and fully faulted her for its "overly embellished and cheerless nature." Unlike the other heavily draped and dreary colored rooms in the eleven room mansion, the kitch-en was, in his words "bright and lively."

He took most of his meals and paper there; in the company of his servants.

Isaac stood up promptly from the kitchen table and pulled out a chair for his sister.

"The food smells wonderful," Thandi declared. She hadn't had a home cooked meal in four days. The ham's pungent smell reminded her of how hungry she was. She smiled back at her polite brother, then sat down in his offered chair.

Tom seated himself just opposite the siblings.

"Thank you," Esther said, flattered. She placed a platter of steaming sliced ham at the table's center. A younger maid, a dark, frail girl, de-livered scrambled eggs and scones with fresh fruit preserves and cream.

Thandi caught the young girl's eyes on her and smiled. The doe-eyed girl smirked back at her, then quickly looked away. She went to the side buffet and got a crystal pitcher of orange juice while Esther brought over hot coffee.

"This is Esther's daughter, Myra," Tom informed Thandi and Isaac.

Myra paused from filling their glasses and gave the pair a smile and polite, acknowledging nod.

"He... Hello," She stuttered meekly.

Thandi could see the resemblance between the mother and daugh-ter. They shared the same large brown eyes and button noses.

After the brief introduction, Esther gave her daughter a tug on her gown sleeve and the two left the room. Isaac helped himself to three slices of ham, three large helpings of eggs, two scones and a tall glass of

17

orange juice. Thandi giggled as he began to shamelessly scarf down the hearty breakfast. Tom followed her gaze to Isaac's full-of-food face. He was fully engaged in what he was doing and unaware of the two staring.

Tom burst out with laughter, causing Isaac to look up in surprise with his mouth half open and jam-packed with eggs. The funny sight of his stuffed cheeks and wide eyes nearly made Thandi loose her eggs as she burst into laughter as well. "Hungry?" Tom teased.

None the wiser, Isaac's thick brows furrowed as he swallowed down another gulp of his orange juice. He stared at the laughing pair for a long moment before it finally hit him. "Forgive me," He said with a chuckle. "I'm absolutely starved."

Though Thandi had managed to keep her manners, she knew all too well how hungry he must have been. The provisions they had packed only lasted for two of the four-day long trip. With only bread and a little water for the past two days, Thandi imagined that all the others who had traveled with them were also in desperate need of sustenance.

She turned to Tom. "Will the others be eating now?" She asked. Her gleeful expression suddenly turned to one of deep concern.

"Of course," Tom assured her. He found it exceptionally sweet and mindful that she'd asked. The morning passed beautifully as the three laughed and shared memories of old times and brought each other up to speed with their present lives.

After breakfast, Tom gave them a brief tour of the renovated mansion. All of the previously dark colored walls were now brightly painted and re papered. The stately home now boasted vibrant shades of blues, creams, and beiges. Even the extensive mahogany woodwork had been remodeled with intricate ivory painted trimmings and moldings. The change of color alone had drastically altered the mansion's former gloomy state.

Tom purposely steered clear of the second floor. He knew that Anna would be in the sewing room at that hour and he had no desire of encountering her ill temperament. Strangely, Thandi felt both apprehensive and anxious as Tom led them up the attic's stairs to their former living quarters.

"I don't think Esther and Myra will mind if I show you to your old rooms," He said, seeming to somehow notice Thandi's apprehension.

He opened the door of the first room on the right side of the narrow hall. Both surprised and relieved, Thandi gushed with delight upon entering. Other than Esther's personal effects and a newly built closet, the room had remained exactly the same as it had been many years past.

Isaac also marveled at the bleak familiarities. The same full sized pine wood bed, trunk, side tables, and bureau...even the then time-worn, hideous olive-colored paper on the walls still remained. Isaac's mind suddenly went to a significant recollection. He eyed the old bureau standing across the room, then started in its direction. Suddenly, he stopped himself sharp and turned to Tom.

"Forgive my manners," He said. "May I?" He gestured a hand toward the chest. Tom and Thandi looked at the chest and immediately knew of his intentions.

"Sure." Tom smiled. "Go ahead."

Isaac promptly walked over and opened the tall bureau's doors. Inside, Esther's garments hung across the wooden bar, and, for a brief second, he felt a spot of guilt for invading the maid's privacy. But he simply had to see it… kneeling on one knee, he put aside the sewing bag and yarn that blocked what he searched for.

Thandi quickly joined him. As she knelt beside him, her gaze instantly went to the special spot inside the chest. Isaac anxiously pushed aside a small black satchel, then the two siblings smiled at each other.

Tom stepped forward upon the discovery.

"Everything up here has pretty much remained the same," He stated. "And always will."

Both Thandi and Isaac shot him a sweet look over their shoulders.

"I never finished it!" Thandi declared upon inspection of her old childhood carving. Her bright green eyes sparkled and she smiled at the youthful memory.

She, Tom, and Isaac were always on their very worst behavior anytime Mr. and Mrs. Lexington Sr. were away, which was often, due to Tom's father's business endeavors.

Haiti had never given much fuss about them, seeing as Master Tom, though only a boy at the time, was "master of the house" in his father's absence. And as long as he didn't bring any hurt to himself or others, she didn't see the harm in him being a boy.

During one of their usual games of hide-and-seek, Thandi carved a little drawing into the bureau's wood while she waited to be found. It had taken Isaac and Tom almost an hour to find her, and she'd become incredibly bored. The three people-like etchings were her depictions of herself, Tom, and Isaac; a faceless trio with just circle heads and squiggly lines for their bodies, arms, and legs. She was the middle figure. She had put squiggly curls on either side of the head for proper identification. Before she could make the finishing touches, Tom had captured her, squealing.

Weeks later, when Haiti discovered the offense, Tom immediately took full blame for the mischief and all was well.

His taking the blame was standard protocol because he never suffered any form of punishment. He was the Lexingtons' beloved son and sole heir. He could do no wrong and the three household rascals took full advantage of that theory.

"We could soon rectify that," Tom said.

Thandi looked from the old, unfinished carving to Tom, puzzled.

Smiling slyly, he pulled something from his pocket. Isaac eyed the object in his hand intensely. With a sharp flick of his wrist, Tom snapped open the one-of-a-kind Whitcliffe switch blade that he'd had in his youth.

Isaac's eyes and face lit with animation. "No way," He gasped. "Is that the old knife?"

Thandi's eyes instantly honed in on it. *It couldn't be the Whitcliffe*, she thought. *Tom had lost it long ago at Hollis Creek...* or, at least, that was what they'd all presumed back then. Tom came even closer so that they could get a better look. "It is!" Thandi exclaimed, shocked. The deep nick on the pearl handle's end proved it so.

Isaac had caused its damage by getting it wedged in a ridiculous entrapment he had built to catch wild rabbits. None of them could ever forget the trusty blade. They had used it regularly on their various wicked capers.

Tom extended the knife to Thandi with a smile, and she took it gleefully. Twisting it from side to side, she examined its distinguishing details.

"However did you find it?" She asked.

"I didn't," Tom admitted. "Old man Hollis returned it to me some years ago." Both Isaac and Thandi looked at him, wide-eyed.

"He said he'd found it on his property years back. And that it must've belonged to one of the Negro scoundrels we owned," Tom explained.

Thandi shook her head in wonder.

"However, I could tell by the way he looked at me that he'd known *exactly* how it'd got on his land," Tom added.

Isaac chuckled at the revelation. He could still picture the old man's face fresh in his mind: his sunken cheeks hot red with anger and those beady black, piercing eyes glowering back at them. He'd hated the three of them thoroughly and with good cause, seeing as how they were always trespassing on his land. But the small river that ran through it was far too compelling for the spirited trio to resist. It wasn't until he had threatened to hang Isaac up in one of his trees that they stopped visiting the creek.

With much enthusiasm, Thandi went about the business of finishing her carving. Tom and Isaac looked on and snickered as she added little eyes, noses and smiling mouths to the already hilarious depictions. Hearing Isaac's infectious laugh behind her made her start to giggle again. She gave the juvenile art another once-over, then stood and proudly straightened her skirts.

"Looks just like us," Tom chided.

Isaac busted a gut again and Thandi shot him a playful glare. Snapping the blade shut, she handed it back to Tom.

"Wait a minute," Isaac said seriously. A sudden, thoughtful look took the place of his smile. Apparently, something of new importance had entered his mind. He began removing Esther's items from the closet's floor with fresh zeal. Tom and Thandi ceased their laughter and watched him. "Have you two forgotten Mama's hiding spot?" He asked them.

Thandi raised a brow, then suddenly it came to her. Haiti had kept her sewing needles and special trinkets in a box underneath the closet's floorboard. Tom and Thandi watched closely as Isaac feverishly began to remove the bureau's floor plank.

Thandi didn't remember seeing the box after their departure from the estate so long ago, and now she wondered if it could indeed still be here after all these years.

Within a matter of moments, her question was answered.

Remarkably, there it was. The three old friends looked at each other with a mixture of surprise and nostalgic sentimentality.

Isaac lifted the dust covered box from its place and sat it down on the floor in front of him. "We must open it!" Thandi declared. She quickly knelt at her brother's side. Intrigued, Tom followed suit and knelt on the other side of Isaac. He removed a handkerchief from his shirt pocket and wiped the thick coat of dust from the box's top and sides. The beautiful, deep cherry wood had remained perfectly intact; however the clasp had become visibly rusted over time.

"Here, you may need this," Tom said. He passed Isaac the trusty Whitcliffe knife, then he and Thandi watched anxiously as Isaac struggled for some time with the aged iron clasp. After a while, he finally freed it open with the blade's tip.

For the first time in what felt like centuries, the three friends set their eyes on Haiti's cherished spool of needles and the now yellowing white handkerchief she'd always carried. The insignificant items they had seen a thousand times before now held immeasurable value and meaning.

Isaac picked up his mother's old hankie and stroked it gently across his cheek. A warm feeling hugged his heart at its touch.

Thandi reached for the pointy spool of needles when suddenly she spotted something she didn't recognize. Amongst the pretty combs and a small hand mirror was a peculiar black velvet pouch. She gave her brother a curious glance then looked at the mysterious bag again. "What is this?" She asked as she pulled it from its place in the box.

Isaac shrugged his shoulders and Tom looked at her with an equally confused expression.

"I've never seen it before," said Isaac.

Without further hesitation, Thandi began trying to unravel the roped ties with her fingernails. The two cords were knotted in a complicated fashion and she struggled hard for some time, trying to loosen them before finally giving up and handing the bag and task over to Isaac.

"I'll have to cut it," He said after careful examination. Thandi gave him an approving nod.

After cutting the ties, he emptied the bag's contents into his hand. Thandi gasped.

To all of their surprise, a golden locket dropped into Isaac's palm. He held it up against one of his big fingers for all to see.

The oval shaped locket hung from a short chain, and it was genuine gold from the looks of it.

"Mother *never* owned any jewelry," Isaac thought aloud.

He stole the words right from his sister's thoughts. Their mother had never owned, and certainly could not afford jewelry. The greatest articles she had owned of any value were her precious needles and her hand painted combs.

Thandi tried hard to recall ever seeing the mysterious locket, but no matter how hard she racked her brain, she couldn't recall one single memory of her mother wearing it or any other trinket, for that matter.

The same thoughts ran through Isaac's mind. He had seen his mother look in the special box countless times and not once had he seen the black bag or the necklace. He would've remembered something so elaborate. He turned to Tom with his eyebrows raised, as if Tom had an answer to the mystery.

The equally puzzled look on Tom's face suggested he hadn't.

"Where could Mother have ever gotten the money to buy something like this?" Thandi asked, taking the locket from her brother's hand. She rubbed its smooth gold between her fingertips and marveled at the beautifully engraved, swirling vines that covered it front to back.

As she twisted the exquisite charm in her fingers, she noticed a thin crease in its side. "I think it opens," She announced. Using her thumbnail, she pried it open.

Inside, there was no picture as one might expect to find; but, instead, there was an inscription etched in fine calligraphy.

She lifted the locket up to her eyes for closer inspection. "Always…" She read the single inscribed word aloud, her voice breathy with amazement.

The three gave each other a look, and soon a series of questions flooded the siblings' already confused minds. Questions like, *How could their mother have left the box behind, especially when it contained something of such significance and value? Had she simply forgotten it in their hasty move? And how on Earth had she obtained it?*

Thandi stared hard at the inscription. *Was it given to her by a lover?* Her silky brows narrowed intensely. *But no slave could afford such an elaborate thing.*

Isaac shook his head. He simply couldn't make sense of the find.

That moment, a highly plausible explanation entered Thandi's mind. The white laborer whom she had been told was responsible for siring her! He just possibly may have given her mother the beautiful trinket.

After all, Haiti had never suggested she had been taken without her consent. In fact, Thandi's mother hadn't given her very much information at all in her father's regard. She had only explained that he was a very handsome and kind man, and that Thandi had more of his features than her own. She had also stated that his time on the plantation had been very brief.

"The white laborer," Thandi announced aloud, as if she had solved the perplexing mystery.

Isaac's brow quirked upward.

"My father, silly," Thandi added.

Isaac's dumbfounded expression slowly melted as he pondered the thought.

Completely clueless, Tom looked on in silence. He personally had never seen the trinket or knew of Thandi's father, for that matter.

Isaac stroked his chin contemplatively, then nodded. *That could very well explain things*, he thought. A small sigh of relief escaped his lips, for secretly his mind had begun to contemplate a far less appealing notion.

"It's very beautiful," Tom said, breaking his slightly awkward silence. "You should wear it, Thandi," He sweetly suggested. Thandi shot him another smile, then stared at the locket again.

"Go ahead, put it on," Isaac nudged her.

She looked up from the charm and into her brother's eyes.

"And just where would I wear it?" She asked mockingly. The mere idea of her or any other slave walking around in servant's frocks and rags, wearing something of that value was definitely laughable. Not to mention the unwanted attention it would bring to her. She already got enough unwanted attention as it was.

With that thought, she suddenly became aware that her mother had probably shared the same sentiment. It would certainly explain why she had never seen her mother wearing it. Yet it gave no explanation as to why she had left it behind.

Tom stifled his ready tongue. He wanted to press further, but quickly decided against it.

Thandi looked at both of the men and smiled thinly. "I'll wear it sometimes," She lied. She dropped the chain back in its pouch, then viewed the other contents. As she looked over the unique painted combs, she thought of Isaac. *He doesn't have any of Mother's belongings*, she thought.

After Haiti passed away, there wasn't much to be passed on other than her dresses and a few knick-knacks. All that she had been given to Thandi.

"You should give these to your beloved," Thandi said, passing the combs to Isaac. "If she has a baby girl, she can pass them on to her." She picked up the box and got back to her feet. The huge smile on her brother's face made her happy.

"Sarah's gonna love them," He said, smiling up at her.

After returning Esther's items to their prior state in the bureau, Isaac stood up with the others. For a final reflective moment, Thandi and Isaac gazed around the room, then made their way back out of the attic apartment.

The remainder of the day fared well, and the three took lunch in the garden.

Again, Tom made his apologies for his wife's repeated absence.

Thandi found it most strange that Anna still felt ill, and yet Tom had made no effort to make sure she was okay. But that was none of her affair and besides, it wasn't uncommon for a woman of her kind to behave in such a manner.

While she gladly waited in the gazebo, Tom showed Isaac the fields and the cotton gin. They talked at length about Tom's expectations for the harvest, and after learning of Isaac's field experience and extensive knowledge of ginnery, Tom quickly decided to appoint him as second overseer alongside Ben during his stay. Naturally, Thandi would work inside the manor under Esther's careful instruction.

But there would be no work for them that day. Tom had insisted upon it. Instead, the three passed the afternoon hours with tea in the garden and much conversation.

As they walked the winding cobblestone pathway, Thandi took in deep breaths of the intoxicating air. The sweet, heavy scents of the garden's magnitude of flowers still lingered as they ventured past the row of familiar mighty oaks.

The three obscured structures Thandi had seen earlier from the bathroom window were far more alluring up close. While Isaac's keen eye admired the modern quarters' interesting design and construction, Thandi found the eight inn-like structures to be most handsome. She had never seen such charming lodgings provided for mere slaves.

Back home, the Negros resided in scantily built log cabins, much like the cabins which existed before the Lexington plantation's improved renovations.

By dinner, Anna's condition had remarkably improved and Tom took dinner with her in the formal dining room while Thandi and Isaac dined with the house servants in the kitchen.

Upon meeting their awkward gazes, Thandi got a strong feeling that, through Esther, they had already been updated on herself and her brother. But still, Esther made their proper introductions.

Three of the six maids seated at the table were just girls. None of them appeared to be more than sixteen years of age. They stared at Thandi often, as if she were the most bizarre thing they had ever laid eyes on.

When Thandi made eye contact with them, they immediately blushed and looked away. All the while, Ben repeatedly stole secret glances of her from across the table.

Though she had detected their eyes on her more than once, the older women mostly gawked at Isaac. They made trivial talk about house duties and tomorrow's menus while each occasionally cast Isaac an inviting gaze or flirtatious smile. Thandi found them all to be amusing.

"How do you like my stew?" Esther asked.

Thandi turned to sing her praises, but stopped abruptly when she noticed that Esther's attention and question were directed solely at Isaac.

He looked up from his heaping bowl and smiled. "It's delicious. Reminds me of home."

Esther smiled widely with pride, but then suddenly her expression turned in a curious manner and she lowered her soup spoon. "About how long are y'all gonna stay?" She asked. This time, her attention made it to Thandi as well, and the two siblings looked to each other.

Madame Lacy said they would be there for as long as Tom deemed necessary to complete the harvest. Having very little field knowledge, Thandi hadn't a clue of how much time that would actually mean.

Isaac had told her it could be a few months or more, depending on the amount of cotton to be harvested, and after seeing the full forty-four acres, Thandi greatly suspected it would be more.

"Well, I'm thinking a few months or more," Isaac casually guessed, for there was no way of being entirely certain.

The average picking season for a large crop such as Tom's normally lasted two to three months, providing one had the proper number of hands. But then came the ginning season, which could mean an increase in their stay by a matter of months if Tom kept them on.

Pondering the matter made Isaac think of Sarah. She wasn't at all happy with him leaving. The two were newly married and they had just learned that she was carrying their first child. He sighed deeply and mulled at a chunk of beef and carrot with his spoon.

Only Thandi had noticed the sudden solemn turn in her brother's jovial expression, and she knew its cause.

Isaac had only been away from Sarah for almost a week, and already he had begun to miss her. Facing the prospect of not seeing her for many months must have been painful for him. Thandi hadn't thought much of the matter until now, and by the look on Isaac's face, she surmised that he hadn't given it much thought before then, either.

"How's it going in here?"

The sound of Tom's voice jolted Thandi from her thoughts. Turning her gaze toward the sound, she met his smiling gaze in the doorway. Everyone greeted him as he entered and took the final seat at the table.

Isaac's smile instantly returned at the sight of him and Thandi was glad. She suddenly had a feeling that he would do just fine. With all the work and Tom's company, his mind would stay consumed and the days would appear shorter. Before long, he'd have Sarah in his arms again.

Tom ran a hand through the sleek curls of his hair and leaned back languidly in his chair.

"I'm simply stuffed. The stew was marvelous," He told Esther.

Both Isaac and Thandi readily agreed and Esther's dark face lit bright with pride and the other two maids passed each other a subtle, but funny look.

Though they had followed her recipe to the letter, Tess and Annie had actually prepared the meal. But, like always, Esther had received the praise.

Thandi looked up from her bowl and found Tom's eyes on her. He had a strange look on his face as if he were staring at something in particular.

"That dress…" He said, pointing a finger at her. "Wasn't that your mother's?"

Thandi looked down at herself, then to him again with a broad smile. "You recognize it?"

"Most definitely," said Tom, nodding.

Its distinctive black eyelet trimming and matching cuffs made the otherwise simple frock especially memorable. And if he remembered correctly, Haiti had made the pretty dress herself.

"It sure is pretty," Esther politely interjected. She especially admired the fine detail of the black eyelet.

"Our mother was quite the seamstress," Isaac stated proudly. "She made garbs even prettier than that."

Thandi immediately cut her eyes across the table to Esther. Wide-eyed and teeth flashing, she held her bread idle in her hands, hanging on Isaac's every word.

"Had she lived, she'd probably have her own store by now," He added.

Again, Thandi examined Esther's countenance. She now had a look of both puzzlement and surprise. The curious maid no doubt wondered how their mother, a slave, could possibly have owned a store without money or freedom.

"Our mother earned wages for the dresses she made for our Missus and all of her friends," Thandi told her. "She hoped to save enough money to move north and open a store someday. Our Missus had promised her freedom...and ours, still...," She added.

Isaac cast his sister a prideful side glance, and in that moment, another idea promptly entered her mind. Upon their mother's death, Madame Lacy told them of the saved wages their mother had entrusted to her. She had also allocated a small monthly wage to them both. After inheriting her mother's craft, Thandi continued to make dresses for the Missus and her socialite lady friends. They already had a fair amount of savings. Perhaps, the sale of the locket would help in their plans to fulfill their mother's dreams.

"I want you to take the locket," Thandi blurted, turning her attention back to her brother's appearance.

He stared back at her with a bewildered expression for a second, then cracked a half smile.

"It's a locket, sister. I think it best that a woman wears it."

Tom folded his lips to stifle his laughter, but still let out an unstoppable snicker. The backward look that Isaac had given his sister was far funnier than his joke.

Thandi smirked and shook her head at the two impossible grown rascals. "No, sillies," She said, scolding them both with her eyes. "I think it would serve a better purpose if we were to sell it." Her eyes locked gazes with her brother's. "We would have more money towards our plans... Mama's plans. Maybe, we'll even have enough now to find some land."

For a moment, Isaac was speechless. He thought on the idea and imagined how very happy Sarah would be. It would be a start towards their family's futures, at least. Madame Lacy had also extended her promise to Sarah and her offspring. Now that one of them had started a family, it was time to bring their mother's dreams to fruition.

"Are you sure?" He asked.

It seemed only right to him that she should keep it. Not only was she their mother's only daughter, but the necklace had likely come from her father as well.

Thandi looked her brother hard in the eyes as if she'd read his niggling thoughts. "I'm more than certain," She assured him.

Tom found the selfless act both sweet and commendable. "Isaac, you couldn't ask for a better sister," He noted.

Thandi flashed him an adorable grin, and caught a glimpse of the curious staff's faces. She had become so enveloped in her conversation with Isaac and Tom that she had nearly forgotten she was still in their company.

"Well, okay, then," Isaac happily agreed. "But I insist that you wear it until we go home." The huge smile that spread across his face deeply satisfied her.

After dinner, Tom and Isaac went off together and Thandi happily retired to the comforts of her room. The grueling trip and all the excitement of the day had left her thoroughly spent. She bid Esther an early goodnight, then made her way to her room as fast as her weary body could get there. She wondered how Isaac could still be so full of energy when she felt so totally drained. Once inside her room, she shut the door and flung herself on the bed. Pulling the covers back would have required more energy than she could give at that moment.

The plush pillows and soft coverlet were instantly soothing. It wasn't long after her head hit the pillow that she was fast asleep.

Chapter 3

Thandi awoke to total darkness and the muffled sound of elevated voices. Concerned, she sat upright in bed and immediately began to fumble in the darkness with the lantern next to her on the nightstand. As the room slowly lit up, the muted voices died down, then suddenly rose again even louder than before.

Though his words were unclear, she immediately recognized the sound of Tom's voice.

Alarm filled her instantly. *What in God's name is going on?* She thought. Without further hesitation, she sprang from the bed and rushed to the bedroom door. Cracking it open just slightly, she did her best to listen in. She tried hard to make out what was being said, or, at least, the general topic, but she could not make any sense out of the voices she heard. Quietly, she ventured out into the dimly lit hall for further investigation. She soon surmised that the sound of Tom's voice seemed to come from the far corner of the house.

Far enough away that she could safely walk down the hall without detection.

Other than the voices, the house was quiet and still. Very few lanterns were still lit in the dark of the night. The brightest light she could see shined from underneath the kitchen door. Thinking of that made her wonder just how long she had slept. It was obviously very late.

When she reached the halls end, she stopped herself cold. A large, obscure figure stood in the darkness just across the parlor. Fearing she would be discovered, she quickly stepped back into the hall's cloaking shadows.

Tst! Tst! She heard a sound and her heart instantly leaped. She frowned in the darkness.

"Tst! Tst, Thandi!" Esther whispered more urgently.

Thandi hesitated for a moment, then reluctantly emerged from the hall's shadows.

"Come here," Esther urged, motioning a hand for Thandi to join her.

Thandi quietly crept across the grand parlor's floor and stood next to her. "What's going on?" She whispered.

30

"They've been arguing for a while, Master Tom and the Missus," Esther informed her in a hushed tone.

A door slammed and the two women looked at each other with alarm.

"Let's go to the kitchen, quickly," Esther directed. Fearing they would be discovered, she scurried away in a hurry with Thandi fast behind her.

Once inside, Thandi immediately took a seat at the kitchen table. "So, why are they arguing?" She asked without a moment's hesitation. Her big, stunned eyes stared keenly into Esther's own, searching for any clues that may be found there.

Esther put a silencing finger to her lips and paused for a spell as she put her ear to the door. She listened for the sound of oncoming footsteps, but heard nothing. Then she turned and looked at Thandi hesitantly, as if she were pondering whether or not to divulge the requested information.

"Well," She broke off, her tone still quiet. "The Missus was all stirred up about..." She paused again and looked Thandi firm in the eyes. "You can't say anything to anybody," She insisted putting her hands on her wide hips and waiting for Thandi's affirmation.

"Well, Master Tom got down on the Missus earlier about how's she treated y'all," She said, shaking her head. "Then the Missus got all stirred up, talking about how she doesn't want niggers in her guest rooms..."

Thandi's heart sank at the unsettling revelation. She had felt the evident animosity that exuded from Anna from the very first moment she looked into her stony gray eyes, but, even so, she hadn't imagined that the earlier display would evolve into this.

"My brother and I are here to be of help, not be a burden!" She thought aloud, frustrated.

"Well... it'll do you good to stay out of her way," Esther warned. "She can be as mean as a snake, especially, when she's doesn't like you."

The disheartening moment of clarity changed Thandi's bewildered expression to a look of vehement dismay. She shook her head disbelievingly. If she had thought for a moment that there would have been trouble in her staying in the guest quarters, she would have immediately declined her room. And Isaac would have most certainly done the same.

For a second, she thought of going to Tom first thing in the morning and telling him just that, but when she looked up at Esther's fretful expression, she was cursedly reminded of the promise she had just made to not say anything about it to anyone else.

Swallowing back the thought, Thandi straightened herself and her pride. She put on a false smile and firmly looked into Esther's wide, beady brown eyes. "You have no worries of me spilling the beans," She stated, "Besides, we won't be here for very long."

Esther's expression softened at her promise, but inwardly, Thandi still seethed.

The kitchen door swung open and the two women immediately turned their attention to Tom's surprise entrance.

Thandi caught a fleeting glimpse of his tempered expression before it quickly changed to one of surprise, then delight. He smiled at her warmly, then shot Esther an acknowledging glance before seating himself at the table across from Thandi.

She returned his smile with a nervous grin, for she was still shaken from the chaos of just minutes before. Esther cast her a forbidding look, then made herself busy with something of sudden importance in the cupboard.

"I knew Esther would be up; she's a relentless night owl. But you?" Tom said. "I imagined you would still be sleeping."

Thandi held her tongue and smiled at him sweetly. She could have told him that the arguing had woken her, but she quickly decided against it. If he wanted to make mention of it, he would, she surmised.

"Can I get you anything, Master?" Esther asked.

"No, nothing for me. Thank you, Esther," He answered over his shoulder. Naturally, he glanced at the bare spot on the table in front of Thandi. He found it strange that there wasn't as much as a glass of water in front of her.

Just then, it hit him. She was likely awakened by his argument with Anna. Why else would she be up at that hour, in the kitchen of all places, if not for food or drink? A twinge of shame needled at him and he suddenly wondered if Isaac was awake as well.

"Would you like something?" He asked, his eyes searching Thandi's blank expression.

"No, I'm perfectly fine," She lied. "Thank you."

Though she tried disguising her troubled feelings with a pretend smile, she could not veil the hint of consternation in her gaze and Tom knew that he had been correct in his previous thinking.

"Well then, how about a late night stroll through the gardens? That is, if you're up for it so late."

Thandi hesitated for a long moment while Tom smiled, watching the play of thought on her face. She soon concluded that a walk would be a welcome distraction from her morbid thoughts. "Sure. I could use the air," She said finally.

She missed the surprised look Esther gave her.

The astounded maid could hardly believe that she had accepted his offer after what she had just told her and what they had just heard. She shook her head in disbelief and made a mental note to speak with the poor, foolish girl about more things concerning Miss Anna and her devilish ways.

***

The moment Tom and Thandi stepped outside and set off for the gardens, Thandi was completely taken aback. The plantation's night scene was breathtakingly picturesque. She looked up at the bright night sky and stared in awe at the uncommonly countless stars. It seemed every star in the universe had come there in attendance that night.

The heady air smelled of gardenias and other fragrant flowers. The only sound to be heard was that of the busy night crickets. A long string of glowing oil lanterns lit the winding cobblestone pathway that ran throughout the garden and beyond.

"I've never seen anything more lovely," Thandi declared.

As she spoke, they passed a wall of tall hedges intertwined with hundreds of radiant white roses. If possible, the garden appeared even more intriguing by night than it had in the daytime with all of its splendor revealed.

"Sure, you have," Tom promptly insisted. He took her arm in his own and smiled, looking deeply into her eyes. "You need only to look in a mirror."

Thandi's face warmed red and she quickly looked away. Tom peered over at her intently as they continued to stroll along. *Was she blushing?* He asked himself. Upon further inspection, he could see that she was. He secretly smiled as he got just what he had hoped for, another glimpse of that heart stopping smile.

But soon, Thandi's face sobered and her brows furrowed as she remembered a much different time.

When they were children, Tom mercilessly teased her about her knobby knees and flat chest. He had regarded her as one of the boys, largely due to her tom-boyish ways and reckless demeanor. But now, today, he looked upon her with new eyes, and apparently found her beautiful.

The very concept of Tom Lexington thinking of her as beautiful was truly laughable, she thought. "Have I changed so much, Tom? Was I so horrid back then?" She asked, her tone teasing, but also serious.

Tom's brows narrowed confusingly and he slowed their leisurely stride to a complete stop before he turned to look at her in a way that made her heart flutter.

She swallowed down the nervous lump which had suddenly formed in her throat and stared back into the intense blue pools of his eyes.

"You're beautiful now. And you were beautiful then," He firmly clarified.

He didn't see how she could come to make such an odd inquiry. From as early as he could remember, she had always been beautiful. Still, to date, she had been the most beautiful girl he had ever seen.

Thandi eyed him suspiciously. She found his answer hard to believe. As they resumed their stroll, she tried putting the subject out of her mind, yet it still nagged at her. *How could he honestly say such things when once he did nothing but mock her unfeminine attributes? Certainly, he's just being gracious,* she thought.

He glanced at her again and she caught his gaze. For a lingering moment, he stared into her eyes. She was indeed breathtakingly beautiful, so beautiful that she naturally compelled all with eyes to stop and stare.

Neither the nighttime spectacle of the stars nor the majestic beauty of the garden compared to her. Her sun-kissed skin seemed to glow beneath the lanterns' soft glowing lights and her full, dark lashes fluttered like tiny black wings above the most bewitching emerald green eyes. Tom's gaze traveled down the smooth of her neck, then for a mindless moment rested upon the swell of her bosom.

Realizing his roguish behavior, he caught himself and tore his gaze away from her breasts. *This is Thandi,* he thought. *How can I regard her in such a manner?* Her dear belated mother had once been his wet nurse for Christ's sake. But, in truth, he had always been especially fond of her, far before she had blossomed so impressively.

Shaking the sordid thoughts from his mind, he returned his attention to their friendly walk like a proper gentleman. His eyes blankly surveyed the scenery around them as a comfortable silence fell between them.

Thandi glanced at him, observing his sudden change in countenance. Though she tried to shake it, she could not dispel the baffling feeling she felt when he looked at her, nor could she quiet the one pressing question that now plagued her mind. Despite of her swelling apprehension, she spilled the words from her mouth before she could stop them.

"If I was beautiful *then*, Tom... why did you taunt me so?"

Taken aback, Tom's eyes once more returned to her. He smiled at the ridiculousness of the question. Even more surprising was the pouty look on her face, which made him laugh. He slowed his steps to a stop and she did the same.

Noticing a garden bench not far away, he gestured a hand in its direction. "Sit with me a while," He said.

Thandi cast him an irritable look before she walked over to a bench and sat down; he straightened his grin right away and he sat next to her.

A glimmer of amazement flashed in her eyes as she looked at him. The streaming light from a close lantern shined down on them like a soft spotlight, illuminating the attractive features of his smiling face.

Though they were friends, she could not help noticing just how remarkably handsome he had become. As a boy, he'd already been good looking, but now, all of his boyish features had finely matured and his former small frame had transformed into a strong, manly physique.

Grinning back at her, he shook his head incredulously.

For a frightening moment, she feared that somehow he had read her embarrassing thoughts.

"I teased you because I was an intolerable misfit back then," He spoke, his ardent gaze fixed on the star speckled sky.

Thandi breathed a small sigh of relief at his reply. Apparently, he hadn't read her mind, after all.

"And, quite honestly, I had a certain fondness for you, though I dared not admit it then."

Thandi's eyes flashed with surprise. Never would she have imagined that he had looked upon her in any way other than just as a friend.

35

God knew he had shown no signs of being attracted to her. In fact, if anything, his behavior had suggested just the exact opposite.

"Young boys have a funny way of expressing their feelings," He noted, shaking his head. A devilish smirk curled the corners of his mouth as youthful memories came to mind.

"A funny way indeed," Thandi countered.

The slight roll of her eyes reminded him of her younger self. She had just as much sass then as she had now. As he remembered, she had rolled her eyes constantly for some reason or another, mostly because he had done something to purposely annoy her.

His infectious grin made her crack a smile in spite of herself. Before long, she found herself laughing alongside him once more. He had that same effect on her when they were younger. No matter how vile he had been or how ticked off he had made her, all it took was a charming smile or funny face to cool her temper.

"You're still so maddening!" Thandi said with a scowl.

As their laughter died away, she stared at him, thinking and wondering if he knew that she too had once held a particular fondness for him, years ago. She always presumed that he had secretly known.

Though she never dared breathe a word of it, she had stuck to him like glue in their youth, even more so than Isaac. They were always exploring or out playing in the woods surrounding the creek. No matter how dirty or bold the adventure, she had tagged along with them.

As her thoughts persisted, he turned to her, and for a split moment, he looked at her in the warm way he had before. But soon he collected his smile and turned his attention back to the majestic heavens.

Thandi followed his gaze and looked up blankly into the firmament, her mind still thronged with the astonishing information. The two sat and quietly gazed up at the stars until Tom suddenly spoke, breaking the silence between them.

"But, in my defense, you did, in fact, have the worst knobby knees," He blurted.

Thandi's jaw dropped instantly. "You're absolutely incorrigible!" She scolded, giving his arm a playful shove and smiling at him, bug-eyed.

"No, seriously," Tom went on with his boyish banter. "Why else would I allow you to win at every single game we played? Especially racing?" He turned and looked her dead in the eyes. "Trust me, it was no wonder you beat me ***each*** and ***every*** time."

Thandi gave him a hard, thoughtful look. As she recalled it, she'd beaten him fair and square and with little effort.

Tom fixed his gaze on her dress covered knees. "Well, I do hope you've outgrown them," He teased. His concerned expression and heartfelt tone held a strong measure of sincerity, even though he was clearly less than serious.

"Stop!" Thandi burst aloud. She could do nothing to contain her laughter. She had indeed had the most awful knock-knees and spindly legs. Tom had discovered them the first summer they swam in Hollis Creek. Like the boys, she swam in her undergarments so she would not destroy her nice clothing. The short knickers she wore stopped just above her knees, exposing her dreadful looking legs.

Thandi gave him a punishing shove to the ribs and, like old times, the two laughed like adolescents for some time.

For Tom, it felt absolutely refreshing to laugh that way again, to laugh so genuinely. He could not remember the last time he enjoyed another's company as much as he had hers and Isaac's.

After a while, their laughter subsided and the busy sound of the chirping crickets filled the air once again. Tom's jovial expression slowly sobered before her eyes. He suddenly looked as if something serious had entered his mind.

"You must forgive me for tonight," He muttered.

Thandi's brows furrowed down in a state of confusion. "Forgive you?" She didn't understand. What on Earth could he possibly need forgiving for? "Whatever do you mean, Tom?" She asked him plainly.

Tom cleared his throat, then swallowed hard. His blue eyes fixed with her haunting green eyed gaze. "Well, I suspect my spat with Anna might have awakened you," He said.

Thandi's eyes narrowed. "You need not make any apologies to me, Tom," She said.

The deep sincerity in her tone and expression struck a chord within his heart. He truly admired her genuine concern for him.

"My marriage isn't the happiest," He frankly admitted.

For a short moment, Thandi sat without words. She was taken aback by his bold confession, but soon her endearing smile resumed. "Really, Tom, we all have our problems. You need not make any excuses for simply being human." She paused for a moment, smiling, then added, "And besides, you're lord of your own house. You could scream and swing from the rafters if you chose to."

Tom shook his head incredulously and grinned as he envisioned himself literally swinging from the mansion's rafters. "I should have taken into consideration the late hour, and I certainly should have respected the presence of my guest."

Thandi's heart warmed at his last word. It was wonderful to see that years and wealth had not changed his unpretentious character. "It's me and Isaac," She reminded him. He need not feel ashamed or put on appearances for them, ever. They were like family and, after all, he was married, and sometimes married people fought. That was simply a fact of life.

A sudden warm breeze swept past them, causing loose tendrils of wayward curls to sweep over the delicate bridge of her nose. Without thinking, Tom swiped them away from her eyes and securely tucked them behind her ear. For a split second, the tip of his fingers delicately touched her skin, and again a strange warm rush secretly flashed through her.

Tom's face warmed with pure admiration of her. *Genuine gentle souls like she and Isaac simply did not exist in Newport,* he thought.

"You have a very beautiful wife," Thandi said with another fetching smile.

Her kind words regarding his ill-behaved wife broke his merry daze. He smiled thinly, then cast his eyes to the shadowy grass at his feet. "If only she were as beautiful on the inside," He said sadly, shaking his head as he looked at the ground. "Anna and I have a very troubled marriage," He continued. "But then, I guess I didn't exactly marry for love."

Thandi sat speechless for a moment. Flabbergasted by his sudden admission, she stared back at him and did not know what to think or say. What did he mean? The pressing question visibly showed in her expression.

"Did you hear of the rumors surrounding my father's death?" He asked her.

She nodded gravely. She could never forget. His father's death had been the reigning topic of discussion in Newport, for quite some time.

"Well, what you may not have heard is the real reason why he took his own life…"

Thandi's eyes widened with curiosity and a little bit of fear at what he might say next. She had heard rumors that Master Lexington had become severely depressed after his wife had abandoned him. The rumors said that on the day he had taken his own life, he had become so drunk and beside himself with grief that he rented an old seedy room amongst the poor and undesirables, and shot himself once in the head with his prized Derringer pistol.

As Thandi recalled, Madame Lacy never spoke on the topic of her brother's death. She had actually overheard the piece of gossip from Ingrid, a fellow servant, who heard the news by way of eavesdropping after their Missus had received a letter.

When she had been bold enough to ask Madame Lacy herself if the rumors were true, she scolded her, saying it was not polite to speak ill of the dead. After that, she never questioned her of it again.

"No," Thandi replied meekly, shaking her head.

Tom looked away as old memories resurfaced. Though he wore a brave face, Thandi could tell that the subject of his father's death still pained him.

She had lost her mother just two years before he had lost his father, so she could certainly relate to the depths of his misery. However, her mother had not died in the tragic way that his father had. She had passed inexplicably, yet peacefully in her sleep.

Tom released a heavy sigh and continued his sad tale. "Just weeks after my father's funeral, I learned he had taken out several large loans against the mill and plantation; loans that were nearing default. My father had invested everything he had, including a sizable amount of my mother's inheritance into an up-and-coming ginnery in the Midwest."

Leaning forward into his lap, he rested his elbows upon his knees. He clasped his hands together and lowered his head. "My father's *friend* ultimately bought all his debts..."

Thandi anticipated more of the story, but suddenly he said nothing. Instead, he looked up and stared gloomily in the mansion's direction. Sensing his turmoil, she considered her next words carefully. Seeing a silver lining in the sad tale, she spoke in hopes of renewing his lost cheer.

"Well, your father had a wonderful friend," She noted.

With his face turned from her, she didn't see the hot flicker that came in his eyes, nor the falsity in the grin he had now fixed on his face.

"His charity did not come without a Devil's price, I assure you," He stated with hard conviction.

Again, he went silent, leaving Thandi hanging on the edge of her seat in a fog of mystery and confusion. Only this time, she simply could not accept his silence.

What on Earth did he mean? She wondered. Swallowing her discretion, she spoke the very question aloud. "What do you mean, Tom? What do you mean by 'the Devil's price'?" She looked at him with an intense air of anticipation.

Tom looked at her, but his answer did not come speedily. For a split moment, she regretted her callous insistence.

"Stafford... Daniel Stafford, my father's 'associate'," He slowly explained. "He was far from a friend to my father, in truth. In my opinion, he was partly responsible for my father's suicide." Emotion crept into his voice and he stopped. He turned his face from her again and spoke out to the stars.

"The poor investments my father made were brought to his attention by way of Stafford, Anna's father. Not only was he my father's friend, he was also his lawyer and advisor. And it was at his advice that my father made the investments," He said, then paused to collect his thoughts.

Thandi was grateful for the pause, so that she could try and make sense of everything she had just heard.

"He had been having financial troubles for some time, and I wasn't at all aware because my mother's family was keeping us afloat. Neither she nor my father ever made mention of any troubles to me, financial or otherwise." He shook his head bitterly. "Not long after he lost his fortune, he started drinking heavily and gambling, throwing good money after bad..." Tom's voice trailed off as he fell deep into his own thoughts. He sighed heavily at the broken image of his father that entered his mind unwelcome. He saw him how he had seen him last, before his death, when he had come home from university to visit that fateful summer.

Tom Sr. was haggard in appearance and unusually sullen. He had insisted that nothing was wrong with him other than lack of rest. Naturally, Tom assumed that marital troubles with his mother had caused his father's sadness. He did not know the true magnitude of his father's despair. He had lost his fortune, his wife, and his son was far away. In hindsight, the three created the perfect storm for misery.

"After my father's death, Stafford bought his debts and assumed ownership of both the cotton mill and the plantation." A lost look appeared on his face as the heavy memories pressed upon his heart. "I was so devastated. My father was gone… my mother had moved back with her family in London. She didn't even bother herself with the shameful business of the funeral. Without my inheritance, I had very few prospects," He paused again, briefly. "But then Stafford made me a convincing offer. An offer that would allow me to save my father's legacy and part of my inheritance."

Wide-eyed, Thandi listened on in astonishment while her heart sank for him.

"In exchange for the deed to the mansion and a partnership in the mill, I was to marry his brat of a daughter, as well as make him an even richer man." Tom shook his head. "Although, he has promised to sell it back, he has also retained twenty acres of the land here, as a way to keep watch over my marriage, no doubt."

Words eluded Thandi. Never would she have imagined such unbelievable grief could befall him. However, her mother once said that pain and tribulation bore no prejudice, that it coveted dark and white, slave and master. Now she understood fully what her mother had meant. When they were young, Tom had been given the perfect life, or at least her youthful eyes had presumed as much. His childhood had appeared most ideal to her. His family had wealth, stature, a lovely estate and vast plantation; all the trappings of a wonderful life. It seemed highly implausible that such misfortunes had fallen upon him and his family.

A flicker of light in an upper window of the mansion caught Tom's attention. It appeared that Anna had finally turned in for the night. He sighed deeply with relief at the comforting thought.

He could not bear another bout with her. He had only consumed three shots of brandy, hardly enough to tune out her silly ramblings. He turned to Thandi and discovered a somber look on her pretty face. "Don't you dare feel bad for me," He said, smiling as he looked into her pitying green eyes. "I have the plantation back and part ownership of the mill. Marrying an ice queen was a small price to pay to preserve my father's legacy."

Tom saw no need in elaborating any further on all the horrors of his father's suicide. The subject of his father's death and his sordid marriage had become profoundly depressing.

41

The slight air of positivity in his tone and the returning smile on his face, though false, renewed Thandi's comfort again.

Suddenly, a warm breeze stirred the leaves of the twin row of oaks that lined the path to the slaves' quarters.

Thandi turned her gaze to them, then back to Tom again. "Well, I'm glad you saved it," She said sincerely. "This place has always been so beautiful." Her voice fell to a whisper as her eyes slowly surveyed her surroundings. Knolls of white roses faintly glowed in the dark along with many yellow bulbs of tulips and other vibrant flowers.

"Indeed," Tom agreed.

For a while, he said nothing else. Like her, he sat silently marveling at the serene surroundings, as if he had just seen it all for the very first time. In a strange way of sorts, he had. Though he had sat on that very bench several times before in other company, never once had he truly noticed the garden's remarkable beauty.

Despite all his family's misfortunes, he still had much to appreciate in the aftermath of it all. Smiling genuinely again at last, he turned to Thandi. "So, what of you?" He asked. "Surely there is some poor beau back home, pining away for you right now as we speak."

Thandi blushed at the forward remark. "No, not hardly," She said, shaking her head firmly at the very idea.

While there were many who wished for a chance at gaining her affections, they dared not attempt to do so, not while under the all-knowing, watchful eyes of Madame Lacy and her painfully doting brother.

After their mother died, Madame Lacy took Thandi and Isaac under her wing and kept them inside the big house instead of turning them out to the slave houses. She gave Thandi her mother's station, which kept her close to her at all times, and she constantly was subjected to Madame Lacy's countless lectures on the importance of acquiring a fitting beau.

Isaac mostly minded the stables and did various odd jobs about the plantation.

Unlike the other Negro boys who had started their field labors as early as age seven, Isaac did not acquire the common duty until he reached sixteen. Even then, the commission had not come at Madame Lacy's order, but, instead, it had been Isaac who constantly requested the miserable toil.

In secret, Madame Lacy taught Thandi and Isaac to read and write just as she had taught their mother. Without question, she had held a particular favor for them. Widowed and childless, Thandi often wondered if it was loneliness that compelled her to the orphaned pair, or if it was the unusual closeness she shared with her mother that had obliged her. Either way, she and her brother were forever thankful for her kindness.

"No, no one's waiting there for me," She said, smiling and revealing that rose-on-bronze blush again. "Isaac wouldn't have it," She said, "and neither would your aunt, for that matter."

Madame Lacy had often reminded her of the importance of keeping one's virtue until one was married. Although she hardly understood how that advice much mattered in the world of *her* kind, she still did as her Missus and brother instructed.

At twenty-two she was still a maid, saving herself for some phantom freed slave her brother imagined for her. Most Negro girls her age, were already married, or at least coupled by now. Though there had been several handsome male servants about Madame Lacy's house, she had avoided them all as if they had the plague, just as her Missus and brother desired, at least that was what Thandi told herself. Under their constant scrutiny, she often wondered how, if ever, she would meet the beau with which fate would suit her.

Another breeze carried the strong scent of the swaying gardenias past her nose. Closing her eyes for a deep breath, she took the smell in. *I could sit in this garden forever*, she thought, smiling.

With her eyes closed, she did not see the tender look Tom gave her. A small grin creased the corner of his lips as he marveled at her beauty and unwavering innocence.

As her eyes opened, he quickly looked away, but not before she caught a glimpse of his intense blue eyes on her.

Suddenly, a strange fluttering sound came from somewhere close by. Startled, Thandi flinched and quickly turned in the direction of the unfamiliar noise. The commotion seemed to come from the trees, not far from where they were sitting.

Thandi peered intensely at the dimly lit oaks; their leafy tops swayed back and forth, rustling fiercely about.

Tom could see a faint look of trepidation in her expression. "It's just the nightingales," He quickly assured her. "We get a large array of different species of birds, due to the flowers, and then of course, all of the trees." He gestured a hand at the old oaks.

Just as he stopped speaking, the rhythmic fluttering sound returned and several birds shot from one oak to the other standing at its side. Thandi smiled brightly at the playful feathered friends.

With this new garden, the plantation was even grander than before. Her eyes sparkled, darting from side to side as she tried following the bird's amusing antics.

Turning her attention to Tom again she gave him a warm smile. "Despite all of it, Tom, you've done really well. Your father would be so very proud of you." Tom held her tender gaze for a lingering moment.

In that moment, she reminded him very much of her mother, Haiti. Thandi's mother had always had comforting words for him whenever he felt dismayed. She had no doubt inherited more than her mother's beauty. She had also inherited her gentle heart.

"And your mother would be astounded to see how wonderful you've become," Tom replied. "You're a tomboy no more!" His charming smile revealed his deep dimples again. "Like your mother, you've become nothing less than a lady."

Thandi returned his warm regard with an even warmer smile. It did her heart good to hear such praise. To be compared in any way to her mother was indeed a very high compliment. The day of her death had been one of the two most horrible days of her life, the second being the day she and her family moved from Tom's father's estate.

Thandi felt a pang of sorrow swell in her heart. Though her mother had been gone for more than eight years, at times, the pain of her loss still hurt as much as it had the day she died. She thought of how Tom had shared the same pain, maybe even more so in his case. It must have been so very hard, tormenting even, to deal with his father's suicide.

Determined to change the mood, Thandi forced the thought and all of its ugliness from her mind. Abruptly standing to her feet, she looked down at Tom's surprised face.

"Still think you can beat me?" She asked him. Her eyes glinted with a spark of familiar mischievousness.

Tom looked puzzled for a moment, then he smiled.

"Of course, I can," He answered. "But I warn you, this time I won't hold back."

Thandi gave him a haughty look. Though he had said he had allowed her to win in the past, she hardly believed it true. She was quite fast then, and she had no doubt that now she could beat him without fail.

"You really shouldn't be so sure of yourself," She scoffed. The smug look on his face suggested he was not the slightest bit concerned with her admonition.

Noting his complacency, Thandi gathered her skirts.

"Well then," She said, returning to him his same confident smile. "Shall we race from one end to the other?" She took a quick look in the tree path's direction, then back at him again. Her bright eyes sparkled with devilish anticipation.

In that moment, she reminded him of her childhood self, the spirited and mischievous tomboy.

"By all means," Tom said with a smirk. He gestured a hand for her to lead the way.

"We'll start at the lanterns," Thandi instructed as she walked over to the first lamppost on the right side of the path's entrance.

Tom looked on as she positioned herself in a runner's stance. Thoroughly tickled, he joined her.

"This will hardly be fair," He taunted. "Maybe I should give you a bit of a head start, seeing as you're at a disadvantage with the skirts." He gave the twisted material in her hands a quick glance.

Thandi wrinkled her nose at his sarcasm. "That won't be necessary," She sharply replied. "I'm gonna beat you, skirts and all, Tom Lexington."

Tom snickered at her utter defiance. He gave her a final cautioning glance that suggested she should probably take him up on his offer at the head start.

Thandi disregarded the look and sharpened her stance. "On three," She announced.

The serious look on her face quickly sobered Tom's callous disposition. Leaning forward, he readied himself for the half mile dash to the other end of the path.

"One..." Thandi called out.

"Two..." She gave Tom one last look.

"THREE!"

Without delay, Tom sprinted forward, taking the lead. When he thought he had enough distance between them, he took a quick look over his shoulder. Hot on his trail was Thandi, just a few steps behind him. He could hardly believe she was so close.

Looking forward again, he increased his speed with new urgency. Either he had lost his youthful luster over the years, or the bourbon shots he took earlier with Isaac had started to take their toll on him. She was hot on his heels, and he was truly giving it all he had.

Thandi pressed forward even harder as the wind licked her face, and her hair, now unbound from its tie, whirled in an all-out frenzy. She was gaining on him fast and Tom could honestly do no more. It was taking all he had in him to maintain the stride he had already achieved. Seeing a flicker of what looked like black ribbon, Tom glanced at his side.

Boggles! He thought. Thandi was nearly right alongside him. Sucking back the thrashing wind, he tightened his chest and willed his body to press forward even harder. He could see the trail's end just feet away at the lamppost marking the path's end.

Just beyond it stood the luminescent white of the slave's quarters and the picket gate which surrounded it. His win was just seconds away. Suddenly, Thandi shot pass him like a bolt of lightning.

Tom slowed to a stop as there was no further need to go on. There, at the finish, stood Thandi, looking back at him with a gloating grin plastered on her face and her hand triumphantly clasped around the lantern's pole.

"Like I said, Tom Lexington..." She paused for a moment to fully catch her breath.

Swallowing hard and inhaling deeply, she tried steadying her heaving chest. "Skirts and all!" She proudly finished.

Exasperated and embarrassingly beaten, Tom bent over and grasped his knees. His heart beat violently as if it would burst right from his chest. Thandi looked on as he desperately struggled to catch his breath. The angst in his expression did little to stop the irrepressible snicker that escaped her lips.

Tom lifted his eyes to her smiling gaze. She was shamelessly reveling in his sorry state of defeat and her own glorious subjugation.

"Are you alright?" She asked, her gloating smile making him wonder if she was sincere in her concern. Her half-hearted tone and expression suggested she hardly felt sorry for his predicament at all.

"I'm just fine," He lied. He forced his weary body upright for confirmation.

"Good. So, then, shall I give you a chance at a tie, and race you back?" She asked.

Tom's eyes grew wide at the mere mention of him running again. His chest burned terribly and his legs felt like jelly beneath him. He might collapse if he attempted to run an inch further.

It was better that he concede now than risk certain humiliation. "How about we walk back together, instead?" He suggested.

Thandi smiled widely. Thoroughly satisfied with her triumph and his piteous submission, she agreed to walk back with him.

The walk back was slow and interesting. Tom shared stories of his time away at gentlemen's school and, in turn, she shared anecdotes with him of her own life at his aunt's estate. They continued to chat and laugh until they reached the mansion.

Once inside, they paused for a breath in the foyer. The two then bid each other goodnight and went their separate ways.

As Tom slowly climbed the stairs to his chambers, he paused for a moment and watched her. Then, as if she knew he was watching, Thandi cast him one last glance over her shoulder before disappearing into the hall's shadows.

Tom smiled to himself, pleased. The gleaming smile on her face had capped off both a pleasurable and painful night.

Chapter 4

The following morning, the welcoming aroma of frying bacon awakened Thandi from her rest. Sitting up in the large bed, she wiped the sleep from her eyes.

A smile slowly curled her lips as the events of the night surfaced in her mind. After a moment, she slid out of the bed and went into the bath. The drapes were still drawn open and the sun was just beginning to come up. Like home, the days there started early.

After washing up, she brushed her hair, then went to the armoire to choose a dress. Just as she pulled a gray frock from the chest, a knock came at the door.

"May I come in?"

"Of course," She answered.

She recognized the head maid's bubbly voice immediately.

"Morning," Esther said brightly, entering the room with fresh towels in hand.

Thandi returned her bubbly greeting with a sweet smile. "Good morning," She said, beaming.

"Master Tom and your brother are taking breakfast in the dining room. They thought I should see if you were up."

"I'll be there straightaway," Thandi assured her. Remembering her mother's necklace, she retrieved it from the vanity's drawer.

After placing the towels in the bath, Esther went to the door. She paused for a breath, casting a peculiar look over her shoulder before leaving the room.

Thandi was puzzled by her odd expression. But then she remembered the disturbing argument she had heard between Tom and his wife.

She had been so enthralled with her time in the garden that she had nearly forgotten the awful event altogether. Putting the unpleasant thoughts aside, she focused back on the moment. Today would be a busy day for everyone, with the harvest officially in full swing. She imagined that she would not see much of either Isaac or Tom once they started work in the fields. She herself would be busy with Esther, learning the different house duties and her assignments.

She put on the necklace and took an admiring look at her reflection. She raised a hand and stroked the smooth gold of the charm between her fingertips. Again, she found herself wondering how her mother had left the precious locket and other prized possessions behind. As she remembered, their move from the estate had been sudden. It was highly possible that her mother had simply forgotten it in her haste. But then, certainly she must have remembered at some point...

Once more, she shook the persisting thoughts from her mind. After quickly fixing her hair and changing into the drab, gray servant gown, she made her way to the dining room and joined the others.

The table was set charmingly. Both Isaac and Tom bid her good morning and greeted her with a smile. Tom stood before Isaac could get to his feet and pulled out a chair for her.

"Oh, my!" Gasped Thandi as Esther sat a generous helping of eggs, bacon, and sweet meal down in front of her. It was more than she could possibly eat, but she made no objection.

"So, I hear you beat the pants off Tom last night," Isaac blurted in greeting.

Thandi's face lit with surprise and she grinned from ear to ear.

She was shocked that Tom would voluntarily share the news of his defeat. He had probably done so to try and save face. Certainly, he didn't want her telling the story first. Her side of it would likely make him appear far less dignified.

"Well, it's good to see you're a good sport, Tom," Thandi taunted; giving him a look that silently communicating her decision to be merciful.

Tom smirked as he knew she was inwardly gloating. "Can you believe this wonderful weather we're having?" He asked, eager to change the subject.

Isaac lifted his eyes above his tilted glass of juice and smiled. It *was* surprisingly warm for early autumn, but not unbearably hot like the previous year. The milder temperatures were a welcomed change, considering the devastating toil the heat had taken on the previous year's crops.

Most parts of the south had suffered from the triple digit heat wave, and nearly all farmers and growers alike had lost their crops due to the long dry spells. Even Tom's Aunt Lacy's plantation had been affected.

"This weather's a blessing," Isaac declared. His gaze fixed on Thandi when something shiny caught his eye. He could see that she was wearing their mother's necklace; though he could hardly see it because it was hidden beneath her collar.

"Your necklace, sister," He said, gesturing a hand towards his own neck.

Thandi promptly looked down at herself. In her haste, she had forgotten to make the final adjustment. She pulled the chain outside her collar and looked up at her smiling brother.

"Perfect," Tom breathed.

Thandi knew without looking that Esther's eyes were on her. One smile in her direction confirmed it.

"That sure is pretty," Esther gushed. Her eyes as big as saucers, she stared intensely.

"It was my mother's," Thandi explained.

Esther paused at the buffet for a moment before cleverly thinking to bring over the pitcher of orange juice. Filling Thandi's glass would give her the perfect opportunity to view the necklace much closer.

As she slowly poured, she eyed the golden locket around her neck. It was very pretty, yet, she wondered how a slave woman could acquire something so costly.

The door opened and Anna entered the room. She froze at the sight of Thandi and Isaac seated at her dining table. All eyes in the room met her piercing glare.

Tom was especially surprised to see her. She never once, in their four years of marriage, had gotten up as early as she had in the past two days. In fact, he couldn't remember the last time he had eaten breakfast with her.

Esther stood frozen, suspended in time. She knew that look on her Missus' face all too well. There was going to be hell to pay, and very soon, by the looks of it.

"Now we have niggers sitting at our dinner table?" Anna asked, nostrils flaring.

Tom looked shocked at first, then outraged. His jaw stiffened with anger and his eyes darkened. Other surprised looks circled the silent room.

Anna gladly met all gazes with an icy, narrow-eyed glare.

"How dare you insult them!" Tom snarled.

He shot to his feet so abruptly he nearly tipped over his chair. Anna took a deep breath and braced herself as he suddenly came thundering towards her. No matter what, she intended to stand her ground. Her heart leaped in her chest as he stopped just breaths in front of her.

"I'll have a word with you upstairs," He ordered. He grabbed her by the arm with such force that she winced.

"Unhand me," She demanded through clenched teeth. Tom's grip tightened as he pulled her with him out the door and down the long hall.

"Let go of me!" Anna repeated as he forcibly dragged her up the winding stairwell to their bedroom and pushed her inside.

Slamming the door shut behind him, he turned and glared at her. His chest heaved and his face was red with anger. Despite his menacing expression and her wild beating heart, she maintained her haughty demeanor.

"You are truly testing my patience," Tom said, scowling in frustration.

"No, you test mine if you think those niggers are going to stay in my household as guests," Anna declared.

"Your household?" Tom scoffed. "The last I checked, the deed to this house is now solely in my name. And I'll have whoever I damn well want in it."

"And you have it by the grace of *my father*! Or have you forgotten?" Anna fired back.

"How could I?" Tom said contemptuously. "God knows you never let me forget." Anna hesitated. "If those niggers are to stay in my house, I'll go to my father's," She threatened.

Tom's face shaped itself into a disgusted frown. "Then I suggest you pack heavy, you spoiled little girl." Stepping aside, he made a clear path for the door.

His careless demeanor and smug countenance further enraged her. Immediately, Anna went to her closets and began gathering her things.

"Then you can have Ben ready the carriage," She affirmed angrily. She half expected him to try and stop her, but he did nothing.

Downstairs in the dining room, Thandi and Isaac still sat shocked and inwardly angered. Isaac pushed his plate aside and rose from the chair. "Well, I'm no longer hungry," He said.

Thandi did the same. Though she had not even begun to eat her breakfast, she could not think of eating a bite, considering what had just happened. In that moment, she wanted nothing more than to leave that table and the house all together.

"I've lost my appetite as well," She said. "I'm sure it was wonderful," She added, putting on a pretend smile for Esther. "Perhaps, I could help you in the kitchen," She offered as she rose from the table.

"And I should probably find Ben," Isaac interjected. "If Tom asks, let him know I'll be in the fields." He gave his sister a wary look before leaving the room.

"Well, I'll take these to the kitchen," Thandi said, lifting the two dishes from the table. She was eager to get out of that room and away from the lingering tension in the air. "I can eat mine a little later." She smiled as she whisked by Esther, pretending all was well.

When she entered the kitchen, she was surprisingly met by the stunned faces of the female house staff, seated around the kitchen table. They were apparently having their breakfast, and by the looks on their faces, she knew instantly that they had overheard everything that just transpired.

Shame and embarrassment settled over her, and she suddenly wished that she had elected to go back to her room. She flashed a nervous smile to the leering women and bid them good morning as she hastily took the plates to a side table.

Esther entered the kitchen with the glasses and pitcher in hand. With one look at Thandi, she could see the unease in her expression. Naturally, she was sympathetic to her.

"I'll put your breakfast in the oven 'til you're ready for it," Esther told her. The cheeky woman gave her a reassuring smile as she walked over. Not so strangely, her presence brought about a small measure of relief to Thandi.

"You ladies about done?" Esther asked. She turned her head to the goggling women and girls at the table.

"I've been done," said Millie. "But I heard all that yelling and was afraid to move."

It was the sort of thing that Thandi would have assumed the servants would have been used to, what with Anna's constantly sour attitude. She wondered if maybe things had been heightened by her and Isaac's arrival. She hoped not, but it was a logical conclusion. As much as she wanted to stay and visit with Tom, she disliked being around that hateful woman.

"Lord, have mercy," Esther's daughter, Myra, said. "I think they might just kill each other one of these days."

"Oh, shush now," Esther said, looking displeased and a bit irritated that they were all fretting so much. She did not like the fighting either, but, as the head maid, she had to do her best to keep the other maids calm and professional, including her young daughter.

"Master Tom is not the violent sort, and Missus Anna is too small to do any damage." She did not sound so convinced of that herself, but it helped to say it.

Unexpectedly, Anna stormed into the kitchen. Thandi let out a small gasp along with the others. "Millie," She said, breathless from her rage. "Get your things. You'll be going to my father's with me." Locking eyes with Thandi, she barked "You!" With a voice thickly coated with venom. "You're the cause of all this. You and that brother of yours. Just who do you think you are?"

Standing just feet from Thandi, she was several inches shorter, even in her heels. The Missus of the manor truly was a pretty little thing, but Thandi could not regard her with anything other than repugnance and slight fear over what further dismay she might cause her dear friend.

"Master Tom invited us," Thandi tried to explain, her own voice just as icy as Anna's. "He needed our help."

Anna waved that away in disbelief. "Oh, how could *you* possibly help him? You're an ignorant, good-for-nothing little nigger girl."

Esther opened her mouth in shock and protest, but said nothing. She was not about to start an argument she couldn't win with the Missus.

Raising her head up and refusing to take any further verbal abuse, Thandi turned to Esther. "Shall we get to work on the morning chores, Esther?" She said. "If you show me what to do, I'm sure I can learn."

Esther's doe eyes went from Thandi to Anna and back again. "Uh huh," She muttered.

As they passed from the room, Thandi wondered if Anna would really take Millie along with her. The poor girl seemed terrified of her.

Though she hardly knew the young girl, Thandi did not think anyone deserved to have to put up with serving Anna Lexington alone.

For Thandi, in a way, it was a relief that Anna did not like her, or want her in her company. Although, it did make things more awkward when it came to Thandi's relationship with Tom.

In that moment, she wished that she could work in the fields with the others. The field hands rarely saw their Missus and she could spend more time with her brother and Tom.

Tom... Thandi lightly fingered the locket around her neck as she walked from room to room, being shown what went where and what needed to be done each morning. Esther was a fast teacher, but she was kind enough to slow down and repeat herself if Thandi got lost. It was easy to get lost when she kept thinking about Tom. His situation was indeed perplexing. *How miserable it must make him to live with such a hateful woman,* she thought.

It would not do any good to think that Anna was jealous of her, but she could not help but think it. As peculiar as it would be, Thandi secretly hoped Anna really would go stay with her father and leave the running of the plantation to Tom for a while. He had clearly had enough of the meddling Stafford's, and could use a break.

But Thandi's hopes were not to come true; at least, not for the time being. By evening time, Anna was still at the house. Thandi helped Esther make dinner. The Master and the Missus were to eat dinner together, a sign that all was well and forgiven. Thandi's heart was heavy as she basted the roasted hen they would be eating.

Once her chores were finished, she went to eat dinner with Isaac and some of the other slaves in the kitchen. They were nice, welcome company and she soon forgot to feel mopey.

Millie gaped when something caught her eye. "My, Miss Thandi," She said, pointing at her. "Where did you get that necklace?"

Thandi reached and clutched it. She smiled shyly at Millie. "It belonged to my mother. It was given to her by my father, I guess."

Sounds of awe filled the kitchen. Thandi felt bashful about it, just as she felt about her eyes and the looks she got from strangers. Isaac seemed to sense how she was feeling and reached over, taking her hand.

"A beautiful necklace for my beautiful sister," He said.

"That she is," Tom's voice said behind her.

Thandi craned her neck around to look at him as he stood, leaning against the door frame and smiling at her. *He's making a hobby of sneaking up on me in doorways*, she thought.

"Aren't you supposed to be supping with your wife?" She asked stiffly. She did not feel like giving any hint about how happy she was to see him again.

Tom straightened up from his leaning. "My wife does not like dining with me much, which is why we don't do it so often anymore. But we did sit together, and I'm happy to say she has apologized for her actions."

Isaac smiled thinly. "Well, that's good of her," He said dryly.

It was not really an apology, thought Thandi, *unless Anna apologized directly to them*. Still, she did her best to smile along with her brother. Tom's wife had not only been rude to her and Isaac, but to Tom as well. Thandi could not believe the way the woman spoke to her husband. A wife was supposed to know her place, and Anna had obviously believed that hers was above Tom's. Thandi knew that it was because she was a spoiled, high born fool, but it still shocked her to see the behavior.

"I would like to officially apologize to all of you," Tom said, "on behalf of Anna. She does not always do well to keep things to herself, and sometimes she says things she doesn't truly mean. But we appreciate all of you, and your hard work."

Thandi knew that this was not Anna's behalf. She did not trust the vile woman, and she wondered what plans she might be hatching that had kept her at the manor. Earlier, she had seemed fully prepared to leave.

Apology speech finished, Tom gave a little bow and exited the kitchen.

***

Four hours afterwards, Tom sat in his study, mulling over the paperwork for the plantation's projected crop yield. For a moment, his thoughts went to Anna and her ugly behavior, but he forced them from his mind. *If only I could buy the old Newport Mill*, he thought. The old building had been badly damaged by a fire, but it was still structurally sound.

He could take a loan against the mansion to fund the cost for its restoration. But how would he ever convince Richmond to sell him the building? Lexington Mills was currently the only operating mill in Newport, and Richmond owned thirty-eight percent of its stock. A nearby competitor would mean less profits. Tom sighed heavily, thinking how impossible it all seemed.

Suddenly, there was a light rap on the door. Tom took a long gulp from his flask and wiped his mouth against his sleeve. He was hoping to be done with social interactions after the past hellacious day. "Yes?" He called.

Anna poked her head in. Anna, the one person he was decidedly against seeing any more of for the day. "Come to bed, my love," She said invitingly. She thought tonight would be as all the others. They would quarrel, make love, and all would be well again.

"I thought I told you not to disturb me in my study, Anna."

"I have my right," She insisted, her voice taking on a syrupy cadence that could not be sincere. "I'm your wife."

"And I have mine as well...to privacy!" Tom pushed the empty flask aside on the table and stormed past her through the parlor and out the front door. He half expected her to follow him, but she did not.

A swift, gentle breeze and the heavy, soothing scent of gardenias met him as he began to walk towards the gardens. The light in the boudoir flickered off, a sign that Anna had given up and gone to bed for the night, alone. Relief set in then, and Tom began to mindlessly walk towards the shed. Catching up with his old friend would put him in better spirits. After all of the uproar about Thandi and Isaac sleeping in the house's guest rooms, Both Thandi and Isaac had chosen to stay in the shed and barn for the night. Tom sighed heavily when he caught the shed in his view. There, too, the lantern had been put out, indicating that Isaac had gone to bed as well. *Maybe he went to the barn to see after Thandi*, Tom thought. He began to walk in the direction of the barn.

He could see the glow from the lantern shining just beneath the barn's door. He began to knock, but then stopped as he heard singing. It was a familiar song that he knew all too well. *Sleep with the Angels* was its name. Haiti had lulled him to sleep many nights with that song when he was a child.

Tom peered into the barn's small window. There was Thandi, removing water from one of the stables, singing happily. How unbelievably beautiful she had become. Slowly, he opened the door so she could hear that someone was coming in.

She stopped singing at once, which hadn't been his intention. "Don't stop," He said gently. "You have such a lovely voice."

With a sideways glance and a flirtatious smile, Thandi continued to sing until, all at once like a wave, he was holding her in his arms. The sudden move took her by surprise.

"Tom?" She said breathlessly, her eyes desperately searching his own.

"Kiss me, Thandi," He whispered wantonly. His lips lightly brushed the warm smoothness of her cheek.

The thought of Tom's wife entered Thandi's mind, but in that moment, she was incapable of resistance. Tom's mouth was suddenly on hers. She could taste the sweet bourbon still fresh on his lips. He kissed her softly at first, then more deeply when she began to kiss him back.

He could feel her body quivering as it pressed against him. He cupped her head in his rough hands, lacing the tips of his fingers in the soft curls of her hair. Part of him could not believe what was happening, but thank God that it was! Fearing they'd be discovered or that the two of them would soon come to their wits, Tom did not want to delay anymore. He could just feel that, at any moment, someone would come in and spoil everything. He moved Thandi against the nearest stable door and quickly lifted her nightgown, drawing it over her head and dropping it to the barn's floor and then went still for a long moment, frozen, as he stared' taking her all in. Her naked body was more remarkable than he could have imagined. His blood quickened and his member hardened. Quickly, he stripped away his clothing and shoes, revealing himself to her fully.

Thandi's eyes widened at the sight of his long, erect member. "Tom," She said in a shaky voice. Before she could utter another word, he kissed her again, his tongue devouring her own until her mind began to swim with a strange pleasure.

"I've always wanted you," He said, breathless. Gently, he ran his finger against the sensitive button between her legs.

Thandi let out a soft moan. He nuzzled his face against the side of her neck. "I want you so badly," He whispered. He pressed her firmly against the stable door and lifted her leg, lowering his hand and guiding himself to her moist entry. He started to enter her and she gasped aloud in shock and pain.

Tom stopped instantly. *Was she?*

"Are you still a virgin?" He asked in a raspy whisper.

"Yes," Thandi croaked.

"Would you like for me stop?" Tom breathed against her ear.

Thandi's mind cried "yes," but her mouth said, "no."

Question answered, Tom continued, first with another deep kiss, then, as gently as he could, he pushed the tip of his member inside her. Her eyes widened and she clung to him with nails digging into his shoulders. She buried her face in his neck and whimpered, resisting the urge to cry out as Tom pushed inch by inch until the thin barrier of her virginity broke. Thandi drew a sharp breath and her body tensed all over. He kissed her again, for it was all she could do not to scream. He waited for her pain to subside, then began moving again inside her, taking short, gentle strokes.

Her loins burned and throbbed as he slowly stretched and filled her. He began slowly thrusting, careful to keep her standing, pressed against the stable door.

"Ahhh!" He groaned. Her virginal walls gripped around him with each movement. No longer able to control his passion, he began to thrust deeper and faster into the warm, wet depths. He shut his eyes, absorbing the splendid feel of her. Before long, the unbearable pain she felt turned to indescribable pleasure and her whimpers changed to moans of passion.

Soon, she could feel something building deep within her. She could feel its pressure mounting to the point of explosion. A shard of fire shot through her.

"Tom!" She cried out his name with a note of desperation in her voice. Her body inflamed with passion, she gritted her teeth and hung on to him for dear life.

"Yes!" Tom grunted, increasing his pace, plunging into her again and again until her body shuddered hard with release; her knees went weak and he caught her in his arms, holding her firm as his own body tensed, then spasmed, spilling his seed deep within her.

He held her in that position for several minutes more, his member still pulsating inside her, and his chest heaving in conjunction with her own. He nuzzled his face in her neck until the stars in his eyes dimmed and went away.

"Now sleep with the angels," He whispered in her ear.

Chapter 5

The following day, Thandi could not look in Tom's direction without blushing. Fortunately for her, he spent most of the morning outside in the fields. It had been difficult for her to sleep much after what had transpired in the barn, and Esther was giving her such weird looks that she wondered if the night's events were written on her face.

Never in all of her wildest fantasies had she imagined Tom coming to her and seducing her. Though she had undeniable feelings for him, she did not fully expect him to return them in such a way; especially, because he was married.

Now that it was a new day and the wool was removed from her eyes, she found herself worrying about what Anna would say or do if she found out. She tried to recollect if she had left everything in order back in the barn. If there was any evidence of the night's actions someone was bound to notice.

"Aren't you finished dusting that portrait yet, Miss Thandi?" Esther asked, arching an eyebrow at her. "You've been scrubbing at it for a long time now."

Thandi looked down at her hand holding onto a cloth as she mindlessly moved it against the portrait's frame. The good thing was that there was no more dust there. The bad thing was that she was drawing undue attention to herself. She stopped scrubbing and gave Esther her best innocent smile. "Why, I'm sorry, Esther. I guess my mind just wandered a little."

Esther eyed her. "Mmm hmm. Come with me and let's make breakfast for Missus Lexington. She's expecting guests this afternoon and wants to be ready to greet them."

Thandi sighed inwardly, wishing she could put something unpleasant in the Missus's food, but knowing full well that she would not.

"What would Missus Anna like?" She asked the head maid. *Other than to see me shipped back to Madame Lacy's, she thought.*

"Bacon and eggs, with a side of grits," Esther answered. "And Missus Anna is partial to a little bit of cheese in her grits."

Of course, the lady of the manor would demand extra flavor in her grits. A braver, meaner girl than Thandi might have spit in Anna's grits, but, instead, Thandi simply set to work making them as requested, knowing that at the very least, Tom would appreciate the effort.

Thandi refused to allow herself to have any sort of silly thoughts about replacing her new mistress, though it *was* an appealing notion. Last night had been amazing, but Tom was a married man: a married white man. She couldn't allow herself to dwell on such foolish fantasies. And, besides, he had been drinking. He was probably regretting his night with her now that he was sober. She vowed right then and there in the kitchen to not let such foolishness happen again.

Once the breakfast was fully prepared, Thandi decoratively arranged it on a tray to personally deliver it to Mrs. Lexington. Perhaps, little nice gestures like this would make her ease up on antagonizing the new slaves.

As she walked past, Esther opened her mouth like she wanted to say something, but thought better of it and closed her mouth again, shaking her head. Thandi hadn't realized how very much she still missed her mother until that moment. Oh, how she wished that she could sit down and talk out her problems with her again. Esther was a sweet woman, but she didn't feel comfortable sharing such secrets with her. Besides, she knew in this instance, keeping mum was the best idea. Gossip buzzed around like flies, especially on plantations like this, with so many people to talk about and so many places to hide, out of earshot, to share rumors.

Thandi did not want to be a rumor. She had spent her whole life trying not to be one.

The staircase had not seemed so long the many other times she had climbed it. Now, with the large tray in her hands, was a different story. She did her best to take her time so as not to let a drop of tea spill. When she reached the top, she lightly knocked on the door to Anna's room and waited. She was not entirely sure what she should say in greeting.

Anna took her time in answering. When she did finally answer the door, she was in a long white nightgown, her long auburn tresses unbound. Thandi raised her eyes from the tray to her, taking her all in as she did so. Tom's wife certainly was beautiful. In sleepiness, she even looked fairly sweet. However, after a little yawn, Anna gave Thandi an irked look.

"What do *you* want?" She asked. She did not have the energy to sound icy, but sounded exasperated nonetheless.

Thandi held up the tray for emphasis. "I made you breakfast. Esther told me you liked cheese grits."

Anna looked at the food, raising her nose a bit in displeasure at the company, but unable to deny that she loved cheese grits. "Did she, now?" She asked, with faux sweetness icing her voice like an arsenic cupcake. "She is so thoughtful. Well, come in and set it down, I guess." She opened the door to her bedroom a little wider so that Thandi could get into the room.

As she walked in, Thandi could not help but gape at the ornate décor of Anna's bedroom. The wallpaper was a delightful shade of pink and her large, white canopy bed took up most of the space. The rest of the space was filled with Anna's white oak vanity and many dresses that were strewn about the room in chaos.

"Set that here, by the bed," Anna instructed her, collapsing back into her soft, feather down bedding and patting her nearby nightstand.

Thandi came over at once and set the tray down.

"Very well," Anna said, languidly reclining in her bed.

Thandi stood there, fidgeting nervously with her fingers.

Suddenly, Anna glared at her. "What are you still doing here? I do not require a watchdog, stupid girl! You can go and assist Esther, or find something else to keep you occupied."

Thandi looked clearly wounded, but she fought back her emotions. With a slight curtsy, she quickly made to leave the room.

"Oh, and before you go," Anna added, sitting up and taking her tea, sipping a tiny drop.

"If I ever see you sitting at the table with my Tom again, I will see to it personally that you're sent back where you came from...*or worse*. Is that clear?"

Thandi made her hands into fists, digging fingernails into her palms without meaning to. She gave a little, barely detectable nod and left the room, closing the door behind her.

The trip down the staircase was much faster, particularly because Thandi's emotions were flying right along with her. The nerve of that woman! All she had done was try to be gracious towards her. There was just no pleasing Anna Lexington. Tearfully, she wondered why she was even staying there. It was Isaac's help that Tom really needed. He had only wanted her there because he wanted to visit with her. *But maybe it would be best if she returned home.*

Before long, she realized that she had marched down the stairs and straight out into the front of the mansion. The smell of gardenias woke her up to her detour and she looked around, in awe all over again. It wasn't hard to see why Tom could not abandon this place and why he'd sacrificed his happiness and married a woman like Anna to save it. Lexington manor was so beautiful, and held so many memories for him. Though it grieved her to think of spending months in Anna's company, Thandi knew she could not leave her brother to suffer here alone.

Just as she was settling in to sniff some of the colorful flowers, she spied Tom walking up the winding path to the house. She straightened up, feeling excited to see him, but, remembering her vow to herself, tried her best to not let on that she felt that way.

"Good morning, Tom," She said brightly. Friendliness was acceptable; they had been friends for so many years. It would be odd if she was suddenly cold towards him, and she felt anything but cold towards him. *My, how handsome he looked…*

He gave her one of his most charming, perfect smiles. "Good morning, Thandi. I thought you were still abed and was on my way to come have Esther wake you for breakfast. Would you like to dine with me?"

The good feeling went away and Thandi looked down at the ground, remembering Anna's threat to send her home if she saw them eating together again. It would have been nice if she did not have to give a hoot about what Anna thought, but, apparently, her staying there greatly depended on staying in Anna's good graces. Thandi knew that her position with Anna was currently tenuous at best, and she did not want to infuriate her any further.

"Oh, uh… Tom, I can't," She replied. "There is much work to be done in the house this morning. I only just stepped outside for a short break. But I could make your breakfast for you, if you like?"

"Nonsense!" Tom argued. "You are my guest."

Thandi let out a little sigh. "I am a slave, Tom," She said. "Or haven't you ever noticed?" A note of irritation could be heard in her last statement and expression.

He looked at her quizzically and folded his arms across his chest. "What has gotten into you? Has Anna said something?"

She didn't say a word but her eyes gave the answer. Tom let out a whistle. "I suspected as much. Thandi, don't let her cow you. She is a hateful, spiteful woman, but she must listen to *me*. This is *my* home, and I say that you and Isaac are welcome to my table whenever you..."

"She said that she would see to it *personally* that I was sent home," Thandi cut in, nervously fidgeting with her fingers again.

Tom raised his eyebrows. He did not seem quite as intimidated as she felt, or even concerned. In fact, he soon was smiling. "And you took that seriously?"

Thandi let her hands fall back to her sides, frustrated by his calmness. She had been worried about things enough as it was, and now Anna was threatening her. She thought Tom would be more understanding. "How else can I take it? She's your wife.

She's a powerful person, or, at least, her father is..."

"All right, all right," Tom said, gently placing his hands on her shoulders to try and settle her down. "I know she irks you, but you should try not to let Anna get to you so. She's been rambling on for years, about one thing or another. I'm afraid it's just her way."

"Oh, but she hates me, Tom," Thandi said sadly.

He raised a hand to her chin and gently lifted it with a finger, forcing her to look into his eyes. "Now, you listen to me, Thandi. No one on this Earth could possibly hate you. I'm certain that everyone who knows you, adores you, though not half as much as I do," He said, smiling. "Anna doesn't know you. She is simply jealous of you. I mean just look at you," He said, his eyes glancing her over. "Is that not so hard to understand? You really must trust me when I say that you have nothing to worry about."

Before she could stop herself, Thandi leaned in and kissed Tom's cheek. It was a short, sweet kiss. When she pulled back to look at him, she realized the error and covered her mouth with her hand. "Forgive me, I'm going to get myself in so much trouble."

Tom laughed and looked around to make sure no one was watching. Thankfully, the field hands were all farther away, occupied with their work, and Anna was not in her usual snooping perch at the window. "We just should be careful," He told her. "Though, I wish we had the luxury of being as outwardly affectionate as I want to be with you."

Thandi's cheeks blushed red. She too, had wished a lot of things, but she was not about to tell him any of them. "I think I really should be getting along to my work," She said, forcing herself back to reality.

Tom shook his head. "I say you shall eat breakfast with me. There will be plenty of work for you to do later, if you so insist. But, for now, let's enjoy the morning together."

Thandi still felt uneasy, dining with him. Although his words had sounded right convincing, Anna's still played in her mind. However, she could not argue with Tom. He was the boss, and she took comfort in the fact that his say outweighed Anna's. "Should I go fetch Isaac from the fields?" She asked.

Tom smiled, shaking his head. "I've already convinced him to come. He'll be on his way shortly." He suddenly gave her a funny, confused look. "And, before we go have breakfast, where is your necklace?"

She reached up to her neck and felt for it, before she remembered that she had forgotten to put it back on.

"Please, put it on. And change into one of your prettiest frocks. It makes me so happy to see you wearing your mother's gift."

Thandi felt defeated, and disappointed in herself for not being able to keep her vow for even a day. "Okay," She said timidly. She went back into the house, careful to avoid the questioning eyes of Esther.

When she appeared in the dining room, her brother and Tom were already seated at the table, but they rose from their chairs as soon as they saw her. Thandi had changed out of her gray work dress and into a prettier blue dress; and she was wearing her mother's locket again. She felt herself blush when their eyes were on her.

"Well, don't you look stunning," said Tom. He went to her and pulled a chair out for her to sit. "Oh, I wouldn't go so far," Thandi blushed. "Nonsense, I've never seen a woman so beautiful," said Tom. Isaac gave a nod of affirmation.

Thandi sat in the offered chair, trying to feel less ill at ease about the whole situation. She did not know where Anna was, and she did not want to bring her up, in case it might jinx her and make the lady of the house appear.

Esther came into the room, carrying a big tray of ham, grits, and eggs. She set it in the middle of the table. Then her daughter, Myra, came in and filled their glasses with orange juice. Thandi wondered what they must think of all this. She could not help but notice the looks of consternation on Esther's and Myra's faces.

"Thank you, Esther," Thandi said, catching her eye.

"You're welcome, Miss Thandi," the maid replied before leading Myra out of the room.

Isaac helped himself to a generous portion of eggs and ham. "You are mighty kind to treat us this way, Tom," He said. "I think your Aunt Lacy will be pleased to hear of it."

Tom smiled. "Oh, don't go boasting too much about me. I am so grateful to have your help. It's the least I can do." He gave both Isaac and Thandi a wink.

Thandi adjusted the napkin on her lap, feeling out of place and anxious.

"Eat, Thandi," Tom told her. "You're safe, I promise. Mrs. Lexington can complain all she wants, but she cannot control how I run my household. There is nothing immoral about a man treating his visiting guests, colored or white, to a decent meal."

She bit her lip and placed some eggs on her plate. She was not so much afraid of getting in trouble for eating at the dining room table as she was afraid of getting in trouble for last night.

Just then, Anna yelled for Millie from the hall as she entered the dining room, smiling to see Tom, but her smile quickly vanished and was replaced by a sneer. "Tom, what are they doing here? I thought we discussed before..."

Tom got up from his chair and went to Anna. "Anna, won't you please have a seat and eat some breakfast with us? You have not truly met my dear friends yet."

She looked at him as if he were mad. "I don't want to meet your *dear friends*. As it so happens, I have written my father about them."

Tom did not let that deter him, but he continued to press her to sit down. He pulled out the chair next to Thandi. "Please, sit. You really should try being more sociable."

Anna narrowed her eyes at him, silently refusing the open chair. "Well, then, more breakfast for us," He said, sitting back down at the head of the table. Anna stood, audibly fuming.

Thandi could hear her heavy breathing. She did not know what Tom was playing at, but she was scared and did not like it.

"I have written to your father as well," Tom declared. "I invited him to come and visit as soon as he can; we have some business to discuss. I assumed that you would write to him after that tantrum you had the other night."

Anna had grown pale. She was clutching the side of her dress, catlike gray eyes glaring over at him. "You have niggers dining at the tables that

65

we eat from and sleeping in our beds. My father is not going to stand for this, Tom. You are running a mad house, now, if you think you can give room and board to people like this. You had better be careful, or he will..."

"You would be wise to not give me your idle threats," Tom interrupted.

Thandi looked down at her eggs, trying hard to just eat them like nothing was wrong, but she did not like this feeling that she was being used.

"Tom, Isaac and I can go," She said softly.

"No!" Tom snapped. "It is Anna who can go."

Thandi's eyes darted to Tom's stern expression. She set her fork down and lowered her gaze to her plate.

Isaac looked over at Anna with big eyes. She was stunned speechless. He watched her face turn red with anger.

"If you cannot be civil towards our guests, you can pack up your things and return home with your father after he gets here. I promised to marry you, but I did not promise..." He cut himself off and ran his fingers through his hair.

Thandi closed her lips tight, inwardly rejoicing at the idea of Anna truly being sent away. Anna eyed her, noticing the locket around her neck.

"This bitch doesn't know her station!" Anna fumed, pointing a finger at Thandi's chest. "You think you're a proper lady just because you grew up here? Do you think you're white? Well, you're not. You are a nigger, and no gold is going to change that. Tom is mine. This house is *mine*!"

She stepped away from the table. "I'll go with my father, if he says for me to go. But I wouldn't be so sure of yourself if I were you. He has been disappointed by the yield the last few years, and he has his own ideas for his portion of the land. Maybe I'll convince him to sell it!" With an angry rustle of her skirts, she left the room.

Tom sat, clutching his fork, his food undisturbed on his plate.

"Tom..." Thandi said, shaking her head. "I do wish you would not place us in this awkward position." The things Anna had said had stung, but, obviously for Tom, they were the sort of words he had grown used to. Anna had not been wrong in what she said. Thandi knew she could not simply put on a nice frock and necklace and expect to be treated like a plantation owner's wife. She knew all too well that she could never have the life of a white woman.

Isaac stared across the table at her. "Maybe Mrs. Lexington is right. Maybe we just ought to go home. It would be nice to see my wife..."

"You shall do no such thing," said Tom. "This has been an ongoing war between me and my wife for years and I refuse to lose my friends in the process. It would be good for her to return home to her parents for now. She is a hindrance to my work here, anyway."

"People will talk," Thandi said.

"Oh, let them talk," Tom replied. He stabbed at a piece of ham and stuffed it in his mouth, swallowing it down with some more ham. "As long, as they're also talking about how well I'm doing here, who cares what they say about Anna and me? Who cares if they talk about the truth?"

Mr. Stafford would care. Thandi was sure of that. As happy as she might have been to see Anna leave the plantation for a while, she was not looking forward to the arrival of Mr. Daniel Stafford, the man to whom Tom owed a great deal, as well as the man who could make him lose it all.

Chapter 6

In about a week's time, the day came when Tom was standing on his front porch, awaiting Stafford's arrival. He was not as happy and excited as he had been for Thandi and Isaac's arrival, but he stood there, anxiously watching just the same. Anna spent the entire morning cooped up in her bedroom, having Millie pack away her belongings into five large suitcases.

Just before Mr. Stafford's expected arrival, Anna made her slow descent down the stairs, stopping near the bottom when she saw Thandi. She was sitting in a chair in the hall near the parlor, intensely focused on her needle work. Anna noticed that she was still wearing *that* locket.

She pouted slightly. "You," She said.

Thandi looked up from her work, genuinely confused. "Yes, Madame?"

"Oh, don't you 'Yes, Madame' me," Anna snapped, stepping toward her, but not too close, as though she was afraid she might catch something. "You're probably happy to see me go. I'm sure you've been just hoping for it. It's probably why you came, to try and steal my husband away from me. Well, don't get too comfortable."

"They're here!" Esther called, coming into the hall and stopping when she saw the two women. She gave a slight roll of her eyes and raised her skirts a smidge so she could walk faster. "Your father's carriage is here, Mrs. Lexington," She told her. She rushed from the parlor and back out to the front porch.

Thandi rose from her chair and carefully placed her needlework down. She cast a quick glance to Anna to see if she would come, too, then headed out to join the others on the porch. It was custom for the immediate staff to come out and greet family upon arrival.

The wind was much stronger than it was when she and her brother had arrived. Tom had to hold his hat on his head to keep it there. When he saw Thandi, he smiled then turned his attention again to the oncoming wagon. Thandi swiped swirling ribbons of hair from her eyes as she watched the carriage approach the plantation.

"It'll be over soon," Tom said. He walked down the porch's steps and to the carriage as it stopped. The carriage driver hopped down from his seat and opened the door for Mr. Daniel Stafford.

The older man was tall and wore a fine suit of light blue. His hair and beard were a most distinguishing white. Tom approached him with a smile, but Mr. Stafford did not smile back. In fact, he looked slightly annoyed that he had been forced to come. Thandi was not much surprised, considering the nature of his visit.

"Daniel," Tom said as he warmly shook his hand. He was ever the welcoming host, even when he was not particularly fond of the guest. Thandi knew that the two men did not have a good history. Tom even blamed the man for his father's death. Yet he had to play nice, to achieve what he wanted.

"Tom," said Mr. Stafford. "I had hoped that we would never be meeting like this, but here we are."

Thandi jumped a bit, startled to suddenly see Anna at her side.

"Pa!" The little woman shouted, running to him. Her hat caught the wind and blew off, but she kept on running until she was in her father's arms. "Oh, Pa, it's so good to see you!"

Mr. Stafford held his daughter, a small smile finally appearing on his once pinched and stern face. "My little Anna," He said as the three of them walked towards the house. "How have you been keeping yourself? You look a bit pale, you could use a little sun."

"Oh, Daddy," She said with a pout. "You know I've never been fond of too much sun. It darkens the skin."

Tom made a funny grimace that only Thandi could see. She tried hard not to crack a smile as the trio walked right past her without giving her a moment's hesitation. Thandi felt relieved. She did not want another spectacle or argument; she just wanted Anna to go away for a while and let the harvest continue in peace.

Tom then led Mr. Stafford and Anna into the study, so that the three of them could have their discussion in private. Esther immediately posted herself near the doorway, but they spoke so low that she could not make out what was being said. She frowned, disappointed that she could not hear the latest news, but she stayed there just the same.

Once she was back indoors, Thandi set right back to work at her sewing. She was trying to make a nice, monogrammed pillowcase for Tom, but her lettering kept coming out crookedly and she had to start over every time she finished.

"I am amazed," Esther said in a whisper. "I thought for sure that they would be yelling at each other. Master Tom and Mr. Stafford are always yelling at each other about something.

They're worse than him and Missus Anna."

Thandi sighed softly and shrugged. She had only just seen Daniel Stafford, but she could tell that he was not a pleasant sort of man. Besides, she had heard enough about him from Tom to know that he was not a nice person.

Esther tisked, shaking her head. "You had best be careful, Miss Thandi," She said. "I don't think it's likely that Mr. Stafford came all this way without your name coming up."

Thandi knew she was right. That did not mean that she wanted to hear it.

"I will be careful," She assured Esther, her voice coming out meekly. She undid her shaky "T" And attempted to stitch it in again. Accidentally poking her finger in the process, she let a yelp escape her.

Esther closed her eyes and shook her head even more. "If you're lucky, Mr. Stafford won't take Anna too seriously. She is always finding things to complain about here."

Anna opened the door and came into the hall, closing it behind her. She was plainly sulking, but when she came close to Thandi, giving her a smirk that could only spell trouble before making her way up the stairs and calling for Millie to come help her with her suitcases.

"Lord, have mercy, she is gonna be the death of that poor girl," Esther whispered disapprovingly. "I hate to see her go. I just know she is gonna be waiting on Missus Anna hand and foot with Mr. Stafford always there, to make sure she is."

Tom opened the study door and stepped out, coming toward Thandi. "May I speak with you?" He said, pulling her to the side. "Daniel wants to speak with you," He said lowly. "I didn't tell him about us, and, of course, you shouldn't either."

"What does he want to speak with me about?" Thandi asked in an alarmed but hushed tone.

Tom sighed softly. "Anna's concerns," He said.

Esther gave her a wide-eyed look as she went to the kitchen, closing the door behind her.

When she entered the study, Stafford was sitting in Tom's chair at the desk table. He looked Thandi over before saying anything. When he did speak, all he said was, "Sit."

Nervously, she did as she was told and sat across from him.

"What is this business I hear about you and Tom sitting at the family dining table together?" He asked, getting right to the point. "It is my understanding that you and your brother are slaves, belonging to the Lexington family. You are not visiting guests. You are servants who may only enter the dining room when serving meals. Is this not correct?"

Thandi bowed her head, feeling guilty even though she knew full well that sitting down to eat breakfast with Tom was nothing to feel guilty for. "Yes, Sir." The lie tasted bitter in her mouth, but she knew that it would be better for both her and Tom if they just let Stafford think he was right.

"My daughter Anna is Tom's wife," Stafford went on. "You will respect that by not hanging about him any longer. He will be focusing on his work. He is not some child friend of yours anymore. It makes me shudder to think that my dear old friend Tom Sr. would have allowed the three of you to play together at all, let alone as often as you seemingly did."

It hurt to hear the name of her former master spoken that way. Thandi wondered how Tom Sr. could have ever trusted this man who sat before her. Just being in his presence made her feel uncomfortable.

"You are to stop this nonsense at once," Stafford demanded. "Anna is coming home with me, to have a vacation from all of this insanity and be with her mother for her upcoming birthday. But meanwhile, my associate, Mr. Richmond, will be along in a few days' time. He'll be here on business. And I'll see to it that he keeps an eye on you and Tom in the process. And, if he catches you going after Tom..."

"I never went after Tom!" Thandi cut in, feeling hot tears sting her eyes.

Mr. Stafford narrowed his cool blue eyes at her and clasped his hands together on the table. Thandi could definitely see where Anna had got that haughty look she always sported.

"I suggest that you see that it stays that way," He said, swatting his hand at her dismissively. "And send Tom back in here."

When Thandi got back to her needlework, she undid the stitches that spelled "T. L." And threw the pillowcase in the corner, letting the tears fall from her eyes.

Meanwhile, in the kitchen, Tom was dealing with Stafford again. He took a seat across from him and wondered what further he had to say on the matter that they hadn't already discussed. Stafford got straight to it.

"I could see right through that girl, and I know you're lying when you say you haven't touched her." He stared at Tom intensely, as if he were looking right into his soul. Tom's jawline clenched, but he said nothing.

"She *is* a pretty little thing," Stafford taunted him. "I certainly can see your dilemma." Tom noticed the lustful sparkle in his eyes.

"But make no bones about it. If this thing between you two continues to persist, I will personally set about on a mission to make your life a living hell."

Tom almost smiled. *You and your brat daughter have already accomplished that,* he thought

"If you were smart, you'd send her home immediately, before your cock gets you into more trouble than you can handle," Stafford went on.

Tom frowned instantly. "Your business with me does not include my personal life," He stated firmly. "And furthermore, I will not send my friends home." He was trying his best to remain calm and cordial with Stafford, but he was beginning to cross the line.

Daniel cracked a half smile and stood up from his chair. "My business *is* my daughter. And you'll do well to remember that."

Meanwhile, Thandi sat alone in her room. She had decided to remain there until after Stafford and Anna departed. She couldn't bear another confrontation with the lecherous man or his equally despicable daughter.

Instead of going to Thandi, though he badly wanted to, Tom went up the staircase to find his wife and say his goodbyes.

After dinner, the Stafford carriage rolled out that evening, a few hours after all of the words had been said and all of the promises had been reaffirmed. Alone on the porch, Tom watched the carriage depart. Thandi closed her eyes and sighed with relief as she heard the sounds of the horses grow farther and farther away.

Rising from her chair, she went to meet Tom on the porch just as soon as the carriage was gone. When she went to the door and looked out its screen, she could see him. He was still standing on the porch, staring out at the empty trail. With Stafford's carriage no longer in view, it was apparent that Tom was troubled. Thandi hesitated in the doorway for a moment, then turned on a heel to return back to her room.

Maybe I should give him some time alone, she thought.

"Thandi," Tom called to her.

She turned around at the sound of his voice. "Yes, Tom," She answered softly.

"Please, join me," He asked.

Thandi stepped out onto the porch, shutting the front door behind her. Without question, she knew that Esther would be snooping close by.

"Will you ever forgive me?" Tom asked. He looked at her with genuine remorse in his eyes. Thandi gave him a bit of a puzzled look. She wondered what exactly it was he was apologizing for.

Was it for the horrid way Stafford and Anna had treated her? Or was it...for last night? "This is as much my fault as it is yours, Tom," She said.

He gave her a little smile, as he knew that was not entirely true. If he hadn't come to her in the barn, they probably would have never...

"Well, I am still sorry," He said. "Will you ever forgive me for all of this? I told Stafford that I have no intentions of sending you home. I guess I was so determined to be rid of Anna for a while, that I did not think of how this could affect you."

Thandi breathed a small sigh of relief. She had worried that Stafford would somehow convince him to send her home, but, despite Stafford's threats, Tom did not waver in his determination to keep her on at the plantation. Before, she had been hurt and angered by the way Stafford had spoken to her, but after seeing Tom's solemn mood, she found herself feeling sad for him despite herself. She put on her best pretend smile, then took a step closer to him, but not too close, for the plantation had many eyes.

"Well, look on the bright side of all this," She said, lowering her voice. "You've gotten rid of Anna for some time. Just as you wished."

Tom smiled instantly. "Ever the optimist," He said, shaking his head.

But Thandi was right. Anna was gone! And would be, at least, until after her mother's birthday. Tom smiled even broader when he thought of how long that would actually mean. *She will be away for more than two weeks, but then there was Richmond to think of. However, he wouldn't be along for a few days yet.*

Thandi cut her eyes at Tom, as if she were reading his thoughts.

He smiled back at her, then looked around, concerned that someone, anyone might hear.

"Meet me at the barn tonight. At midnight," Tom told her in a hushed tone.

His words reminded Thandi of the many games of hide-and-seek they had played together in the barn. She blushed, thinking of what it was used for now. By turning in early, she was able to avoid the staff's worried expressions and Esther's questions.

Later that night, when the time came to meet Tom, she became nervous and afraid. There, alone in her room, she had time to reflect on the day's events *and* Stafford's threat. She had decided that it would be best not to meet Tom, even though she had wanted nothing more than to be in his arms again. She truly loved him, and his true happiness meant more to her than her own.

If they were to be found out, it could bring consequences that could ultimately destroy him. As time passed, Thandi lay awake in bed, staring at the ceiling, wondering if Tom would be angry with her, or if he would understand her not coming.

Suddenly, she heard a slight knock at the bedroom door. Her heart leaped and her mind snapped to full alert. "Yes?" She called out softly.

She watched as the door knob slowly turned and the door opened. To her surprise, Tom slipped in, shutting the door closed behind him.

Thandi sprung upright in bed. She called out his name, but her lips did not move. She sat inaudible as he walked over, their eyes never wavering from their connection. He stopped suddenly, just a couple of feet from the bed and began to disrobe.

Thandi swallowed her nerves and tried calming the millions of butterflies in her stomach.

When he had shed the last of his clothing, he rushed to her, kissing her deeply, savoring the taste of her as he unlaced her nightgown. He slid the sheer garment off her shoulders and pulled it downward until she lay completely naked. He cupped her breast in his hand and suckled her nipple. His other hand went to the warmth of her crotch, his fingers gently drumming against her until she was wet and moaning.

He tossed the pillows to the floor, then gently pushed her flat on the bed. Thandi shut her eyes as he trailed hot kisses from her breast to her belly. She gasped when he suddenly licked the sensitive button between her legs. Over and over, stroke after stroke, he licked and tongued the throbbing flesh. Thandi moaned and writhed against his eager mouth.

"Tom!" She cried out his name, her voice full of warning.

Throwing caution to the wind, Tom picked up his pace. Thandi pushed at his head and shoulders, but he did not waver in his erotic assault. Instead, he began to suckle the pulsing flesh until her body began to shudder and convulse with her sweet release. When her body fell limp, he mounted her.

She held onto the bedding as he pushed his girth inside her, thrusting and growling low in his throat. It was hard to keep quiet, it felt so overwhelming.

As he moved in and out, back and forth against her, he grabbed hold of her waist with his strong hands and she began to match his own movements. She winced, taking all of him and driving him deeper inside. She opened herself wide, burying her fingers into his back and her face into his neck as she felt him throbbing deep inside her.

Her long curls spilled over his broad shoulders as blinding pleasure overtook her and his body tensed and released with her own. For several moments, they lay still, embracing as he lovingly stroked her back.

After a while she sat upward and turned to him. "I love you, Tom," She whispered.

Tom wiped a single tear from her face and smiled. "I love you more," He said.

Thandi gazed at him with love filled eyes, and she wondered if he truly knew just how deep her love ran, that what she had felt was more than just a crush all those years ago. She had adored him her whole life long.

She loved him now… she loved him then.

***

Two days later, Thandi worked in the flower gardens. She brushed away a stray tendril of hair from her face as a soft autumn breeze blew her wavy long curls into a frenzy. Gathering the long locks, she tossed them over one shoulder and resumed planting a small rose bush.

"You should use a hair tie," an unfamiliar voice said behind her.

The voice startled her and her heart leaped up into her throat when she turned around to discover the unknown man. He was tall with thick, black hair and dark brown eyes, and he was dressed in the most fetching and ornate suit Thandi had ever seen. It was black and appeared to be made of crushed velvet. She had never seen any gentlemen on a plantation wearing something like that.

"Forgive my intrusion," He said. He had a slight European accent that somehow managed to make his every word sound seductive. "My name is Victor Richmond. I am an associate of Tom's and *Mr. Daniel Stafford*. He sent me to oversee some business while he is away."

He gave her a smile that made Thandi feel as though he knew all of the goings on between her and Tom. The way he looked at her made her uncomfortable, like he was familiar with her without having seen her before.

"And who might you be?"

Thandi stood up, grabbing her long hair and pulling it back forward. She felt defiant about letting it be loose now that he had suggested tying it back. "I'm Thandi," She said, softer than she expected.

Mr. Richmond chuckled and put his hands on his hips, regarding her. Thandi now wished she were wearing something other than her thin, white slip of a dress. She had not wanted to get dirt on her nice dresses, but now, she felt awkward with his hungry eyes on her. "Are you always this shy?" He asked her.

She knelt back down and grabbed the garden spade, digging into the dirt around her freshly-planted bush as though she were preoccupied.

"Are you looking for Tom?" She asked, quickly changing the subject. The last thing she wanted to talk about with this man was herself. She could not trust an associate of Stafford's, even if he did have an attractive accent and an appealing sense of fashion.

Richmond smiled and followed suit. "As a matter of fact, I did come here looking for Tom. Where is he? Have you seen him?"

Thandi patted the dirt firmly around the roots of the rose bush, then began to dig another hole. "He's been gone for most of the day now, but he's due back any minute. You're welcome to wait in the parlor for him, if you'd like."

Victor Richmond continued to grin at her and shook his head slowly from side to side. "I guess I will wait in the parlor, then." He walked towards the house, looking back at her several times before finally making his way inside.

My, Thandi thought. *So far, this Richmond fellow seems far more pleasant than Stafford!* She wanted to feel relieved that he seemed to like her, but, instead, it made her feel sort of scandalized. Richmond looked at her the way a gentleman was not supposed to look at a lady. But then, she was no lady.

And she'd grown used to being looked at by strangers like something "other"; like something tantalizing. However, she only wanted Tom to look at her that way.

She wondered how much longer he would be.

When she finally heard the familiar sound of his carriage approaching, she rushed out to the front path to greet him. He disembarked and quickly came to her side.

"Let's have lunch in the garden, shall we? It's such a beautiful day," Tom began.

"I don't think that would be a good idea," Thandi interrupted, shaking her head from side to side. "Especially, since sometimes important people arrive unexpected while you're away."

Tom pulled back just enough to look into her face. He seemed confused for a moment, but then the realization dawned on him. "Richmond?" He asked, incredulous. "Richmond is already here? When did he get here?"

"He got here just a few minutes ago, as far as I can tell," She said, crossing her arms in front of herself and feeling as though she surely must change clothes before meeting with that man again. "I was planting rose bushes and I told him to wait for you in the parlor."

Tom looked from her to the house and his jaw tensed slightly. "Well, I suppose now is as good a time as any to greet him." He was tired from his meeting and the journey back home, but one could never rest long on his plantation. Things just always tended to come up unexpectedly.

He gave Thandi his arm and walked with her into the house. She modestly cut away from him once they were inside.

"Richmond!" Tom said, his voice full of surprise, even though he had been told of his arrival. "How long have you been waiting for me?"

"Not long," Richmond said. His gaze went to Thandi.

"Well, I hope you haven't been bored much."

"One could not possibly be bored when they're in the company of such beautiful ladies," Richmond responded.

Esther stood nearby, always on hand to take care of a guest's needs, and she blushed and giggled at the compliment.

Thandi smiled at Tom lovingly, before disappearing down the long hall. She reappeared sometime later wearing a form fitting, but very modest, rose pink frock.

"May I help you with anything, Master Lexington?" Esther asked.

Tom returned Esther's bright smile. "No, I'll manage just fine. Thank you, Esther."

Esther eyed Thandi and cleared her throat. Heeding the warning signal, Thandi followed the plump maid into the kitchen.

Tom extended a hand, gesturing for Richmond to follow him into his study. "So, what has brought you here, business or *otherwise*?" Tom asked, pouring himself a drink. He paused over the second glass. "Brandy?"

Richmond smiled charmingly. "No, no, none for me, thank you." He waited patiently as Tom settled himself in his seat.

"A bit of both, actually. I thought we could talk shop as well as address Daniel's suspicions of you and that very fetching young girl. Not that any of it is my business," He said, throwing up a hand. "But I think I can already see where he might get his ideas."

Tom leaned forward a bit in his chair, eyeing Richmond suspiciously. "And just what is it that you think you see?"

Richmond smiled slowly. "Well, just from the parlor window, I would say I saw the faces of two lovers when you arrived. Daniel also feels that you are not as entirely invested in our partnership as I'd like to believe. He thinks your heart is not in it. Is that so?"

Tom looked darkly at Victor. "How could my heart not be in it? Just as my heart is in every brick and stone of this place. This plantation and the mill are my birthright; your *associate* has taken that from me. He owns the controlling interest in the mill and he requires a hefty percentage of the plantations yield each year. He is lording himself over my plantation. My *home*. If he had his way, I'd do nothing but work for him, and be his daughter's simpering little husband."

Richmond looked at him, running his fingers through his thick, dark hair. "Tom, I'd like to think of you as my friend. But Stafford is my friend, as well. Now, you two had an agreement."

"Agreeing to something under duress is not really an agreement," Tom argued.

Leaning back in his chair, Victor looked at Tom's drink glass. "I've changed my mind. I think I will have some of that brandy."

Tom stood up immediately and poured Richmond a glass.

"I do wish there were something I could say or do to help you with your predicament." Richmond said, swirling the liquid around in the glass a few times before taking a long sip.

"There is *something* you could do," said Tom. "Do what you do best: do business with me."

Richmond furrowed his dark brows as he looked over at Tom. "Business with you? What business?"

"There is something that I have had my eye on for quite some time," Tom said, sitting on the edge of his seat in his excitement to share. "The old Newport Mill...if you aim to sell it."

Richmond did not have to think long to know why Tom would have an interest in the mill; however, he did wonder how he thought to buy such a prime piece of real estate, and, more importantly, he wondered how Tom could even imagine that he would sell it.

"You must be kidding," Victor said seriously. "I make an excellent profit from my shares at Lexington Mills. Why on Earth would I jeopardize that by selling you the mill and making you my competitor?"

"I've given that thought, as well," Tom said. "If you don't want to sell it outright, you could enter into a partnership with me. Lexington Mills profits would hardly be affected. The old mill is closer to Bridgeport and Fenton, two major farming cities. The farmers there currently take their business to Steinway simply because it's closer than Lexington. I'm certain that if we were to restore the Newport mill, they'd bring their business to us and other surrounding cities as well. Before the fire, the mill had thrived and I'm certain it could thrive again." He paused a second. "You don't even have to think about it right now. You're welcome to relax here for a while. Make yourself at home so that Stafford really thinks you're out here spying on me. I've saved a considerable sum of cash over the past few years, and with my proceeds from this year's yield, I'm certain that I can come up with an asking price. All I ask is that you'll consider it."

Victor smiled into his eyes.

"You're the best businessman in Newport," Tom added. "If there is anything that I can do for you to help make the deal more appealing, please, do not hesitate to mention it."

Richmond leaned back in his chair, swirling his drink again before taking a final big gulp of the dark brandy.

"I can think of something," He said. "But I will stay here a while longer and think of it some more."

With that, the two men rose to their feet and shook hands.

Chapter 7

Over the next few days, it seemed that wherever Thandi went, Victor Richmond was right there, watching her. She found him staring at her as she did her usual chores and she even felt his eyes on her from the windows when she worked inside the gardens. The only other person who seemed to notice his focus on her was Esther, and she did not make the situation any better, what with her raised eyebrows and impish grins in Thandi's direction.

Though it was not entirely clear to her what the man was doing at the plantation, it was evident that he was going to be there for a while. Tom spent much of his time with Richmond now, sitting in his study or out on the veranda, sipping brandy and discussing real estate and other business matters. Whenever Thandi was nearby to serve them cakes or announce the next meal, she caught snippets of their conversation.

Richmond would somehow always catch her eye, and wink at her. She frowned back at him constantly to make sure that he knew she did not like him. He was Stafford's spy and his presence made her uncomfortable. And now, apparently, Tom was doing business with him!

She could not wait to get Tom alone so she could discuss things with him, but the trouble was that he was almost never alone anymore. Whatever he was plotting with Richmond seemed to give him a new burst of energy. He was always working on something, be it planning with Victor or discussing the harvest with Ben and Isaac.

It seemed the only one of them she could find alone was Richmond. She would run into him in the halls and end up dutifully offering him tea or fresh linens and hate herself in the process.

"You don't like me, do you, Thandi?" He would often say in response, letting a laugh escape him.

Really, it went far beyond simply not liking the man. She did not trust him, and she did not understand what he was possibly gaining from befriending Tom. She could not find the chance to ask him, and she was certainly not going to ask Richmond.

"You're as jumpy as a jackrabbit whenever Mister Richmond is around," Esther noted one evening. "Master Tom trusts him, so there's no reason to be scared of him."

Thandi shook her head dismissively. "I'm not afraid of him. I just don't like the way he looks at me."

This was only a partial lie. Victor Richmond always looked at Thandi as though she was not wearing any clothing. She was used to receiving lustful looks from men, but they were hard to ignore when the lustful man was in her presence nearly every moment of every day.

Thankfully, one evening before supper, Thandi found Tom alone in the parlor. He was sitting with the day's mail in his lap, reading over something. She felt sorry for interrupting, but she saw no other opportunity. She stood in the doorway and softly cleared her throat, hoping that would be enough to get his attention.

When Tom looked up, however, she instantly felt guilty. He had tears in his eyes and a look of utmost concern.

"Tom?" She asked softly, moving closer and gently placing a hand on his broad shoulder. "What is it? What's wrong?"

He looked back down at the letter. "It's Aunt Lacy," He said, his voice shaky. "She's sick. She's dying."

"What?" Thandi asked, breathless.

Tom handed the letter to her and put his head in his hands. Thandi quickly read it over.

Lacy Lexington had come down with scarlet fever. Despite her doctor's best efforts, she was not expected to recover.

Thandi was heartbroken. Ms. Lexington had always been so kind to her and Isaac. She had treated them almost as her own children. Thandi's eyes welled with tears. "Oh, Tom," She said sadly, wrapping him in a gentle hug. "I am so sorry."

He gratefully held her tightly and let himself cry a little, but he was soon on his feet. "I have to go to her," He declared. "I have to go see her before it is too late."

"But Tom..."

Before Thandi could even try to stop him, he was out of the room in search of Esther.

"Please, pack my things," He told Esther as soon as he had found the trusted housekeeper. "I must go to my aunt, at once."

Esther was bewildered. "Yes, Sir," was all she could say. She turned to Thandi and gave her a questioning look. She would not get answers from Tom, but she could get them from Thandi. The two went to Tom's room and began gathering his clothing.

"Aunt Lacy is dying, Esther," Thandi told her, trying to keep her voice down. "She has scarlet fever. The letter told him that it's too dangerous for anyone to be around her, but do you think that will stop him?" She bit her lip. She did not want Tom to leave and put himself at risk, but she also knew that there was no stopping him when he put his mind to something, especially when it came to his loved ones.

Slowly shaking her head, Esther tutted. "He'll have you and me to take care of him if he comes back sick. And if we get sick, well… that's not important."

Thandi was not worried at all about herself. She did not want Tom to get sick and die, not now that she had him back in her life. She was devastated for Aunt Lacy, but she couldn't help but worry about Tom's safety.

Once the suitcases were packed and brought downstairs by the two women, Richmond took them and headed outside to Tom's waiting carriage. The Lexington's coach driver, Luther, was at the helm, and he did not look so eager to go. He was no doubt worried about the sickness that awaited him as well.

"Give your aunty our love, you hear?"

Esther said as she and a sulking Thandi followed Tom.

"Thank you, Esther," He replied. His voice was a monotone and his brow was set resolutely.

Thandi thought of Isaac and how he hadn't known about Madame Lacy. "Tom, wait," She pleaded. He stopped and turned to her, his face solemn. "Isaac must know. His wife could be in danger."

Tom hesitated for a moment, pondering whether or not he should bring Isaac along. If his friend were to become ill and die he would never forgive himself, but if he did not take him, Isaac would never forgive him if his wife fell ill and he hadn't gone to her. Tom turned towards the fields. "I'll go to him," He said. With that, he walked to the fields at a fast pace. Thandi looked on as he approached Isaac. The two men talked for a moment, then walked back quickly to the house together.

Thandi could see her brother's troubled expression as he raced by her and the others and into the house. Shortly after, he came out with his luggage in hand. Thandi's heart plummeted to her stomach. Suddenly, she wished that she'd not even made mention of Isaac.

Tom would've been on his way by now without him. She hated herself for having such a selfish thought. Of course, Isaac had to go to

Sarah, she was his wife; it was his duty. Still, she could not help feeling afraid for him and Tom.

Suddenly, Richmond spoke from behind her. "Don't worry about a thing, Tom," He said.

"I'll make sure this place stays running properly."

Tom shook his hand and Thandi could feel the color drain from her face. She did not want to be left alone with *Mr. Victor Richmond*! Sadly, she watched Tom step into the carriage. Isaac gave her a hug and said his goodbyes. Tom gave her one last look just before the carriage pulled out. A small smile curled the corners of his lips and she could see his love for her in his eyes.

Luther shouted a loud "hiya!" And then they were off on their way away from Thandi and the house… off towards what only God knew awaited them.

***

The ride to Aunt Lacy's plantation was longer than Tom remembered, perhaps owing to the fact that, in the past, the ride had been fun and exciting for him. He remembered riding there to visit as a boy and delighting in the sight of passing farmlands as he and his father made their journey for family functions. Sometimes Thandi had come along with him, and he wished that she could be with him now for the hardest journey, but he could not risk her safety, no matter how much he'd wanted her with him. Rain splashed down in the mud alongside the carriage's wheels and did not help his mood.

Under the circumstances, neither Isaac nor Luther were much for conversation. Tom kept telling himself that the letter might have been exaggerated and his aunt could pull through and everything could end up just fine. But telling himself that and believing it were two different things. When Tom's carriage finally arrived, it was pitch black outside. Aunt Lacy was probably not even awake at that hour, but he had to see her regardless. He alighted from the coach and Luther brought along his suitcases. Isaac did not bother to grab his luggage. He headed to the house immediately, going first to his pregnant wife.

Once inside, Tom sent his driver to a spare bedroom while he immediately showed himself to his aunt's bedchamber.

Tom's beloved aunt was lying in her bed and appeared to be asleep. The lamp was out and a soft glow from the lights outside offered the only illumination in the small but well-furnished bedroom. He was about to turn and take his leave, assuring himself that he could come back to her, when she suddenly awoke.

"Tom?"

He rushed to her side and took her hand. "Yes, Aunt Lacy, it's me. I came for you."

Aunt Lacy opened her eyes a bit to look at him. She did not smile, but he knew she was happy to have him there. He gave her hand a gentle squeeze. "I am glad to see you," She said, "but you should not have come, Tom. You could become ill, too."

Tom shook his head. "I could not let you be sick alone. I would never have forgiven myself."

Lacy exhaled a raspy sigh. "You've always been so noble... like your father." A thought suddenly struck her and she opened her eyes wider, as though feeling the weight of something for the very first time. She tried to sit herself up in bed, but she was too weak and immediately fell back.

"Lie still," Tom instructed, giving her forehead a gentle pet. She was burning up. It was not surprising, but her evident fever made the situation all the more real to him. His auntie was dying. Tears welled up in his eyes, but he would not let them escape. He did not want her to see him cry. It would only bring her more grief.

Gulping back hard, she took a ragged breath before speaking again. "Tom," She said, her voice now mostly a whisper. "Tom, I have something important to tell you... something I should have told you years ago..."

"Shhhh! save your strength," Tom said, stroking her hand. "Whatever it was, it isn't important now."

"But it is important," She argued softly. She took another ragged breath and he realized that she was crying. The gray skin on her face was now glistening with fallen tears. "Tom..." She said again, ever so slightly tightening her grip on his hand. "Your father did not kill himself because of money or land..."

Tom sighed. "Aunt Lacy, I don't want to talk about this," He said. Rumors and opinions about his father's suicide had plagued him for so long that he wanted to stop thinking about it forever. "I don't want to discuss that rat Stafford while you're..."

"He died because of love, Tom."

85

A confused look came over Tom's face. "Because of my mother?"

She slowly shook her head "no." "Your mother had given up on him long before, long before your father had fallen in love with Haiti."

This statement sent Tom reeling. "Haiti?" He asked disbelievingly. The gentle woman had always treated him as though she was his second mother, but he had always attributed that to her kind, loving nature. He would never have thought that she and his father...

"It killed him when she died," his aunt went on. "He couldn't live with himself knowing he had sent her and her children away." Tom fell back a little in the bedside chair. He simply couldn't believe what he was hearing.

"But, honestly, it was the only thing he could do after your mother had learned about them." Tom looked dazed as he tried processing the shocking news.

My father had been in love with Haiti. His Slave. Thandi's mother!

He immediately thought of Thandi. He supposed that he and his father were similar.

"When he sent her to me, the poor thing was devastated," Aunt Lacy continued. She stopped speaking as her mind went back to that time.

"Tom," She said more firmly after a moment.

He straightened himself up and gently squeezed her hand. "Yes, Aunt Lacy?" He answered. He could tell from her eyes and the cold feel of her hand that she did not have much time left. "Yes, Aunt Lacy?" He asked again, wishing he could have more years with her.

"Thandi..." She whispered, her grip on his hand loosening. "Thandi was his daughter."

Tom went numb, and the world closed in around him. "Whatever do you mean?" He asked.

"Yes, Tom. She is your sister," his aunt whispered. She closed her eyes and took in another labored breath. "You must see after her... and Isaac," She said.

Tom felt a pang in his chest as her words still echoed in his mind. *Thandi was his daughter...your sister!*

***

Life at the plantation under Victor Richmond's rule proved to be less horrific than Thandi anticipated. Although he was still much more flirtatious and forward than she would have liked, Richmond spent most of his time in the study, preoccupied with his own affairs.

He did not conduct business the same way Tom ran his affairs. Whereas Tom could be seen working out in the fields alongside the slaves, Richmond chose to let the workers handle their tasks once they were assigned. He dressed in fine suits and expensive shoes and rarely walked into the dirty fields. Instead, he sat in the office and handled whatever paperwork there was to be done. Thandi figured that there must be a lot of paperwork, since Tom was usually splitting his time between several different tasks at once. She wondered if Tom had already spoken with Richmond regarding the Newport Mill, as he had once mentioned. With all that had been going on, she hadn't had an opportunity to talk to him much at all.

Regardless of their business, she still could not stomach the fact that Richmond was there. She and Tom had not shared any time together since his arrival, and Anna would be back at the plantation soon. She knew that Madame Lacy was deathly ill, and that it was dangerous for even Tom and Isaac to go, but she still wished Tom would have invited her.

She did not have the opportunity to say goodbye to her mother. And now she would not be able to say her goodbyes to the woman who had cared for her in her stead.

Nearly two weeks later, Thandi lay in bed crying one evening when she heard a light knock on the door. She did her best to wipe away the tears from her cheeks. "Come in," She said.

The door opened and Esther came inside. She stopped short when she saw the pained look on Thandi's face.

"What is it, Esther?" Thandi asked solemnly.

Esther hesitated for a moment, then unfolded a paper she was holding in her hand. "I'm afraid I have bad news," She said regrettably.

Fearing the worst, Thandi sprung upright in bed.

"It's Madame Lacy," Esther said. "She's passed on."

Tears welled again in Thandi's eyes. She opened her mouth, but all that came out was a partially stifled sob.

Esther came to her at once and wrapped her motherly arms around her. "Aww, Miss Thandi, it's going to be all right. Master Tom and your brother will be back, as soon as they can be."

Sniffling, Thandi closed her eyes, appreciating the embrace. "I should have gone with them," She said mournfully.

"Aww," Esther said, smiling a bit and rocking Thandi sympathetically. "But I'm sure Ms. Lacy would not have wanted you to go and put yourself in danger. And I'm sure she knew you loved her, too," She added.

"I did love her," Thandi said, crying softly. "I just wish none of this ever happened. And I hate being here with this Richmond fellow. I want him to leave."

Esther shushed her. "Master Richmond is in charge here while Master Lexington's away. You better not say such things, in case he hears you."

Thandi pouted. "I don't care if he hears me. He should not be here. He's Stafford's…," She stopped herself; she had almost said too much. "I just don't like him," She finished plainly.

"Well, do you hate being here with me?" Esther asked as she released Thandi from her arms, and looked into her teary green eyes.

"No, of course, not," Thandi replied.

"And as far as Mr. Richmond, well, I can't see why you don't like him. He seems to like *you* just fine," Esther stated with a matter-of-fact tone in her voice.

Thandi wiped the tears from her face and frowned.

"Well, I suppose you won't be moving back to Missus Lacy's," Esther said, changing the subject.

Thandi looked up at her. She hadn't thought of what would happen if Madame Lacy died. *Who would run her plantation?* Suddenly her mind began to fill with questions.

"You'd do best to stay in good graces with Master Tom's associates and family, even if you don't like them, especially when you just may be here indefinitely now." With that said, Esther rose from the bed. "Now, dry your eyes and come help me set the table for Master Richmond's dinner. If he says anything to you, just bow and don't let it get to you."

Reluctantly, Thandi did as she was told. She went to the kitchen and helped prepare supper for Victor. He had requested roasted duck, and it was Thandi's job to set it on the table for him. The table was lavishly laid out, even though he was the only one who would be dining there. Thandi sadly wondered who might be preparing Tom's supper. She hoped that he was keeping himself fed. And she hoped that he and her brother would be on their way home to her soon. *She had missed them so terribly…*

"The food looks marvelous," Victor spoke.

Thandi shook her thoughts and smiled faintly as she filled his glass goblet with red wine. "Obviously, I cannot possibly eat all of this by myself," He said, gesturing his fork at the large roasted duck that centered the table. "You simply must dine with me," He said, smiling.

Thandi's eyes grew big at his request. She did not want to be alone in the same room with him, let alone, have dinner with him.

"I don't think that would be a good idea," She quickly protested.

Victor began to cough violently. Covering his mouth with his napkin, he tried desperately to compose himself.

Instinctively, Thandi rushed over and handed him the glass of red wine. "Here, drink this," She said. She looked on slightly concerned as he struggled to gather himself.

"Forgive me," He said, clearing his throat. "I've been a little under the weather as of late." Thandi gave a small nod, then turned to leave the room.

"Wait," called Victor.

Thandi turned to face him. "Yes, Sir?"

"Why?" He asked.

"Why what, Sir?" Thandi asked, raising a questioning brow.

"Why wouldn't it be a good idea?"

Thandi hesitated a moment, as she did not have a ready answer. She lowered her gaze from his probing eyes, then slowly looked up again. "It simply would not be appropriate, sir," She answered flatly.

Richmond smiled coyly as he adjusted his napkin on his lap. "I'm sure it wouldn't be the first inappropriate thing to happen in this house," He coyly remarked.

Thandi's nose flared and her brows furrowed, expressing her obvious disdain for him. She now wished that she had allowed him to choke. She could tell by his condescending tone and smug smile that he was referring to her and Tom's relationship.

Chapter 8

Days later, Tom returned home. At the first distant sound of galloping hooves, Esther rushed out to the front porch. Ben was already there. He stood sentry on the veranda, waiting for the first sight of the carriage so he could help Master Tom with his luggage and anything else he might require fresh off the road. Thandi took her place on the veranda, watching the road along with Ben and Esther, even though she was meant to be in the kitchen, preparing a light appetizer before dinner. She believed Tom would forgive her for wanting to be one of the first to greet him and Isaac.

Sure enough, when the wagon approached, Thandi took off running. Ben started walking towards the wagon, but stopped with a large grin on his face when he saw her take flight. He followed her at a quick pace, but he was not even going to attempt to run with her. As soon as the carriage settled, Thandi stopped beside it, bouncing on the balls of her feet in anticipation for the door opening. There was a long pause that she did not particularly like. For a flash of a moment, she worried that Tom or Isaac was ill and would be needing Luther and Ben's assistance in coming out to the house. The door to the carriage finally opened, setting her mind at ease, but only for a moment.

She had expected a warm smile, but when Tom disembarked the carriage, he gave her a solemn look for half a second, then looked away, focusing his eyes on the middle distance. *Aunt Lacy,* she thought.

"Tom…" She said softly, reaching out to give him a sympathetic hug.

But his gaze and attention stayed focused away from her. When Ben approached, he finally gave a bit of a smile. "It's good to be home," He said. "There's still another suitcase, Ben."

Ben smiled. "On it, Boss," He said.

Rather than linger any longer, Tom continued on his way up to the house. Thandi watched as he walked away without so much as looking in her direction.

Isaac, she thought. She turned her attention again to the wagon. Both doors were open on either side and she could see inside. Isaac was not inside, nor was he around anywhere to be seen. Alarmed, Thandi looked around until her eyes found Luther.

"My brother," She said. "Where is he?"

"Isaac stayed on, Missus," He answered. Thandi's heart sank at the news. Though, she had half expected that he would stay on for some time, she still hoped that he'd return with Tom. Richmond greeted Tom on the porch, then the two men went inside the house. Thandi worried about what might be going on in Tom's mind. There was so much she wanted to ask him, but she had no idea how to ask, or if it would be appropriate for her to do so just now. Auntie Lacy was *his* auntie, after all, not hers. As kind as the woman had always been to her, she had to let Tom grieve however he saw fit. And he had to be able to do it alone, if he so chose.

She decided that the best thing to do was to give him some pleasant news. She got the opportunity to do so when she found him in the kitchen drinking a tall glass of water. "You must be famished," She said to him.

He looked at her briefly, then turned to place his glass on the side table.

"Well, not an awful lot has happened while you were away, Tom," She began, thinking of the best pieces of news she could share. "I hear the crops are far greater in number than the previous years. And it won't be much longer before the hands have cleared the fields. At least, that is what Ben says," She added nervously. "The other day, he said they sowed about one hundred more stalks than last year's record."

Farming cotton and other such crops was not exactly Thandi's forte or even interest, but she had to share the news with him anyway. Perhaps it would make him look a little happier. Tom stared blankly into the kitchen sink.

"The weather is changing," He said.

Did he sound cryptic or was that just Thandi's imagination?

"I had faith that things would turn around. I always do," He said. He finally, slowly, turned his blue eyes toward her. He appeared as though he desperately wanted to say something.

Thandi opened her mouth to prompt him, but then he looked away again.

"Where's Richmond?"

Oh, hang Richmond! Her thoughts screamed. *Haven't you missed me, Tom? Why can't you look at me?* She thought.

"In… in your study," She said quietly, stricken by his ambivalence. "He's in your study, working on… something."

She suddenly felt ill. She had almost forgotten that Tom and Richmond were working together now. The happiness at Tom's return had made Richmond's presence seem at an end.

Tom wasted no time and went straight to his study to confer with Richmond. Thandi took a seat on the settee in the foyer, wondering what they were discussing, now. She could not understand Tom's odd behavior towards her. She understood that he was deeply saddened by his aunt's death, but she couldn't help feeling that there was something else.

Esther found Thandi there, and greeted her with her hands on her hips and a disapproving look. "Your peanut soup must be scentless," She said sharply. "Since there is no smell of it coming out of the kitchen."

Thandi felt as though she had been whipped. First by Tom, then by Esther. "I'm sorry, Esther. I'll start it right away. It's only… I wanted to greet him as soon as he got home."

"Mmm hmm," Esther said gruffly, not removing her hands from her hips. "Well, he's got to eat," She said plainly.

"I know," Thandi replied timidly. She reluctantly went into the kitchen to begin making the soup as planned. She doubted very much that Tom would have much of an appetite for it, what with the strange way he was acting. But what Esther said went. There was also Mr. Richmond's appetite to consider, though Thandi felt loathe to do so.

When she rapped on the door to the study to announce that their soup was ready, the conversation between Tom and Richmond stopped.

"Come in," Tom said.

She opened the door and looked in. Richmond sat in his chair and grinned over at her while Tom looked addled. Thandi did her best to ignore both of their expressions. "Sorry to interrupt you, gentlemen, but I have prepared some soup for you if you would like to come down to the dining room. Dinner will be ready later on."

"My, my," said Richmond. "That is awfully nice of you, Thandi."

She gave him a small smile. She would've rather that the compliment had come from Tom, but she genuinely appreciated it all the same.

Tom looked at her thoughtfully, unsmiling. When she caught his gaze, he quickly shifted his eyes away from her again. Thandi's heart sank to her stomach. It was clear that he did not want her company, although he seemed to be perfectly content with Richmond's.

He almost seemed to be singling her out, as if he were angry with her for some unknown reason. "Yes, thank you, Thandi," Tom said stiffly. "We'll be along in a few minutes."

Thandi looked at him again, and again he avoided her eyes. Swallowing her hurt, she gave a small curtsy and left the men to their work. When she had left the room, closing the door behind her, Richmond turned in his chair so he was facing Tom fully. "That girl is one of your best kept secrets. I'm surprised you are able to get any work done around here, with her in your home."

"I do my work just fine," Tom countered.

Victor's dark eyes seemed to flash. "But your wife doesn't like her. Her presence here is obviously causing rifts in your marriage."

Tom did not want to have this conversation, especially, not now, but he knew that Victor would persist with his questioning until his curiosity was satisfied. "There is nothing between us," Tom finally answered.

Victor narrowed his eyes a bit at the information. "So, why keep her here, if it causes your marriage trouble?"

Tom poured himself another drink as he considered the true answer to his question. *He'd kept her there simply because he wanted to. And because he loved her, and she meant more to him than his sham of a marriage.* But it wouldn't serve him good to speak so honestly.

"You know how women can be. Anna is just jealous of her. I've known Thandi and her brother since we were children. They are good friends. And they've done nothing to offend her. I shouldn't have to throw them into the streets simply because my wife wishes it."

Stroking his chin thoughtfully, Victor leaned back in his chair. "You know," He said. "I have been thinking more on your proposal for the old mill."

Tom sat up in his chair, smiling a genuine smile for what felt like, and was, the first time in weeks. "You have?"

"Yes," Richmond answered. He took another small sip from his glass. "However, I must say that I'm not entirely certain if another partnership would be wise for me. I'm already stretched pretty thin as it is."

Tom straightened himself up in his chair. "I can pay you for the building outright. Just tell me your terms," He said.

Victor ceased to swirl his drink around.

"It isn't an issue of profit for me, Tom. I don't *need* money. I already own practically half of Newport as it is. But there is something that you have that I don't… something that I have not had for many years."

Tom gave him a confused look. He could not think of what that could possibly be. Victor Richmond seemed to already have everything a man could possibly want. Foolishly, he wondered if Richmond might want to relieve him of his wife, since he seemed so interested in her happiness. She was undoubtedly beautiful, and a man with as much power as Richmond would surely be able to get her to behave like a good wife should. Tom silently prayed that Anna was what he was after.

"Thandi," Richmond blurted.

Tom blinked at him, shocked. "Thandi?"

Victor nodded. "Thandi. Give her to me and you will have your mill."

Tom's body stiffened at his words. He was visibly taken aback by Richmond's request. This was not something that he could have considered. *After so long without her in his life, he couldn't imagine sending her away, especially now that she didn't have to return to Aunt Lacy's plantation.* Tom checked his thoughts. How could he even allow himself to think this way now? The ugly realization of what he had learned flooded his mind again. *Thandi was his half sister. His father's daughter.*

"Is it a deal?" Richmond asked. He downed the last of his bourbon, then sat the empty glass down on the table.

Tom hesitated a moment longer. The thought of him giving Thandi over to another man still did not sit well with him. And besides, Thandi would never agree to go with him, anyway.

"I would have to talk it over with Thandi, and see if she agrees," He said finally.

Richmond felt slightly defeated. *Well played,* he thought, seeing as how he knew that Tom knew she would not go willingly.

"Very well." He smiled and looked to the door, then to Tom again. "We should probably go and have some of that delightful smelling soup." He stood up from his chair and Tom did the same.

As they walked to the door of the study, Richmond suddenly slowed his steps then stopped and turned to him. "Oh, there is just one other thing," He said, holding up a finger. "I'd like to take Thandi out for a ride tomorrow. That is, if you have no objections, of course."

It seemed that Richmond had a few tricks of his own. He knew that Tom could not deny him such a simple request. *Especially, since there had been nothing between him and his **friend**.*

Tom forced a phony smile. "But, of course," He said, giving his blessing.

"Thank you, Tom," Richmond said brightly. He gave him a thankful pat on the shoulder then started towards the door again.

Thandi sat outside the dining room with her needlework after serving Tom and Victor their peanut soup and bread. As she hoped, she could overhear their conversation. First, the two men discussed business matters, then Tom shared with him his plans of attending his aunt's funeral and the reading of her will. Thandi's heart sank. She didn't want Tom to leave her so soon again. *But certainly, he would allow her to pay her last respects.*

As the clattering of dishes came to an end, she stood up and set her work down before going into the dining room to take away their bowls for cleaning.

She caught Tom's eye briefly, and for the first time since his return, he gave her a sweet smile. However, there was a note of sadness in his smile, but that was not so unusual after what had happened. She returned it, giving him a little nod.

"Dinner will be ready soon. Esther is working on it, she said."

Victor shared a glance with Tom. "It won't be necessary to prepare dinner for me," He said. "I must be off today on a matter of business."

Thandi remembered herself enough to give a slight curtsy. "I shall be sorry to see you go, Sir," She lied.

Tom's smile faltered at that. "Oh, I shall be back soon enough," Victor said with a note of zeal in his tone. "I've got Tom's permission to take you out for a ride tomorrow."

Thandi turned her head sharply and looked at Tom. Victor could plainly see the look of disappointment and even anger in her eyes.

So, this was what went on behind the closed door in the study, Thandi thought. Tom looked away from her, unable to face the hurt and betrayal in her eyes.

"Very well," She heard herself say in a monotone. "I will be ready, Sirs!"

With that, she turned on her heel and briskly left the room. Only she did not go to the kitchen to help Esther with their dinner as she had been instructed. Instead, she ran out to the gardens where she could be alone and away from Tom and his lecherous new friend. Warm tears slipped down her cheeks as she began to walk in the gazebo's direction.

Why would Tom allow this to happen? He's behaving so strangely. What had she done to make him treat her this way? Had he tired of her? And now sought to pass her to another suitor to ease his guilt? The questions plagued her mind.

Heartbroken and dispirited, she stepped into the gazebo and lay down on the bench. She could hear the workers in the distant fields as they sang a familiar uplifting song that she had not heard since she was a child.

Somehow, she still remembered the words:

Though my back is breaking
 Lord! My feet are aching
Sweat's coming down like rain on me, but
I'm still a believahh! Ohhh ohhh
All this pain I'm taking Oh! But I'm not forsaken!
'Cause I know my God's got ah perfect plan for me!
And I'm still a believahh! Oh ohhhh!

Thandi closed her eyes and tried listening to the sweet hymns from the fields instead of her miserable thoughts. As a child, she often hid in the tall stalks of wheat as she watched the workers and listened to them sing. After a while, her tears ceased to fall and she drifted off to sleep.

Soon after, Tom found her there. He sat across from her so as not to wake her. The tear stains on her cheek were proof that he had hurt her deeply. He felt a tug at his already heavy heart. As he had searched for her, he tried thinking of what he would say to her when he'd found her.

He could not possibly tell her the truth. She would be too devastated. He wanted to protect her, spare her the torment and pain of knowing. Yet, he had to put a stop to their affair immediately. He could not avoid her forever, nor did he want to.

Feeling a presence, Thandi stirred in her sleep and her eyes fluttered open and focused on him. She frowned as recognition and memory flooded back. She sat upright immediately and brushed out the wrinkles from her dress.

"May I help you, Sir?" She asked him. Her newfound formality and clipped gaze spoke volumes.

Tom sighed deeply. He deserved her anger. He swallowed hard, knowing he was going to have to hurt her even more.

"I wanted to talk to you," He said.

Thandi looked back at him with contempt in her eyes. "Yes," She answered dryly.

"First," Tom said, starring squarely into her piercing green eyes. "I'd like to apologize for my behavior earlier. I have not quite been myself lately."

Thandi gave him a sharp look. She couldn't have agreed more with his statement.

He lowered his eyes, then leaned forward, clasping his hands between his knees. "There's just been so much craziness the past few weeks that I can hardly make sense of it all."

His words were heavy with grief. He stopped speaking a moment and shook his head. He looked up at her again, and he could see some of the anger leave her eyes. *But still, that does not explain the morrows ride with Richmond. Why on Earth would he wish her to go riding with another man?* Before she could part her lips to ask that very question, he spoke as if he had mirrored her thoughts.

"Victor questioned the nature of our relationship," He said to her.

Thandi seemed hardly surprised. It seemed the two had talked a great deal since Richmond's arrival. Tom dropped his eyes to his hands in his lap. "I told him that there was nothing between us, though, I doubt he believed me. I believe he's requested the ride with you, to test me. To see how I'll react."

"A test?" Thandi blurted.

Once again, she did not like feeling like she was being used, nor did she want to be a part of Richmond's little game.

"But if it makes you uncomfortable," Tom continued.

"No," Thandi cut in. "If it will convince him of that, then I will go." Greater than her loathing of Richmond was her compassion for Tom.

Tom sat speechless for several seconds, gazing at her, evidently touched by her selflessness. "You are truly remarkable," He said. His face softened with a familiar smile.

"Yes, I am," She agreed jokingly, glad to see that his dark mood had improved.

"Tom," She said, smiling. "I've missed you so much," She confessed. She wanted desperately to cross the space between them, to kiss him, and feel his strong arms around her again. If only they were somewhere private, she would show him just how much she'd missed him.

Slowly, Tom's bright smile faded and the light in his eyes dimmed as his thoughts turned again to reality. Thandi's own smile faded as she noticed the return of his solemn expression.

"Tom," She said, her voice filled with genuine concern. "Are you alright?" She asked, giving him a quizzical expression.

"I'm fine, but there is something that we must discuss."

Thandi leaned forward in anticipation. "I don't know an easy way to say this," He started.

Alarm swelled in Thandi's chest as her thoughts went immediately to her brother. "Isaac," She said. "Is he ill!?"

"No, Isaac is fine," Tom quickly assured her. He hesitated for several seconds before speaking again. The seconds felt like hours. "I'd like to discuss us," He said finally. Thandi swallowed hard. His serious tone and grim expression made her heart leap.

"We can no longer see each other. At least, not intimately," He said. Thandi's face went still at the shock of his words. As the realization of what he was telling her set in, her heart sank within her. She looked at him with confusion and hurt in her eyes. "Have I done something wrong?" She asked, her voice breaking, and her sad eyes searching his face.

"It's not you, Thandi. It's my marriage," He said solemnly. His face seemed to darken with his words. "I was wrong to come to you." His voice faltered, and it was a moment before he was able to continue. "To seduce you. I should have never crossed that line between us."

A profound sadness filled Thandi as she continued to listen. She could hardly believe what was happening. He had seemed so pleased before...she didn't know what she had hoped, but she certainly had not imagined that *he* would end their relationship.

"I'm not a happily married man, but I am married, all the same," Tom went on, pulling her from her thoughts. She sat numb and unable to speak.

It hurt him to see the stunned look on her face, the pain and disappointment in her eyes. He hated lying to her, but he knew no other way. He cursed himself for hurting her, but he could not let his inner turmoil show on his face.

Tears stung the back of Thandi's eyes but she forced them away. She couldn't unravel in front of him. She turned and looked to him.

"It's for the best," She said bleakly doing her best to smile, as her heart was breaking and her world crumbled around her.

Chapter 9

As she walked back to the house, Thandi felt as though her heart was bursting. She went directly to her room to be alone. She lay on the bed and let her tears flow freely, surrendering to the pain as she thought of Tom and all that had transpired.

Her thoughts went back to the night they'd last made love, to his words, to the love she'd seen his eyes, and to the love she saw there still. *He loved her*... of that she was certain. She'd felt it in the way he looked at her, in the way he kissed and touched her. She understood that he could be troubled in conscience because of his marriage, but yet she selfishly wanted him to be with her despite of it.

Thandi cursed the thoughts in her mind. How could she think herself justified in thinking such a thing? *Did she truly expect him to cast aside his virtue, and continue on with their affair? Or had she foolishly believed that he would leave Anna and be hers and hers alone? How naive she was*, she thought. Her thoughts were interrupted by a light rap on the door. She sighed deeply, not wanting to face anyone at that moment. She sprung upright in bed and wiped away the evidence of her tears.

"Yes?" She called.

"May I come in?" Esther asked.

"Yes," Thandi reluctantly replied. She turned her gaze to the door as Esther entered.

"You didn't snap those peas like I told you..." Esther stopped speaking mid sentence when she saw Thandi's face. Despite her efforts to dry her tears, she could not wipe away her somber expression. "You alright?" Esther asked with deep concern in her voice.

"I'm...I'm okay," Thandi sputtered, looking down as if she were trying to avoid Esther's probing eyes.

"Well, you don't look all right," Esther said straightaway. "You want to tell me what's ailing you?

"It's nothing," Thandi told her.

"It's something," Esther persisted in a factual tone.

Thandi shook her head, knowing that Esther would continue to badger her until she gave an answer. "I...I cannot say," She said in a low voice, casting down her eyes.

"Is it about Master Tom?" Esther asked, almost knowingly.

Thandi's eyes flashed. "Why, no," She lied.

Esther looked her over speculatively. "You don't have to keep nothing from me, child. I already know about you and the master."

Thandi looked up at her with surprise. Shock and shame drained the color from her skin.

"Whatever do you mean?" She asked, her eyes wide.

"Well, I heard you and Master Tom in here the night before he left," Esther said.

She gave Thandi a look that suggested that denial on her part would be useless. Instead, Thandi surrendered to the truth.

"Well, that will never happen again," She said, her heart and voice heavy with sorrow.

Esther hesitated before speaking, as if she were deciding on her words. "Master Tom is an honorable man. If he's ended things between the two of you, then you should be glad," She said. "Things would get only worse between him and the Missus, which would make things even worse for you."

Thandi sat stunned, shamed, and speechless. She didn't want to hear Esther's advice, though she knew that she was right. No matter how much she loved him, Tom was not hers to have. He belonged to Anna; even if their marriage was miserable, even if he had loathed her. None of that had mattered. The relationship between herself and Tom was over, and his interest now was only for friendship. She knew that any endeavors to change his mind would be useless.

She shook her head from side to side. "I am so ashamed of myself," She muttered.

Esther laid a hand on her arm and looked at her earnestly. "You need not be ashamed, child," She said. "We cannot control who we love or whether our hearts will be broken. It's just how life is." She hesitated a moment before speaking again. "But I do know that Master Tom loves you...I knew it pretty early on."

Thandi's eyes grew large at the admission.

"I could see it in the way he looked at you. I ain't never seen him look at the Missus that way. And I ain't never seen him smile as much as he has since you've been here."

Thandi took comfort in Esther's words. She had confirmed what she already knew in her heart. *Tom had indeed loved her.*

"You mustn't be angry with him, either," Esther continued. "He's just doing what's best for the both of you."

Thandi's eyes sank to her lap. "You're right," She sadly conceded. If only she could go on as if nothing had happened between them. But she had to go on, she had to accept what had happened and move on. It would do no good to wallow in self pity and melancholy. She straightened her shoulders and turned to Esther. "Thank you for your kindness," She said, standing up with a warm smile.

"Well, come, now," Esther said as she stood up. We should be getting dinner started."

For the remainder of the day, Tom mostly stayed in the fields and he took his meals alone in his study. It was plain that he was purposely trying to avoid Thandi. She felt crushed, but she kept busy, trying to push aside her thoughts of him. But that night, as she lay alone, with no distractions, she could think of nothing else.

The following morning, Thandi awoke to Richmond first and foremost on her mind. Today, he would come for her. How she dreaded the thought of their riding together... *of being so close to him.*

At breakfast, Tom barely touched his meal. His absent manner was quickly observed by Esther, who asked with deep concern. "Are you alright, Master?"

"Yes," He replied. "I just don't have much of an appetite this morning."

Esther could see that something was truly troubling him, and after her talk with Thandi, she knew what that something was. His somber mood certainly didn't go unnoticed by Thandi.

Though he greeted her with a kind "good morning," He avoided eye contact as she helped serve his breakfast. After a few bites, he pushed his plate aside before Esther could make any further inquiry and hastily returned to his study. Thandi's heart hurt all over again. His coldness and indifference towards her was torture.

Tears stung at her eyes, but she wouldn't let them fall. *How much longer will he behave this way?* She wondered miserably. How she missed the way they had been before. The way they laughed and talked so easily. She missed the way he joked and smiled at her constantly, and, more than anything, she missed the connection between them.

Though she knew she had to lose him as her lover, she desperately did not want to lose him as her friend. She tried to distract herself from her feelings with various household chores, and when they were done, she started to tend the garden. She felt relieved when Esther said that the roses could use some pruning. She knew with certainty that there was no work to be done in the garden, and that Esther was merely being kind by temporarily sending her away from the tensions of the house.

The strong scent of gardenias filled Thandi's senses the moment she stepped outside. She walked slowly, inhaling deeply, letting the warm aromatic breeze pass over her.

Inside the house, Tom stood at his study window with a glass of brandy in his hand, lost in his thoughts, when suddenly, outside the window, a flash of movement caught his eye.

"Thandi," He thought aloud. He stared out the window, watching as she walked towards the garden, her long hair swirling in the wind behind her. *My God, she's so very lovely,* he thought. He hated himself for thinking it. Hated himself for still having feelings of lust in her regard. *His sister's regard!*

"Beautiful out, isn't it?" Someone said from behind him.

Tom turned in surprise. He had become so engrossed in his thoughts that he didn't hear Victor knocking. "I'm so sorry, I didn't hear the door," He said.

Victor gave him a funny smile, as if he had known exactly why he'd been so distracted.

"May I offer you something?" Tom politely asked. He finished off his drink then went to the cabinet for a refill.

"No, it's far too early for me," Victor replied. "And besides, I'll need all my wits for today's ride."

A slight perplexed frown creased Tom's forehead. "I had nearly forgotten," He said. He went back to his chair and looked across at Victor. Neither of them spoke for several seconds, then Victor spoke.

"Well, we should probably be off, now," He said pointedly.

Tom nodded faintly and Victor exited the room. Tom sank back in his chair and silently brooded, his eyes cast down meditatively upon his drink. Even though he knew Thandi had no desire for Victor, it didn't stop him from feeling jealous. He hated the thought of her being with someone else; even if he could never have her.

At Mr. Richmond's request, Esther sent a servant to get Thandi, and another to fetch his horse. He waited eagerly, looking on in the courtyard, awaiting her appearance. Soon after, she walked up the garden path; the expression on her face telling. She looked less than happy to see him, but it was what he'd expected. Though she'd showed evident dislike of him, he still found her utterly intriguing. Besides, he quite liked her feisty manner, and he'd always loved a challenge.

Thandi stopped short several feet in from him. He smiled instantly into her eyes, causing her heart to flutter in her throat. There was something in the way he looked at her...or through her, that unnerved her so. She stared at him briefly, then gave a small half curtsy. "Sir," She said, nodding.

Victor looked her over, his smile never leaving his lips. He could see that she'd put no effort in dolling herself up for him. She wore the same drab servants gown from the day before, and her long unruly curls hung wild.

If only she knew how it made her look even more desirable, he thought as the servant boy brought his horse around.

The beast was a beautiful animal, and Thandi couldn't help but notice the horse's remarkable shiny black mane. The horse snorted and nickered as the boy dismounted.

"This here is Belle," Richmond said, stroking the mare's side. Thandi visibly dropped her guard a little, betraying the first sign of interest he'd seen in her. *Even if it was for his horse.*

"She's beautiful," She said. She moved closer and reached out, stroking the horse's long, sleek nose. Belle sniffed and snorted at her hand and she smiled.

"She likes you," Richmond said. He helped Thandi up unto the saddle, then mounted. Taking the reins in his hands, he kicked Belle into a gallop and they rode away from the Lexington plantation.

As they rode, following the main road, Thandi remained silent and withdrawn. She did her best to ignore Richmond's very presence as she concentrated her attention on the landscapes: passing meadows and woodlands. As they neared a familiar crossing, Thandi stared intensely.

"Hollis Creek," She muttered aloud.

Victor slowed Belle to a trot. "You know this land?" He asked.

Thandi's eyes lit behind him with amusement. "I know it very well," She breathed. A small smile creased the corners of her mouth as she slowly looked around. Everything in sight had remained just as she remembered. Nearly a mile of tall majestic oaks and coned trees outlined the private stretch of land. She shielded her eyes against the bright glare of the sun, and tried peering beyond the trees. Suddenly, the wind swept the treetops, sending the smell of creek water past her nose. "It must still be there," She said to herself.

"What must still be here?" Victor questioned.

"The creek," Thandi answered, not realizing she had spoken aloud.

Suddenly, Richmond veered his horse to the left, off the trail, and towards the trees.

"Where are you going?" Thandi asked, concerned.

"To investigate that creek you mentioned," Richmond answered.

"You mustn't," Thandi warned. "This is private land."

Ignoring her warning, he dug a heel into Belle, compelling the horse into a gallop straight for the creek. "I don't think the owner will mind if we take a brief look around."

Thandi raised a questionable brow. She knew if old man Hollis was still alive, he would care very much.

She told him of how she played in the woods and creek as a child, and of the countless times she'd been run off by a shotgun wielding Mr. Hollis. She even pointed out a nearby no trespassing sign, but Richmond simply ignored it.

The nerve of this man! She thought. He seemed to have absolutely no regard for the danger he was putting them both in. As they came upon a small path in the woods, Thandi could hear the unmistakable sound of the creek's bubbling water. As they drew closer, the sound of rushing water grew louder, and soon her eyes caught sight of the creek. Her lips parted and her eyes widened with delight as she looked around at the tranquil surroundings. Richmond led Belle to the water's edge to drink her fill as he dismounted.

When he reached up to help Thandi down, she gave him a scorching look. "As I told you, Sir, we shouldn't be here. This is..."

"I know, I know. **Private land**," Victor interrupted.

"Exactly," She retorted sharply. Victor smiled at the trace of irritability in her voice.

"We will be just fine," He said, reaching up for her again.

Thandi folded her arms across her chest in defiance. "And how can you be certain of that?" She asked him.

Unable to contain his smile, Richmond answered, "Because I am the owner of this land."

A few seconds elapsed before Thandi spoke again. "How so?" She asked in a surprised and disbelieving tone.

The sound of Victor's chuckle filled the air around them, and he watched as her expression changed from curious to furious. "Well, I bought it from the former landholder of course," He said in a kind, but condescending tone.

The grin on his face widened as he again lifted his arms in attempt to assist her. She flashed him an irritable look, then leaned forward and allowed him to lift her down from the horse. He held her waist for a moment longer than required before placing her feet on the ground.

Thandi moved quickly away from him. He watched intently as she slowly began walking alongside the creek. She stopped and stared at her reflection in the crystal clear water. The last time she had done so, a pig-tailed girl had stared back at her. A slow smile crept upon her lips as childhood memories surfaced in her mind. The creek had been her favorite play place, in spite of "Old Man Hollis."

Thinking of which, Thandi turned to look at Richmond again. "Sir, do you really own Hollis Creek?" She asked.

Victor smirked at the question. "Yes, I really do, and please call me Victor," He said.

Thandi bashfully dropped her eyes from his gaze and turned her attention again to the water. She bent her head to study the tiny gold and silver fish swimming around. "You're very fortunate to own it," She muttered.

"Yes, I am," Victor said. His eyes scanned the beautiful nature around them. "It'll be a shame to cut down this forest," He said with a sigh.

Thandi's gaze darted to him as a shocked look appeared on her face. "You plan to destroy these woods?"

Her unfavorable reaction took Victor by surprise. "Yes, I have plans to clear and cultivate two hundred of the three hundred acres," He said in a matter-of-fact tone.

Thandi's eyes lit with a spark of anger. "How can you destroy something so beautiful?" She exclaimed, throwing her arms wide to encompass the breathtaking landscape.

Victor marveled at the unexpected display of emotion. Not only was she beautiful, but she was bold and spirited. *Just the way he liked them.*

"This land is prime for agriculture," He said, looking around him. "The soil is rich, and the creek provides a natural water source for irrigation. I could either farm the land myself or lease it in parcels to farmers for good profit."

He talked as if Thandi had an interest in his business prospects when she couldn't care less about farming or profits. It was the forest that she cared about.

"I will never understand man's greed," She said, shaking her head. "Always in pursuit of more than what you need." She stopped her words, fearing she had overstepped her boundaries and said too much.

Victor smiled as if he found her anger amusing. "You should think of it differently," He told her. "There's nothing wrong with wanting more for yourself."

Thandi couldn't hold her tongue. "Yes, but at what cost?" She found herself saying. It wasn't just Hollis Creek that she cared for. For years, she'd watched farmers cut and burn the forest routinely. They grew crops until the land was no longer fertile, then simply abandoned it.

Much of the land's natural beauty was, and still continued to be, destroyed that way. "I fear that someday all of Carolina will look like wasteland because of men like you."

Victor smiled inwardly. All he could think of as she spoke was how beautiful she looked standing next to the water. "I somehow doubt that will ever happen," He said with a chuckle. "You needn't worry. More trees will be planted when men *like me* are done with the land."

The look he gave her made her feel silly and childish for her remarks. She scolded herself mentally for not biting her tongue as she should have.

"As I said," He continued in a more serious tone. "I plan to clear two of the three hundred acres. The creek and surrounding woods will remain perfectly intact."

Thandi silently sighed in relief.

"You're welcome to visit the land whenever you like."

Thandi turned her gaze to him, and he could see the hostility leave her eyes. "That's very gracious of you, Sir," She said.

Smiling, he quirked a brow and shook his head.

"Forgive me." She paused. "*Victor.*"

The sound of his name coming from her lips pleased him greatly. It was a small accomplishment, but an accomplishment all the same.

"When you're ready, we can resume our ride," He said.

Thandi lingered a moment longer, taking in the sights, then allowed him to assist her in mounting the horse.

Chapter 10

The afternoon ride was surprisingly pleasing with Victor showing her various acres of his land and a breathtaking hill top view of his elaborate lakeside estate. She couldn't help but be impressed. Which, she strongly suspected, was the reason he had taken her on the ride. He liked her. She knew that. But nothing could change her perception of him. He was Stafford's friend and spy, and for those reasons alone, she didn't like him.

From what she'd seen, he seemed like a man that was accustomed to getting what he wanted. *How disappointing it must have been to be rejected by a mere slave,* she thought.

When they returned from their ride, they found Stafford's carriage stationed in front of the mansion. Thandi's heart sank instantly. It was apparent that Anna had returned home from her visit and she certainly possessed no desire to see the vile woman.

As she and Victor dismounted Belle, Esther came out to meet them. As she approached, Thandi noticed at once the troubled look on her face.

"Is anything wrong?" She asked, feeling a surge of unease. Before Esther could respond, Daniel Stafford appeared in the doorway.

"Well, there you are," He said to Victor, smiling from ear to ear. His gaze and wide smile then darted to Thandi.

She dropped her eyes from his gaze instantly. Looking again to Esther, she could see that her troubled expression had grown darker at Stafford's appearance. Victor smiled up at his friend before handing the reigns over to a servant boy.

"There's much work to be done, Miss Thandi," Esther said.

She gave Thandi's dress sleeve a tug, then made haste up the stairs. "Excuse me, Sir," She said to Mr. Stafford. Thandi stood close behind her with her head hung low and her gaze locked to the porch's wood floor.

Stafford quickly stepped aside, allowing Esther to enter, but when Thandi attempted to pass, he suddenly blocked the doorway again. Her heart leaped into her throat as she accidentally bumped into his chest. She took a take step back so fast she stumbled a little.

107

"Forgive me, Sir," She said, her voice low and trembling. Her heart pounded as he stared for a long moment before finally stepping aside.

Once inside, Esther quickly led her to the kitchen, where they found Myra standing at the kitchen sink.

"You can see to something else. We got the kitchen chores," Esther told her, sending her daughter away. When she felt she was no longer in earshot, Esther started in. "Miss Thandi, I overheard a most terrible thing," She said. She spoke in a low frantic tone.

"What is it?" Thandi asked, alarmed by her manner. Silently praying that nothing had happened to her brother or anyone else back home. Color flushed from her cheeks at the very thought of it.

"I overheard Mr. Stafford talking to Master Lexington," Esther began. "He says he's got some kind of legal papers proving he's the owner of you and your brother. He was talking about taking you back with him!" Esther exclaimed.

Thandi shook her head, as if trying to make sense of the information.

"That can't be possible," She said firmly. "You must have heard wrong, Esther," She added.

"No, no, Miss Thandi," Esther said with firm certainty. "I heard him just right," She went on. "He said that when Master Tom's daddy died, he not only bought the plantation, but he gained ownership of his slaves, too."

Thandi's eyes widened in astonishment. *But even if that were true, how on Earth does this apply to me and my brother?* She thought. Madame Lacy was their owner, and their mother's, too. Certainly, Esther had overheard something wrong in her eavesdropping. *I'll go to Tom straightaway and clear up the matter*, she thought.

"I'm certain you're wrong," Thandi said.

She placed a reassuring hand on Esther's shoulder, then set off after Tom. Upon reaching his closed study door, she stopped. Sighing deeply, wondering if he were alone. She hadn't seen Anna yet, and Stafford and Victor could very well be with him. Knocking lightly, she nervously waited.

"Come in," Tom answered through the door.

He looked up at her as she entered, shutting the door behind her. She paused a moment, staring into his solemn expression.

"Please sit," He instructed. She crossed the room and sat down across from him at his desk. A glass of bourbon sat in front of him and he held several papers in his hand.

"There is something that we must discuss." Both his expression and tone were heavy.

A wave of panic washed over Thandi. She knew something was seriously wrong. She could tell by the sound of his voice and the grave way he looked at her. Instantly, her thoughts went to Esther. Her eyes then darted nervously to the papers he held, then back to him again.

"Yes?" She said, urging him to continue.

Tom sucked in a deep breath then exhaled wearily. "Anna's father has made a very serious claim," He started.

He paused for a breath staring down at the paperwork he held.

"He claims to be the rightful owner of my father's slaves."

He paused again, looking up at her, then to the papers again. "He has brought this sales agreement to prove his allegations."

Thandi gave him a puzzled look. "What does that mean?" She asked, confused.

Tom swallowed hard, staring into her wide-eyed gaze.

"As owner..." His words broke off, and he paused again, his grief clear in his voice and eyes. "As their owner, he would also become owner of the slaves' offspring."

Thandi still looked confused. "And what exactly does that mean?"

Tom looked at her with piteous eyes. "It means, that if these documents are, in fact, legal, then Daniel is the true and lawful owner of you, Isaac, and all the others my father owned."

Tears started to well in Thandi's eyes.

"But Madame Lacy *was* our owner," She quickly retorted. "She even promised my mother our freedom."

"Yes," Tom said. "But Daniel questions the legality of the ownership. If my father gave your mother to my aunt without proper papers, then Daniel could possibly have a legal right to her offspring."

Thandi glared at the papers clasped in his hands. "May I see them?" She asked.

Tom handed them over to her and watched with a heavy heart as she viewed the documents intently. When she finished reading she looked up, and stared hopelessly at him.

"How can this be?" She asked, tears spilling from her eyes.

A sudden knock on the door stopped her next words.

"Yes?" Tom called out.

"May I come in?" Victor asked through the door.

Thandi wiped the tears from her face and stood up, preparing to leave the room.

"We will finish this very soon," Tom promised.

Thandi hid her saddened face as Victor entered, keeping her eyes directed toward the floor and avoiding his gaze as she moved from the room. Upon exiting the hall, she saw Anna on the stairwell. She paused in the middle of the staircase smiling down at her triumphantly. Thandi slowed her stride and frowned. It was apparent that the witch was fully aware of the matters at hand, and that she had most certainly had a hand in it. Thandi dismissed her gaze and increased her pace.

"Stop right there!" Anna commanded, stopping Thandi in her tracks. Thandi stopped and looked her squarely in the eyes.

"Come, draw my bath," She ordered, a snide look curling her ruby lips before she abruptly turned and walked up the stairs, leaving Thandi standing hot with anger.

Though she hated it, she had no choice but to do as she was told.

When she entered her room, Anna was already disrobing. Thandi made haste to the bath, only to find the tub already filled and the strong scent of lavender oil in the air.

"Oh, yes," Anna called out from the bedroom. "I forgot, I had Millie draw me a bath already."

Somehow, Thandi doubted that was true. She was clearly antagonizing her as usual. Eager to leave, she stepped from the bath and started for the door.

"I didn't give you permission to go," Anna snapped.

Thandi stopped and turned to her. "Yes?" She muttered.

Anna gave her a long scowling glare. "It's 'Yes, Ma'am'," She corrected.

Unlacing her bodice, she removed the last remnants of her clothing. Thandi looked away quickly. "I think I'll have you wash me," said Anna crossing the room as naked as the day she was born, and entered the bath.

For a moment, Thandi stood motionless, her cheeks flushed with anger. Gathering herself, she went to the bathroom where Anna was already settled in the large marble tub, waiting.

"Get that sponge," She said, pointing to a nearby shelf. "And give me my drink," She added.

Thandi followed her gaze to the glass of brandy that sat within arm's reach of her. She got the sponge and handed her the glass. Anna took a sip, making a sour face.

"I can't see how my husband likes this so much," She declared.

Thandi's brows raised at the comment. Gathering her hair, Anna leaned forward, drawing her knees to her chest. "Wash my back," She ordered.

Thandi hesitated a moment, seething.

"Well, get on with it!" Anna snapped.

Dipping the sponge in the soapy water, Thandi proceeded to wash her, moving with slow, delicate strokes.

"Are you dumb?" Anna snorted. "Harder! I should have had Millie bathe me!" She ranted.

Gritting her teeth, Thandi clenched the sponge and applied more pressure.

"That's better," said Anna, closing her eyes, a faint smile on her lips.

"Go lower," She breathed. Thandi made a face as she did so. She moved the sponge vigorously up and down her lower back.

"That's enough," Anna announced after some time. Stretching out her long, slender legs she leaned back against the tub, submerging her body fully in the hot water. She let out a long, relaxed sigh as the water enclosed around her. "Hmmm," She moaned. "You know my mother's always saying a nigger ain't good for nothing, but I, myself, agree with my daddy. Without y'all, who else would pick our cotton and wash our asses?" She giggled.

Thandi did her best to keep a straight face and show no reaction. "Will that be all, Ma'am?" She asked in her best submissive voice.

Anna looked her over and smiled. "Has my Tom told you the latest news?" She asked. Her red brows quirked upwards as she awaited Thandi's response.

"Yes," Thandi muttered.

"Then you understand that you are my father's property?"

Thandi stood silent, staring at the floor without attempting to answer.

Anna dipped down in the water, then up again. "You are a stubborn little nigger," She said. "My mama's gonna have herself quite a time breaking you." She paused, swinging a long leg over the edge of the tub.

"She keeps a short leather whip for our niggas back home. My daddy gave it to her on her thirty-fifth birthday. Can you imagine such a gift?" She laughed.

Thandi's stoic expression broke at her words, and Anna could see the fear in her eyes.

"It would do you good to change your attitude. My mama especially hates your kind. Niggers that look like us. It's an abomination, she says."

Though Thandi tried hard not to react, Anna could tell by the agitated rise and fall of her chest that she was thoroughly vexed. Satisfied she'd made her point, Anna dismissed her.

Thandi turned and quickly left the room, accidentally slamming the door behind her in her haste. Esther turned to her when she entered the kitchen. She knew from the look on Thandi's face that she had most likely gone and talked to the Master. Thandi could no longer hold back her tears as they flowed freely down her cheeks.

"I'd like to go to my room for the evening," She said, tearfully wiping her face.

Esther resisted the urge to question her. She could see she didn't want to talk about it. "That would be just fine," She told her. "Me and Myra can handle the chores."

Leaving the kitchen, Thandi started down the hall. To her surprise, she found Daniel Stafford seated in the foyer. By the smile on his face and devilish look in his eyes, Thandi knew that he had been waiting for her. She lowered her gaze from his seedy eyes and continued to walk slowly.

"Hold on there, girl," He said, stopping her.

Thandi reluctantly stopped at his command. She kept her eyes to the floor as he stood and walked towards her. A chill ran up her spine and her flesh crawled as he approached her.

"Well, well. Here you are," He said, settling himself uncomfortably close in front of her. He stood so close, she could feel his breath on her face. She kept her gaze steady on the marble floor.

"Look at me, girl, when I address you," Stafford quipped.

Thandi lifted her gaze to his, and her heart dropped.

He could tell she'd been crying by the redness of her eyes. *Obvious-ly, she had already talked with Tom,* he thought. "Have you had a word with our Tom?" He asked coyly.

Thandi didn't answer his question, but he knew the answer.

"I'm gonna have myself a really good time with you," He said hus-kily.

He brought a hand to her face, brushing her cheek with his long fingers.

Thandi shuddered at his touch.

He licked his lips, relishing in her fear. He looked her over, his lustful gaze slowly raking over every inch of her lovely form. *Oh, how he couldn't wait to see her naked,* he thought. He felt his cock harden as his gaze momentarily rested on her heaving chest.

Thandi's eyes darted around the room, desperately searching for a means of escape.

"I'm gonna fuck you," He told her. "I'm gonna fuck you *so* hard."

Thandi took a step back from him. The tears she held, now spilled uncontrollably.

"Daniel," a voice called out from the hall's shadows.

Thandi looked up and Stafford turned in the voice's direction. Strangely, she felt a surge of relief as Victor appeared from the hall.

"I was just coming to find you," Victor said to Daniel. "Tom would like a word with you."

His fun spoiled, Stafford gave Thandi a small smile, then followed Victor down the hall to Tom's study.

To calm her heart, Thandi deeply inhaled a steadying breath of air as the two men disappeared from sight. Quickly, she made her way to her room, locking the door behind her. She went to the basin and washed her face clean of Stafford's revolting touch.

***

Stafford settled into one of the chairs across from Tom in his study.

"I'd like to have the documents reviewed by an attorney," Tom said.

Daniel smiled coyly. "You forget that I *am* an attorney, Tom. I can assure you, that another attorney will not find anything different. You're only putting off the inevitable. But I've got time," He finished.

"I've suggested to Tom one of my own attorneys," Victor said.

"Your attorney?" Daniel said, with a note of surprise in his tone. It seemed to him, that Victor and Tom had become fast friends as of late.

"It doesn't matter," Daniel said, waving a hand. "The outcome will be the same. I've always known I legally owned the slaves here, Tom. But seeing as how you've got my Anna, I saw fit to leave them here. You know, Tom, you should really be thanking me instead of brooding over this. As I've told you, I have no interest in the brother or the others. It's just Thandi that I want." He paused for a second to watch Tom's expression. "But if you insist upon making this a problem, then maybe I should just take the whole lot of them."

Tom's jaw clenched, his expression steely. "That won't be necessary," He said in a bitter tone. "But I see no harm in verifying the documents."

"No, no, Tom, there's no harm in it at all. However, doing so does imply that you don't *entirely* trust me."

Tom said nothing to deny the statement. *Oh, how he wanted so badly to reach across that desk and punch that sly grin right off Daniel's face!*

"With the girl gone," Daniel continued. "Maybe now you can focus back on what's important." He paused for a second. "Like keeping my Anna happy for starters."

Victor could see the tension building in Tom's expression. "If you'd like, we can ride into town tomorrow morning," He said, interjecting himself into the conversation. "To consult with my attorney."

Tom turned to him. "I would appreciate that," He said.

"Well, tomorrow, after you two are done verifying what we already know, I'll be by to collect the girl," Daniel said, rising from his chair. "Meantime, I think I'll stay in town for the night. There's a poker game going that I simply must attend." With that, Daniel started towards the door.

Midway out of the room, he suddenly stopped and turned to Victor.

"What's the name of your attorney? I may as well accompany the two of you, since I'll already be in town."

For a moment, Victor hesitated. "George Peterson," He replied.

"Oh, yes, George," Daniel noted in remembrance. "So, what time shall we meet?" He asked.

Victor glanced at Tom's bitter expression, then back to Daniel again. "Eleven would be good timing," He replied.

Daniel gave the pair of men a long smile, then exited the room.

Later that night, Tom sent Esther to fetch Thandi. He told her of his plans to meet with Victor's attorney the following morning, but the news did little to calm her nerves.

With all the thoughts going through her mind, she wouldn't be able to sleep.

***

The next morning, she appeared in the kitchen, pale and tired. She had no appetite for breakfast, and said very little, except in response to Esther or the other servants. Seeing her mood, Esther decided she would not ask questions. Instead, she gave Thandi some time alone, and saw to it that Millie and Myra did the same.

Meanwhile, Victor and Tom rode into town. When they arrived at Peterson's office, Stafford's carriage was already there, which came to no surprise to Tom, since Stafford was eager to get his hands on Thandi. *And even more eager to make him miserable.*

Upon entering the office, the first thing Tom noticed was Stafford. He was sitting across the desk from a stout, red-bearded older gentlemen. After a few pleasant exchanges and introductions, the attorney came straight to the point.

"As I understand, you have some documents you'd like me to review," He said to Tom.

"Yes," Tom answered. He pulled the papers from his vest and handed them over.

"Please, be seated," Peterson said, gesturing a hand towards the chairs next to Daniel.

Tom allowed Victor to sit first, taking the seat next to Daniel. He wanted to put as much space as possible between himself and Stafford. He watched nervously as the lawyer looked over the documents, his eyes slowly skimming each paragraph. Meanwhile, Stafford sat coolly with a small confident smile plastered on his face. When he'd finished reading, Peterson looked up from the papers and looked Tom in the eyes as he started to explain.

"Everything is perfectly in order," He said. "Without question, Mr. Stafford is the legal and rightful owner of Tom Lexington, Senior's slaves. The slaves and their offspring were included in the sale of the plantation," He added.

115

Tom stood silent for several moments. "But if my father had given one of those slaves to another prior to the sale..."

"Yes," Peterson said, cutting him off. "Daniel has explained the situation. If your father turned a slave over to another party without taking the proper legal channels, then those said slaves would rightfully be owned by Mr. Stafford."

A hint of a smile crossed Daniel's lips. "And if I were a betting man, and I am," Daniel added. "I'd bet that my dear friend did no such thing. He wasn't himself for some time," He said, brushing a speck of lint from his expensive black suit. "In fact, he was a total mess towards the end."

Tom's face turned red and his hands formed into fists at his sides.

Sensing the imminent fight that was bound to ensue, Victor again interjected. "Then it appears that you must inquire with your aunt's lawyers," He said to Tom, gaining his attention.

"Yes," Tom replied after a moment. The reading of his aunt's will was just a week away. He had planned to leave in two days' time, but now, under the circumstances, he decided that he would leave the following morning. "I will leave for my aunt's tomorrow," He stated.

"Well, don't be too long," Daniel said, standing. "I am very anxious to collect what's due to me."

Tom gave him an icy glare.

Daniel said his goodbyes to the gentlemen and promised to return in two weeks before exiting the office.

As he and Victor returned to the plantation, Tom sat silent in the coach. His mind was full and his heart heavy. Misery swelled within him at the prospect of Stafford taking Thandi. His mind raced with thoughts of possibilities and outcomes. He even pondered the thought of running away with her if the worst were to happen. He simply couldn't allow her to end up in Stafford's clutches. The very idea made him sick to his stomach. He had hoped to have news that would make her feel more at ease at least, but he had nothing more than what they'd already known. If a contract could not be found between his father and aunt, then Daniel would come to claim her.

When they reached the plantation, Tom and Victor parted ways. As he walked up the steps to the mansion, the door opened. He smiled weakly when he saw Esther.

"I need to speak with Thandi," He told her, pausing momentarily in the foyer to hand her his overcoat and hat. "Please, send her to my study."

Thandi found the study door wide open. Tom sat at his desk with his face in his hands, unaware of her presence. He looked as if the weight of the world rested squarely on his shoulders. She moved into the room and closed the door.

"Tom," She said softly.

He looked up and their eyes met. "Esther said that you wished to see me," She said.

Standing, Tom walked over to the window and looked out over the garden. He didn't want her to see the worry in his face. If he looked as though he were falling apart it would surely heighten her fear. She'd been through so much unpleasantness. He would spare her as much grief as he could.

"I'm afraid that I must leave in the morning," He started. "The attorney has advised me to obtain the contract between my father and aunt."

"So, then there *is* a contract," said Thandi.

Tom noted the note of hope in her voice. He turned his head slightly and put on a faint smile. "Yes, possibly," He said, but his eyes and tone were unconvincing, extinguishing the spark of hope that had ignited within her.

She walked over and stood closer to him. "And if there isn't?" She asked.

"Well, we mustn't assume the worst," He said, turning to face her.

"Please, let me go with you," She said, staring earnestly into his eyes. "I miss Isaac terribly, and I'd like to attend Madame Lacy's services."

She heard him exhale as he turned his gaze out the window again. Silent seconds passed.

"You should be ready by dawn," He said finally. He intended to be gone before Anna awakened.

Thandi felt a small measure of relief that she'd soon be leaving. She couldn't bear to be left alone with Anna again. The very thought of it had made her grow pale.

"I will be ready," She agreed.

When she got back to her room, she immediately started packing.

She thought to herself of her brother and all the others she'd soon see. Isaac had always made her feel safe, and she needed to feel that more than ever right now. Even if it were only temporary. A knock at the door interrupted her.

"Miss Thandi," Esther's muffled voice penetrated the door.

"Come in," Thandi called out. She continued packing as Esther entered.

Esther stood, watching her for a moment, her hand still holding the door handle.

"Master Tom said for me to see to your packing," She said.

Thandi looked up at her, then down again at the saddlebag of clothes on the bed. She shook her head in thought of Tom. With everything going on, he still treated her as if she were a guest. "Thank you, but I don't need any help." She tried to keep the emotion out of her voice.

Esther looked worriedly at her. "Don't you worry, Miss Thandi, I knows everything gonna be alright."

"If I have to, I'll run," Thandi said firmly. "I couldn't imagine a more horrible thing than having that man as a master."

Esther gave her a stricken look. "Now, don't you go talking like that! You'd be hunted if you run away! Don't you worry," She said, turning to go. "If there's a contract, you best believe Master Tom gonnna find it."

"But what if there isn't?" Thandi replied, looking up at her.

"If there isn't, I'm sure Master Tom will figure something out," Esther said exiting the room, leaving Thandi alone with her thoughts and worries.

That night, Thandi lay awake, unable to sleep, wallowing in her misery, willing the dawn to come.

At first light, she sprang to her feet. The room was still dark as she hastily attired herself. Gathering her bags, she quietly ventured into the hall. When she reached the foyer, Tom was already there. He gave her a smile, then reached for her bags, hoisting them over his shoulder.

Outside, the carriage was already waiting with Tom's luggage already put on the back.

As they entered the carriage, Esther came with a large basket of food.

"This should get you through," She said in a hushed tone, handing it over to Thandi. As soon as they were inside, the driver swiftly took off.

118

A long silence followed, broken only by the sound of the horse's galloping hooves and the coachman's occasional commands.

As the carriage rode north, Tom stared out the window blankly, his thoughts a million miles away.

As she watched him, Thandi wondered what he was thinking, but, then again, she already knew. He glanced up after some time to find her staring back at him.

"Are you okay, Tom?" She asked, her eyes full of worry.

"I'm fine," He said, his smile as false as his lie.

"Are you really?" Thandi asked, her emerald eyes boring into him.

"I will be when this is all behind us," He said, more truthfully.

Smiling thinly, she felt little comfort hearing his words. She told herself that he would protect her. *But how could he, if he held no claim to her?* She thought.

The very thought of Stafford terrified her. She shuddered inwardly, remembering his repulsing words. She would rather die than go with him.

"Tom?" She said.

Turning his gaze from the window, he looked into her eyes. "Yes?" He replied.

She hesitated a moment. "Tom, if the worse should happen, promise me that you won't let him take me," She pleaded. "I could remain home with Isaac, and never return to the plantation again."

The fear and desperation in her eyes and voice gripped his heart. Suddenly, he got up and sat next to her, taking her hands into his own.

"I know that all of this is terribly hard, but please try not to worry," He said. "You have my promise that I will do everything possible to keep you from him...no matter what I must do."

The soothing feel of his warm strong hands holding hers, calmed her. The sincerity in his eyes and his words were unmistakable. A long yawn escaped her mouth, and she batted her eyelashes heavily.

"Get some sleep," Tom said, encouraging her to rest her head on his lap.

Smiling sweetly, she did so. She closed her eyes and let her mind drift where it would. Within moments, she was fast asleep.

Tom gently removed a strand of hair from her cheek. He couldn't help but marvel at her. She looked so peaceful; almost angelic, as the sunlight poured through the windows, illuminating her beautiful face. It had been awhile since he'd been this close to her. He'd kept his distance out of fear of what might happen, because he felt unable to trust himself. For weeks, he had warred with his thoughts of her, and the horrid secret he held. It had been torture not to go to her, not to comfort her as he wanted. *How alone and helpless she must have felt*, he thought. *How afraid she must have been.*

As his eyes wandered over her sleeping face, he thought of his promise to her. No matter the outcome, he would protect her somehow. No matter the cost. *Of that, he was certain.*

Soon, the carriage approached Hollis Creek. Tom watched intently as the scenery long familiar to him passed by.

As he took in the sight, memories of his time of innocence came to mind, bringing a smile to his lips. He could still picture himself as a boy, running through the woods with Thandi and Isaac alongside him, laughing and playing without a care in the world. But those days were now long gone.

Chapter 11

Days later, they entered his aunt's estate. Isaac was overjoyed to see them, but the happiness was short lived when Tom informed him of Daniel's claims.

That evening, the three of them carefully searched through his aunt's belongings. For hours they searched, to no avail. Every room, other than the maid's quarters and kitchen, had been searched thoroughly. Tom had reassured them by saying that the contract was likely in his aunt's lawyer's possession.

In three days' time, the reading of her will would be held there in the mansion. He said that he would speak with her attorney at that time regarding the matter.

With Madame Lacy's funeral scheduled for the morrow's morning, Thandi's reunion with Isaac and the others was bittersweet. There were no smiling faces or cheerful banter as was customary at Fairview. A deep sadness and silence now permeated the air. The slaves all wore long faces, expressing their feelings of loss and love for their beloved mistress.

The following morning, many people arrived for the services, including several slaves who stood on the outside around the chapel's gates. Both Isaac and Thandi accompanied Tom inside the church.

Thandi did her best to ignore the stares and glares of the many white people in attendance. They stared at Isaac mostly. The expressions on their faces were readable. They were, without doubt, offended with niggers sitting in the pews of their church, but none dared to say a thing to Tom.

Two days after the funeral, the attorney arrived at the mansion for the reading of the will. Tom waited in the sitting room along with two of Madame Lacy's closest socialite friends.

Surprisingly, at the request of the attorney, both Isaac and Thandi were called into attendance.

The two women, Lady Tolbert and Madame Rigby, mumbled amongst themselves, casting glances in their direction.

Thandi didn't have to wonder what they were talking about; she already knew. They were obviously curious as to why two slaves were there, and she herself wondered the same.

121

Clearing his throat, Attorney Davenport spoke. "Well, it appears that everyone is here," He said, adjusting his spectacles. The room fell silent as he began reading the last will and testament of *Lacetta Marie Lexington*...

"To my beloved nephew, Thomas Richard Lexington, Jr., I hereby leave my plantation, Fairview, and all of its furnishings, one hundred thirty-two acres of land, sixty-four slaves, and twenty thousand dollars. To my dear friend, Mrs. Annette T. Tolbert, I leave my prized silver flatware, china, and crystal. To my dear friend, Mrs. Diane Rigby, I leave my dresses and pearl broach. To my beloved church, North Creek Presbyterian, I hereby leave one thousand dollars to be entered into the church's benevolence fund.

"And to Thandi Boran," the attorney said. "I leave my mother's ring, and I do, hereby upon my death, give her freedom, thus making her a free slave.

"And to Isaac Boran, I leave two hundred dollars; his mother's savings, and I do, hereby upon my death, give him his freedom, thus making him a free slave." Tom, Isaac, and Thandi all looked to each other at once.

Thandi's face lit with happiness. She looked in Isaac's eyes and they both smiled wide.

Strangely, Tom did not smile along with them. He turned his attention back to Davenport, his face and expression unreadable. When Davenport finished reading, Tom stood and walked up to him, and Thandi watched in confusion as the two men shared hushed words, then exited the room.

"Can you believe this, Sister?" Isaac exclaimed. He threw his arms around her and hugged her tight.

We're no longer slaves, but free! He thought.

Tears of happiness and relief sprang to Thandi's eyes.

Releasing her from his hug, Isaac held her at arm's length. "I've gotta tell Sarah!" He exclaimed and bolted for the door.

Thandi stood stunned as the two women left the room. Soon, the sound of snorting horses broke her from her lethargy. She crossed the room and looked out the window to see Tom and the attorney standing alongside Davenport's carriage. They exchanged inaudible words, then shook hands.

Tom stood on the walkway for several moments as the carriage departed, then turned to enter the house.

Smiling, Thandi walked away from the window and went to find him. As she descended the stairs, he crossed the foyer. He looked up at her bright face and paused.

"I was just coming to find you," She said, smiling. When he did not return her smile, her own faded. "Is there something wrong?" She asked.

"I'm afraid so," Tom said, slowly. "I need to find Isaac," He continued. "You should meet us in the sitting room."

As he walked away, Thandi stood momentarily dazed with confusion. *How could he not be pleased?* She thought. *She and Isaac now had their freedom, and he had inherited a great deal of wealth.* Shaking her thoughts away, she headed back to the sitting room, where she waited. After several long moments, Tom and Isaac entered the room.

Isaac walked over and stood next to her. She could tell by his expression that he too had been confused by Tom's strange behavior and the request for this meeting.

"What is it, Tom?" Isaac asked.

Tom lowered his eyes for a moment, then looked up again at Isaac.

"I spoke with Davenport." He paused momentarily, finding the words on his tongue hard to say. "He said that he was never made aware of a contract between my father and aunt." He paused again, sighing heavily before continuing. "It appears that there *was* no contract," He said finally, his gaze shifting between the two.

Thandi narrowed her eyes in confusion. She didn't see how any of that mattered now.

"But we have our freedom now, Tom," She said. His eyes saddened at her words.

Unexpectedly, the same feeling of foreboding she had before washed over her.

Tom sighed miserably. "He explained that if there isn't a contract or written agreement to prove legal ownership of you two and your mother, then the will can be contested."

Silence followed as the realization of his words sank in. Taking a breath, Thandi fought back tears that threatened. Isaac turned away, but not before she saw the tears in his eyes. Her heart sank for him, despite herself.

For so long, their freedom had been promised to them. For years, it had been all he could think of. He had made so many plans for their future.

Tom's heart wrenched with guilt. *It wasn't enough that he'd caused them so much trouble*, he thought, *but his foolish actions had now cost them their freedom.*

"I am so sorry," He said heavily. He searched for words to comfort them, but knew there were none.

"I intend to have a talk with Daniel," He stammered. "Somehow, someway, I will fix this."

"You bear no fault in this, Tom," Isaac said, turning to face him.

His words stung at Tom's conscience.

Thandi remained silent, her own guilt weighing heavy in her heart.

Stepping forward, Isaac placed a hand on Tom's shoulder then somberly left the room.

Tom looked up into Thandi's misty green eyes. "Please, don't cry," He said gently. He walked over to her and wrapped his arms around her, holding her tight.

"I made you a promise, and I fully intend to keep it," He said holding her a moment longer before releasing her and kissing her sweetly on the forehead. Looking into her eyes, he gave her a reassuring smile.

"I will be leaving the day after tomorrow, and I want you to remain here with Isaac," He said.

Thandi did not protest. In fact, she felt relieved that she would not have to return.

"I'll be back as soon as I've cleared the air with Stafford. There's much business here that I must attend to."

Thandi smiled inwardly at the thought of his returning. Although she didn't want him to leave, she knew that he must.

***

On the morning of his departure, dark gray clouds threatened rain. Both Isaac and Thandi had insisted that he wait, but Tom had insisted upon leaving. Soon, a light mist turned to drizzle, then to steady rain that beat on top of the coach's roof and against its windows. As the rainfall increased, the driver slowed the horses to a steady pace. Staring out the carriage window at the gloomy scene before him, Tom hoped that the weather would soon improve. Before long, his thoughts turned again to Thandi, and his promise.

Thandi had been a threat to his precious daughter's marriage, but now that she'd returned home, maybe now he would put an end to all of this foolishness, he thought. How he dreaded talking to him and hated being completely at his mercy. But Tom knew he had no other choice. For Thandi, he would beg, if necessary. He gritted his teeth at the very thought. If talking failed, he was prepared to offer him money in exchange for Thandi's freedom.

He would also require Isaac's as well, though Daniel said he'd had no interest in taking him. He couldn't trust him to keep his word. And, more than anything, he wanted to give Isaac and Thandi the freedom they longed for.

Money, Tom thought. *That's the one thing that Daniel loves most.* With the money from his inheritance and the upcoming yield profits, Tom could make him a sizable offer...*one he couldn't refuse. And there would still be more money to purchase the Old Mill.*

For the first time since the reading of the will, he had truly given thought to his inheritance.

The Fairview plantation and its 132 acres of land was valued at 67,000 dollars, according to Davenport. There were also the slaves and the yearly yield from the sugar cane, tobacco, and wheat. A small smile creased his lips. Finally, he would no longer be under Daniel's thumb!

After several hours, exhaustion finally overtook him and he drifted into a deep sleep.

Chapter 12

Days later, when he finally arrived home, Anna came out onto the veranda.

At first glance, Tom could see her reddened face set in an expression of anger. He simply ignored her and walked into the house in search of Esther. When he entered the kitchen, Esther looked up from a bowl of peas she was shelling.

"Master!" She exclaimed, grinning wide. She stood immediately, wiping her hands on the sides of her apron. "I didn't hear your wagon. Are you hungry? You must be starved!" She exclaimed. Pulling a chair from the table, Tom plopped down into the wooden seat.

"I am, indeed. And tired as well," He said, sighing and running a hand through his hair.

"I'll make you some sandwiches and tea right away," Esther said, rising from her chair. She put the kettle on to boil, then fetched a platter of cold meats and cheese.

"Made the bread fresh this morning," She chimed, turning to the pantry. As she did so, Anna entered the kitchen.

"I'd like a word with you," She said to Tom.

Esther paused for a breath, reading the anger on her face, then quickly resumed her sandwich making.

"Not now," said Tom. He threw up a dismissive hand, without so much as looking her in the eyes.

Anna's blood boiled at his nonchalant attitude. "Where's the girl?" She asked, straining to keep her temper.

Tom turned to face her.

"She's returned home like you wanted. Maybe now you can be happy," He said. His eyes warred with hers for tense seconds before he turned his back to her again.

Esther kept busy with slicing the cheese, pretending not to hear them.

"Hardly," Anna seethed. "And I can assure you that my father won't be happy, either."

"She's gone, and yet, you *still* aren't satisfied," said Tom, shaking his head.

He gave Esther a faint smile as she sat the sandwiches and tea down in front of him.

"Yes, but she isn't very far, now is she?" Anna said snidely.

"She's at her home, where she should be," Tom said, turning to her again. "And, in case you haven't noticed, I've just returned home from my aunt's funeral. I'm tired, hungry, and mourning. Would it trouble you to have a little heart?" He said, turning again to his lunch.

Anna stood fuming a moment longer, before finally storming away. If she was expecting him to come after her, she was mistaken. Without giving her another thought, Tom took a large bite of his sandwich, then followed it with a careful sip of the hot tea.

"Esther, will you have Myra draw me a hot bath, please?" He asked, taking another bite.

"Yes, Sir," She replied, leaving the room.

Tom planned to take a long nap after his bath. The seats of the coach had been hard on his back, and he felt a little sore and stiff. *Today I'll rest,* he thought. *And tomorrow, I'll ride out to see Stafford instead of awaiting his arrival.*

***

Later, Tom awoke in the darkness of his room. The sound of thunder boomed and flashes of lightning flickered through the windows. Feeling a presence, he turned to find Anna there in their bed. He had obviously slept longer than intended. Careful not to wake her, he slipped from the bed and quietly crept out of the bedroom. Once in his study, he lit the lantern and poured himself a glass of bourbon. The low fire burning in the fireplace did little to warm the large drafty room.

He walked over to the fireplace and threw another log into the dying flames. For several minutes, he stood watching as the flames grew larger and the wood crackled and popped.

"Tom?" A voice called, breaking his trance-like state. He turned to find Anna standing in the doorway. "Are you hungry? You slept through dinner," She said.

Tom hesitated a moment, his eyes fixed on her own. "No… no, thank you," He stammered. He walked over to the desk and retrieved his drink.

Anna stepped into the room and shut the door behind her.

"May I have one of those? It's hard to sleep with the thunder," She asked, eyeing the glass in his hand.

Tom walked over and handed it to her, then went to the cabinet to pour himself another. Walking back to his desk, he took a large gulp of the strong drink.

Grabbing the decanter of bourbon from the cabinet, Anna took the seat across from him at his desk. She filled his half empty glass, then watched as he downed it in one gulp.

"You're drinking a lot more these days," She said, refilling his glass again.

"No more than usual," He said, giving her a wry look.

Anna twisted her lips at the snide remark as she lifted her glass, taking a small sip.

She made a sour face that made him smile faintly. Placing the glass down on the desk, she leaned back in the chair.

"I had expected to accompany you to your aunt's funeral," She said, looking him square in the eyes. "But you left me behind without so much as a goodbye, and took *her...*" She broke off her words, swallowing the lump of emotion in her throat and then reached for her drink and took a longer sip.

"It's hurtful and embarrassing the way you treat me, Tom" She said. Her eyes reflected a hint of pain.

"Why would I bring you along, with me knowing the way you feel about Thandi? You and I have been at odds from the moment she arrived," He said.

"Exactly!" Anna quipped. "She's made nothing but trouble for us, and you treat me like an enemy, instead of your wife."

Tom shook his head, and tossed back another drink. "You are truly unbelievable," He said.

"Am I?" Anna asked, raising her eyebrows. "Can you honestly tell me that you haven't touched her?"

"And what good would it do if I did?" Tom asked. "You will believe what you will, no matter what I say." He refilled his glass and walked over to the window. He sipped his bourbon as he stared at bolts of lightning flashing in the dark sky.

Anna turned in her chair to face his direction. "Then swear on your aunt's grave that you haven't been with her," She said, breaking the momentary silence.

Tom said nothing. Staring into the distance, he smiled wryly and shook his head. Her profound lack of shamelessness and basic human decency never ceased to amaze him.

Anna could feel his disappointment and resentment, and painfully regretted the words that came from her mouth.

"I won't play these silly games with you," Tom said without bothering to turn and face her.

"I'm sorry. I shouldn't have mentioned your aunt in that way," She muttered. She hesitated a moment considering her next words. "It's just that it's been so long since you've touched me. How can I *not* believe something is going on?"

Tom could feel the bourbon taking effect. It seemed the room had now grown hotter with each passing second. He finished his drink and sat the empty glass on a side table. Still in his day clothing, he unbuttoned his shirt collar, then went to his chair.

Feeling slightly drunk, he leaned back and looked across at her. "Our problems existed long before Thandi ever came here," He said, his words sounding slightly slurred.

"Yes, but there was nothing that we didn't work out some way or another," She said and gave him a familiar sultry look along with the teasing smile that always weakened him. Sensing his vulnerability, she rose from her chair and walked around the desk to his side.

"Don't you miss me?" She asked seductively, her eyes wandered down his body and up again.

She bit her lip, holding his eyes in her gaze. With his mind clouded by the alcohol, Tom could not formulate words to speak. His silence and the obvious bulge in his trousers was all the answer Anna needed. She smiled inwardly, proud to see that she still had that effect on him.

Stepping up to him slowly, she removed her robe from her arms and let it fall to the floor, revealing to him a very sheer gown.

The ample mounds of her breast strained against the thin fabric, and her stiffened nipples showed clearly beneath. Tom took in a deep breath, attempting to gain control of himself while Anna, unrelenting in her pursuit, sank to her knees and began to unbuckle his belt. He attempted to stop her, but, in his drunken state, he gave up the second she put his cock in her hot mouth. She teased his shaft with long rhythmic strokes of her tongue, savoring the salty taste of him. As she slowly sucked him, she could feel her cunt throb, the need to feel him inside her growing more and more. Tom groaned as, inch by inch, she took him in deeper and deeper, until her throat could stand the length of him.

"Please," He growled. His mind was a fog; void of all thought and conscience.

Soon she could feel his cock pulsating, He clasped her head in his palms and she knew that he was dangerously close to ejaculation. She stopped abruptly and rose to her feet.

Lifting her gown, she straddled his thighs and pushed his penis halfway inside her. "Ahhh!" She gasped, arching her back against the momentary pain. Gently, she began to move upon him, working her hips slowly up and down until he filled her completely. Soon, she could feel him pulsing within her. Tossing her head back, she began to ride him harder and faster. "Yes!" She cried breathlessly. She could feel her climax building, her cunt throbbing and burning deep. She thrust harder and harder, her inner muscles clenching and releasing until finally she exploded with ecstasy.

"Thandi!" Tom groaned against her shoulder, his hands clenching her hips as he released his heavy load.

Anna's heart leaped, then plunged as the realization of what he said hit her like a ton of bricks.

"You bastard!" She cried, smacking his face hard.

Tom looked up at her stunned, his brows furrowed, conveying his utter confusion. Still drunk, he didn't understand what he had done to upset her. Grabbing her robe, Anna stormed from the room, slamming the door behind her.

Chapter 13

The following day, Tom rode out to Stafford's plantation. All morning, his mind reeled with recollections of the previous night's events. He had tried apologizing to Anna, but she was angry beyond reason. She'd locked herself in their bedroom, refusing to see him.

Tom was met at the door by Stafford's butler. The tall negro guided him to the back lawn where Daniel sat, having his noon tea.

"Why, Tom, what a great surprise!" Daniel said, peering over his teacup. "Please, have a seat," He said, his eyes shifted to the white iron-rot chair across from him. The butler stood by, awaiting his next orders. "Would you like a spot of tea?" Daniel asked.

"No... no, thanks," said Tom.

"Maybe something a little stronger?" Daniel said, smiling.

"Oh, no, no, thanks." Tom shook his head.

After all he'd drank last night, he couldn't imagine having another drink.

With a flick of his wrist, Daniel dismissed the butler and reached for one of the scones on a platter in the center of the table.

"So, I take it you're here to discuss our little situation," He said before taking a bite of the flaky pastry.

"Yes," Tom replied with a nod.

Daniel chewed his food thoroughly, then sipped his tea.

"So, did you find a contract?" He asked, staring intently into Tom's blue eyes.

For a moment, Tom didn't answer. "No," He said finally, dropping his gaze from Daniel's face, then looking back again.

A trace of a smile crossed Daniel's lips. "I didn't think you would," He said, taking another bite of the delicious scone.

He took his time consuming it before speaking again.

"So, then, when will I be able to collect the girl?" He asked.

Tom swallowed hard, trying to clear the nervous lump in his throat. He suddenly regretted that he had not accepted that drink. "Well, I'd hoped that we could further discuss things," He said.

Daniel's thick white brows raised curiously.

131

"I have returned Thandi to Fairview, so there will be no more problems with her and my wife."

Daniel sipped his tea and smiled wryly.

"So, then you've returned her to a home that you now undoubtedly own?" He said, placing the cup down on the table again.

Tom did not answer him for several seconds. He knew exactly what Daniel was doing and implying. He also knew that he couldn't allow him to get under his skin. It wouldn't do good to argue with him. Not with Thandi's fate on the line.

He straightened himself in his chair and stared across the table into Daniels large eyes. "I have, in fact, inherited my aunt's estate, which brings me to another possible remedy to our situation." He paused momentarily. "I'd like to make you an offer for both Isaac and Thandi," He continued.

A look of intrigue crossed Daniel's face and Tom knew that he'd grabbed his attention.

"And just how much would that offer be?" Daniel asked, picking up his tea once again, taking a sip.

"Two thousand," Tom said flatly.

Smiling, Daniel wiped his mouth with a linen napkin. Tom's offer was, in fact, impressive. A buyer could purchase fifteen slaves or better for that price. But something told him that Tom would be willing to go even higher.

"Well, I don't know, Tom. I've quite been looking forward to having the girl here. And I've already been more than fair with letting you keep all the others..."

"Five thousand," Tom interrupted.

The large number took Daniel by surprise, rendering him momentarily speechless.

"Well, that's certainly an impressive offer," He said after a long moment. "But I think I'll take the day and think it over. I can come as early as tomorrow with my answer."

Tom's heart shrank. He had hoped to settle the matter now, between the two of them, without the possibility of interference or meddling from Anna. He grimaced inwardly in thought of what she would undoubtedly tell her father.

Suddenly he felt less hopeful.

"So, tomorrow, then?" Daniel questioned, breaking Tom's brief reverie.

"Yes," Tom answered. He stood and extended his hand. "Tomorrow, then," He said, forcing a fake smile. Daniel shook his hand without bothering to stand, then watched as Tom walked away.

The whole ride back, all Tom could think of was Anna and how he desperately needed to smooth things over with her before Daniel's arrival. Though he had offered him a small fortune, he knew that there was still cause for worry if Anna were to get in his ear.

There was only one thing Daniel Stafford loved more than money, and that was his precious daughter. He acted as if the sun, moon, and stars all revolved around his little girl. Tom knew that no amount of money could measure greater than the influence she had over him.

When he arrived home, he found her in her sewing room. She looked up from her needle work and glared as he entered the room.

"I can understand that you are angry," He said. "But I ask that you forgive me. I was drunk and completely out of my head."

"Well, if you were *out* of your head, as you say, then your so-called friend was most certainly *in* it," Anna replied snidely.

Tom had no words. He knew in that instance that nothing he could have said would've made a difference. He could only hope that Daniel's greed would outweigh his loyalty.

"Well, again, I am sorry," He said repentantly.

Anna dropped her gaze back to her needlepoint as if he had never entered the room.

***

The following morning, Tom awoke at dawn. He turned in bed to find Anna's side empty. The weight and agony of his situation came upon him again as he remembered that she'd chose to sleep in a guest room. Desperately needing a release from his thoughts, he dressed in his work clothes and set off for the fields. Tedious work had always helped him get his mind off his troubles.

Ben smiled wide when he noticed Tom walking up the row with his blade and sack. "Morning, Boss!" He chimed.

Tom smiled back as he put on his work gloves, preparing to join him.

"We been missing ya out here," Ben said as he approached. The big bright smiles of the other hands around him proved his words true.

"I brought you these," Tom said, pulling a second pair of gloves from his sack.

"Aww, Boss, you know me. I works better without 'em," Ben said.

Tom glanced at his hands, and they appeared to look just as bad as they had before he left. Both of Ben's hands were covered in cuts, callouses, and open blisters.

"I insist that you wear them," Tom told him, handing him the gloves. "We can't have blood on our cotton. Now can we?" He added.

"Ain't no blood on 'em. They done healed up pretty good," Ben said, showing his palms for proof.

By noon, the sun was blaring and the hot winds gave little comfort against the scorching heat.

Thirsty and famished, Tom took his lunch outside with Ben and the others.

"Can you believe it? We's almost done," Ben beamed, taking a seat on the tree stump next to him.

Tom looked up from his meager bowl of corn stew, and looked out at the nearly barren cotton fields. A great feeling of accomplishment washed over him, bringing a small smile to his lips.

But the smile on his face was short lived when he saw Daniel's carriage entering onto the plantation's trail.

Ben eyed the wagon as well. "You need help with anything, Boss?" He asked Tom.

Tom sighed heavily, his eyes fixed on the oncoming carriage. "No, Big Ben," He said, shaking his head. "Nothing short of God himself can help me right now."

Chapter 14

Tom walked to the house and made Esther aware of Daniel's arrival. He went out into the courtyard and waited to welcome him. As the carriage grew closer, he began to feel tense again.

The carriage came to a stop and he approached.

Before the driver could jump down and open the door, Tom stopped him with a halting hand. "I've got it," He said, opening the door.

To his surprise, Victor sat inside across from Daniel. "I hope we are in time for lunch," Daniel said, grabbing his cane.

"Hello again, Tom," Victor said. His expression and bland smile told Tom he was aware of what was going on. "Victor." Tom nodded in acknowledgment, smiling back.

"I'm sure there's plenty of food left over," He stated, as he assisted Daniel down from the coach.

"My, what in God's name!" Daniel cried, wiping dirt from his white day gloves. Tom looked at his palms and noticed dirt on his right hand.

"I'm sorry," He said. "I've been working in the fields all morning."

Daniel pulled off his gloves one finger at a time. "I will never understand why you go out into the fields at all!" He fussed, shaking his head. "You have niggers here, just for that purpose!" He went on.

Tom swallowed his words and followed him up the porch stairs, listening as he continued to ramble on.

When they entered the house, Esther met them at the entrance, taking their hats and jackets.

"Esther, please prepare some lunch for our guests," Tom instructed.

"Yes, Sir. Would you like something as well?" She asked.

Tom gave her a brief smile and nod. He wasn't hungry, but he didn't want to explain that he had already eaten with the field hands.

"Papa!" A familiar voice called out.

Tom looked up to spy Anna walking towards them. Daniel turned to meet his daughter with open arms.

"Pumpkin!" He said lovingly, squeezing his arms around her tight. When he released her from his embrace, she looked up at him with intense doe eyes.

"May I have a word with you, Papa, alone?" She asked. The tone in her voice told him something was wrong and Daniel gave her a curious look.

"But, of course," He said. He turned to Victor and Tom. "I'll see you two in the dining room shortly."

"Certainly," said Victor who gave Daniel a short nod, then looked to Anna.

"Good afternoon, Mrs. Lexington," He said, greeting her with a charming smile.

"Please forgive my manners. Good morning, Mr. Richmond," Anna replied.

Her gaze shifted briefly to the wounded look on her husband's face, then back to her father again. Taking his hand in her own, she proceeded to lead him down the long hall.

In the dining room, Tom took a seat at the head of the table.

"I hope you don't mind my coming. Daniel insisted that I come along," Victor said, now that they were alone.

"No, of course, not." Tom smiled. He was, in fact, glad to have a buffer between himself and Daniel. *Especially now.*

A long silence fell between them as both men retired themselves to their own thoughts. Tom sat imagining the conversation between Anna and her father. She was probably telling him everything. Probably crying on his shoulder at that very moment. He sighed at the thought of it.

From the first moment he'd realized what he had done, he'd felt genuinely remorseful. It wasn't his intention to hurt her. Nor did he ever intend to fall in love with Thandi.

"Master?" Esther spoke, jarring Tom from his condemning thoughts.

"Yes," He responded, looking up.

"Should I fetch Master Stafford, Sir?" She asked.

"No," said Tom. "I imagine he'll be joining us in just a moment." Esther nodded dutifully and left the room, closing the door behind her.

Victor turned his attention to Tom upon her exit. He looked at Tom, smiling a caring smile. "So, how have you been holding up?" He asked, making conversation, *and* out of genuine concern.

"I've been fine," Tom lied, forcing a smile.

Given the present circumstances, Victor knew that wasn't entirely true. He looked at Tom for a long moment before speaking again. "I had a talk with Daniel." He hesitated a breath while viewing Tom's expression. "That was a considerable offer you made. I think he will very likely take you up on it," He said.

Tom's face visibly brightened. He wasn't surprised at all that Victor had known. He had already suspected that Daniel had told him of their discussion. However, he was glad to hear that Victor felt he would accept.

"Has he said something to make you think he will?" He asked.

"Well, no," Victor said. "But I could tell that he was seriously considering it. And I did urge him to do so, as well."

A small spark of hope triggered within Tom's chest at his words. He had hoped that his offer would be compelling enough to make Daniel finally lose interest in Thandi, but knowing that Victor had a say in the matter, on his behalf, made him feel all the more confident.

"Thank you," He said, smiling.

Abruptly, The dining room door opened and Daniel entered the room. He looked at Tom with a stern expression before taking a seat at the opposite end of the table. Within seconds, the door sprung open again and Esther poked her head inside.

"Should I serve now, Master?" She asked.

Tom nodded his head. He looked to Daniel and found his eyes already on him.

"I doubt I'll have much now. I seem to have lost my appetite," Daniel said, his eyes never leaving Tom's own.

In that instant, Tom's hope faded. He knew by the look in Daniel's eyes that Anna had told him everything. An uncomfortable silence filled the room.

"Well, I, for one, could eat a horse right now," Victor jested in an attempt to lighten the mood.

Daniel gave him a dry smile, then turned his attention to Tom again. "Well," He said abruptly. "I guess we should get to the point of my being here."

Tom's chest tightened with apprehension.

"As you know, my main concern is for my daughter and her happiness..." He stopped speaking as Esther entered the room again, carrying a tray of soup bowls and sandwiches. Myra followed behind her, bringing fresh squeezed lemonade. Daniel held his tongue until they had gone from the room and shut the door.

"As I was saying," He resumed. "My daughter's happiness is what's most important to me." He paused, fixing his gaze on Tom's face. "As it should be to you," He continued. "After much consideration, as generous as it is, I've decided to reject your offer."

A look of surprise came over Victor's face. He glanced over to Tom and saw his expression darken. He had sensed a change in Daniel's mood from the moment he sat down at the table.

"I can assure you that your daughter's happiness is not at risk," said Tom.

"Can you?" Daniel swiftly countered. He gave Tom a piercing look from under raised brows.

Tom spoke cautiously, knowing that he could not afford to risk angering Daniel any more than he already had. "I can understand your concern, but there is nothing for Anna to fear other than her own active imagination."

A look of disbelief crossed Daniel's face. For a long moment, he said nothing.

Victor sat silent, stirring his soup, watching the exchange between the two men. "So, was it my daughter's imagination when you cried out the name of your nigger *friend?*" Daniel, finally blurted.

His fear now realized, Tom's face flushed red with embarrassment and his heart plummeted within his chest. He glanced at Victor's stunned expression, then back to Daniel again.

"As I tried explaining to Anna, I'd had far too much to drink..."

Daniel threw up a hand, stopping Tom's next words. "Please, spare me your pathetic explanation," He said with a look of irritation. "As we all know, a drunk tongue speaks a sober mind."

"You have my word there will be no further problems," Tom returned.

"Your word?" Daniel said sardonically. "I have no faith in your words or your promises. You gave your word to love and honor my daughter, and yet we are sitting here, now, having this conversation."

Tom frowned slightly, realizing that no explanation or apology would be of use.

"And, despite what my daughter has told me, the fact that you're willing to go to such lengths to keep the girl lets me know all I need to know. It also lets me know that the girl has got to have quite a piece of tail on her," He added in a voice laced with lust.

"I won't permit you to take her," Tom said boldly.

Smiling, Daniel dipped his spoon into the bowl of piping hot mushroom soup. "And just what can you do to stop me?" He asked, looking up into Tom's stern eyes. "If you don't bring her back immediately and turn her over, then I'll simply be forced to bring in the law." He stopped to blow his soup and cool it. "Either way, I get the girl," He finished.

The tension in the room grew thicker in an instant.

Tom's face warmed with anger. Pushing his bowl away, he dropped his napkin on the table.

"Then I guess there is nothing further for us to discuss," He said, glowering at Daniel.

Victor noted the contemptuous expressions on both men's faces.

"Other than business, I think not," Daniel said harshly, before lowering his head to his bowl and continuing to eat as if nothing had happened.

Tom stared at him for seconds longer, then abruptly stood and stormed from the room.

After he left, Daniel turned to Victor. "Can you believe him?" He said, smiling.

The two men exchanged glances, then resumed eating in silence for several minutes before Victor finally spoke.

"I have an alternate solution to your troubles," He said, breaking the silence and looking down the table into Daniel's eyes.

Daniel lowered his spoon and eyed him suspiciously. "And just what might that be?" He asked.

"Sell the girl to me," said Victor.

Astonished, Daniel raised his brow. "Sell her to you?" He said, repeating Victor's words.

"Yes," Victor answered, nodding. "I could use some companionship, and it would free you of your problems with Tom."

Daniel slurped his soup loudly.

"Well, this is turning into one hell of an afternoon," Daniel said, smiling wide. "I knew you favored the girl, but not this much," He chuckled, sipping his lemonade. "Save your money my friend, I promise to share."

Victor took a long sip from his glass, then looked to Daniel with serious eyes. "There is something that I haven't shared with you," He said. "Something that I haven't shared with anyone." His words broke off, and his face took on a grave expression. Seeing his countenance, the smile dropped from Daniel's face.

"I am very ill," Victor said. He looked to Daniel with painful truth in his eyes.

"What is it?" Daniel asked, his deep concern evident. Victor dropped his gaze to his bowl.

"Cancer, I'm afraid," Victor said softly.

There was a momentary silence. "How long have you known?" Daniel asked sadly.

"For almost a year, now."

"Is there a cure?"

"None that have been known to work," said Victor. "My doctor is currently treating me with iodine and tonics, and he has me on a special diet that I refuse to follow," He answered smiling.

No longer hungry, Daniel lowered his spoon into his bowl. "I am sorry to hear this," He said.

"Don't look so grim," Victor said, smiling. "I'm too stubborn to die, but I could use a companion now."

Daniel swallowed hard, considering his next words.

"Yes. Yes, certainly," He stammered.

"Just how much did you have in mind? He asked.

"Five thousand," Victor answered. "The same offer as Tom's."

"But Tom's offer was for both the girl and her brother. You'd only need to pay half as much," Daniel pointed out to him.

"Yes, but I think I'd like the brother as well. I could use a good hand when it comes time to clear the fields surrounding Hollis Creek."

"So, what are your plans for the land? Do you still intend to lease it?" Daniel asked.

"Yes, but, because of my illness, I plan to lease the land annually," Victor explained.

Daniel fell silent for several moments. "I think that we could be of help to each other," He said finally. "I'd like to lease that land myself. Lease it to me at a fair price, and I'll be more than happy to accept your offer for the girl and her brother."

Victor smiled ruefully, thinking of how terribly cunning Daniel was.

"You have a deal," He told him, grinning from ear to ear.

"Okay, then," Daniel smiled, finishing his soup.

***

Meantime, Tom had started to pack his things in his room. He wasn't sure what he was doing. He was no longer thinking rationally. All he knew was that he had to get to Thandi. He had to keep his promise and keep her safe. *Maybe he could hide her. Move her far away from Newport. He would figure things out after he'd arrived at Fairview,* he thought. As he gathered some shirts from the closet, a knock came at the door.

"Who's there," Tom called out.

"Tom, it's me," Victor answered through the door. Tom hesitated a moment, then dropped the shirts onto the bed and unlocked the door.

"May I have a word with you?" Victor asked. Tom nodded slightly, then stepped aside, allowing him entrance. He shut the door and locked it behind him.

Victor eyed the bags and clothing strewn about the bed. "Are you leaving?" He asked.

"Yes, I'm going to Fairview," said Tom. He resumed packing, stuffing his shirts into an already crammed bag.

"We need to talk," Victor told him.

Tom paused, and looked to him. "What is it?" He asked thickly.

Victor hesitated to answer. He knew there would be no easy way to tell him about his agreement with Daniel, but, hopefully, he could make him see that what he did was for the best. "I've had a talk with Daniel." He paused again, taking a deep breath and exhaling. "I have asked him to allow me to purchase the girl." He paused again, noting the surprise in Tom's eyes. "He has agreed to sell Thandi to me… and her brother as well, for the price that you offered."

Tom stood, visibly taken aback.

"I hope that you aren't too upset with me, but I can assure you that it is the only way to stop Daniel from taking Thandi. Running away is certainly not an option," He said, eyeing the many bags on the bed. "I still intend to sell you the mill, and, as for Thandi's brother, I have no intentions on taking him; I only did it as a favor to you." *And to Thandi,* Tom thought sorely. "After the deal is done, I'll have my lawyer draw up the necessary papers for change of ownership."

"How good of you," Tom said, his anger evident in his clipped tone. "I'll see to it that you're paid at the end of it."

Victor sighed heavily. "I can understand your anger, but I do hope that you will get past it and see that this is truly for the best. This is the only reasonable option there is."

"Reasonable for who?" Tom asked.

Victor paused for a moment. "For Thandi," He said plainly. "I can

141

give her a good life, Tom. A life worth having. Would you rather see her with a man such as Daniel?"

Tom frowned at the very notion. For weeks, he had been beyond worry with the very thought of that. He had imagined every possible horror that could happen to Thandi at Daniel's hands. He couldn't allow Daniel to have her, no matter what. He had promised to keep him from her and to keep her safe, and he was prepared to do anything to keep that promise, no matter the repercussions. But he knew that Victor was right. He could hide her away somewhere, but what kind of life would that be? A life in fear, always looking over her shoulder.

"You'd be welcome to visit anytime you like," Victor stated.

For a while, Tom said nothing. Victor could see from his face that he was weighing his words carefully.

"How long before you take her?" Tom said, looking up into his face with a wounded gaze.

"I'm not sure when Daniel and I will close the deal, but I imagine that it will be very soon." He hesitated, pondering. "Perhaps, in two weeks," He said finally. "I can send for her then."

Tom lowered his eyes and swallowed hard. "Very well, then," He said sadly.

Victor nodded in silent agreement, then turned and left the room.

Chapter 15

Days later, Tom made the trip to Fairview. Breaking the news to Thandi was the hardest thing he'd ever done. She broke down in front of him and sobbed uncontrollably. It was all he could do not to throw caution to the wind and run away with her.

Isaac had been angry beyond words. The bittersweet news of his impending freedom gave him no satisfaction. He didn't think it was right that he would be freed and his sister would remain enslaved. The two siblings had never once been separated, and Isaac had no knowledge of this Mr. Victor Richmond. He had insisted upon riding back with Tom and Thandi. With such short time before she left, he wanted to spend every possible moment he could with her.

Esther had been elated upon their arrival. However, her happiness was short lived and turned to sadness when she learned of Thandi's troubles.

Soon, the dreadful day came when Victor's driver came to collect her. He arrived in an elegant black carriage with the initials V.R. embossed in gold lettering on its doors. Victor had sent his best carriage to ensure her comfort.

Thandi stood solemnly in the courtyard with Isaac and Esther at her side as Tom and the coachman loaded her luggage into the carriage.

"Master Tom says you won't be far away. An hour's ride at best, so we'll be able to see you pretty often," said Esther. She put on her best sweet smile and placed a comforting hand on Thandi's shoulder.

Isaac brushed a falling tear from her cheek.

"If it's all right with Mr. Richmond, I'll come to visit you as soon as I'm freed," He told her.

Thandi looked up into his large brown eyes. "Promise?" She said solemnly.

"I promise," He said.

He wrapped his long arms around her and hugged her tight against his chest. He pressed a loving kiss to her forehead and released her. They both turned their gazes to Tom as he approached.

Thandi could see the pain behind his eyes, despite his attempt to smile.

In spite of herself, her heart ached for him. She knew he'd blamed himself for what happened, but it wasn't his fault. At least, not entirely.

Tom glanced up at the house, he could see Anna standing in an upstairs window looking down on them. Following his gaze, Thandi turned and saw Anna peering back at her, a wicked grin curling her lips. She quickly turned her attention back to Tom.

"I will be visiting you very soon," He said, his gaze holding hers. Thandi blinked back her tears and smiled faintly.

Tom had to resist the urge to hug her. Instead, he smiled reassuringly then turned towards the waiting carriage.

"Wait!" Cried Esther. She thrust a basket of biscuits and strawberry preserves into Thandi's hands.

"You ain't barely ate a bite in days!" She cut in, before Thandi could refuse.

Both Isaac and Tom walked Thandi to the carriage. Dismissing the coachman's assistance, Tom helped her up inside.

"You be good, you hear?" Said Isaac. "And remember, I'll be to see you soon. I just may bring Sarah along with me," He said, smiling.

Thandi looked tenderly into her brother's eyes and smiled lovingly and then looked again to Tom.

They held each other's gaze for a long moment, their eyes speaking all the words left unsaid, then, with much pain, Tom collected his courage and closed the carriage door.

The driver took off at a fast trot. Thandi watched Isaac and Tom from the window until their figures disappeared from view. Suddenly, a pang of realization hit her again. Sinking back against the cushioned carriage seat, she gave way to despair until she cried herself asleep.

"Madame...Madame." Thandi heard a voice call.

Her eyes fluttered opened and met the coach driver's gaze. She sat upright and straightened her dress. "Forgive me," She said, shaking herself from her momentary daze. She took his offered hand and stepped down from the coach and onto the walkway in front of a very large and elegant mansion. Her eyes widened in surprise as she slowly took in her surroundings. Even more beautiful than the mansion was the large enchanting silver lake overhung by weeping green willows. The hilltop view of Victor's estate had been impressive, but up close it was breathtakingly stunning.

"Well, here you are," a familiar voice called.

Thandi turned to see Victor making his way down the mansion's front steps. Instantly, the feeling of wonder faded, and her fears and apprehension returned.

He nodded briefly to his driver and stopped in front of her. Observing her red swollen eyes and sullen face he frowned.

Despite her grievous mood, he put on a smile. "I've been looking quite forward to your arrival," He said, his tone oozing with European charm.

Thandi gave him a sharp look, but otherwise said nothing.

Victor brushed off the look she gave him, and smiled. "Come on, I'll show you to your room. Henry will see to your bags."

He reached for her hand and Thandi hesitated before reluctantly taking it. Victor smiled to himself, silently noting her stubbornness and fiery eyes.

As they entered the mansion, Thandi's mouth fell slightly agape. Her eyes slowly roved around the very large high ceiling foyer. The tall ivory walls were trimmed in rich gold, and a long white marble winding staircase cascaded from the second floor to the parlors massive white marbled floors.

"After you've settled in, I can show you around. Maybe after dinner," Victor said.

Thandi shut her mouth quickly. Without being conscious of it, she'd briefly forgotten her melancholy and anguish of before.

"Follow me," said Victor.

He led her up the stairs and down a long wall-papered hallway. Suddenly, he stopped at a door on the left. He went inside and Thandi followed him. Like the foyer, the room was absolutely stunning. It was, by far, larger than any bedroom she'd ever seen. And also, like the foyer, the room, it boasted bright ivory walls with gold molding. Rich gold drapes trimmed in white piping adorned the windows. And bright rays of sunlight shined though the balcony's glass double doors. Centering the west wall was a large marble mantelpiece with an open hearth. At the opposite end of the room sat a large four poster bed, encircled by a sheer white canopy.

"Thank you, Corin," Victor said.

Thandi turned around curiously to find a young maid staring back at her.

"I took the liberty of having a bath drawn for you. This here is Corin," said Victor.

The girl curtsied and smiled shyly. "Good afternoon, Madame," She said.

"It's very nice to meet you," Thandi replied with a weak smile.

"If there is anything you need, please, feel free to call on Corin. She will be your personal servant," said Victor.

Thandi's eyes darted to him at his last words, then back to the girl again.

"I don't imagine I'll need much once you've shown me around," She told him.

"The private bath is just beyond that door," Victor said, pointing. "I've also taken the liberty to buy you a few garments. I only hope that I guessed correctly at your measurements."

He walked over to a double door closet and opened its doors. Inside, a long row of dresses hung perfectly neat on wooden racks.

"I particularly like this," He said, pulling out a stunning blue silk dress. "I will buy you shoes after you've been fitted, but, for tonight, we will have to manage." Thandi gave him a questioning look.

"Dinner is served promptly at eight. I'd like it if you wore this dress tonight."

With that said, Victor draped the dress over a nearby chair, and he and the girl left the room.

Just moments later, Henry came with her bags. She glanced at the clock on the mantel piece. *Six-fifteen,* she thought. She picked up the dress from the chair and held it at arm's length.

It was the type of dress that highborn ladies wore, not a slave. She glanced at the other dresses hanging in the open closet. *If Victor plans to buy my affections, it will never work,* she thought.

As expected, the bath was also very lovely. Thandi stepped into the tub and sank down into the hot water. She deeply inhaled the soothing scent of the lavender water and exhaled. She felt as if she could stay in the tub forever, but the water soon turned tepid and then cold, and her forever was over.

She stepped out of the tub and dried off. After taking a glance at the clock, she began to move with haste. It was now seven-thirty and her hair was dripping wet. She hadn't realized she'd spent so much time in the bath. She gathered her under garments from the bed, then pulled a corset from the closet and placed them on the chair with the dress.

She stood before the mirror and began to vigorously dry her hair. When she finished, she dressed quickly and fashioned her hair into a modest bun.

Upon completion, she looked herself over in the full length mirror. She stared at herself for a long moment as if seeing herself for the very first time. The dress looked beautiful, and it fit her body like a glove. She touched a hand to her cleavage, feeling overexposed. She now strongly suspected that was why it was Victor's favorite.

With just minutes to spare, she put on her best shoes and started for the door. When she reached the foyer, she realized that she had no idea where the dining room was.

She crossed the floor and walked down a long hall with several doors leading to both the left and the right. Hearing chatter, she stopped at a set of double doors on her left. Before she could knock on the door it opened, and Corin appeared in the doorway.

"I was just coming to announce dinner, Madame," She said. She stepped aside, allowing Thandi entrance to the dining room.

At a beautifully decorated table sat Victor. He looked up at her and smiled as Corin steered her to her chair.

"You look amazingly stunning," He said with a grin.

Thandi stared back at him in silence. She briefly took in his dapper brown suit, then shifted her gaze to the room's grandeur. Although, she didn't want to be there, she couldn't help admiring the place thus far.

Her gaze settled on an intriguing statue in the far corner of the room.

"That is Hygieia, the Greek goddess of health," Victor said.

Thandi studied the sculpture a moment longer, then turned her attention back to the table.

"Do I make you that nervous?" Victor asked with a slight smile on his lips. The question forced her to look at him.

"Whatever do you mean, Sir?" She replied.

"I mean, that it seems you have a hard time looking at me. So, I imagine that either I make you nervous, or that I'm too hideous to look upon. And again, please call me Victor. Sir is far too formal between us now, don't you think?"

Before she could answer, Victors gaze shifted towards the door as two female servants brought in their meal of roasted quail with orange sauce, peppered potatoes, carrots, and shallots. Another server entered with wine and bread. When they were gone from the room, Victor looked to her again.

"So?" He asked, lifting a questioning brow.

"No, I am not nervous," She lied.

"So, then I *am* hideous," He said, smiling.

For a brief second, he could see a hint of a smile play on Thandi's face.

"You don't like me, do you, Thandi?"

She pouted a little. "I don't think it matters," She said dryly.

"It matters to me," He said. "I don't want to release you from the pain and judgment you've suffered with the Lexington's only for you to be unhappy with a brute like me. So, tell me why don't you like me? I mean, other than the fact that Daniel and I are partners."

Thandi lowered her gaze and didn't answer.

"If you give me a chance, I think you'll find that I'm quite the opposite of my associate."

"You mean, your *friend,*" Thandi said, finally lifting her eyes to meet his gaze.

"Well, I wouldn't exactly call Daniel my friend. We are more so business partners."

Thandi gave him a smart look, then picked up her fork. Though she hadn't eaten a proper meal in days, she wasn't the slightest bit hungry. With so much clouding her mind, she had almost forgot about eating all together. However, at that very moment, she needed to do something to distract her from his probing gaze. She poked at a few of the carrots with her fork, willing herself to eat.

"You really shouldn't feel so downtrodden about what's happened. It's fate that has brought you here."

"*Fate?*" Thandi said in a cold tone. "Forgive me, but I don't think *fate* has had anything to do with my being here."

"You make it sound as though I've kidnapped you." Victor remarked, sipping his wine.

Thandi looked at him glowering. "*Haven't* you?"

Victor chuckled in that dark, flirtatious way that she despised. "Actually, I'd like to think that what I've done, is free you," He said.

Thandi ceased to mull at her food and glared up at him.

"And just how have you freed me? As I was told, you purchased me at a hefty price. That makes me your property. Your **slave**."

"What that makes you is lady of this manor," Victor interrupted. "And what I freed you from was yourself. Tom is a fine, admirable fellow, Thandi, but he is also married. You two can deny it all you want, but it's clear you have feelings for each other. I don't even doubt that he loves you, but what happiness could he ever give you?" He paused a moment, allowing her a chance to answer, but she said nothing. "Why waste your precious youth pursuing what you can never truly have?"

His words stung her deep, partly because they were true.

"This isn't exactly the worst place to be. Especially, when you consider your one other option."

Thandi lowered her eyes again. She knew he was right. Anywhere was better than being with the Stafford's. She knew that she should have been grateful to him for freeing Isaac, and for saving her from Stafford. She also knew the true source of her resentment for him. He wasn't who she had wanted. He wasn't and could never be Tom.

"Forgive me, I'm being ungracious," She muttered. "I am, in fact, grateful for what you have done."

"Yes, but you aren't happy," said Victor. "I do hope to change that."

"So, what are your expectations of me?" Thandi asked, swallowing hard.

"I expect you stop sulking, eventually. And to embrace this new life that you have." He paused briefly. "And to, perhaps, someday embrace me in your heart as you now do another." Thandi's eyes darted up to him, her expression suggesting that would never happen.

Victor smirked inwardly. "I tell you what," He said, straightening himself up in his chair. "I'll make you a deal. Stay here a year with me. If you're still not happy at the end of that year, then you can leave. *With* your freedom."

Thandi's face brightened before his eyes.

"There is, however, one condition."

Thandi frowned, but she wasn't at all surprised that there was more.

"I'd expect you to act as my companion, and not my enemy. I don't expect that you will fall in love with me, but I do expect to have an intimate relationship between us."

Thandi's face flushed white.

149

"However, if you do happen to fall in love with me and stay, that would make me very happy."

Thandi said nothing, but sat silent in thought. She knew that, no matter her answer, it wouldn't change her present circumstances. She also knew that, no matter what, she would never come to love him. It sickened her to think that she would have to sacrifice her body for her freedom, but, in the end, she would be free. Free of him. Free to go back to Fairview with her brother. Free to...she shook the thought away.

"You give your word you'll let me go?" She asked.

"Of course," said Victor. "I always honor my promises."

Something in his eyes told her that he would be faithful to his word. She believed him, but it did nothing to ease her fears of what was to come. *A year. A year,* she thought. To her, it sounded like a lifetime.

Chapter 16

When they finally finished their meals, he showed her around the mansion and introduced her to the staff. To her surprise, there were only five maids, one butler, two drivers, and a single gardener. Thandi found it hard to believe that only a staff of nine ran such a large manor. She walked along in awe as they moved through all of the mansion's 14 rooms. She particularly liked the leisure room. There was a piano and harp, as well as a table set with playing cards and an ivory chess set. Everywhere she looked, there was beauty. Expensive sculptures, splendid furnishings, and paintings adorned every room.

In the study, one painting in particular struck her breathless with surprise.

On the tall robin's blue wall facing her, there was a massive portrait of a beautiful aristocratic woman in a captivating gold gown. Something else about the woman captivated Thandi, too: her skin was as brown as mocha.

She slowly approached the portrait, taking it all in with each step, walking cautiously as though she could possibly disturb the painted woman forever immortalized within it.

The woman's deep caramel eyes looked out of the paint, out of the frame, and, seemingly, directly into Thandi's soul.

"My wife, Elena," Victor said tonelessly, following her gaze.

Thandi stifled a gasp. She did a double take of the painting, and stepped even closer to it.

"But she is negro," She muttered, her tone expressing her surprise.

"Does that shock you?" Asked Victor.

"Well, of course, it does," Thandi quickly replied. "But how can that be?" She asked, confused.

Victor turned and stared into the ghostly eyes of the beautiful woman staring back at him.

"Although there could be no legal marriage between us, Elena and I had our own unofficial ceremony. It was very private. No family or friends... just our personal staff ." His words broke off, and he smiled as he reflected back on that joyous day. "For all points and purposes, our marriage was as real as any. Even better," He added.

Thandi looked to him as if seeing him for the very first time and then turned again to Elena's portrait. In a strange way, he resembled his mother. The two shared the same complexion, large brown eyes, and long flowing raven black hair. "She is very beautiful," She said softly.

"Yes," Victor said, a heavy sadness etching his words. She turned again and met his warm gaze.

"Whatever happened to her?" She asked hesitantly. "Is she alive?" She knew the answer immediately from his grim expression.

"I'm sorry. That was nosy of me."

Victor shook his head a little. "It's not. She died of small pox 15 years ago." Thandi turned back to the painting and a comfortable silence fell between them.

"Do I somehow remind you of her?" She asked. Her eyes searched his own.

Victor hesitated to answer, and she could tell that he was pondering the question. "Yes, in a way, I suppose. The two of you share the same stubborn temperament," He said, smiling.

Thandi gave him a pouty look. "I can only imagine the scrutiny and scandal you two must have endured," She said heavily.

Victor smiled. This was the sweet side of her that he wanted to see more of. "When you obtain enough wealth and power, men tend to turn a blind eye to things they otherwise wouldn't," He stated. He paused a moment, giving Elena a long, loving look. "But even so, nothing and no one could have prevented me from loving her," He said, his eyes never leaving the painting.

A look of admiration flashed over Thandi's face.

"Perhaps tomorrow I can show you the gardens. I imagine that you could use some rest tonight."

Thandi tore her gaze away from the portrait. In truth, she hadn't slept a full night in several weeks. "Yes… yes, I could," She answered.

With that, Victor offered her his arm, and she took it. He escorted her to her bedroom door where they paused momentarily. Thandi looked up nervously into his eyes, and he smiled, as if he knew exactly what it was she was thinking.

"You have the most incredible green eyes," He said. The intense way he looked at her made her heart flutter within her chest.

"Well, goodnight," He said. He wanted to kiss her, but restrained himself.

Unable to tear her gaze away from the intensity of his eyes, she lingered for moments longer. "Well, goodnight, then," She said finally, breaking the spell that held her.

"Yes, goodnight," Victor replied. He stood for seconds longer as she entered the room, closing the door shut behind her.

As he walked towards his room his smile grew larger and larger in thought of her.

***

The following morning, Thandi awoke to the sound of knocking on her bedroom door. She opened her eyes and winced at the bright morning light that came through the half drawn drapes. She glanced at the clock over the mantle, surprised to see that it was ten-forty. Quickly standing, she put on her robe and slippers, then went to the door.

As she'd expected, it was Corin.

"Morning, Madame." She curtsied.

"Good morning, Corin," Thandi replied.

"Did you sleep well Missus?" She asked.

"Yes, very much so," Thandi said, taking another glance at the clock. She stepped aside, allowing Corin to enter.

"Master Richmond instructed me not to wake you," She explained. Thandi smiled at his thoughtfulness.

"Is there anything I can do for you?" Asked Corin.

"No, you needn't make any fuss over me, Corin. I'm quite used to doing for myself." The maid gave her a peculiar look, then smiled just slightly.

"Yes, Madame, but Master Richmond has instructed me to see to you as lady of the manor."

"I'm no *lady*," Thandi cut in. "I'm just a slave like you, Corin," She told her.

"Forgive me, Madame, but I'm not a slave," Corin said respectfully. Thandi turned to her with a surprised look on her face.

"What do you mean?" She asked. "You are free?"

Corin nodded her head in reply. "We *all* are here," She said. Thandi stood visibly taken aback.

"Were you freed by Victor?" She asked.

Again, Corin nodded her head. "Master Richmond has given us all

153

our papers. We work for pay, and our food and lodging are free. Master Richmond is a very gracious man."

Thandi lowered her eyes to the floor for a few moments, as if she were processing the information.

Suddenly, she felt even more confident about her deal with Victor.

He will free me, she thought. "Thank you, Corin," She said finally. "But there's nothing I need," She said. "Perhaps you could draw my bath each day, and keep fresh water for the basin. That would be enough."

"Yes, Madame," Corin nodded, dutifully. "When you're ready, Master Richmond would like for you to join him for breakfast," She said.

"Tell him I shall be there straightaway," Thandi told her.

Even after Corin left the room, she still stood frozen in a state of wonder.

More and more she was beginning to realize that there was more to Victor than she had perceived.

Feeling well rested, she dressed hurriedly and headed for breakfast.

When she entered the dining room, she found Victor already there, waiting.

"There you are, I wasn't sure if I should instruct the staff to prepare lunch," He said.

"Forgive me. I haven't gotten much sleep as of late," Thandi replied.

The servants immediately brought coffee, orange juice, toast, bacon, scrambled eggs, sweet meal, and chopped fruit.

"You look stunning," said Victor, casting his daily paper to the side. Thandi smiled at him.

"Thank you. You look very handsome yourself," She countered, letting her eyes rove over his fancy black suit.

"I was thinking that perhaps today we could do some shopping. Maybe buy you a few more dresses and get you fitted for new shoes."

Thandi gave him an incredulous look and shook her head.

"It would be a waste of your time. No store is going to cater to a mulatto."

"Oh, they'll cater to you just fine. I know the owners personally," He said. "Besides, they'll probably mistake you for a white woman," He said half joking, but mostly serious. "Trust me, you'll be just fine," He assured her.

After breakfast, he proposed a walk to show her around the gardens. As she'd imagined it would be, the gardens were splendid. Bursts of colorful flowers and trees with interesting forms and shapes spanned for two or more acres of the massive tree enclosed garden. Even the grass seemed lusher and greener than any others she'd seen before.

Victor had accredited its vibrant appearance to the natural water source being so near, and to the talented hands of Jonah, his gardener.

They took their lunch at a table near one of the garden's four fountains. There they talked of many things, but mainly of Victor's past life in London. Shortly after lunch, they boarded the coach and headed for town. There, everything went well just as Victor had assured her. The store owners were very pleasant to her, some too pleasant and she had found so many things to her liking.

Outside of a few sidelong gazes from a couple of snooty white women, she had managed to survive the trip unscathed. To Thandi's surprise, she was beginning to find Victor's company more pleasant than she could ever have imagined.

Victor of course, was happy to see that her mood had improved and was thoroughly enjoying her company.

In the lady's store, just for a moment, he'd seen her smile a genuine, wide, radiant smile he'd never seen before. *Something was beginning to shift between them*, he thought. At least, she no longer appeared to hate him. It wasn't love, but it was certainly a start to something positive between them.

With Henry's assistance, he placed at least a dozen shopping bags on the seat inside the carriage. With so many bags, Thandi had no other choice but to sit beside him. After seeing the clever smile on his face, she quickly surmised that he had put them there purposely.

"Thank you," She said as the carriage took off at a slow trot.

"It was my pleasure." Victor smiled.

As they rode on, Thandi cast her gaze out the window and watched the town's scenery slowly pass by. She found herself intrigued by all the new stores, café, and restaurants that had developed there since her childhood.

"Are you hungry?" Victor asked, breaking the silence that had fallen between them.

Thandi nodded her head. "A little," She said prompting Victor to call on Henry by tapping his silver cane on the carriage floor.

"Yes, Suh?" Henry replied, bringing the carriage to a halt.

"Take us to the Watercrest," Victor instructed him.

Within minutes, Henry slowed the horses again to a stop.

Curious, Thandi peered out of the window and saw that they had reached a restaurant.

The more modern faced building stood out amongst the older shops and taverns along the strip.

"I hear the food here is splendid," Victor noted.

Thandi looked up at the sign on the awning that read, *The Watercrest.*

"Ready?" He asked. He extended his hand and she took it.

Suddenly, he remembered something. "Wait," He said. He leaned forward and grabbed one of the bags purchased from Pearson's Shoes.

"Wear these," He told her. He pulled a shoe box from the bag, and handed it to her.

Thandi gave him a sweet smile. He'd picked that particular pair out personally. The peach suede matched perfectly with her peach colored day dress.

She slid off her old worn boots and slipped on the dainty new heels.

"Perfect," said Victor.

He gave her a long admiring once over, then exited the carriage.

Once inside the restaurant, the maître d' greeted them personally and they were immediately seated at a table in the center of the full dining room. With wide eyes, Thandi looked around at the elegant surroundings. Seeing so many white faces in one room made her feel slightly nervous.

"So, what would you like?" Victor asked. He picked up his napkin from the table and placed it neatly on his lap.

Thandi picked up her menu and began to glance through it. "I think I'll have the broiled chicken," She said after a moment.

"Good selection. I think I will have the salmon myself."

"But you haven't even looked at your menu," said Thandi, as a waiter walked over to take their orders.

"Good evening, Mr. Richmond," He said, bowing his head.

Thandi raised a puzzled brow. Victor had given her the impression that he hadn't eaten there before, but it was apparent that the waiter had known him.

Victor took the liberty to order for them both.

In addition to the chicken and salmon entrées, he also ordered a bottle of a very old French wine.

"And for dessert, Sir," the waiter asked.

Victor hesitated a moment. "Do you like chocolate mousse?" He asked.

"I can't say that I've ever had it."

Victor smiled at the note of sarcasm in her tone. "So, tell me, what are some of the things you like to do," He asked, making conversation.

Thandi hesitated a while, as if pondering her answer.

"I like sewing, mainly. I picked up the hobby from my mother."

"And? Surely there must be more."

Thandi lowered her eyes to the table in thought for a long moment.

"And I adore music," She said finally, looking up at him with those bright green eyes.

"Ah! Now, there's a hobby. What instrument do you play?"

Thandi smiled broadly. "None," She said, thinking of how Missus Lacy had once told her she was all thumbs when it came to playing the piano.

"I like listening to music. My former mistress played the piano often," She explained.

"Perhaps," said Victor. He stopped speaking as the waiter returned with their glasses and the bottle of wine. "Perhaps I can play something for you tonight," He resumed after the waiter had gone.

Thandi smiled, but said nothing. Her true attention was on the dark haired woman sitting at the table in the left corner of the room. The woman had been ogling her for a while.

Thandi scanned the room to see if anyone else was staring. She found other eyes on her. All of which looked away when she met their gazes.

"You seem preoccupied," Victor said, breaking her reverie.

"Forgive me," She said softly. "But people are staring."

Victor glanced around the dining room and saw the eyes of Giles Morton and his wife, and, also Mr. Archer from the press. Their eyes met and they all smiled and nodded in acknowledgment.

Victor smiled back at them, then turned his attention to Thandi again. "If they're staring, it is because you're the most beautiful woman in the room," He said reassuringly.

Somehow, Thandi doubted that was the case.

Especially, for the dark haired woman. Victor turned his head following the direction of her fixed gaze.

When he looked into the woman's eyes, she smiled faintly, then quickly looked away.

"Madame Buckley. She's an old friend," He said, reaching for his glass.

"An old, *intimate* friend?" Thandi asked, before she could consider her words.

"That was quite some time ago," Victor said, smiling at her boldness.

Thandi hated herself for asking the question. *She didn't care about his personal affairs*, she told herself.

"You should drink your wine. It'll help you relax," Victor suggested. "I don't see how you can be so at ease," Thandi said lowly. "If one of these white folks stare at me long enough, we will both be thrown out by the ears or worse."

Victor belted out an unstoppable laugh. "I'm sure that won't happen," He said.

Thandi shook her head from side to side. "And just how can you be certain of that?"

"Because the owner would not allow that to happen."

Thandi gave him another incredulous look. "Don't be so certain of yourself," She warned.

"But I *can* be certain of myself," Victor said smiling. The Water Crest is *my* establishment.

Chapter 17

After they arrived back at the estate, Thandi went into her bedroom.

"Thank you," She said to Corin and Sophie as they brought in her shopping bags.

"Would you like for us to put these away now, Madame?" Corin asked.

Glancing at the number of bags, Thandi nodded. "Yes, please," She replied.

She pulled an elegant silk gown from the linen bag that she carried, and held it up to herself in the long mirror on the wall. She did her best not to act too thrilled in the store, but she had greatly adored the gown above all the others. With its soft champagne color and beige lace up its sides, it strongly reminded her of a gown that Madame Lacy had worn.

"Should I hang that in the closet, Madame? The armoire is full," Corin asked.

"Yes, thank you," Thandi replied, passing her the dress.

"Master Richmond has informed us that you two have eaten, but if you become hungry again, there's dinner ready," Corin informed her.

"Oh, no," Thandi smiled sweetly, shaking her head. "I'm quite stuffed. I couldn't imagine eating another bite tonight."

"Would you like a bath drawn now?" Corin asked.

"No, thank you. I think I'll rest a bit now," Thandi said.

She glanced over at the clock on the mantel. *Seven thirty.* It was hardly late. *Perhaps, I'll rest for an hour, then visit the sewing room,* she thought.

After the maids finally left the room, she slipped off her pretty new shoes and flung herself onto the bed. She closed her eyes, succumbing to the inviting effects of the wine from dinner. Soon, her mind drifted aimlessly, somewhere between sleep and wakefulness. Never had she felt so peacefully blissful, and carefree.

After a short time, she heard a sound; a sweet sound.

She opened her eyes hazily, blinking as she tried to focus.

Still, she heard it; the soft sound of a piano playing. Drawn by the mysterious melody, she got out of bed and slipped on her shoes. After a quick glance at herself in the mirror, she set out in search of the music's source. The music grew louder with every step as she walked down the hall.

As she grew closer, she realized the music was coming from the music room Victor had shown her. She slowed her steps as she approached the open door on the left side of the hall. When she reached the doorway, she saw Victor seated at the piano, playing. He stopped abruptly as his eyes met hers.

"Well, hello there," He said, smiling.

Out of habit, Thandi gave a small curtsy and returned his smile as she entered the room.

"You really must stop doing that," He said, shaking his head.

Please, don't stop. That sounded quite lovely," Thandi said.

Victor smiled warmly as she came over and stood next to the piano. As she'd requested, he resumed playing.

Thandi stood entranced, absorbing each sweet note as the haunting melody filled the room. The piece was dark and eerily beautiful; the most beautiful music she'd ever heard. Her heart fluttered as the piano boldly surged, then faded sweetly again.

The piece seemed to tell a story. *A story of love, and love lost*, she imagined. She swallowed back the heavy lump in her throat and batted back a tear that threatened to come. When the melody slowly faded away, she exhaled deeply, as if the music had finally released her from its hold.

"What were you playing?" She breathed.

Victor smiled up at her. "Actually, it's a piece I wrote. I never gave it a title. But perhaps I should."

A look of surprise and wonder came over Thandi's face. "*You...* you wrote that?"

Victor gave her an incredulous look and broad smile. "Is that so surprising?" He asked.

"Did you write the piece with Elena in mind?" She asked innocently.

Victor's smile faded, then appeared again. "Yes," He answered softly. "I wrote it shortly after her death. It was a very hard time in my life." He paused for a moment, and then said, "Music helped me make it through."

160

Thandi smiled piteously, thinking of how deeply in love he must have been to write such a moving piece.

"Come, come, sit," He said, patting the empty spot on the piano bench next to him.

Thandi's heart swelled at the request. Apprehension showed clear in her face as she cautiously sat beside him. The two were very close. So close, that their arms slightly brushed and she could smell the inviting scent of his cologne.

"Would you like to learn a simple scale?" He asked.

Thandi shook her head. "No, I'm quite impossible to teach," She warned.

"Don't be silly, anyone can learn" He said and began playing a slow, simple tune.

Thandi looked on, watching his hands in fascination. She could tell by his ease that he'd been playing for some time.

"When did you learn to play?" She asked.

He turned his gaze to her, his hands never leaving the keys. "I learned pretty early on," He said. "My mother started my lessons when I was just five. Her greatest ambition was to be the mother of a child prodigy," He said, smiling.

Thandi smiled, too. "So, what happened?" She asked. "Why did you *not* pursue a career in music?"

Victor stopped playing and turned to face her. "Because my father had other ambitions for me," He said. He held her gaze for a heart stopping moment. Brown eyes boring into green. "Put your hands on top of mine," He said after a moment. He placed his hands on the piano keys then looked to her again.

Thandi's eyes widened. Her former nervousness returned and she lowered her eyes from his penetrating gaze. Then with great hesitation, she did as instructed.

Smiling, Victor moved their hands, positioning them correctly on the appropriate keys. The feel of his hands beneath hers, and the long row of black and ivory, vividly reminded her of past times. No matter how hard Madame Lacy had tried to teach her, she simply could not grasp onto her teachings.

"Relax your fingers," He said, sliding closer to her.

Thandi's heart beat quickened at the feel of him against her.

He must have sensed her unease, because again he told her to relax. "Be careful not to press down, just watch the keys that I press," He said.

Thandi took a deep breath and did her best to relax her hands and steady her racing heart.

When ready, he tentatively pressed down on one of the keys beneath his right fingers, and then again on another.

Thandi watched their hands closely as the loud notes rang out, echoing into the air.

Suddenly, he stopped, then repeated the movement; slowly at first, then faster until the repetitive strokes created a melodic sound. "Now, you try," He said removing his hands and looking into her eyes.

Thandi hesitated a moment, then turned her gaze upon the keys again. Nervously, she attempted to copy his movements.

"That's it. Don't stop," He said, smiling.

Suddenly, he placed his hands on the keys to the right and began to play. As he did, Thandi continued to stroke the keys on the left. To her surprise, the combined notes created a sweet melody. Her eyes lit with delight.

"It sounds beautiful." She smiled, a note of wonder in her voice.

Victor smiled back at her, then turned his attention again to the keys. "Now, you try it all alone," He said, removing his hands from the piano completely.

Thandi's smile fell away and she withdrew her hands from the keys. "I can't," She said.

"Yes, you can," said Victor, his stern tone suggesting that he wouldn't accept no for an answer.

Thandi hesitated a moment, then turned and studied the keys. Placing her fingers on them delicately, she took a deep breath, then slowly began. For a moment, she did well, but when she attempted the second chord she couldn't remember the sequence of keys and the notes jumbled up.

"As I told you, I can't," She said, sounding discouraged.

She removed her hands from the piano and placed them in her lap.

"You shouldn't give up so quickly. Besides, you almost had it. Try again. Only this time, play the scale a lot slower."

Thandi made an irritated face, then reluctantly complied, placing her hands again on the keys. Again, she started to play. This time, she played slower as he'd suggested and focused hard. To her surprise, she finished the short piece without a single error.

"Marvelous." Victor smiled. "Now, again, but this time a little faster."

Feeling a bit more confident, she studied the keys once more, then started. Amazingly, she finished again without flaw.

"And you said you couldn't learn!" Victor exclaimed.

Thandi smiled a little, feeling proud of herself.

"I could teach you to play, if you like."

Thandi smiled back into his eyes. "Yes, I'd like," She said.

He held her gaze until she finally looked away. "So, so far, have I proven myself to be the monster that you imagined?" He teased, breaking the brief silence that had fallen between them.

"No… not yet," Thandi chided. "But what I don't understand is…" She stopped.

Victor stared back at her, anxiously awaiting the rest of her response. "What you don't understand is, what?" He nudged.

"What I don't understand is why a man like you, would want a woman like me as a companion," She said, her tone suggesting that she wasn't just speaking of herself, but of Elena, too.

"A woman like *you,*" Victor repeated, shaking his head from side to side.

"Yes… a *negro*. A *slave*," Thandi said. "Why on Earth would you want a slave, when you could have someone far better suited for you. Someone like the likes of Madame Buckley."

Victor's face lit with amusement. "Do you mean someone *white?*" He asked.

Thandi nodded hard. "Yes."

"Come with me," He said, rising and taking her hand.

He led her out of the room and down the long hall to a room on the right.

Thandi paused in surprise as they entered. She could tell instantly that the room belonged to him from its masculine decor. The butterflies in her stomach returned when her gaze fell upon the room's huge four poster bed. She looked to Victor as he crossed the room and took a picture from the mantel.

"These are my parents," He said, handing her the picture.

Thandi lowered her gaze to the portrait and stared for a long moment.

"You strongly resemble your father," She said, her eyes never leaving the picture. "And your mother is quite lovely. Are they still in London?" She asked, looking up at him.

"No, they both died years ago," Victor said sadly.

Thandi truly felt saddened by his loss. "I'm so sorry," She said, handing the picture back to him.

Victor gazed at the photo for a moment then turned it over.

Thandi looked on curiously as he removed the backing from the frame and set it aside on a nearby table.

"*This* is my true mother," He said, removing a small photograph from the frame. Oddly, the smaller photo had been hidden behind the portrait of his parents.

Thandi gave him a puzzled look as he handed her the picture.

Upon first glance, she could see that the young girl in the photo was *not* the woman in the picture with his father. In the picture she now held, was a beautiful young girl with long dark hair and sad brown eyes. Thandi looked up at Victor. "I don't understand," She said.

"The girl in that photo," He said, glancing at the picture in her hand. "That young girl is my *real* mother."

A puzzled frown creased Thandi's brows.

"That girl," Victor said, glancing again at the picture she held. "She was a mulatto slave named Lily. She was owned by my father."

"Your *mother*!?" Thandi said, unable to conceal the shock in her voice. Her eyes shifted to the picture, then back to him again.

"Yes," Victor nodded. "Before my father died, he confessed a secret to me. A secret that he had promised my mother he'd never share with me or another. He turned the picture around in his hands and gazed down at his parents' faces.

"According to my father, my mother was unable to bear children. He said that she had desperately wanted a child, and that he himself wanted an heir. He said that my mother had wanted me so badly that she alone devised a plan that would give them the child that they both longed for." He could see that Thandi was listening intently.

"They moved to the states so that they could purchase a female slave. For a year, they looked for my mother. They attended endless auctions." He paused a moment, staring into the familiar eyes of his mother. "He said that it was my mother who chose Lily. She wanted Lily because she was young and likely very fertile, and, more importantly, she had been the lightest skinned mulatto girl they'd ever seen."

Thandi cringed unconsciously.

"With my mother's blessing, my father impregnated her. She was just thirteen...still a child." He shook his head in disgust, imagining again how terrifying things must have been for her. "After she delivered the baby, my mother claimed the child as her own. They kept Lily on at the estate for two years so that she could nurse me. When they no longer needed her, my father sold her off and my parents moved back to London and presented their new son to society as their very own." He paused in thought.

"My father made me promise to never tell my mother that I knew. When I asked him about the reason for his confession, he said that he wanted to leave this world with a clear conscience, and that he had always wondered about the girl." He paused again staring solely at his father's face.

"His dying wish was for me to find Lily. To purchase her back, no matter the cost. He gave me the name of the man he sold her to, but, by the time I found him, she had already been sold off to someone else."

Lowering the frame, he looked up into Thandi's wide-eyed gaze.

"The bill of sale had been lost over the years, so there was no way of finding her. In the end, I liquidated my father's estate and holdings and moved here in hopes that maybe someday, somehow, I would see her. I imagine that is why my father had that picture taken of her. His conscience...it must have plagued him all those years."

He shook his head, put the picture aside, then turned again to Thandi. "So, as you can see, you and I have a lot more in common than you thought," He said.

"Does anyone know?" She asked, the words caught in her throat.

"No, of course, not. Until now, I've never uttered a word of this to anyone. Not even to Elena."

Thandi knew that had to be true. He wouldn't have had the privileges and wealth he had now if people had known.

"How long have you kept this secret?" She asked.

"I've held this secret for more than twenty years."

Thandi's shocked expression turned to a look of disbelief and sadness. She gazed upon the photo of his mother a moment longer, then it gave it back to him.

He set the picture on the table, then turned to her again. Some of her bewildered look remained on her face.

"Everyone has their secrets," He said.

Thandi didn't like the way he looked at her when he said it.

Smiling warmly, his gaze slowly lowered from her eyes to her neck. "I've been meaning to ask you," He said, stepping towards her.

Thandi's heart dropped to her stomach.

"Where did you get this?" He asked.

A shudder ran through her as he lifted the locket from between her breast, his hand brushing the bare skin.

"It was my mother's," She answered nervously.

"It's quite beautiful," He said, eyeing the locket's beautiful swirling vines. "As are you," He noted, lifting his intent gaze to her eyes.

Thandi could feel her unease rise and her heartbeat quicken. He touched her cheek gently, his fingers lightly caressing the smoothness of her skin. Without warning, he bent his head and kissed her lips.

"Don't!" She said, pulling back from him.

Victor's frowned in confusion by her reaction.

"Forgive me. I didn't mean any harm," He said sincerely. "I must have somehow gotten our conversation confused yesterday. I had thought we had an agreement."

Thandi went still at his words. She dropped her eyes to the floor. *Victor is right. I did agree. And even if I hadn't, it wouldn't matter*, she thought. "We do," She uttered somberly, lifting her sad gaze to his eyes.

"If you'd give me a chance, I could make you very happy. Even if that happiness is only for a year," He said, his voice and expression beseeching.

He could see the hesitancy in her eyes; the uncertainty, the fear.

Tenderly, he stroked her cheek, his thumb tracing the soft line of her bottom lip. Gently he cupped her chin with his fingers and lowered his mouth again to her lips and kissed her gingerly. She shut her eyes in surrender, her chest rising and falling with trepidation.

Suddenly, he lowered his hands to her waist and pulled her closer. He could feel her shaky breath against his lips. Again, he kissed her, this time more slowly, then deeply, clutching her head in his hands, his fingers tangled in the soft curls of her hair. Then, suddenly, he pulled away from her lips and began to suckle the sensitive curve of her neck.

Thandi gasped, unable to fight the heated sensation that shot through her. She felt his hands on her back, his fingers busy with the buttons and ribbons of her gown. When she finally was naked, he picked her up and carried her over to the king sized bed.

For a moment, he gazed upon her; a long admiring gaze. Then he stripped off his clothing and climbed into the bed, pulling her into his arms.

He kissed her lips, her neck, her shoulders. Then he rolled on top of her. A surge of panic shot through her at the feel of his hard member against her thigh. She braced herself against the bed as he parted her legs with his own and pushed inside her.

"Aahhh!" She cried in pain, her hands gripping the bed covers. She could feel herself stretching and burning as he filled her. "You're too large," She cried against his chest.

Victor lifted himself up onto his elbows and looked down into her teary eyes.

"Relax," He whispered. He pressed a kiss to her forehead and slowly withdrew himself from inside her as he kissed her lips; trailing kisses down her neck, to her breast, then even lower to the soft nest of curls between her legs.

She closed her eyes and sucked in a breath as she felt his tongue began to stroke and soothe the aching folds of her feminine flesh. Soon he had parted her lips with his fingers and found her hidden pearl.

Thandi squirmed against the bed as he closed his lips around the sensitive nub of flesh and began to suckle. Within moments, he could feel the sweet bud swelling between his lips. The sound of her soft moans heightened his hunger. He moved his mouth and lifted her hips, thrusting his stiff tongue deep inside her tight opening.

He loved the taste of her: sweet and salty. He could feel her walls contract in response around him. She moaned and writhed against the bed. She could feel heat and tension building deep within her. Soon, a rapture overtook her, rendering her mind and body no longer her own.

She arched her back with a groan and he could feel her thighs begin to tremble against his face. He held her steady, his mouth and tongue sucking and licking her feverishly.

"God!" She cried out, unconsciously clutching the curls of his hair in her fists.

He tightened his grip on her waist and thrust his searching tongue even deeper inside her.

She moaned aloud, almost desperately, as her body trembled hard with release.

He lapped up her sweet flowing nectar until she ceased to tremble and stroked his thumb over her slick folds and bud. She was soaking wet. *Now, she is ready for me*, he thought.

He climbed on top of her again and gently pushed the tip of his member inside her wetness. She gave a small gasp as he pushed deeper, slowly inching his thick length inside until he filled her completely. Her moans and whimpers were muffled against his neck as he began to move inside her, slowly at first, then faster and harder until she cried out. He groaned with pleasure as he felt her hot walls clenching and releasing around him. Though she cried for mercy, he did not cease his assault. Instead, he gripped her hips and drove himself even deeper inside her.

Soon, strangely' the pain became pleasurable. She clawed at his back and kneaded his shoulders, moaning into the heat of his chest. Soon, he groaned and shuddered against her. She could feel his member pulsing inside her, his heartbeat thundering against her breast, its frantic rhythm matching her own.

When his spasms ceased, he pressed a kiss to her panting lips, then rolled off of her as he drew her into his arms to hold her close, gently caressing her, until they both fell asleep.

Chapter 18

The following morning, Thandi soaked in a hot tub of water, her body sore and her mind at war with her own plaguing thoughts. The aching between her legs was a strong reminder of the night's events. Although Tom had given his blessing to her present arrangement, she still couldn't help feeling as if she had betrayed him.

Though it grieved her to think of it, she knew that deep down a part of her had enjoyed Victor's lovemaking. *Some dark, carnal side,* she thought. Even now, flashes of their night together kept coming to mind, haunting her conscience. And although she had tried to put him out of her mind, her thoughts still clung to Tom. She missed him and she missed Isaac. She even missed Esther's constant snooping and needling.

Days quickly passed, then weeks, and, finally, a month with no word from either Tom or Isaac. She had begun to worry, but Victor had assured her they were just fine. He said that Tom had often inquired about her and that Isaac had now had his freedom.

Although she was relieved to hear such good news, she was still slightly disappointed that they had not come to visit her yet.

She thought about the two of them constantly, and, with each passing day, she missed them more and more. Even now as she stood at the library window, gazing out over the lake, a small smile curled her lips as she pictured their smiling faces.

"A penny for your thoughts," Victor said from behind, his unexpected voice causing her to jump. She turned from the window and met his smiling gaze.

"Good afternoon," She said softly.

Despite her poor attempt at a smile, he quickly detected her somber mood. Over the past few days, she had become increasingly sullen and detached. She was undoubtedly homesick, which was why he strongly suspected that the news he had for her would surely lift her spirits.

"We have visitors," He said. "It is your brother...and Tom."

He watched her expectedly as her chin lifted and her face brightened with an enormous smile.

"They're here!?" She gushed.

He heard the life in her voice and saw the excitement spring into her eyes. "Yes," He smiled, arching a conspicuous brow. "They are waiting for you in the parlor."

"Well, then, I must go!" She said, grinning from ear to ear.

She breezed past him, leaving a light scent of jasmine in her wake.

He followed behind her as she hurried down the hall toward the parlor.

"Isaac!" She squealed when she saw her brother's smiling face. She immediately ran to him and threw her arms around him. "Tom!" She said surprised.

Tom stood up from the corner settee and smiled wide. She wanted to run and hug him as well, but thought better of it. Instead, she smiled warmly into his eyes.

"I was beginning to think that the two of you had forgotten me," She said, releasing her hold on her brother.

"Never," Tom said.

He held her gaze as he stepped next to Isaac. His eyes unconsciously slid from her face down her body and back up again. If possible, she looked even more lovely than she did just a month before. Draped in a form fitting silk emerald green dress, she was the perfect vision of beauty. Even her hair was done up in curls and interwoven green silk ribbons. Tom inwardly marveled at her perfection. He could see that Victor had spared no expense on her.

"Do you intend on staying for the night, or longer, perhaps?" Thandi asked.

"Yes, *how* long will you stay?" Victor asked, joining her side.

Tom looked to Victor and his smile fell away.

"Just for dinner, as we discussed," He answered.

A confused look came over Thandi's face and she turned to Victor. "You knew they were coming?" She asked him.

"Yes. Tom and I discussed their coming just last week. I thought that it would be a nice surprise."

"It is. This is the best surprise ever," Thandi said, her eyes beaming.

"Well, there is still time before dinner," Victor said, turning to Tom and Isaac. "Perhaps, I can interest the two of you in a brandy?"

"No, none for me, thank you," said Isaac. He was apparently eager to spend time with his sister.

"Then you, Tom?" Victor said, shifting his eyes to him. "Certainly, you won't suffer a friend to drink alone."

Tom smiled thinly. He wanted to decline as well, but it would be impolite. "Just lead the way," He said.

Victor's smile broadened, and he placed a hand on his shoulder. "Good, then! Besides, we have business to discuss."

To that end, Tom followed him towards his study while Thandi and Isaac went for a walk along the lake.

As he followed behind Victor, Tom looked around.

"This place is quite impressive," He noted.

Like Thandi, Tom stared with intrigue at the high painted ceilings and massive chandeliers.

"Maybe someday I can give you the official tour," Victor scoffed.

As they entered a long hall, he pointed out a shield bearing his family's crest before stopping in front of a door halfway down the hall that he opened.

"Please, have a seat," He said, gesturing towards the chairs at his desk as they entered. Tom went and sat as Victor walked over to the cabinet to make their drinks.

"Here you are," Victor said, handing him a glass of brandy before taking a seat behind his desk.

"Thandi looks well," Tom said.

He sipped his drink looking at Victor over the rim of his glass.

"She *is* well, Tom. She's quite well," He added. "However, as you can tell, she misses the two of you very much."

Tom said nothing. Instead, he gave a half smile and swallowed a large gulp of his drink. "So, what business do we have?" He asked, changing the subject.

Victor raised a brow. "Did you forget?" He opened his desk drawer and pulled out some papers. "This is the contract for the Old Mill."

"Oh, yes, of course," Tom replied. He had been so distracted by Thandi's appearance that he'd nearly forgotten the true nature of his visit.

He shook his head to himself, then reached into his jacket pocket, pulled out an envelope, and slid it across the table.

Victor looked inside and saw a check written for thirty thousand.

"This is double my asking price," He said, confused.

"Sell her back to me," Tom uttered. He swallowed the nervous knot in his throat and looked Victor square in the eyes. Naturally, Victor was taken aback.

"You can't be serious," He chuckled.

"But I am," Tom said. "Thandi should have her freedom as her brother does. And she should be home with her family."

"And with you?" Victor cut in.

Victor finished his drink and put the glass down on the table.

"Look, Tom, there's no need for the whole horse and pony show. At least, not with me. You're in love with her, and it's grossly obvious that she is in love with you. The two of you might as well admit as much."

Tom lifted his glass and sank back in his chair. "Even if that were true, I could never have her, not in that way," He said.

"So, then why would you wish to take her away?" Victor asked. "She's free to visit her brother and the others as often as she likes. She deserves a chance at true happiness."

"And you think you can give that to her?" Tom interrupted.

"Yes. In time, I could," Victor said plainly.

"But what of her freedom?" Tom countered. "Her happiness is what's most important to me. You can give her the world, but she would never be happy as your slave." Victor gave him a smart look.

"It's interesting that you say that, because Thandi and I have already discussed the subject."

Tom looked surprised.

"She **will** have her freedom. In fact, she will have it in a year's time," Victor added. He picked up his empty glass and went back to the cabinet for a refill.

"If she chooses to leave when that time comes, I won't stop her," He said. Returning with the entire decanter, he sat down again. He refilled their glasses, then settled back in his chair.

"So, then, as you can see, there's no need for the extra money."

Tom was stunned speechless. He watched blankly as Victor took another gulp from his glass. Curiosity flooded his mind as he wondered what had happened to make him reach such a strange decision.

"Here you are," Victor said, Smiling, he pushed the check back across the wide oak desk.

"I'm sure you'll need all that extra money for renovations and production." To Tom, his smile seemed a bit disingenuous.

After dinner, Tom joined Thandi and Isaac for another walk along the lake.

The three of them talked and laughed as Victor nursed a drink and watched them from his study window. With all that he had, he couldn't help feeling slightly envious towards Tom when he saw Thandi's smile. She was smiling bright and wide. Smiling in a way that women do, when they're in the company of the beau they love. He knew that smile all too well. He'd seen it a million times on Elena's face, and now he aspired to see it again on the face of another.

***

As the weeks went by, Tom's visits increased. And each time, he brought Isaac along with him.

Victor found himself wondering if Isaac had in fact missed his sister so often, or if Tom had brought him along using the guise of sibling love to see her himself, without causing suspicion.

Naturally, Thandi had been elated. The three mostly spent their time together horseback riding along the scenic trails of Victor's 354 acre estate. They also visited Hollis Creek, and went for long walks throughout the surrounding woods.

For a time, all had seemed well, until one evening Victor found Thandi in tears after Tom and Isaac's departure.

"What is the matter?" He asked, though he strongly suspected that he already knew the answer. *She had most likely learned the news of Anna's pregnancy,* he thought.

He'd heard the news himself from Daniel just days earlier, after he'd bumped into him in town.

"I'm fine," Thandi lied, wiping away the tears from her face.

"No, you're not fine," said Victor. "Perhaps, I should stop Tom's visits."

"I'm sure that won't be necessary," Thandi snapped.

He could hear a measure of bitterness in her tone. "I suppose Tom has told you about Anna," He said.

Thandi's eyes flashed up at him in shock. She paused for a moment, staring wide-eyed, then turned away to hide the hurt and embarrassment in her eyes.

"Yes," She admitted. "I'm actually very happy for him," She said; the words nearly choking her.

"Somehow, I doubt that is true," said Victor.

Thandi turned abruptly, her eyes flaring and her face flushed red with anger. "How dare you to presume to know my feelings. You know nothing of me," She hissed.

"Oh, I know enough," Victor countered. "I know that you are foolishly wasting your tears and hopes on a man that you could never have as your own. At the very best, you could be his mistress or his whore. However, I sometimes wonder if that just may be enough for you."

Thandi's eyes flashed with rage and her tears sprang anew.

Victor could see that his words had deeply hurt her, but he did not regret them. He was no longer interested in sparing her feelings. For her own good, she needed to hear what he'd said and more.

"And just what am I to you, if not your whore? Bought and paid for," Thandi said. "You speak as if what you're doing is any better; buying slaves for affection. But then, I suppose the apple doesn't fall too far from the tree, as they say. Maybe you're just like your father!"

Regret filled her almost instantly when an angry look crossed over Victor's face. She knew that she had gone too far, but it was too late; the vicious words were already said, and she could not take them back.

"Maybe you're right," Victor said, his tone as cold as ice.

Suddenly, he stepped forward and grabbed her by the arms. Thandi tried to pull away, but could do nothing against his strength. He pulled her to a chair, spun her around, and bent her over it.

"No, don't!" She cried.

She tried pushing herself up, but he pushed her back down and threw her skirts over her hips, tearing off her undergarments in the process. She jerked and thrashed beneath him, but he pressed against her, his hands fumbling with the buttons of his trousers.

Soon she felt the head of his member pushing into her flesh.

"Aghh!" She cried out as suddenly with one merciless hard thrust, he entered her. He gripped her hips and pushed forward, burying himself inside her tight channel until he filled her to the hilt. She groaned aloud against the throbbing pain that invaded her loins.

"It hurts!" She cried out to him, but her cries seemed to fall on deaf ears as his hands gripped her hips even tighter and held her steady as he began to plunge in and out of her.

"Please!" She pleaded over and over, her hands clutching desperately at the arms of the chair. Despite her wails and whimpering, he proceeded to thrust inside her, driving deeper and faster, pumping her soft flesh vigorously. Soon, her cries filled the room and beyond as he began pounding her relentlessly.

She squeezed her eyes shut and clenched her teeth, trying to shut out the pain.

"Oh, God," He groaned.

She could feel his peak fast approaching as he sped up his rhythm. Then, with great relief, she felt him shudder hard inside her. Breathing heavily, he released her hips and withdrew himself from her.

Collapsing against the seat, Thandi tugged down her skirts and pulled herself up, wincing at the discomfort between her legs.

"I... I'm sorry," said Victor.

Thandi turned her face from him and lowered her eyes. She didn't want to look at him, and she certainly did not want to hear his apology. She just wanted him to go away and leave her there alone. She kept her teary eyes to the floor as he fastened his trousers, and straightened his clothing. As he stood, staring upon her silently, Victor's heart sank with deep regret. He so wanted to hold her, to apologize for the terrible thing he'd just done. But he knew that in that moment, there was nothing he could say or do to make things better except to leave.

"Perhaps, tomorrow we can talk things over," He said to her.

Thandi's scorn filled eyes darted up to him, then fell away again.

Victor stood there a few seconds longer, then reluctantly left the room.

Chapter 19

The following morning, Thandi stood at the mirror in her open robe and viewed the black and blue bruises on her knees and legs.

"Should I add the oil and salts, Madame?" Corin asked from the bath's doorway.

"Yes, plenty, please," Thandi replied. She closed her robe quickly against Corin's curious eyes. She could tell from the girl's wary expression that she had been fully aware of last night's sordid events.

"You could use more towels," Corin said as she walked back into the bathroom to add the salts and oil. Moments later, she returned, holding a bundle of the previous day's dirty linen.

"I shall be right back," She said, smiling sweetly.

Thandi gave her a nod of affirmation as the maid left the room and then turned her attention back towards the bath, dropping her robe and stepping into the tub. The fragrant hot water soothed her aching body instantly. She sank down into the water, allowing it to envelope her almost completely as she released a deep sigh and shut her eyes, wallowing in the tempered water's much needed comfort. Suddenly she heard the room's door open.

Corin was returning with the towels, she thought; feeling the young maid's presence there with her in the bathroom. She opened her eyes to speak to her and jumped from surprise at Victor's appearance.

"Forgive me, I didn't mean to startle you," He said.

Thandi hugged her knees to her chest and wrapped her arms around her legs. She could see that he was holding an armful of towels.

He glanced down at the towels then up again into Thandi's stony gaze. "I ran into Corin, in the hall," He explained.

He placed the towels on a shelf, then turned again to face her.

"I'd like to apologize again for last night."

Thandi dropped her gaze at his words.

"My actions were inexcusable," He continued. "I never should of..." His words broke off as he noticed the bruising on Thandi's knee. Instantly, he frowned in disgust at himself.

"I hope that perhaps, somehow, you can forgive me, but I will fully understand if you cannot. I certainly will never forgive myself."

Thandi stared down into the water as if he weren't in the room. She didn't want to listen to his words, or hear his apology. She didn't want to hear it last night, and she didn't want to hear it now. All she wanted was for him to go away and leave her alone.

"You have my promise that it will never happen again," Victor said lowly and released a grievous sigh as he turned towards the door.

Thandi waited until she heard the room's door shut, then sank back down into the tub. A pressing feeling of hopelessness and sadness overcame her as her thoughts turned back to Tom and the news of his expectant child. Although it may have been foolish, until now, she had still held out the hope that someday, somehow, she and Tom would be together. Oh, how she hated herself for being so fiercely naive. How she hated the way her heart ached for him. As much as she despised the thought, she knew that Victor was right. Tom wasn't hers. He never was… and never would be.

As much as it hurt, she knew that it was time that she accepted reality: Tom would never leave Anna. Not now that she was to have his child. She knew that he would never suffer his child to be raised by that awful woman and her father, no matter how much he loved her, or how much he despised the two of them.

But even with everything that had happened before, only now did she truly believe that. Tears sprang to her eyes as her mind and heart fully absorbed the cold realization.

When she finished bathing, she toweled herself dry and went into the room. Upon entering, she immediately noticed a large bouquet of red roses on the bedside table. She walked over to examine them closer and noticed something else. A mysterious black case with gold trim lay beside the crystal vase. She picked it up, and ran a finger over the soft velvet of the case. After a moment's hesitation, she opened it. Immediately, her eyes grew wide and she gasped.

Inside the case was a glittering emerald and diamond necklace. The piece was stunningly beautiful, and was undoubtedly very expensive.

Thandi shook her head. *Isn't that just like him, to think that he can buy my forgiveness*, she thought.

She snapped the case closed and placed it back on the table.

Her only solace was that now she had understood why Tom had ended their affair so abruptly. All of his strange behavior had now finally made sense.

At the same time, Tom was thinking of her. He had thought of little else since their last encounter. Over and over he saw her face in his mind. The way she looked at him when he told her of Anna's pregnancy. The light had instantly dimmed in her eyes and her smile slowly fell away.

For a long time, she had said nothing. Then she put on her best attempt at a smile and offered her congratulations. She had even promised to stitch the babe's first blanket and booties.

Even though she would not express to him her hurt and disappointment, Tom knew her true feelings. Shortly after she made an excuse about suddenly feeling ill, thus bringing their visit to a very early and graceful end. Tom had been shocked when he learned of Anna's pregnancy.

For Anna, it was the most joyous of news, while Tom couldn't have been more displeased. For him, it was the final nail in his coffin. Because now that there was a child to consider, he could no longer entertain the thought of leaving his marriage.

Before he had been in better spirits. With the purchase of the Old Mill and the news of Thandi's future freedom, things had seemed to be turning around for the better. But now, once again, he was dismayed.

During the following weeks, Thandi did her best to keep her distance from Victor. Although, her coldness towards him had hurt, he was glad to see that she no longer kept herself locked away in her room. Instead, she spent hours alone in the library and often rode through the woods accompanied by Corin and one of the male staff.

He tried to speak with her several times, but she would only ignore him. Although physically she was there with him, he missed her. He missed her smile and their talks. He even missed watching her fingers stroke the keys of the piano during their lessons, and how she pouted whenever she messed up.

Lately, he had begun to wonder if she would ever forgive him, if she would ever speak to him again. As he pondered that very thought one Sunday afternoon in his study, the sound of trotting hooves broke his thoughts.

He went to the window and drew back the curtain. Below, he saw Tom's carriage coming to a stop in front of the mansion. He sighed heavily and watched as the driver jumped down from his post to open the carriage door. Seconds later, a figure disembarked, and then another.

He could see that it was Thandi's brother Isaac, and a very pregnant negro girl from the looks of it. He was surprised to see that Tom had not come. Though he presumed that Thandi was most likely already doing so, he set off to meet Isaac and his companion. When he reached the parlor, as expected, he saw Thandi wrapped inside her brother's embrace.

"You look as if you're ready to burst!" She said jokingly to the girl.

The two laughed merrily and embraced each other.

Victor was glad to see the genuine smile on Thandi's face again. Even if it was only temporary.

After Thandi made the introductions between Sarah and Victor, she elected to have lunch with her guests in the garden room. Victor wasn't at all surprised that she hadn't included him, but, to Isaac, it seemed a bit odd that she had not.

In fact, he had felt the tension between them almost immediately. When they were all seated in the garden room, Sarah looked around in absolute awe.

"I never thought I'd see a place more lovely than Madame Lacy's," She said. Thandi smiled back at her.

"Yes, this place is very beautiful," She said. Her words sounded lifeless. "So, how much longer?" She asked, her voice coming alive again.

"Almost two months still!" Sarah replied grievously.

"Well, that isn't too much longer. Perhaps, I can come and visit for a while after the babe is born. And, if possible, I could stay for a while and help out until you're up and well again."

Sarah's face lit with delight. "Yes, of course!" She said excitedly.

Thandi smiled, then suddenly frowned. "I'll just have to ask Victor," She said.

Isaac gave her a smile. "It would be nice to have you," He stated.

At that moment, the maids entered the room with their lunch. Thandi smiled sweetly at Corin as she sat down a large platter of pastries and cucumber sandwiches. The other maid, Tess, carried the tea platter.

"It looks delicious," Thandi said. She particularly liked how the sandwiches were cut into small, neat diamond shapes.

"Here I go again," said Sarah as she placed a hand beneath her large belly. "If you could just point me in the direction of the facilities," She said.

"Certainly, but Corin can take you," said Thandi.

Corin escorted Sarah to the bath and Tess left.

Isaac was glad to have the time alone with his sister. He had wanted to give her Aunt Lacy's ring as directed by Tom, and more importantly, he wanted to speak with her about what he had recently learned.

"How have you been?" He asked her.

Thandi smiled at him sweetly, then reached for the sugar bowl.

"I've been well," She smiled.

Isaac smiled back. He didn't doubt that she had been, but it wasn't her physical wellbeing that he questioned. "I have something for you," He said, reaching into his vest pocket. He took out a small red ring box.

"This is for you," He said, handing it over to Thandi. "It's Madame Lacy's ring."

"Oh, yes!" Thandi said. She took the case and opened it. Her face lit with a smile on seeing the pearl and diamond ring. It seemed hardly believable that she had come to acquire so many beautiful and expensive things. "I still can't believe she left this to me," She said.

"I can," said Isaac. "She loved you like family."

Thandi put the ring on her finger and it fit perfectly. Then she remembered their mother's locket hanging around her neck. She unhooked the necklace's clasp and gave the locket to Isaac.

"Are you sure?" He asked.

Thandi didn't hesitate to answer, "I'm absolutely certain."

"How are things with you and Victor?" Isaac asked.

Thandi looked up at him with surprise. Seconds passed before she could formulate an answer. "Things are well between us," She lied.

Isaac smiled flatly, as if he hadn't altogether believed her answer. "He loves you," He said to her.

Thandi gave him a questionable look.

"Victor, I mean," He clarified.

Thandi froze for a matter of seconds. In that instant, she knew that he had known about Tom. "Perhaps," She answered lowly, picking up the teapot and pouring their tea.

"Tom has told me that you're to be freed in a year," Isaac stated; changing the subject.

"Yes," She answered, her tone thick and matter-of-fact. "At least, that is what Victor has promised."

"So, will you return or will you remain here?"

"If I am freed, I will most definitely return home," She answered sharply.

"Well, we would all be happy to have you, but honestly sister, I don't see why you'd want to give this all up. What has happened for you doesn't happen for our kind."

Thandi gave him a dry smile. She started to tell him about what had happened to her, but then Sarah entered room. Perhaps, it was just as well, she thought to herself. It wouldn't do any good to have her brother worrying over her.

"I can't get over how beautiful this place is! Isaac, have you used the facilities? I felt like a queen on a throne!" Sarah exclaimed, taking her seat again.

Thandi nearly lost her tea as she tried to stifle a laugh. She had missed Sarah's humor. Not only was she pretty, but she was smart and funny. She could easily see why her brother had chosen her.

After lunch, Thandi showed Sarah around the mansion while Isaac joined Victor in the parlor for drinks. As she walked from room to room, she thought of Isaac's words to her and of how he had likely known about her and Tom's affair.

She also wondered what he and Victor were talking about, though she strongly suspected she already knew. When she finished showing Sarah around, they joined the men in the parlor and said their goodbyes shortly after.

When her company was gone, she was left alone again with her thoughts. She thought of what Isaac had said to her about Victor. And about the strong possibility that Isaac had somehow known about her and Tom's affair. But how? She wondered.

She wondered if Tom had told him, or if he had put it together on his own. Either way, she was almost certain that he knew. She could only imagine what he must have thought.

Suddenly, she felt very ashamed. It was no wonder to her that he'd preferred Victor over Tom. She knew that he would never approve of her seeing a married man, no matter whom that man may be. He had always had such great expectations, such high hopes for her. But never in her wildest dreams would he have imagined her living a life such as the one she led now.

And neither would she, for that matter. But despite the luxury and the fancy lifestyle, she would have much rather preferred to have her former life back. And she would've much rather preferred to have a say in her own life and to make her own choices.

Oh, how she couldn't wait to have her freedom! It was all she could think of now. She thought constantly about how life would be once she'd returned home again. She imagined that Isaac would want to move almost immediately.

She wondered how her life would be in the north. She had heard so many good things about it. However, she hardly looked forward to the bitter cold winters. She had heard much about that as well.

Just months before, she had felt saddened and perplexed when she thought of leaving Carolina.....when she thought of leaving Tom.

But now, she almost looked forward to going away; to putting all the ugliness that had happened behind her.

A fresh start in a new land seemed just what she needed to move on and forward with her life. It wasn't enough just to reside miles away from Tom. She still thought of him constantly and still saw him, though seldom anymore. She imagined that if she were to move so far away, she would probably never see Tom again.

Feeling an oncoming bout of melancholy, she shook the depressing thought and forced her mind to something happier…someone.

A crooked smile creased the corners of her lips as she now thought of Sarah.

Sarah was fast becoming the sister she never had. Thandi simply adored her, and her constant humor had always kept everyone in merry spirits. Sarah's uplifting company was just what Thandi had needed.

At least, I'll have Sarah and the baby to keep myself busy, she thought. As well as *my plans with Isaac.*

Thandi sighed heavily. She was sick and tired of thinking. Perhaps, she could help Corin and Sophie with the Christmas decorations, she thought. She had seen them with Estelle in the halls, hanging garland and bows. But on second thought, she decided against it. As lovely as Corin's voice was, she just wasn't in the mood to hear her singing her Christmas hymns. In fact, she wasn't in the mood for anything.

Besides, without her brother and the others back home, it didn't feel much like Christmas at all. Her thoughts wandered to Madame Lacy. Christmas had been her favorite time of year.

Each year, she would decorate the mansion and throw large parties. She even allowed Thandi to attend as a guest and not a servant. Those were happy times. But now those times were gone forever and would never return again.

"Thandi?"

Thandi looked up, meeting Victor's gaze.

"Forgive me, the door was open," He said.

"You don't have to make apologies to me. It's your library," Thandi replied.

Although, she had pardoned him, he could tell from her cold eyes and tone that she couldn't have been less happy to see him. She cast her eyes on a book on the table and picked it up.

"I'm going into town, and I'd very much like for you to accompany me. Perhaps, we could have lunch at the restaurant?"

Thandi exhaled deeply. She didn't want to accompany him. Nor did she want to sit across from him and dine as if nothing had ever happened. She was still angry with him and fully intended to stay that way.

She didn't answer him right away, instead she leafed through the pages of the book. "I'm not hungry," She lied, when in fact she was starving. That morning, she had hardly touched her breakfast.

"Well, then I must insist that you come. It'll do you good to get out and get some fresh air."

Thandi looked up from the book and into his dark brown eyes. He could see that she was displeased with the fact that he could so easily order her to do his will.

"Well, if I must," She replied grimly lowering her gaze again.

"Perfect, we will leave in an hour or so. That should be plenty enough time to change," Victor noted.

Thandi didn't respond and she didn't look up again until after he'd left the room.

The nerve of him! She thought, after he'd gone.

She glared at the door, and sat the book back down on the table. If she was to be forced to go with him, she wouldn't bother to change. She was now glad that she had decided to wear one of her old drab frocks earlier. The pale gray dress matched her mood, and she didn't care if Victor liked it or not.

When an hour had passed, she met him in the parlor. Though he wanted to, Victor said nothing about her attire. Instead, he decided to play her game and say nothing about it.

"You look beautiful," He said. A devilish smirk slightly curled the corners of his lips.

Thandi shot him a vexed look as she collected her coat from Corin. Soon after, the two of them boarded the awaiting coach and set off for town. Thandi kept silent throughout the whole ride. To avoid looking at him, she stared out the coach window.

Victor smiled ruefully to himself, thinking about how impossibly stubborn she was. But soon she would be unable to avoid him and she would have to talk to him. At lunch, she would have to sit across from him and look him straight in the eyes.

Thandi flashed a glance at him as if she had read his mind.

He grinned at her, his brown eyes twinkling with mischief and amusement. She quickly looked away and stared out the window again.

After some time, they entered the busy town and slowly passed through the streets until they reached the Water Crest.

Like before, once inside, they were immediately seated at Victor's table. Thandi glanced around at all of the fancy dressed women and instantly felt uncomfortable. She suddenly sorely regretted her decision not to change.

How silly I must look, she thought. How very plain and out of place.

Her eyes passed over the many faces in the room. Then, suddenly, her gaze came to a stop and rested on a single woman.

Thandi's heart dropped. The woman was Anna.

And she was seated with Tom at a table in the far left corner of the room. As if she sensed someone were looking, Anna turned and their eyes locked. The two looked at each other with cold regard.

Thandi tore her gaze away from her. She wanted to get up and leave the restaurant, but she couldn't. How would she possibly explain herself to Victor? And exactly where would she go? There was nothing that she could do. Nothing other than hope and pray that they would not come by their table.

"Are you okay?" Victor asked, the sound of his voice breaking Thandi's reverie.

"Yes," She said. The fact that she'd smiled told him that something was off. Something had her distracted.

He turned his gaze toward the direction she had looked. Almost immediately he saw Anna. She was staring right at them. Tom, too, had now noticed them. He smiled nervously at Victor and waived. Victor smiled back.

Then, just as Thandi had dreaded, Tom stood up, and so did Anna. Her heart leaped as the two began to walk over. Victor rose to greet them.

"Well, what a nice surprise," He said to Tom. Tom smiled, then glanced to Thandi, then back to Victor again.

"Yes, it is," He said, returning Victor's smile. Anna shifted even closer to Tom.

"Anna," Victor smiled. "As always you look positively radiant," He said.

Thandi frowned at the compliment and kept her eyes on her menu, as if she couldn't care less about what Anna was wearing. But, in fact, she had already seen the olive green form fitting number as Anna walked over.

"Well, I'm afraid I won't look so flattering in the next few months," Anna returned.

Thandi frowned again.

She stared hard at her menu, not seeing anything.

"Oh, yes," smiled Victor. "The two of you must be so thrilled."

"We are!" Answered Anna.

Tom said nothing but gave a hint of a smile.

"Actually, we are having a small dinner party this weekend to celebrate," Anna continued. "I was certain that we sent an invitation."

Thandi glanced up from her menu at Victor.

"No, no, I don't believe we have received an invitation," Victor lied; knowing full well that he had in fact received the invitation several days earlier and had concluded to say nothing to Thandi.

"Perhaps, the two of you would like to join us," Victor offered.

Thandi's cheeks flushed hot red and Tom could see the horrified look on her face.

"No, we've actually just finished our lunch," He said.

Thandi was relieved to hear it. It was enough that she had to dine with Victor.

"Well, you must come to dinner this Sunday, at seven," Anna quickly interjected. "And you're more than welcome to bring a guest," She stated.

Her gaze went to Thandi, then back again to Victor. Thandi could tell that she was gloating. And she could tell by her haughty tone that she had now felt confident that she had neutralized the threat to her marriage.

"Well, then, we both shall see you then," smiled Victor. He placed a friendly hand on Tom's shoulder, and then both Tom and Anna were off.

During lunch, Thandi sat silently eating. Victor attempted to engage conversation, but his effort came to no avail. He didn't have to wonder at what Thandi was thinking, or of whom she was thinking of. Strangely, his heart went out to her, in spite of himself.

Chapter 20

The carriage ride home was just as quiet. Victor remained silent, leaving Thandi to her thoughts. When they finally arrived back at the estate, she immediately took leave to her room, where she remained until dinner, where the table was shrouded in silence once again.

He watched as she ate and wondered if things would ever change, if she would ever come around. While he knew that what he'd done was wrong, he knew that there was more to the source of her anger and hatred. He was beginning to wonder if maybe he was wrong to pursue her.

It seemed that he had underestimated her love for Tom. She loved him madly. She loved him in a way that only first loves do... foolishly, blindly, and wholeheartedly.

It would probably take a lifetime to win her heart, and, in all likelihood, he didn't have that kind of time, he thought. Perhaps, he should let go. Perhaps, he was being selfish. True love was rare, and he'd already been fortunate to find it once. Maybe it was greedy of him to want that love again.

The days passed quickly, and soon the day of Anna's dinner was upon them. Victor wore an old suit. However, it was hardly old in reality, since he'd only worn it once. But not Thandi. Though she'd objected, he bought her a new dress. And not just any dress. The dressmaker swore that it was an original and the only one of its kind in Newport.

Victor bought her new shoes as well, even though she had others that she hadn't even worn yet and that would've matched perfectly. For the party, he wanted her to look like a queen.

He wanted everyone in attendance to gawk and stare at the most beautiful woman in the room.

He knew that would make her happy... for it would certainly get Anna's goat.

Slowly Thandi began descending the stairs. His mouth fell open at the sight of her. Her beauty never ceased to amaze him. The garnet colored silk dress hugged her every curve like a second skin. What was even more surprising was that she wore make up; just a hint of rouge on her high cheekbones and a deep burgundy stain on her lips. She wasn't just beautiful, she was striking.

"You look incredible," Victor said.

Thandi's face brightened, and, for a flash of a moment, he saw a hint of a smile.

They arrived at Lexington plantation just after seven-thirty. Thandi could tell from the number of carriages that the party would not be as small as Anna suggested.

Just as Victor had imagined she would, Thandi wowed the room with her entrance. Victor gave her satin gloved hand a squeeze of comfort as Thandi nervously looked out at the many faces looking back at her. The grand hall was filled with fancy dressed white people.

"You'll be fine, I promise," said Victor, as if he'd read her thoughts.

With one look into his eyes, Thandi felt her fear fade. There was something in the way that he looked at her that made her feel safe. He gave her another reassuring smile, then began to lead her through the crowded room of distinguished guests.

He stopped several times to greet friends and introduce them to Thandi. Thandi returned the smiles and shook the hands of socialites and gentlemen. Never in her wildest of dreams would she have imagined herself hobnobbing with white elites.

If only my mother could see me, she thought. *She would be so very surprised.*

Thandi looked around and smiled. The soothing sound of violins played, and a huge fire burned in the hearth. New satin blue drapes hung from the tall windows, and new rugs covered the floors. Even the staff was dressed in what looked like new uniforms.

Anna had obviously gone all out to make the night special.

Soon, Thandi spotted Mami and Myra; they were serving champagne and hors d'oeuvres to the guests.

"Victor!" Thandi heard a familiar voice call. She turned to see Tom and Anna walking toward them.

"Well, there you two are," said Victor, smiling brightly.

Thandi forced a smile in greeting as Tom looked at her. The two of them locked eyes and Thandi felt her heart flutter. Oh, how she hated that he still had that effect on her.

"Well, this is hardly a small party," Victor said.

Thandi smiled a little. It was as if he'd read her thoughts again. She cast a glance at Anna, then looked again to him.

"Well, dinner should be starting shortly," said Tom. "We took the liberty of reserving seats for you at the table." He looked again to Thandi as the dinner bell sounded.

"Well, then, shall we go?" Tom smiled as he turned and headed for the dining hall and Anna followed.

Thandi felt relieved, but only for a moment. As she walked along-side Victor, she saw Daniel Stafford. He was conversing with a friend of Victor's. "Dr. Gordan," Thandi remembered. He had visited Victor quite often.

An attractive blonde older woman stood at his side. Thandi presumed that it was Daniel's wife, the equally wicked Mrs. Margret Stafford. She cringed in remembrance of the things Anna had told her of her mother.

Once they were inside the dining room they were seated right across from them at the center of the table, while both Tom and Anna took their usual places at opposite ends.

Thandi didn't have to wonder who had arranged the seating. She was certain that it was Anna. Tom would never have done so, she thought.

Both Victor and Daniel exchanged words of greeting and Victor introduced Thandi to Daniel's wife.

"Pleased to meet you," Thandi smiled.

Her polite greeting went unreturned as Lady Margret simply ig-nored her and went about straightening her utensils on the table as if she weren't there. Victor gave Thandi's back an encouraging rub as he promptly struck up a conversation.

"So, you must be elated now that you are to become a grandfather," He said to Daniel. Thandi frowned inwardly at the choice of topic.

"Why, we're downright ecstatic," Stafford beamed. His face bright-ened with the words. "Margret and I were just speaking with your friend, the doctor, about seeing after our Anna."

"Well, Gordan is an excellent doctor, I wouldn't trust anyone else with her care," Victor returned. The stiff look on Lady Margret's face had softened with the talk of her future grandchild.

"Well, I myself am thinking of hiring a full time live-in nurse to take care of her. I don't trust these darkies to see to her properly." Her gaze went to Thandi, then back to Victor again.

Thandi noted the devilish smile on her lips. For in that moment, Mrs. Stafford had strongly resembled her daughter in more ways than one. She could see exactly where Anna had acquired her vile attitude. *She had inherited it from both sides*, she thought.

The sound of a clanking glass came from the other end of the table. "Quiet, please," Tom said.

After the room hushed, he stood and raised his glass. The staff had already filled all the guests' glasses with champagne.

"First and foremost, I'd like to thank you all for coming. I am honored to have you join us in the celebration of my wife's pregnancy." Shocks of happy surprise circled the table, and congratulations and well wishes followed.

"To our child," Tom said as he looked at Anna's beaming face, and then back at the crowd at again. He took a sip from his glass and everyone else did the same.

Thandi took a long sip from her glass. Oh, how she wished the night were already over.

She had known that it wouldn't be easy to be there around Tom and Anna, but she didn't imagine it would be so hard. Perhaps, it was Tom's apparent happiness that had bothered her. She felt somewhat ashamed. She should have been happy for him, but she wasn't. And she didn't want him to be happy, either.

I shouldn't have come, she thought. But there was no way that she could have declined without raising a question from Victor.

Tom sat down again after he'd finished his toast, and the guests resumed chatting. The men began to talk about business and current affairs, while the women exchanged flattering compliments and niceties. Thandi suddenly smiled as Esther and the rest of the waiting staff appeared with their soup and bread. She wanted to get up and greet her, but she knew she should not. She couldn't. Not in the presence of her current company.

"Madame Thandi," Lady Davenport started.

Anna pretended to choke a little on her apple cider.

"I must say that your dress is unlike any I've seen around. The hue is just lovely."

"Yes, Madame Thandi," Anna said mischievously. "Where ever did you find it?"

Thandi's smile fell away as she looked at Anna.

"I don't know, you'd have to ask Victor," She said.

"Sanderson's," Victor answered. "The new boutique in the square." Anna slurped her soup.

"Well, the dress itself is very pretty, but the color is a bit too risqué for my taste," She said.

Thandi smiled politely in spite of the underhanded comment.

"Well, I must visit the store soon. I'm looking for the perfect dress for my Ida's wedding," Lady Davenport beamed.

All the ladies went on to discuss the matter, and Thandi was glad for the change of subject. She had started to fear that everyone would begin to sense the tension between she and Anna. She only hoped that she could get through the night without issue.

Esther sat a bowl of soup down in front of her and Thandi smiled up at her. Esther returned her smile with a little wink.

As Esther walked away, Thandi picked up her spoon and leaned forward, deeply inhaling the pungent scent of the potato and leek soup.

Suddenly, she felt ill. She lowered her spoon and leaned back in her chair. Swallowing hard, she tried to force back the nauseous feeling.

"Are you okay?" Victor asked. He had seen the troubled look on her face.

"I feel a bit nauseous." Thandi paused and swallowed back the sickness again. "I think I could use some air," She said after a moment.

"Certainly," said Victor. He immediately rose from his chair to assist her.

"Are you alright?" Asked Mrs. Davenport, putting her hand to her heart.

Thandi forced a smile and nod, but didn't speak for fear of puking all over the table. She stood as Victor helped her from her chair and she hurried out of the dining hall. As the sick feeling came on again she quickened her steps down the long hall, while Victor followed worriedly behind. When she reached the parlor, she covered her mouth with one hand as she urgently opened the front door with the other, racing out onto the porch and down the front steps. When she reached the garden, she could no longer hold her sickness and doubled over, vomiting into a small bush.

"My, you are ill!" Victor said, rushing to her side. He pulled a loose strand of hair from her face as she started to vomit again. When she finally stopped, he pulled a kerchief from his jacket and gave it to her.

"Thank you," Thandi said. She wiped her mouth and stood upright again.

"Was it the soup?" Victor asked.

Thandi shook her head confused.

"I'm not sure… I mean, I didn't eat any, but the smell was rather strong."

Victor's brows furrowed in a puzzled expression. "Perhaps it's just a case of the nerves," He said.

"Is everything well?" A voice called out from behind them. They both turned and saw Tom walking up to them.

"Yes, I do believe so," Victor said. He looked at Thandi with a look of uncertainty.

"I'm fine," Thandi told them, straightening her dress.

"Are you certain?" Tom asked, his eyes filled with concern.

"Yes, I'm fine, now," Thandi assured him. An awkward silence fell between them.

"Well, I do think it would be best if we retired early," Victor said, breaking both the silence and Tom's locked gaze.

"Given the circumstances, I'm sure everyone will understand," Tom said, looking again to Thandi. Standing there with her in the garden brought back the fond memory of their race.

"Well, then, if you could just have Esther collect our coats," said Victor, breaking the reverie.

"Of course," Tom answered.

He paused a moment, then turned and walked back to the house.

Once he was gone, Thandi turned back to Victor. "I'm sorry for ruining your evening," She said sheepishly.

"Nonsense," Victor said. "You're saving me from a night of boredom, and possibly, bad soup."

Thandi laughed a little, and he was pleasantly surprised.

As they walked towards their carriage, Tom brought out their coats himself. Thandi had hoped to say goodbye to Esther before leaving, but it appeared she wouldn't get the chance. "Please, do say goodbye for me to Esther and the others," She told Tom.

"Certainly," He said. He looked as if he had wanted to say more, but he didn't; watching as Victor tentatively helped with her coat.

As Thandi rode back home, she felt both relieved and embarrassed.

She wondered if Anna and the others were talking about her and Victor's abrupt departure. She imagined Anna gossiping, saying bad things about her, and the other women standing around listening, their faces filled with shock and even disgust.

"Are you truly feeling better?" Victor asked. His voice broke her thoughts.

"Yes, much," She said. She did, in fact, feel much better.

Perhaps, it was nerves as he had suggested, she thought.

"You should still try and eat something. When we get back, I'll have the kitchen prepare you something lite," Victor told her.

Thandi looked at him with a small thankful smile. And, for a second, her eyes warmly lingered on his before turning out the window once more.

Chapter 21

Days later, a messenger came with the surprising news of Isaac and Sarah's baby's birth. The child's arrival had come very suddenly, leaving Isaac no time to send warning.

Thandi frowned at the news, but then smiled in the same breath. She had so wanted to be with Sarah at the time of the babe's birth, but that no longer mattered.

All that mattered was that the child had been born healthy. *My brother's daughter and my niece!* She thought happily.

Oh, how she couldn't wait to meet her…to finally see the face of the child she had imagined for months.

"May I visit my brother?" She asked Victor. For him, the request came as no surprise.

"How long would you like to stay?" He asked, looking into her bright gaze.

"A couple of weeks. A month, maybe," She said casually.

Victor furrowed his brow at the latter part of her answer. Thinking of his upcoming busy schedule he knew that he wouldn't be able to accompany her.

"Two weeks," He answered, firmly. If she stayed any longer she wouldn't be back in time for Christmas, he thought. Though she hoped to stay longer, Thandi's face lit with happiness and he was pleased.

In just three days' time, she was off to Fairview. Since he couldn't accompany her, Victor sent both Corin and Jonah in his place.

Although, Thandi would have much rather preferred to go alone, she didn't put up a fuss. Besides, she did like Corin, and the trip to Fairview would be long and otherwise quite lonely without some company.

When they arrived at Fairview, Isaac greeted his sister with a huge smile and an even bigger hug.

"I had hoped you'd come straightaway," He said.

Thandi could tell that he was happy to see her, even relieved.

"Sarah, where is she?" She asked, without delay.

"She's in bed upstairs. She's taken mother's old room," Isaac answered.

Thandi left her bags to Corin and the coachman, and followed him through the parlor and up the stairs. When she approached the open bedroom door, stopping short at the sight of Tom. She was surprised to see him there in the room.

"Sister!" Sarah called when she saw Thandi, extending a hand to her from the bed.

Tom turned fully from the window with a surprised look on his face. "Thandi!" He said, smiling. "What a pleasant surprise."

For a second, Thandi stood frozen, staring back at him, before turning her attention to Sarah again.

"Sarah!" She exclaimed, shaking off the shock of his presence.

"Hello, Tom," She said to him with a smile as she crossed the room.

"Oh! Sarah," She smiled, taking her hand as she sat next to her on the bed. "How are you feeling?" She asked, her voice filled with concern.

"Better. I really had a time of it," Sarah answered.

Isaac placed a hand on Thandi's shoulder, then sat down in a chair next to the bed. "Well, I shall see after you while I'm here," Thandi said, sweeping a braid from Sarah's face.

"And how long will that be?" Sarah asked brightly.

"A couple of weeks, though I wish it could be longer," Thandi answered. She made a disappointed face, then put on a smile again. "So, where is my little niece?" She asked, smiling.

No sooner than she stopped speaking, the maid Alice entered the room. She was holding a small white bundle in her arms.

"The baby!" Thandi thought aloud. She quickly stood and went to the basin to wash her hands. When she finished, she quickly sat again, and Alice placed the babe in her arms. Thandi's face immediately lit with delight.

"Oh, she's so beautiful," She said, looking down at the infant cradled in her arms. She flashed a glance at both Sarah and Isaac, then returned her attention again to the babe. "She looks like you both," She said, examining the little one's sweet features.

"I think she has mama's eyes," Isaac said.

Thandi looked intently into the baby's dark brown eyes, and a huge smile came to her lips. "Yes, she does," She exclaimed brightly. "What is her name?"

"Odessa. After my mother," Sarah answered as the babe started to fuss.

"I think it's time for a feeding," Sarah noted.

Thandi smiled down at the little one, then handed her over to her mother.

"Well, I think I'll take my leave now," Tom said. He nodded to everyone, then left the room.

"I think I shall as well," said Thandi.

She gave Sarah's arm a loving squeeze then made her exit, leaving them some privacy.

In the hall, Tom turned at the sound of her footsteps as she entered. When he saw her face, he stopped in his tracks and smiled. Thandi smiled back at him as she caught up to him.

As she walked to him, she could once again feel the nervous butterflies returning in her stomach. He held her gaze as she quickened her steps. When she encountered him, they began to slowly walk together.

"I didn't know you were coming, I would have had a room prepared for you," said Tom.

Thandi smiled in response. "I had just received the news and thought I should come straightaway," She said.

To her surprise, Tom took her arm as they walked down the stairs. "Are you hungry?" He asked. "Alice just made lunch for us."

"Yes, thank you," Thandi replied. She had in fact still felt famished, even though she'd just eaten with Corin in the carriage.

Not long after they sat down at the dining table, Isaac came in and joined them.

As usual, he was wearing his famous white smile; only now, it was beaming bright with pride and joy.

Thandi felt relieved that he had joined them. For she didn't entirely feel comfortable with being alone with Tom. She didn't want to have a personal conversation with him, to discuss herself or hear any more news of his personal life. She was still too hurt. Too bitter. And she knew that she couldn't trust herself, or her emotions. She would most likely end up saying something she would later regret.

"You look well," said Isaac. He sat down, looking her over. "I heard you had taken ill."

"Yes," Thandi, answered, dryly. She had hoped to forget that embarrassing night all together. "However, I think it was just a bad case of the nerves. There were so many people…"

Her words trailed off intentionally, she didn't see the need to elaborate on the subject any further.

"Well, has Tom told you about the crop turn out?"

Grateful to talk about something else, Thandi quickly shook her head no.

"Well, it was thirty percent higher than last season." Thandi's mouth dropped open with surprise.

"And that's just at Lexington," Isaac continued. "We saw a fifteen percent increase here."

Tom gave him a proud look. "Yes, business has been good," He agreed.

"You must be very proud," Thandi said to him. "That is far more than you expected."

"We've also started the reconstruction of the mill," Tom added as Alice brought in the shepherd's pie and set it on the table.

"That looks wonderful," Thandi smiled. "Alice, would you please ask my companion Corin, if she'd like to join us?" She asked.

Though she doubted Corin would still be hungry, she thought it would be kind to extend the invitation.

Alice nodded with a smile and left the room. As she left, the maid Lily brought in a pitcher of fresh lemonade. Moments later, Alice returned to announce that Corin had graciously declined.

Over lunch, the two men talked business while Thandi scarfed down two generous slices of pie, three biscuits, and a tall glass of lemonade. Afterwards, she felt very tired. More tired than she'd ever felt before.

"If you two will excuse me, I think I'll retire now. I could use a hot bath and a bit of rest," She said.

"Annie's fixing up your old room. I imagine she should be done by now," said Isaac.

"That is, if you want it," Tom interceded. "You could take one of the guest rooms if you like."

"No, my room is just fine." Thandi smiled.

She had in fact preferred her old room, the place where she'd spent a large part of her youth.

After her bath, she rested for several hours, then awoke feeling refreshed. She sat up on the side of her bed and looked around at the familiar surroundings of her old room. Nothing had seemed to have changed; everything was still in its place, just as she had left it. Her gaze went to the doll sitting on the mantle.

Addy, she thought, smiling. Her childhood doll. She stood up and went to the mantle to get her.

As she held it in her hands, examining the loose black button eyes and stringy yarn hair, she found that she missed it. Though she had been an avid tomboy in her youth, she'd still played with Addy from time to time. However, she did so mostly in secret for fear that the boys would tease her.

As she stood examining the old doll's loose eyes, holes, and tattered clothing, a thought suddenly came to mind.

Perhaps she could mend it and pass it on to little Odessa.

Yes! Thandi thought, smiling. It would be the perfect gift! And maybe, someday Odessa could pass it on to her daughter, and so on.

She went to the trunk at the end of the bed to look for sewing thread and a needle. After rummaging through its contents, she found that there was none there. She looked over at the clock on the table. It was just after four in the afternoon, and dinner wasn't for several hours.

I will check in on Sarah and the baby, then go to the sewing room to make the doll's repairs, she thought.

After spending an hour catching up with Sarah and doting over her new niece, she did just that. It took less than an hour, and it turned out very well. However, the doll still needed a good washing. After dinner, she would get it all cleaned up and set it by the fireplace to dry overnight. She wanted to give it to Sarah tomorrow, hopefully after breakfast, if it was dry. But, for now, she wanted to visit with her old friends, Alice and Annie. The two were likely in the kitchen preparing dinner at that time. Deciding to go in search of the women she got up from her chair and left the room, taking the doll with her.

"Thandi!" Tom called as she walked down the hall towards the kitchen. She stopped and turned to him.

"Tom," She answered.

"And... Addy," Tom added, smiling as he walked up to her.

Thandi blushed brightly, glancing down at the doll. When she looked up again, Tom was grinning widely.

"Still playing with dolls," He teased, his eyes fixed on the rag doll clutched in her hands.

"No," Thandi said sheepishly. "I plan to give the doll to Odessa," She explained. "I've mended it, but it still needs cleaning," She said, holding it up so that he could see.

Tom glanced the doll over.

"I'm sure that Sarah will absolutely love it," He said. "So, where are you off to?" He asked.

"I thought I'd go to the kitchen and visit with the girls," Thandi replied. "Perhaps, I can give them a hand with dinner."

"Well, I was very much hoping that I could speak with you alone this evening, seeing as how I'll be heading back to the estate tomorrow morning."

Thandi looked up at him in surprise. *Why,* she thought. *Why now after I've just gotten here?* Though, she wondered, she didn't dare allow herself to ask the question.

"Well, certainly," She answered coolly. "We could talk now before dinner, if you like."

"No rush," Tom smiled. "We can talk alone in the study after. That is, if that's okay with you," He added pointedly.

Thandi hesitated to answer, wondering what it was he had to say to her that needed privacy. "Certainly," She answered, smiling faintly.

"Well, then, I shall see you at dinner," Tom said.

After he left, Thandi went to the kitchen. As she'd suspected, both Alice and Annie were there preparing supper. Annie smiled widely when she saw her.

"Well, I don't know whether I should hug you or bow," She teased as Alice turned from the stove and saw Thandi as well.

"I was wondering how long it would be before you came to visit," She said, smiling.

She wiped her hands on a rag, then went to Thandi for a huge hug. As the two women embraced, Annie joined them.

"My! Just look at you. You look like a real lady," Alice said.

"Yes, you do," Annie agreed emphatically, looking over her fancy dress and shoes. "You look just like a proper white woman," She added.

Thandi giggled as the two embraced. "Well, aren't looks deceiving," She said, letting go.

"So, I hear that you now live in a mansion twice the size of this place and far grander," Annie said.

Thandi laughed at the expression on her face; her eyes were as big as saucers.

"And don't forget the lake," Alice quickly noted.

"Thandi, you must be so happy." Annie smiled.

The smile on Thandi's face fell a little. "Yes, the mansion is very big," She replied.

"We also hear that your master is not only very rich, but very handsome, too," Alice said, with a devilish little smile.

Thandi's face turned red. "Yes, I guess he is," She reluctantly responded. "Well, something sure smells good in here," She said abruptly, hoping to change the subject.

"That's roast beef and vegetables you're smelling. And apple pie, too," Alice said, turning her gaze to the oven.

"It should be done, now," said Annie. She grabbed a long fork from the counter and went to the oven to check. The meat poked tender, and was perfectly browned, and the potatoes and carrots were tender as well. But not too tender, just as Master Tom had liked.

"It's ready," Annie announced. "We just need to slice the bread," She said, looking over at the fresh baked loaf on the table.

"Let me," Thandi offered, crossing the room to the kitchen drawers and removing a bread knife. After slicing the bread, the three of them went about setting the table. For Thandi, it felt like old times to help Annie and Alice. And, even more so, it felt good to be home again.

At dinner, Isaac and Tom both mostly discussed shop as usual, while Thandi eagerly ate her dinner. Never before had she remembered a roast tasting so good. The potatoes seemed to melt in her mouth, and the taste of the carrots seemed so rich. Before she'd realized it, she'd eaten two helpings and still had room for pie.

After dinner, she went to her room to freshen up, then she was off to the study.

As she walked, she could feel her heart racing, its frantic beat drumming in her ears. Though she tried hard to calm her nerves, she couldn't help feeling nervous, knowing that she was about to face Tom alone. Seeing that the door to the study was ajar, she went in. Tom was standing by the fireplace, his hands in his pockets and his back to her, totally unaware that she was there.

"Tom," She spoke, making her presence known. He turned at the sound of her voice.

"Thandi," He answered, smiling. She shut the door, then turned her attention to him again.

"Come, have a seat," He said, gesturing to the wing back chair next to the fire. Thandi hesitated a moment before crossing the room and taking the seat.

"Would you like something to drink? Perhaps, some wine?" Asked Tom.

"Yes, wine would be nice," Thandi answered. She hoped it would help settle her nerves.

Tom walked over to the cabinet and pulled out a bottle and glass.

"Esther misses you very much," He said from over his shoulder.

A smile broke Thandi's lips that he did not see.

"I miss her, too," She said softly. "Very much so."

Tom turned, gave her a smile, then poured himself a glass of brandy. Afterwards, he picked up both glasses and walked over to Thandi's chair.

"Here you are," He said, handing her the goblet.

She thanked him and raised the glass to her lips, taking a long sip. Tom drew up the matching wing back chair, and settled himself down comfortably with his drink.

"So, how have you been," He asked.

Thandi cast her eyes downward, then up again.

"Well," She said, feigning a smile.

"And Victor. I imagine that he is treating you well," He said. His statement sounding more like a question.

Thandi hesitated to answer, thinking back on the night Victor took her. "Yes, he treats me well," She answered after a moment.

She didn't care to tell him about the incident between them. And besides, it wouldn't have mattered. She was Victor's property now, and he could do with her anything he wanted. She shifted her gaze to the fire and downed another gulp of the much needed wine.

Tom could sense her discomfort. He'd known that she was upset with him, even though she did her best not to show it.

"Tell me, are you upset with me?" The question moved from his thoughts to his tongue.

Thandi turned her gaze on him. Again, she hesitated to answer, then slowly shook her head. "No. Why would I be upset with you?" She asked.

Her slightly condescending tone suggested that he knew exactly why she would be.

"You are angry with me," Tom said tenderly.

Thandi sighed, but said nothing. Instead, she took another sip from her glass and stared into the fire's flickering flames. Her silence had confirmed his words. He knew that she had been upset with him for the way things ended between them.

"You have every right to be upset," He said.

Thandi's gaze shot from the flames and into his eyes.

"I miss you, Thandi," He said to her. Her heart flipped inside her chest.

"I miss the way that we were before all of the craziness." He paused as though carefully thinking of what to say next. "I just wish that we could put everything behind us and find a way to be like we were before."

He paused a moment before continuing.

"Before I screwed up," He said. "I worry that I have ruined our friendship."

For a moment, Thandi sat frozen, staring back at him. Tears watered in her eyes, but she kept her composure, refusing to let them fall.

Friendship, she thought. The word stung like a slap in the face. "We will always be friends," She said to him, though her heart was breaking.

"If only the circumstances could have been different," Tom said. His deep sincerity showed in his eyes.

"It's fine," Thandi told him. She did her best to sound convincing. "I just want to see you happy, Tom. I want that more than anything."

Tom's heart sank at the tenderness of her words. If only she knew just how much he'd meant what he'd said. If circumstances had truly been different, he would've risked it all to have her. But fate wouldn't allow it. She was forever forbidden to him, now that he'd known the truth. Shamefully, and more than often, he found himself wishing he'd never learned the truth at all. If he hadn't, the two of them would likely be together somewhere faraway. Perhaps, with Isaac and Sarah. Tom tossed back the last of his bourbon, shutting out the foolish thoughts.

"Are you happy?" Thandi asked.

The question took Tom by surprise. He looked at her and she stared back at him, her eyes challenging him to tell the truth. Though he knew the true answer, he dared not say it.

"I suppose I am," He half lied. "I have the mill now, and Fairview. Also, business has been better than it's ever been."

Thandi couldn't help but notice that he made no mention of his wife and future child.

"Then I am happy for you," She said, smiling bravely.

After a moment's silence, Tom spoke again. "No matter what happens, I will always see to your care."

If he meant to comfort her with such words, he was failing miserably, Thandi thought. But she didn't want to make him feel guilty, or responsible for what had happened. Nor did she want his pity. She only wanted what she couldn't have. She wanted him.

"I'll be fine, there's no need to worry about me," She said bravely.

"But I do worry," said Tom. "And so does Esther. There isn't a week that goes by that she doesn't ask about you. She was very glad to see you at the party."

Thandi smiled instantly. "I was happy to see her as well," She said. "I had hoped to spend some time with her, but then… well, you know," She said, embarrassed.

Tom chuckled, remembering that night. "When I think of that poor rose bush," He teased.

Thandi laughed at the heartbreaking look on his face.

When their laughter faded, their eyes met, and again, silence engulfed the room. The only sound was that of the fire's crackling flames and their own beating hearts.

"Perhaps, I could arrange a visit," Tom said after a moment.

A confused look crossed Thandi's face.

"With Esther," Tom explained. "I'm certain that Victor wouldn't have a problem with her coming to visit."

"Yes!" Thandi said brightly. "I would like that very much."

"Well, then, I shall see to it." Tom smiled.

Another silence fell between them and Thandi could now feel the effects of the wine coming over her. She felt warm. The temperature in the room had seemed to rise twenty degrees in just a matter of moments.

"I think that I should go lie down now," She said, placing her empty glass on the table next to her.

"Are you okay?" Tom asked.

"Yes," She said reassuringly. "However, I believe the wine has started to get to me," She smiled and rose to her feet.

Tom stood as well. "I should walk you to your room," He said.

"No," She said, putting up a hand as if to stop him. "I'll be fine, but you mustn't leave tomorrow morning without me seeing you off," She told him.

Tom nodded and watched as she left the room, shutting the door behind her.

As she walked down the hall and began to cross the parlor, Thandi began to feel even more strange. She suddenly felt dizzy and very unsteady.

"Ma'am! Ma'am!" She heard a voice calling.

Struggling, she lifted her lids, straining to see the blurry image in front of her.

"Corin," She murmured as her image slowly came into focus.

A second later, Tom was there. He saw her stretched out on the parlor floor, and the girl Corin kneeling over her.

"What happened?" He asked, rushing to Thandi's side.

"I don't know. I just found her," Corin nervously explained.

"Thandi, are you okay?" He asked, pulling her up into his arms.

"I...I don't know," Thandi stammered. "I was walking, when suddenly I became really dizzy. Then the room seemed to be spinning around me." She looked dazed, confused, and very pale.

"We should get you to bed at once," Tom said worriedly.

"Thandi!" Another familiar voice yelled.

She turned in Toms arms to see Isaac rushing down the stairs.

"What happened!?" He asked like the others, his tone filled with alarm.

"I believe she fainted," Tom informed him.

"I will go fetch the doctor," said Isaac.

"Don't... that won't be necessary," Thandi said. She pulled herself up in Tom's arms, then slowly, with his assistance, she rose to her feet.

"I'm quite alright now," She said, straightening her composure. "I do believe it was a combination of the heat and wine that brought the spell on," She said to Tom. The concerned look on his face still remained.

"Still, it wouldn't hurt to have a doctor look at you," He said, turning to Isaac who gave an affirming nod and immediately left the house while Tom helped Thandi to her room.

After he pulled the bed covers back, she sat down and watched as he tentatively removed her shoes.

"Now, lie down," Tom ordered. He placed a rolled pillow under her neck, then touched her forehead with the back of his hand.

"Well, you don't seem to have a fever," He said with relief.

"Excuse me, Master," said Corin. She was standing inside the open doorway. A second later, Alice joined her side. "Is there anything I can do?" Corin asked.

Thandi could see the worried looks on their faces.

"Yes, water," Tom said. "And perhaps a damp cloth," He added.

With their instructions, the girls were immediately off, leaving them briefly alone.

"Really… all of this fuss is unnecessary," said Thandi.

"It's quite necessary," said Tom. "I wouldn't feel comfortable leaving without knowing that you're fine."

Soon, the girls reentered the room bearing the water and cloth.

After Thandi had finished a glass of ice water, Tom applied a cold towel to her head. Pulling up the only chair in the room he sat next to her by the bed, staying with her until the doctor arrived and then waited outside her room with Isaac.

After some time, the doctor opened the door and stepped into the hall to speak with them.

"Well, she is fine," Dr. Granger told them. Both Isaac and Tom instantly smiled with relief.

"So, it was the wine?" Tom asked.

"Partly," The doctor replied. "The girl is in a delicate state right now, and should not be drinking wine or any other alcohol for that matter," He noted. Tom gave him a questionable look.

"The pregnancy," Doctor Granger said pointedly. "The girl is pregnant."

Shock gripped Tom. He glanced at Isaac and saw his equally surprised expression. "Are you sure?" He asked, facing the doctor again.

"Yes, I'm pretty certain. She's early on. Perhaps, a month or two at best. It's difficult to say for certain," He explained . "The girl has been having abnormal monthlies, she says."

Tom's expression went blank as an alarming thought suddenly came to mind.

Two months, he thought to himself. Was it possible? His heart leaped within his chest.

"May we see her now?" Asked Isaac.

Tom's thoughts broke off at the sound of his voice.

"Certainly," said the doctor.

Isaac went into her room, while Tom saw to the doctor's payment.

After he'd seen the doctor to his carriage, Tom returned to Thandi's room.

On entering, she looked up at him with sadness in her eyes. He noticed that Isaac wasn't in the room. Nor were the maids. For the time being, he and Thandi were alone.

"I spoke with the doctor," He said as he approached her bed.

Thandi gave him a glum look, her eyes glossed over with tears. "I can't believe it," She said lowly.

Tom took her hand into his own and gave it a comforting squeeze. Although he felt fearful, he did his best not to let his anxiety show.

"Well, at least now, I know you're not dying," He said jokingly.

He had wanted to make Thandi smile, and for a few seconds she did.

"Dying would probably be better," She said, her expression again turning grim.

Tom hesitated a moment then asked the one question that was heaviest on his mind. "Is the child mine?" He asked.

Thandi looked at him for a long moment then shook her head. "I'm not sure," She muttered. She drew a deep breath, and exhaled. "The child could be Victor's," She said. Tom lowered his eyes and sighed as his mind digested the truth.

Before now, he had been content, not knowing if there had been a union between them. Though he thought it, and even expected that it would eventually happen, he didn't know for certain as he did now. A series of feelings flowed through him. Fear, guilt, jealousy...anger. The anger he felt was towards himself, and himself alone. For even if the child were not his, he had still felt responsible for the pregnancy. After all, it was he who had made her go with Victor...

"Tom," Thandi spoke. She could see the worry forming on his face. "Are you angry with me?" She asked.

Tom looked at her instantly and said, "No." "None of what has happened is your fault," He told her.

"What will I do?" She asked.

Tears rolled down her face, and he wiped them away.

"What will we do," Tom corrected her. "No matter what happens, I won't leave you to face this alone," He said.

"Victor," Thandi muttered. She looked away, thinking of him.

He would certainly presume that he had sired her child. More tears swelled her eyes as she thought of the possibility.

"Does he know about us?" Tom asked. Thandi shook her head. "No, but he has his suspicions," She said.

"Everything will be fine; we will figure this out," said Tom. He rubbed her hand and gave her an encouraging smile.

"And how can you know that?" Thandi asked, despair heavy in her tone.

Tom began to speak, but then a knock came to the door, interrupting their conversation. He hesitated to answer, still looking into Thandi's eyes.

"Come in," He called after a moment. He turned to the door to see Sarah and Isaac walking into the room.

Thandi sat up and wiped the tears from her face as Sarah approached. "You should be in bed," Thandi scolded her.

"Nonsense, I've been in bed long enough," said Sarah. "Besides, I've been looking for any excuse to break free of that jail," She said, smiling.

"Tom, may I have a word with you?" Asked Isaac.

The smile on Thandi's face fell away at the sight of her brother's serious expression.

"Of course," Tom answered as he turned to follow Isaac out of the room.

"Tom!" Thandi called after him.

He stopped and turned to face her.

"Will you still be leaving in the morning?" She asked.

Tom hesitated, thinking of the busy weeks ahead. "Yes, I have several business commitments that I must see to," He said regretfully. "But I will come to visit you very soon."

"Remember, you must not leave without me seeing you off," Thandi said, sadly.

Tom nodded in agreement, then walked over to the bed, bent over and kissed her on the forehead.

Thandi watched him as he followed Isaac out of the room and into the hall, leaving the women alone.

As she sat with Sarah, she wondered what they were talking about. She felt certain that she and her pregnancy had been the topic of their discussion. After Sarah had gone, she lay in bed, still wondering if Tom and Isaac were still together. It had been nearly an hour since they'd left the room. She thought to go and look for them, but quickly decided she should not. She remembered Isaac's stern face and tone. He had obviously wanted to speak with Tom alone.

She bent her head and looked down at her belly. She still couldn't believe it. *A baby*, she thought. *How could I have ignored the signs?*

Chapter 22

The following morning just after day break, she was awakened by Alice informing her that Master Lexington would soon be leaving. Thandi quickly rose from the bed, put on her robe and slippers, and set off to find him.

He's likely in the dining room, waiting for me at breakfast, she thought.

As she walked down the stairs and out onto the parlor floor, she stopped in her tracks at the sight of him. He was standing at the hall closet, already dressed in his coat and hat and apparently, ready to leave.

Thandi's heart felt heavy. She had hoped to have a little time with him before he left, but that didn't seem likely now.

"Good morning," She said, walking towards him. Tom turned to her and smiled warmly.

"Good morning," He returned.

"Have you already had breakfast?" Thandi asked, puzzled. She glanced at the grandfather clock nearby, then back at him again.

"No, I'm not at all hungry," said Tom. "And, besides, we must stop in town for supplies. I'll likely have a bite to eat while we're there."

"And Isaac? Where is he?" She questioned, looking around. Normally, he was up by five. It was now well after six.

Tom's gaze dropped to the unfastened buttons on his coat.

"He's probably still sleeping," He said, buttoning up.

"Still sleeping?" Thandi repeated in her head. Perhaps, he had been up all night with little Odessa, she thought.

One of the staff boys brought up Tom's bags, and Thandi could hear the sound of his carriage settling into position out front. She sighed with disappointment.

"Will you come visit soon?" She asked.

Tom could hear the emotion in her voice and stepped up to her, shortening the distance between them. "I promise, I'll come and see you as soon as possible," He said. "Please, don't worry." He stepped even closer to her. So, close that she thought he may kiss her. She wanted him to kiss her. And she wanted to kiss him.

"We shall talk very soon," He said cupping her head with his hands and pressed a long kiss on her forehead. Thandi shut her eyes, enjoying the soft feel of his kiss. But then, all too soon he was gone, leaving her once again.

As he rode alone, Tom's thoughts were of Thandi and the child she carried.

He thought also of Isaac and the conversation they shared. Isaac had questioned him about Thandi's pregnancy, asking him point blank if he had fathered her child.

Tom had answered truthfully, and naturally, Isaac was upset. Other than love, Tom had no defense for his actions.

He knew that Isaac had every right to be upset, for he had put his sister in an impossible predicament.

Surprisingly, Isaac suggested that they keep their affair secret, and to allow Victor to raise the child as his own, even if he had in fact not fathered the child.

It was the best thing for everyone, and, most certainly, the best thing for the child, he argued. He said that he was concerned with what might happen to Thandi if Anna learned of his indiscretions. And he also reminded him of all he stood to lose in the event of a divorce. And there was another child to think of: his wife's child. Tom's child. Not to mention, Lexington Mills, his father's company. Stafford still held controlling interest. Exposing the truth would do more harm than good, he had insisted. After he'd finished his argument, Tom felt defeated.

He had promised to seriously consider Isaac's point. He knew that Isaac had been right about everything he said. However, he simply couldn't imagine another man raising his child.

If it is my child, he thought grimly. Suddenly, a heavy feeling of shame overcame him as it finally struck him that he had possibly sired a child with his own sister. He shook his head, thinking of the terrible mess he'd made and of all the grief he'd caused Thandi. He thought of how Anna would react if she learned the truth. A separation would be inevitable, and Daniel would undoubtedly do everything in his power to ruin him. Or even worse, they would turn his own child against him.

And then, there was Thandi. How could he possibly ask her to do such a deceitful thing? She would be hurt that he could even make such a request.

Either way, it was an impossible situation. Perhaps, Isaac's solution was best, he thought.

Victor was in love with Thandi, and he would undoubtedly love the child. With him, she could have a better life. The kind of life she deserved.

***

Back at Fairview, Thandi was preoccupied with her own plaguing thoughts and feelings. From the moment she'd learned that she was pregnant, she could think of nothing else.

At breakfast, Isaac was unusually quiet, and during lunch, he took to the fields.

Thandi had the distinct feeling that he was angry with her, and she already knew why. She thought of how disappointed he must have been. For he had hardly said more than a few words to her since his rather lengthy conversation with Tom.

In the meantime, everyone else was so excited for her. The news of her pregnancy had spread throughout the manor overnight, and everyone she saw extended their congratulations and well wishes.

She had put on a smile and pretended to be pleased, but inside, she felt anything but happy. Fear was the one emotion she felt most. She was afraid of what would happen in the event that Tom was the father and everyone became aware. Anna would undoubtedly be beside herself with anger, and Victor would know that she had lied about her relationship with Tom.

And if the child turned out to be Victor's, she knew he'd never let her go as he had promised. Not with his child.

But even worse was her fear of becoming a mother. Strangely, she had never imagined herself with a family of her own. For so long, it had been just her and her brother, but now Isaac had a family of his own. And now soon, so would she.

Thandi turned over in bed and wiped the tears from her face.

So much had changed so fast. It was all too much… It was all too overwhelming.

After a moment, she heard a knock at her door. She glanced at the mantle clock as she thought it was nearly time for dinner. More than likely, Alice had come to notify her. Or perhaps it was Corin. Since she'd learned of her pregnancy, the girl had checked in on her constantly.

Either way, she wasn't in the mood to see anyone at the moment. She turned again and buried her head in the pillow, hoping they would go away. But then, seconds later, she could hear the doorknob turning. She removed the pillow and turned her gaze towards the door as Isaac entered the room. Quickly, she wiped away the last evidence of her tears and sat up straight.

"Were you sleeping?" Isaac asked, though he could clearly tell she'd been crying.

"No, just resting until dinner," said Thandi.

"Well, I was hoping we could talk a minute," Isaac said, shutting the door.

"Certainly," Thandi replied, smiling thinly. As he walked over, she coughed to clear the nervous symptoms she could feel coming on.

"How are you feeling?" He asked, sitting in the chair closest to her bed.

"I'm feeling quite well," Thandi answered. She met his gaze, trying to read his expression. *Was he angry with her? If he was, it didn't show in his eyes. At least, not yet*, she thought.

After a moment's hesitation, he spoke. "I had a talk with Tom," He said.

Thandi tensed, knowing what would follow next.

"I know that the child could be his."

Thandi inhaled a deep breath and released it slowly.

"Yes," She muttered shamefully. She dropped her gaze to the bed, unable to look at him.

"I know that you love him, Sis," He continued.

Thandi lifted her eyes at the tenderness in his voice.

"But he isn't yours to love," He said firmly. "Think about it, Thandi. After everything you've been through, do you honestly think Anna and her father would leave you in peace? And Tom will not leave her. Not now that she's having his child. Never could he openly acknowledge you or your baby. At the very best, you could be his mistress. Is that what you want for yourself? Or more importantly, is that what you want for your child?"

Thandi's eyes watered and she looked away, but not before he saw the hurt on her face.

"I know that this must be hard," He continued. "But you must make the best of your situation."

Thandi turned again to face him, and he looked into her teary green eyes.

"Do you not think that I have considered all those things?" She asked. Tears spilled down her cheeks and she wiped them away. "I just can't do what you're asking. To deceive a man into raising another man's child as his own. It is wrong, Isaac," She said, shaking her head at the very thought.

"But you don't know that for certain. The child could very well be Victor's," Isaac countered. "What other real choice do you have right now?" He asked.

Thandi went silent. The truth of his words hurt her deep. She knew he was right. What other choice was there? Unlike him, she wasn't free. Even if she wanted to go away and raise the child on her own, she could not. She was still a slave. Still Victor's property. And the child would be also.

Suddenly, an overwhelming sense of hopelessness overcame her and she began to weep.

"Oh, no, don't cry," Isaac said. He got up from his chair and sat down next to her on the bed. "Everything will work out," He said, placing his arm around her. "Everything will be just fine."

Thandi doubted that was true. How could anything ever be fine again?

She shut her eyes and snuggled her face into her brother's shoulder. Despite her despair, it felt good to have him hold her. With him, she had always felt so very safe.

Soon, it would be time to leave Fairview and go back to Victor again.

***

When she arrived home, Victor greeted her with great joy. She could tell how much he missed her, and found herself wondering why that was when she had done nothing to encourage his attentions. In fact, she had done just the opposite, and even still he pursued her.

Isaac had said that he loved her, but even if he did, she had not felt the same. Perhaps, she could have, if her heart hadn't already belonged to another.

She had started to tell Victor about the baby at lunch, but found herself unable to say the words. Tomorrow morning at breakfast she would talk with him she decided, but for now, she did not want to think on it. Right now, she just wanted to think of nothing except the beauty around her.

"Giddy up, Belle!" She called firmly.

The mare immediately took off in a slow gallop down the wood's trail. Thandi looked behind her and saw Jonah. As expected, he increased his own horse's speed, shortening the distance between them. As the cool wind blew through her hair, she took in the sights of the passing oaks and lush green foliage.

"Go, Belle go!" She ordered. The horse increased her speed, leaving Jonah and his horse far behind. A wicked smile spread across Thandi's face as she heard Jonah yelling at his horse to go faster. She yelled again and Belle bolted. As the forest flashed by and the wind licked her face, Thandi smiled. In that moment, she felt free of her worries and sought to fully enjoy her ride.

As they approached a fallen tree, Belle stopped abruptly. Neighing loudly, she reared up, throwing Thandi backwards.

She screamed as she flew through the air and landed hard on the ground. Sitting up slowly, she winced at the pain in her back and arm.

"Madame Thandi!" She heard Jonah scream. Within seconds, he was there. "Are you hurt!?" He asked, dropping to the ground beside her.

"My back hurts a little... and my arm," She said, touching where she'd felt the pain.

Jonah glanced at her arm and saw the scrapes and bruises. "Can you stand up?" He asked, his face and tone filled with worry.

"I believe so," said Thandi.

With his assistance, she got to her feet.

"Does anything feel broken?" Jonah asked.

Thandi shifted her shoulders and shook her head, "No."

"I'll take you back on my horse," Jonah said and went over to the now calm Belle and proceeded to tie her to a tree.

"I'll come back for her in a few," He said walking over to Thandi to help her up onto his horse. When they arrived back at the house, he helped her inside.

"What in God's name!" Victor cried, taking in her torn dress and bruises.

"Madame Thandi took a fall from her horse," Jonah said quickly.

"I'm quite fine," Thandi cut in. "I think Belle experienced more of a scare than myself. There's a large fallen tree on the trail. I fell off the horse, but I'm fine. I'm just a little sore is all."

A frown creased Victor's brow. "Well, you hardly look fine," He said, examining her bruises.

Corin appeared at that moment, a stunned look came over her face when she saw Thandi.

"Madame!" She shrieked.

"I'm okay," Thandi said immediately.

"You seem fine, but I think you should still see a doctor," Victor said, looking at her arm.

"Nonsense," Thandi smiled. "It's just a few minor scrapes..."

"But what about the baby?" Corin blurted.

Thandi's heart dropped. She could see the puzzled expression instantly forming on Victor's face.

"You're pregnant?" He asked in amazement

"Yes, I was going to tell you tomorrow at breakfast, but now Corin has already imparted you with the news," Thandi said looking to Corin and giving her a wry smile.

"How do you know? Are you certain?" Victor asked all at once.

Thandi swallowed hard. "Yes, I saw a doctor at Fairview," She told him.

"Well, that settles it, you're definitely seeing Gordan," He said.

"Should I fetch him now, Masta?" Jonah asked.

"Yes, right away," Victor instructed.

"But, Belle," Thandi said, thinking of her horse still in the woods.

"I'll send another hand to get her, Madame," Jonah said.

"Well, let's get you cleaned up and in bed," Victor said assisting Thandi upstairs to her room as Corin followed.

Dr. Gordan arrived about two hours later. After examining Thandi, he met with Victor.

"She appears to be fine. There's no broken bones. Just external scrapes and bruises. And yes, she is pregnant," He added.

Victors face lit with delight.

"How far along?" He asked.

"She's very early. Just a month or slightly more," Gordan said.

Victor beamed at the news. He had always wanted a child. For years, he had tried to conceive a child with Elena but could not.

"I've cleaned and dressed her bruises. She should get some rest; and no more horseback riding," He concluded.

"Yes, of course," Victor responded.

"And you, how are you feeling?" Gordan asked.

"I've been well," Victor said. "The tonic has been working perfectly."

"Well, then, I should be going. I have another patient I must see to."

"Of course," said Victor escorting the doctor out to his waiting carriage. When he returned he found Thandi crying in her room.

"What is wrong," He asked, although, he suspected he already knew the answer.

"I didn't expect this to happen," She sobbed.

What she said was true, but secretly there was more. Unlike the other doctor, Dr. Gordan had seemed more certain of how far along she was. And, if he was right, there was no doubt that Victor had fathered her child.

He went and sat down on the bed next to her. "I can understand how you feel," He said, gently.

Thandi gave him a bitter look, but said nothing. The look in her eyes said it all. Victor knew that she blamed him for the pregnancy, and she had every right to. Still, he wished she could be happy. If only she would give him a chance, he would devote the rest of his life to satisfying her every want and need.

"Please, don't cry," He said, wiping the tears from her face. "I promise I'll give you a good life." He paused a moment, placing his hand gently on her belly. "Both of you."

Chapter 23

The following morning, Corin came to check on her, and to give her Victor's orders that she must stay in bed. He had left early for a business meeting, she explained.

Thandi looked at the clock and saw the time. It was just after ten a.m. She couldn't believe she had slept so long. She threw back the covers and quickly got out of bed. Suddenly, she felt sick to her stomach. She quickly covered her mouth and ran to the bathroom. Alarmed by her behavior, Corin immediately followed her.

Pausing in the open doorway, she watched Thandi vomit into the basin. When the nauseous feeling passed, Thandi rinsed her mouth and slowly collected herself. "Would you like some bread and crackers? It'll help settle your stomach," Corin said.

"Yes," Thandi muttered. "I don't think I could stomach anything else."

Corin immediately left the room and Thandi climbed back into bed. Her stomach still felt uneasy, and she thought that she would vomit again. She stayed in bed all morning, feeling miserable and waiting for the sickness to pass.

After lunch, Victor arrived back home. The first thing he did upon setting foot in the door was go to Thandi. As he approached her bedroom door, Corin was leaving the room.

"Master," She nodded.

Victor gave her a smile and entered the room. His cheerful smile remained as he saw Thandi.

"Finally, you're awake," He said.

Thandi's head turned at the sound of his voice.

"Yes," She answered dryly. "May I ask, how long I must stay in this bed?"

Victor pretended not to hear the irritation in her voice as he walked over to the side table and poured her a glass of water. Next to the pitcher was a silver platter. He lifted its lid and saw the crackers.

"Lunch?" He asked, raising a brow.

"I was very nauseous earlier," Thandi explained.

"Would you like something now?" Victor asked.

He extended the glass of water to her, and she sat up.

"Yes, Thandi returned. I'd like an answer to my question. Just how much longer must I stay in this bed?" She repeated firmly.

Victor smiled at her cleverness. "Until I'm satisfied you're okay," He answered smartly.

Thandi turned her head to the window and he could see that she was upset.

"Gordan said that you should rest for a few days. He'll be back on Wednesday. We shall see how he feels then."

The frown on Thandi's brow darkened. "Can I bring you something to eat? You must be starving," He asked.

"No, thank you, Corin is bringing stew," Thandi answered, not even bothering to turn and look at him.

Victor suppressed the urge to sit down next to her. He wanted so very much to touch her, to stroke her face and hair. But he feared that she would reject his touch.

Later that afternoon, he personally brought her dinner. And that evening he brought her warm milk and a snack.

The following morning when she awoke, Thandi vaguely remembered him coming into her room. He had sat by the bed and watched her while she slept. Strangely, she had felt comforted by his presence.

Days later, Dr. Gordan returned to re-examine her. She had no bleeding or signs of fever, and had appeared to be in good health, he said.

However, he had still suggested that she remain on bed rest for a few days longer.

Naturally, Thandi was upset with the recommendation. She had already been confined to her bed for three days now. If she remained there any longer, she feared she'd go mad.

Victor, of course, had no objection. In fact, he seemed pleased with the doctor's decision and had promised she'd follow his orders.

As they departed her room for Victor's office, Thandi stared angrily at the pair.

Over the next four days, despite Victor's constant efforts to please her, she'd remained in a sour mood. Finally, on Sunday morning, he gave permission to cease her bed rest.

Thandi could hardly wait to be free of her room. She immediately bathed and dressed herself, then set off for a walk around the lake.

Unlike the last time she'd walked, the air had grown much colder.

Despite the frigid temperature, she chose to remain outdoors. After a while, the chill was gone. She had become so engrossed with the enchanting lake that she no longer felt the cold air. Squatting down, she picked up a rock and threw it far into the lake's still waters.

"It's a bit nippy out, don't you think?"

Thandi turned to see Victor walking over.

"You should get inside before you catch cold," He said.

Thandi released a heavy sigh. She wasn't ready to go back.

Victor walked closer to her and extended her his hand. Thandi hesitated a moment before taking it and the pair began to walk back towards the house, hand in hand. Strangely, she no longer felt uncomfortable at his touch. Perhaps, she was getting used to him. Or perhaps, deep down on some subconscious level, she was beginning to accept her fate.

Christmas came just two days later. Although, she hoped he would come, Thandi doubted she'd see her brother. As she stood in front of the massive Christmas tree in the parlor, she thought of him. And as much as she hadn't wanted to, she also thought of Tom.

The tall decorated tree fondly reminded her of one she'd seen as a child. Like the one before her, it had been heavily dressed from top to bottom in gold ribbon, crystal ornaments, red bulbs, and bows.

She and Tom had helped her mother and the staff with the tree's decoration. Isaac had been sick in bed with a cold. Sadly, that was their last Christmas at the Lexington plantation.

"So, are you ready to open your gifts?"

Thandi turned to see Victor walking towards her.

"There are so many," She said, turning her gaze to the small mountain of gifts that circled the tree.

Victor laughed heartily. "Well, they all aren't for you," He said.

Thandi blushed with embarrassment and turned her gaze to the tree again.

"The gifts are all labeled," said Victor.

He walked over to the tree and picked up a large gift. "Here you are. This one is yours," He said, placing the box in front of her.

Thandi slowly glanced over the expensive gold wrapping and large red bow, then proceeded to delicately tear away the paper.

"Well, that's no way to open a Christmas gift," Victor chided. Grabbing a smaller box, he read her name. "Now, this is the proper way to open a gift," He stated carelessly ripping away the box's paper like an overzealous child.

Thandi giggled at his silly behavior. This was a side of him she hadn't seen before.

"Shall I open it?" He asked, looking down at the box's white lid.

Thandi nodded her approval and he lifted it the lid, revealing an exquisite feathered hat.

"Oh my!" She gasped, marveling at the unique brown feathers.

"Now, it's your turn," Victor said, eyeing the box in front of her.

Smiling, Thandi swiftly tore away the paper and lifted the box's lid. Much to her surprise, inside was a luxurious fur coat. She pulled it out and held it up in her trembling hands. "It's... it's gorgeous," She said, wide-eyed, her voice filled with awe.

"Matches the hat," Victor replied. "Seeing as how you like to walk in the winter, I thought it necessary," He smartly concluded.

"But I have nothing for you," Thandi said sadly.

"Well, that isn't true. You've already given me the greatest gift a woman could ever give a man." His gaze dropped to her midsection and then up to her eyes.

Thandi smiled thinly, turning her attention back to the coat. "Thank you. It's absolutely beautiful," She said.

Her genuine gratefulness could be heard in her voice.

When she'd finished unwrapping her gifts, she counted eight dresses, six pairs of shoes, two hats, three petticoats, a set of gold combs, and a magnificent pair of diamond earrings.

Never in her life had she received such elegant gifts. Victor had obviously spent a small fortune.

For their Christmas breakfast, the staff served them with gold platters of bacon, eggs, grits, cold ham, imported cheeses, fruits, nuts, scones, and spreads. Four beverages were served: hot tea, fresh milk, cider, and eggnog.

Dinner had been just the same. A small feast of various meats, vegetables, fruits, cakes, and breads were served. Only this time, the staff had joined them. It had been tradition for the staff to join the table at Christmas in Victor's home, as well as at Thanksgiving and Easter, he told her.

All throughout dinner, he and the staff talked and laughed. Thandi, however, had very little to say; she had been too busy enjoying her meal.

The evening passed quite pleasantly. They played games, shared stories, and listened to music. Victor played several Christmas songs and two captivating pieces by Strauss and Chopin, but it was Corin's angelic voice that had been the night's highlight. She sang a beautiful hymn titled *Now the Wait is Over*, that brought the house to tears. At eleven o'clock, Thandi retired for the evening.

When morning came, she opened her eyes, remembering the events of last night and a small smile creased her lips as she recalled Corin's singing.

She got out of bed and walked to the bathroom. As she walked to the basin, she caught a glimpse of herself in the mirror. She turned to face her image when suddenly the reality of her situation hit her again. She was pregnant. Pregnant with Victor's child. She lowered her eyes, thinking of the freedom she would never have.

***

At breakfast, Victor told her of his plans to throw a New Year's Eve party. He said that it would be a small tasteful dinner, followed by a few fireworks, and a classical band. Surprisingly, the thought had pleased Thandi. He had suggested that she invite her family, and that they should all wear their very best. Victor had even offered to send money to ensure it.

The thought of seeing her family again so soon filled Thandi with happiness. So much so that she didn't even think of whom else would be in attendance.

On the morning of New Year's Eve, several decorators and vendors arrived early to set up for the party. Everywhere she turned, someone was busy with preparations for the night's festivities. She stood and watched in amazement as the workers slowly transformed the mansion's lower level into a spectacle like she'd never seen before.

Outside, Victor monitored the work for the fireworks.

"More!" A man on a ladder, yelled.

Thandi stared up at him, intrigued. He was hanging white and gold ceiling drapes into a most interesting design.

Around six-thirty, she began to get dressed. The guests weren't expected until eight o'clock, but she had wanted plenty of time to prepare.

When she entered her room, she saw her gown lying across the bed. Corin had already laid out her new dress. Keeping with the party's color scheme, Victor had bought himself a new white suit, and for her, a sleeveless white gown with shimmering gold accents. The dress fit her perfectly, accenting her every curve.

Sitting at her vanity, Thandi examined herself in the mirror.

The diamond earrings that Victor had given her sparkled in her ears, and the gold combs held her hair perfectly in place. A soft smile parted her lips as she stared at her reflection.

"Thank you, Corin. My hair looks wonderful," She said.

For the party, she had allowed the maid to dress her hair into an elegant bun.

"You look beautiful, Madame," Corin said, standing behind her when a soft knock sounded at the door.

"Come in," Thandi called out.

She turned in her chair to see Victor entering the room. For a second, she froze, staring at him. He looked exceptionally handsome in his white-tailored suit and polished white dress shoes. His gold kerchief and bow matched well with her long gold gloves and shoes. "You look very handsome," She told him.

Victor smiled at the compliment and began walking towards her.

"You don't look so bad yourself," He said.

As he came closer, she could see that he was holding something sparkly in his hands.

"I thought that this would complete your look," He said, slipping a necklace around her neck.

Thandi looked into the mirror and she could hear Corin gasp from behind.

At the same time, her eyes lit with wonder and her jaw fell slightly agape. Touching her hand to her neck, she slowly traced a finger over the long string of diamonds. For several seconds, she could say nothing. She stared mesmerized by the shimmering gems.

"You shouldn't have," She said, looking up at his reflection.

"I've spent nothing. It was Elena's," Victor said.

Thandi looked into his eyes in the mirror and smiled sadly. "Only tonight," She said.

Victor smiled warmly and nodded in agreement.

Through her room doors, she could hear the music from downstairs. The band had already started.

"Will you be needing anything else, Madam?" Corin asked.

Thandi turned around in her chair and looked her in the eyes. "No, nothing," She said, smiling.

Corin smiled back and left the room. As the door shut behind her, Thandi turned again to the mirror and caught Victor's gaze.

"Well, I guess I should go and check on things," He said.

Thandi gave him a smile and off he went.

Soon after, she made her appearance downstairs.

At the front double doors stood Victor and a uniformed butler, ready to greet their guests. She gave him a small smile as she passed through the parlor and into the hall. Soon, the distinguished guests began to arrive and the mansion quickly came alive with the sound of laughter, music, and inaudible chatter. Everyone was dressed to impress in fine suits and high-fashioned gowns.

With so many people, Thandi hoped that she could blend discreetly amongst the guests. As she aimlessly moved through the crowd, she suddenly saw Tom. He was talking to a blonde haired gentleman. With him, of course, was Anna. She held his arm, smiling proudly.

Both of them wore blue and white attire; she in an off the shoulder blue gown and he in a black suit with matching blue bow tie, and kerchief. There was no doubt that the two were a handsome pair.

Thandi shook herself inwardly and turned around in the other direction. She knew that she would have to face them any moment now, but she wasn't ready for it to happen. As she started to walk away, she saw Victor coming toward her.

"Hiding from me?" He asked, walking up to her.

She shook her head and took his offered hand.

They walked around the room arm in arm, greeting their guests one by one. Thankfully, she didn't have to speak much. Sensing her fear, Victor did all the talking.

"You know, you'll have to get used to this someday," He said when they were finally alone for a fleeting moment.

"I don't think that I could, ever," Thandi stated, her eyes scanning the many faces in the room. Oh, how she wished her brother were there.

She had sent him an invitation, but received no response. Still, she had been hopeful. Even now, she found herself looking for his face in the crowd.

"Victor!" A familiar voice called.

Thandi turned to see Stafford approaching. Sighing heavily, she looked away. "Excuse me. I'm going to visit the powder room," She quickly informed Victor.

"Certainly," He said, releasing her hand.

She hurried off, leaving before Daniel could approach them. She didn't look back, nor did she make eye contact with the many goggling eyes that stared upon her.

Never could I get used to these people, she thought. *And never to Daniel Stafford.*

"Thandi!" Someone called loudly.

Suddenly someone behind her touched her shoulder. She stopped, turned around, and looked directly into Tom's eyes.

"Can we talk somewhere?" He asked.

Thandi hesitated a moment, then nodded. "The drawing room, we can talk there," She said.

She led the way and Tom followed. When they entered the room, she looked around to make sure that no one else was around. Although the room was dimly lit, she could see that they were alone.

"Dinner will be starting soon," She said, turning to him.

"Yes, we won't be long," Tom said. "So, how have you been feeling?" He asked.

"Exhausted, mostly. And the morning sickness is horrible. But otherwise, I've been fine," Thandi said.

"Thandi," Tom began. "I've been giving our situation a great deal of thought. I think that I should talk with Victor. He, of course, will be upset, but he is a very reasonable man. If the child is mine he can return you back to me; whatever the price. You could live at Fairview until I've made other arrangements. Anna would never have to know that..."

"Stop!" Thandi said, cutting him off. She simply couldn't hear anymore. *My brother had been right*, she thought sorely.

Tom stared back at her confused.

"The child is Victor's," She said.

Tom stood speechless for several seconds. "How do you know?"

"Victor's doctor examined me. Like the other doctor, he said that I am very early. Even earlier than Dr. Granger suggested."

She paused, drawing a deep breath. In those seconds, she could see the confusion slowly leave Tom's face.

"He believes I am no more than five to six weeks," She said.

Tom went quiet for a moment. He dropped his gaze to the floor and shook his head.

When he looked up again, Thandi did not see a look of relief in his eyes as she'd expected, but, instead, she saw a look of remorse and possibly even disappointment. "So, then Victor is pleased?" Tom asked.

"Yes. Very much so," Thandi answered lowly.

A heavy silence fell between them; a silence filled with unspoken words.

"We should probably be getting back, now," Thandi said after a moment.

Tom nodded slowly. "Should you need anything, you only need ask," He said.

Thandi swallowed back the lump of emotion in her throat, and smiled. "I know that," She said bravely.

She turned towards the door to leave when suddenly Tom grabbed her hand pulling her against his chest. Her face flushed as he briefly held her face in his hands and stared deep into her eyes and pressed a long kiss to her lips. A final kiss.

When he released her, neither of them said a word.

"We should go now... separately," Thandi said after a moment.

Tom gave her a wry smile and nodded in agreement.

She stepped back and gave him a long look before finally leaving.

Minutes later, Tom left the room. As he walked back to the dining hall, his mind reeled with confusion. Strangely, he felt deeply saddened. He touched a finger to his mouth, remembering the feel of her lips. *Why did I do that?* He thought. He knew that he was wrong to kiss her. But even more troubling was how much he'd enjoyed it. How much he'd missed it.

He forced the thoughts out of his mind as he neared the hall's doors and entered. The dinner was just beginning and the guests were being seated.

"Tom!" Anna called, spotting him at the door.

As he walked towards the table he was quickly assisted by one of the staff.

"Where were you?" She asked as he sat down next to her.

"I went for some air," Tom said, avoiding her gaze.

As he adjusted his napkin, he stole a glimpse down the table and saw Thandi. She was seated next to Victor at the opposite end. Far from him and Anna. And even further from Stafford and his wife. Tom strongly suspected that Victor had divided them all purposely, and rightly so.

He had been apprehensive about going to the dinner; about what would happen. He had even warned Anna to be on her best behavior. Although, he doubted she'd disobey him, he still felt better with the distance between them, and so did Victor, obviously. As the main course started, the room quickly filled with chatter and merriment.

Though the lamb was marvelous, Tom hardly touched his plate.

"Is there something wrong?" Anna asked. "You've hardly touched your food."

Tom looked down at the idle fork in his hands. "I guess I don't have much of an appetite," He said honestly.

Anna gave him a strange look then continued to carry on her conversation with Madame Ballard.

Tom glanced down the table again and saw Victor and Thandi talking. Victor looked so genuinely happy, so genuinely in love that Tom couldn't help feeling jealous. Victor had everything he ever wanted: wealth, power, respect.

But above all those things, he had Thandi. The one true love of his life.

After the main course dishes were cleared, Victor stood to make a toast.

"To a very happy, healthy," He paused a moment and turned to Thandi. "And fruitful New Year," He finished.

As he turned back to the crowd of guests, everyone applauded and cheered. Everyone but Tom, that is. His mind had been too consumed with his pressing thoughts.

After dessert, the guests gathered again in the drawing room. Victor stood in the room's center with Thandi at his side, surrounded by friends and acquaintances.

"Victor, I must say you've truly outdone yourself this time," said a red haired gentleman.

"Yes," Madame Pulford interjected. "The place always looks so beautiful."

As she spoke, they were joined by Daniel and his wife. Thandi cringed inside as her eyes met with Stafford's, for he was smiling like a cat with a canary.

"With a place so large," Madame Pulford continued, "I imagine you spent a small fortune on decorations."

Victor smiled and lifted his champagne glass to his lips.

"Speaking of a place this large, when will you ever marry a proper girl and fill it with the sound of little pattering feet?" Lady Margret, asked.

Thandi's face flushed red as she looked to Victor.

"Funny that you ask," Victor said.

Inwardly, Thandi prayed that he wouldn't reveal her pregnancy.

"As it appears, my companion and I are expecting," He announced.

Thandi's heart sank.

"Well, that is wonderful!" Madame Pulford said brightly. Others began to express their happiness for Victor while Anna and her mother stood in shock.

Tom also stood silently. He could hardly believe what Victor had just done. He had just told a large group of Charleston's elite that he had sired a child with his mulatto lover.

The man was truly fearless. Truly fearless indeed, Tom thought.

"Well, that simply isn't the same," Lady Margret returned. "I meant that your house should be filled with white children: proper heirs," She added.

Thandi fumed silently as the women began to gasp, wonder, and whisper. Never before had she felt so humiliated.

"Well, while I do thank you for your concern, Lady Margret, I think that I shall fill it with whatever color children I like," Victor said plainly.

At that moment, everyone around them went silent.

"Daniel, if I can have a word," Victor said, looking to Stafford.

"But, of course," Daniel nodded.

"If you'll excuse me," Victor said to Thandi.

Reluctantly, she nodded her approval and the two men left the room.

"If you all will please excuse me, too," Thandi said, then hurried out of the room.

Tom felt a pang of guilt grip his heart. He desperately wanted to go after her, but he knew that he could not. Not with Anna and her mother standing guard.

Meanwhile, when they entered the study, Victor walked straight to the liquor cabinet, poured two glasses of bourbon and handed one to Daniel.

"So, tell me, you old dog." Stafford smiled. "How is she?"

Victor gave him an incredulous look.

"The girl," Stafford said pointedly. "How is the girl in bed? I mean, she must have a good piece of tail on her, seeing as how you've already gotten her knocked her up," He said, smiling ruefully.

Victor lowered his glass and turned from the mantle. The previously pleasant look on his face was now more serious.

"How she is in bed is of no concern to you. And she certainly should no longer be of concern to your wife and daughter," Victor said firmly. "I simply won't stand for any more attacks on her."

Daniel's smile instantly dropped and his jovial red cheeks flushed white as Victor's words sunk in. He lowered his glass to the side table. "Are you serious?" He asked, taken aback.

"I am," said Victor. His eyes and tone left no question.

Daniel stared back at him in disbelief.

"If I or my wife have offended you, then I do apologize. However, you can't expect people to treat the girl like a white woman," He laughed.

"No, I cannot. But I can expect you and others to treat her with common decency and respect."

Daniel shook his head in wonder. "What is it about this girl that makes you and Tom so crazy?" He asked.

Victor matched his wicked grin with a menacing frown. "Perhaps, you didn't hear what I said," He snapped.

Daniel's face turned red as he began to puff up in indignation. Victor had obviously hit a sore spot.

"So, then you are serious," Daniel said, his tone heavy with disbelief. "You are putting this girl, this nigger girl, before our friendship?" He paused a second as if he were awaiting an answer. "I mean, of course, I can understand your wanting her, how could any man not? But you go too far with all of this. Dressing her in jewels and fancy clothes; presenting her on your arm. She's a beautiful piece of mulatto ass, my friend, and nothing more," He stated.

"You should leave now," Victor said as he placed his glass on the mantle and turned back again, glaring into Daniel's eyes.

"So, you'd seriously risk our friendship over this girl?" Daniel asked, surprised.

"Yes, but I won't have to, because from this point on, you and I are no longer friends," Victor said as he shoved his hands into his jacket pockets and awaited Daniel's departure.

For a matter of seconds, Stafford sat speechless. Then he slowly stood, stared a moment at Victor, then started towards the door. As he gripped the doorknob, he stopped and turned back. "Well, then, I guess I shall contact you if there is business," He said.

Victor gave him an agreeable nod.

Daniel then turned to the door again. He began to turn the handle but stopped and once again turned to meet Victor's piercing eyes.

"You know, I didn't say anything about you selling the mill to Tom. But since you and I have been so candid with each other tonight, I think you should know my feelings on the matter. You knew that I wanted it, and yet you sold it to Tom. I do pray that you stay in good health, old friend. I worry about what would happen if you were gone."

Before Victor could respond, he opened the door and disappeared.

Victor didn't have to follow him. He knew exactly what he meant. His words were a threat. A threat against Thandi.

Thinking of her, he quickly returned to the dining hall to find her nowhere in sight. Daniel and his family also appeared to be missing. Several of his friends and counterparts approached him, but he quickly dismissed them all. He needed to find Thandi. He knew that she was upset.

He walked out of the dining hall's doors and headed towards her room. When he reached her door, he knocked and waited. Receiving no answer, he knocked again. Still, there was no response. He opened the door and entered. The bed was empty. He looked around the room and saw the open balcony doors and a frightful feeling came over him. A feeling which made him so afraid that he ran to the doors and nearly jumped outside. Thandi spun around at the sound of his entrance.

"Are you okay!?" Victor asked.

Thandi could see the alarm in his face. She looked over the terrace and back again into his eyes. "Did you think that I would jump?" She asked.

Victor gave her an uncertain look.

"Well, you need not worry," She said.

Feeling slightly embarrassed, Victor straightened his suit and ran a hand through his slicked back hair. "Are you angry with me?" He asked her.

"Actually, yes. How could you do that to me?" Thandi began. "You should not have told those people about my pregnancy. I am not one of you!" She snapped.

"One of you?" Victor said. "Think of what you're saying. You and I are no different."

"Oh, but we are," Thandi said, looking all around her.

"This is your life now," Victor said firmly.

"This isn't my life. I'll never be one of those ladies downstairs. And there will always be people like Anna and her mother to remind me of exactly who and what I am."

"Who you are? It isn't the color of your skin that defines who you are. You are a beautiful woman. A woman that I am proud to have as a companion. A woman that I am proud to have as the mother of my child," He said. He took a step closer, his eyes searching hers.

"Your guests are waiting," Thandi said coldly.

Victor took a step closer.

"Let them wait," He said gently lifting her chin, and kissing her softly on the lips.

Chapter 24

Life went on as usual at the estate as the days passed. It seemed as if all had been forgotten; however, for Victor, nothing had been forgiven. Thoughts of Daniel and their conversation constantly played in his mind. Although he had no fear of Daniel, or any other man, for that matter, he did fear the unknown.

As long as he was alive, he knew that Thandi would be safe. *But what if he were not?* He thought. *What would become of Thandi and his child?*

Before, he hadn't given much thought to the future. But now, after his bout with Daniel he could think of little else.

Over the next month, he saw very little of Daniel; he had seen him only once at a business meeting and again, briefly, in town. Victor also noticed that he and his wife no longer frequented the restaurant, which suited him just perfect.

Thandi, too, had been grateful that they were no longer friends. She no longer had to deal with them or their behavior. Life had been peaceful without them in it. However, she did miss Tom. The memory of his kiss still lingered in her mind. She knew from the way he'd kissed her that he was saying goodbye.

For her own sake, and for the sake of her child, she had to move on with her life. She knew that. The time had come. But what she didn't know was, how.

She still thought of him. Yearned for him. Thankfully, the tears had stopped. Though she'd felt heavily saddened at times, she had not cried. Perhaps because there were no tears left.

As time progressed, so did Thandi's waistline. In just two short months, she could see a small change to her pregnant belly. The morning sickness had gotten better, but the fatigue had still persisted. Dr. Gordan visited regularly; at least once a week. But then, he had always visited often, even before Thandi's pregnancy. He and Victor had appeared to be very close. And Thandi often found herself wondering what it was that they talked about so often.

Each time that the doctor would visit, he and Victor had spent some time locked away in the study. But then Victor was a peculiar man.

There was still so much to learn about him, Thandi thought. And perhaps now she could. Now that she had begun to move on from the past.

In early spring, Isaac came to visit. He had been glad to hear that the child was Victor's. He had been even happier to hear that she had decided to accept her life there. He told her that he no longer wanted to move away, that he could never leave her behind and go so far away. Besides, he and Sarah were happy at Fairview and Tom was paying him a good salary.

Thandi questioned his sudden change of heart. She knew that he truly hadn't wanted to remain in Carolina. For as long as she could remember, he had dreamed of moving North. She knew that he was giving up his dreams to stay close to her.

Just a week after his visit, a messenger arrived with a telegram from Esther. She had requested permission to visit Thandi. Victor, of course, agreed. When she arrived two weeks later, Thandi was happy to see her.

While Corin prepared sandwiches for them, the two had tea in the sitting room.

"You look so beautiful," Esther said, looking her over. As she looked into Thandi's smiling face, she noticed that something about her appearance was slightly different. Not only was her skin glowing, but it seemed that she had put on a few pounds since she'd seen her last.

She squinted her eyes at Thandi and her jaw dropped. "Oh, my! You are pregnant!" She blurted.

Thandi gave her a startled look. "How did you know?" She asked.

"Well, I overheard the Missus and her lady friends talking about the New Year's Party." Thandi shook her head, but she wasn't surprised.

"Not to mention, you've put on some weight, and your skin looks as smooth as a baby's bottom."

Thandi giggled at her last remark.

"Master Tom told her I was going to visit family. If she knew I was coming to see you, she would've never let me come."

"Well, I'm glad that you have," said Thandi, sipping her tea.

After a moment, she glanced up to find Esther staring at her strangely.

"Is something wrong?" She asked concerned.

Esther looked as if she wanted to say something, but wasn't sure if she should.

"What is it, Esther?" Thandi asked, her voice rising.

"It's nothing," Esther said, shaking her head. "Just something silly that crossed my mind," She said, waving her hand as if waving away the thought.

"Well I'd like to hear it just the same," Thandi said. She lowered her cup, awaiting Esther's answer.

Esther lowered her eyes, hesitated, and looked up again.

"Well, I couldn't help wondering if," Again she paused. "Well, wondering if Tom was the father," She finished in a hushed tone.

Thandi shook her head in wonder.

"No, the child is Victor's," She said in an equally low tone.

"I'm sorry, there I go, being nosy," said Esther.

Thandi shrugged. "It's fine," She said. She had come to expect that from her. However, the question had still come as a surprise. "How long will you stay?" Thandi asked.

"Three days. The Missus wants me back in time for some luncheon she's having. Ever since she found out she was expecting, she's been throwing parties and giving dinners like all of Charleston don't know already."

Thandi chuckled, nearly spilling her tea.

After lunch, they talked some more as she showed Esther around the mansion. Esther had been astonished by everything she saw and even more astounded by her quarters. Thandi had put her in the best guest room, which had a balcony and king-sized bed.

Over the next two days, they spent their time together talking, laughing, and sewing, mostly. On the morning of the third day, Esther returned home. Thandi, of course, was sad to see her go, but Esther assured her that she would visit again.

And so, the days passed. Spring came and went, and Thandi still hadn't seen Tom since the New Years' dinner. It seemed that he too had moved on with his life, as if he and she had never existed. Even though months had passed without seeing him, Thandi still felt connected to him. But then, she always had, and perhaps always would.

***

Thandi felt the baby's first flutter at four months and at six, she felt the babe kicking and moving strong in her womb. Thandi had felt both afraid and amazed by the feeling of life inside her.

Victor had been elated, always wanting to feel her stomach and talk to the unborn child. He had even started converting one of the guest rooms into a very large nursery. Thandi could see the excitement on the faces of everyone around her.

For the first time in many months, she felt at peace with her life.

No longer had she been moody. In fact, it seemed that her bitterness toward Victor had faded altogether. Perhaps, it was the upcoming birth of her child that swayed her feelings. Or, perhaps, it was a combination of time and his unwavering love. Whatever the reason, Victor couldn't have been more happy. Everything was going better than he'd hoped for.

Everything but his health, that was.

The coughing bouts he'd suffered months earlier had come back even worse, and he suffered with a dull pain in his back and chest. Still, he hadn't made Thandi aware of his illness. He didn't want her to worry. Everything had been going so well. Besides, Gordan had started him on a new tonic from Britain that was said to work wonders.

I will be fine, he thought. *I have too much to live for to die.*

As he sat with Thandi in the sitting room, Corin came into the room.

"Excuse me, Sir. There was a messenger," She said, handing Victor an envelope.

"Thank you." He said, smiling

As she walked away, he turned it over and opened it, withdrawing a short letter. As he read it, his face grew grim.

"My God," He muttered.

Tom had written to inform him that he wouldn't be able to make their upcoming meeting; that his wife was ill and had suffered a miscarriage. Victor's heart sank within him. He could only imagine how devastated they must have been. He thought of Thandi and their unborn child. If anything were to happen to them, he would be heartbroken.

"Is everything all right?" Thandi asked, seeing his grave expression. Victor looked up from the letter and into her eyes.

"No, I'm afraid not," He said sadly. He lowered his eyes, folding the letter in his hands.

"The letter is from Tom," He said, looking up at her. "Anna has lost the child."

For a second, Thandi went numb with shock. "How awful," She said sincerely.

"We should send our condolences," Victor said.

"Yes," Thandi readily agreed.

For a long moment, they sat in an odd silence. Then Victor stood up and went over to her. He bent down and placed a loving kiss on her forehead and left the room.

After he was gone, she sat for a long time thinking…of Tom, of Anna, of their child, and of everything that had happened. She ran her hands over her swollen belly, thinking of the precious life inside her. As much as she had despised Anna, her heart still went out to her.

***

After learning such terrible news, Victor had wanted to take every precaution to ensure the healthy arrival of his own child. For Thandi, travel had no longer been permitted, nor could she continue to go for her usual long walks.

She didn't mind the restrictions. She was willing to do whatever it took to protect her unborn child. As the days went by, she thought of Tom constantly. She worried about him, but there was nothing she could do except pray that he was okay. She thought of writing him, but she feared that Anna would find her letter and she didn't want to cause any trouble or grief; there had been enough of that. And so, she just went on each day hoping and wishing that he would soon visit.

Her wish came true about three weeks later, when Tom came to the estate to discuss some business matters with Victor. A look of surprise came over his face when he saw her very pregnant belly. And for a split second, his smile fell away, then came again when he looked back up into her eyes.

Thandi felt bad for him, thinking of how hard it must have been for him to see her now. She hadn't thought of that before.

Perhaps that was why he hadn't come to visit, she thought.

After he met with Victor, the two of them talked for a short time in the sitting room.

"How have you been?" He asked her. She smiled at him lovingly.

"I've been fine," She replied. "And you, how are you?" She asked gingerly.

He dropped his gaze to his lap and up again. "I've been all right. I've been keeping busy with work at the mill," He said weakly.

Thandi gave him a sweet smile.

"And Anna? How is she?" She asked.

Tom inhaled deeply and sighed. "She is feeling better," He said, smiling thinly, dropping his gaze again. "She took the loss very hard."

He paused for a moment, thinking back to the morning she gave birth. "He was stillborn," He said sadly.

Thandi's heart sank within her at the thought. Unconsciously, she touched her stomach. When she looked to Tom again, she saw his eyes on her belly. "I'm so sorry, Tom," She said sincerely.

He looked up again into her eyes and gave her a solemn smile.

Before either of them could say another word, Victor walked into the room. "I nearly forgot to give you this," He said to Tom, handing over some papers.

"Oh, yes," Tom said. He folded the papers and tucked them into his pocket. For a moment, the room filled with silence. "Well, I should probably get going," Tom said finally as he stood up to leave. Thandi felt disheartened, she had wanted to spend more time with him; but she did not protest his leaving, for she had understood why he would want to go.

***

Two weeks later, Thandi went into early labor; she wasn't due for almost another month. Dutifully, Victor sat at her bedside and held her hand as they awaited the doctor. Meanwhile, the live-in midwife he'd hired was there to assist in his stead.

As the pains came faster and stronger, Thandi screamed and yelled, squeezing Victor's hand. "Where the Hell is Gordan!?" Victor fumed, looking towards the door.

"We won't need him," the midwife said coming to the bed again to check Thandi. "It won't be long now," She said encouragingly.

Thandi grimaced and clenched her teeth as another pain hit her. "Ahhh!" She screamed in agony.

Victor swallowed hard with fear. He felt helpless! He didn't know what to do. Except be angry at Gordan for taking so damned long to get there! Perhaps, if he were there, he could do something to help her.

The pain became more and more unbearable, tears spilled uncontrollably from Thandi's eyes. She was tired, so very, very tired., Another labor pain suddenly struck her and she screamed again.

"Push, Madame!" The midwife yelled.

Victor's heart pounded. He could hear its beat in his ears.

"I can't! I can't!" Thandi cried, panting.

"It's almost over. You've got to push, darling," Victor said.

Leaning forward, Thandi gathered all her strength and pushed as hard as she could. Moments later, the strong sound of a baby's cry filled the room.

"It's a boy!" The midwife announced.

Victor's face brightened instantly. He looked to Thandi and saw a smile on her face.

"You did it!" He said, kissing her hand as the midwife swaddled the baby before placing him in his mother's arms.

Thandi stared down into her son's face, tears welling in her eyes. He was beautiful. So perfectly beautiful. *And white!* She thought to herself with a smile.

His little eyes were squeezed shut and a tiny fist was balled tightly. Never before had she felt so amazed by anything, or anyone. The babe began to wail and kick in her arms.

"I think he's hungry," the midwife said.

"Yes, of course," said Thandi. She pulled down the left shoulder of her nightgown and offered her nipple to the babe.

Almost immediately, he latched on to it, sucking greedily.

"He's already strong," Victor said proudly.

Thandi looked up at him and smiled.

"Would you like to hold him after he's finished?" She asked.

"More than anything," Victor smiled.

Once the babe had stopped feeding, Victor carefully took him from Thandi's arms. He gazed down at the infant, his eyes absorbing every feature of his angelic little face.

"He certainly has your straight, dark hair," Thandi said.

Victor flashed her a smile, then looked back down at him. The baby's eyes fluttered open. He almost seemed to be staring at Victor.

"His eyes are open now," He announced as the boy stared up at him with the most amazing green eyes. For a long moment, Victor went silent. He stood holding him with a small smile on his face. "He has your eyes," He said finally.

Thandi moved forward to see him and instantly she groaned in pain.

"Lay back," Victor scolded as he placed the baby back in her arms.

"What will we name him?" Thandi asked.

Victor hesitated, as he thought. "Caleb," He said after a moment.

Thandi gave him a puzzled look. She was thoroughly surprised that he had not answered "Victor."

A knock sounded at the door.

"Who is it?" Victor called out.

"Gordan," the doctor called back.

"Come in," Victor yelled; gazing intently at the door, awaiting Gordan's entrance.

No sooner than he entered the room, Victor began to question his tardiness. "What took you so long?" He asked. Frustration was clearly heard in his voice.

"I was in the middle of delivering Lady Thompson," Gordan answered, immediately walking to a nearby basin to wash his hands.

"Thank you, I'll take it from here, Clarissa," He said to the midwife.

"I didn't expect to be on call this soon. Thandi's early," He said, coming to her bedside.

"Thank God we had Clarissa," Victor said.

"Well, friend, I'm here now," Gordan smiled. "And I'm afraid, I'll have to ask you to give me some time alone with my patients."

Victor gave him a vexed look.

"I'll be back soon," Victor said to Thandi. He smiled down at Caleb, and placed a kiss on the top of Thandi's forehead before leaving the room.

Chapter 25

They were visited by a number of friends and family over the following weeks. Everyone had been in awe of little Caleb. Especially Tom. Thandi had been surprised by his visit. From the very first moment he laid eyes on Caleb, he could not stop staring. Thandi watched his expression as he held him.

His eyes were filled with wonder. "What is his name?" He asked.

Caleb Richmond," Thandi replied.

Tom turned to her with a confused look on his face.

"Victor gave Caleb his freedom so that he could legally bear his name," She explained.

"And you?" Tom asked.

Thandi did not answer. Instead, she simply smiled and shook her head. "No."

Tom smiled thinly, and turned his attention back to Caleb.

"He's a fine boy. He favors you; he has your eyes," Tom said, smiling.

"Yes, everyone says that," Thandi beamed.

"Was he early?" Tom suddenly asked.

"Yes, by weeks," Thandi replied. "Dr. Gordan believes that it may have been the fall I suffered early on in the pregnancy that brought on the early labor."

Tom frowned. "You had an accident?"

"Yes, a minor fall from my horse very early on," Thandi replied. "I'm just grateful that Caleb..." She stopped speaking when s he noticed Tom's sad expression and she suddenly remembered.

"Please, forgive me. That was very thoughtless of me," She said.

"You need not apologize. You should be grateful to have him," Tom said, smiling.

His eyes lingered on hers for a moment before turning back to Caleb. He touched his tiny hand and the infant boy grabbed a hold of his finger and squeezed.

A broad smile instantly came across Tom's face, and his eyes lit with delight.

Thandi smiled too as she watched him. She could tell that he was genuinely smitten by her son.

After a moment, he sighed heavily and gently placed Caleb in her arms.

He met her gaze, and she knew what that meant, It was time for him to go.

He left, promising to visit again soon.

The entire ride back home, Tom thought of Caleb. Pictures of his tiny face flashed over and over in his mind. He thought of how he felt when he held him, of how he still felt now.

He had felt such a strong connection. He had felt the same connection when he held Nathaniel in his arms. He closed his eyes as if closing out the thought.

What was he doing? Caleb was Victor's son. He had to put his suspicions to rest. Besides, there was an explanation as to why Thandi had delivered early. Perhaps he was just grieving. Perhaps deep down he had just wanted Caleb to be his son. Loosing Nathaniel had been hard; and still was.

***

And, so, life went on, relatively pleasantly, until a year later when Victor suddenly fell ill. Thandi was taken by surprise one evening when, out of nowhere, he suddenly doubled over and collapsed in pain. It was then that she learned about his illness.

So much had made sense to her now; Gordan's frequent visits and their secret conversations, Victor's persistent cough and the strange drink that he drank religiously.

She felt guilty for the horrible way she'd treated him. Although their relationship had improved enormously since Caleb's birth, she still felt guilty about how she had treated him before.

He had deserved so much more from her. More than she could bring herself to give. Now, she found herself wishing that she could go back in time and do things over.

If she could, she would do things so much differently. But then, there had been many good times, also; especially after Caleb was born. The boy had brought Victor so much joy. He had brought them closer than Thandi had ever imagined possible.

Somewhere, over time, she had come to love Victor. Truly love him. Until now, she hadn't realized just how much.

For weeks, he lay in bed moaning from the pain. Gordan and several other doctors administered different treatments and medicines, but still, his condition did not improve. His health had declined drastically; so much so that Gordan and the other doctors said his case was hopeless, and that she should prepare herself for the worse.

On August 15th, the worst happened. Victor passed away quietly in his sleep.

Thandi was grateful to have the chance to say goodbye. That morning, she had told him just how much she loved him, and that she would always. Even in his grievous state, the words had brought a smile to his lips.

That night, he gave her an envelope. Inside the envelope were her freedom papers.

As she held them in her hands, more tears welled in her eyes. Somehow, now, the freedom felt bittersweet. She no longer cared about her freedom. In that moment, she only wanted him back. Him, and nothing more. Her only solace was knowing that he knew she loved him.

He had told her that he knew, that he had finally felt it in his heart and that he was dying a happy man. After he was gone, she cried and cried for days. Her only comfort in her bereavement was Caleb.

After the funeral, she was approached by Victor's attorney, George Peterson. He asked if she could please meet with him at his office in town on that upcoming Monday at three o'clock for the reading of Victor's will.

On that day, she saw Tom and several other faces from the funeral. But one face in particular stood out to her, the face of Daniel Stafford. He sat up front and center with a proud look plastered on his face and frowned instantly when he saw her.

"What, is this?" He asked, flailing a hand in the air. He looked to Peterson and the two other men that stood on opposite sides of him.

"She's in the will," Peterson said to him. "Please, Miss Boran, have a seat," He said, gesturing to the open chair next to Daniel's.

Thandi moved the chair over several inches, then sat down.

"You've got to be kidding me," Daniel laughed.

"Well, it seems that everyone is in attendance. We will now start the reading of the will," Peterson said, ignoring him.

A dead silence filled the room. Everyone sat quiet and very alert.

Thandi could feel Daniel's eyes on her, but she kept her gaze straight ahead. Her nerves were on edge, but she refused to let it show. *If ever she had to be strong, now was the time*, she thought. Now that Victor was gone, she had to stay strong for Caleb.

"Let me first begin by saying that we thank you all for being here," Peterson started. "I'm sure some of you may be wondering who these two other gentlemen are," He said, gesturing a hand to his left and right. "This here is Attorney Carl Briggers, and this is Attorney Richard Jameson. Both of these gentlemen also have last will and testaments from Victor. They shall each read them separately after I've concluded the first."

A wave of whispers filled the room then settled to quiet again

"Known by all men by their presence, that I, Victor Xavier Richmond, of the county of Bulford and state of South Carolina, being of sound mind and full age, do make, publish, and hereby declare this to be my last will and testament in the manner following: first, I nominate and appoint Thomas R. Lexington as executor of my estate." Stafford straightened up in his chair.

"I hereby give and bequeath to him, Thomas R. Lexington, my estate, all real property, and land, other than the one hundred and twenty-four acres known as Hollis Creek. I also bequeath to him, Thomas R. Lexington, all debts owing to me with relation to my business, land, real property, and interest holdings. I also bequeath to him, Thomas R. Lexington, all my shares in the Lexington Mill Company."

Daniel stood up from his chair and Peterson paused momentarily looking up at Daniel's angry face, then lowered his eyes to the document again. Thandi glanced at Tom and saw his shocked expression.

"And to Thandi Boran, a female slave, I give and bequeath to her, again, her freedom. I also bequeath to her, Thandi Boran, two-point-one million dollars..." The room instantly went into an uproar.

"And all my personal belongings!" Peterson read on in an elevated voice.

"This is outrageous!" Daniel yelled. He turned to Tom and met his gaze. Turning to Thandi he said, "You won't see those shares." He said. "And no court's going to give a nigger that kind of money!" He finished.

"There's three wills," Peterson said.

Stafford turned his attention to him again, his face red hot with anger.

"All three are the same. And all three are iron clad."

Stafford stood, fuming. He turned to Tom again and saw a smug smile on his face.

"You're an attorney, Daniel, aren't you?" Tom asked.

Stafford stormed out of the room, and Peterson continued on reading the will. In the end, Victor left Thandi the creek, and Caleb a large sum of money that would be available to him upon his twenty-fifth birthday or before, if he should marry. Certain items and monetary amounts were given to others in the room. Thandi sat stunned, her heart and mind racing. She could hardly believe what she'd heard. After all three wills were read, Peterson handed Tom a sealed envelope, then concluded the meeting. Tom turned the envelope over in his hands and tore it open. As he read the letter's contents, tears formed in his eyes.

"Are you okay, Tom?" Thandi asked, concerned.

Tom looked up at her, tears falling from his eyes. "I've never been better," He said, handing her the letter.

Thandi lowered her eyes to the paper and read…

Dear Tom:

I suppose you and many others are baffled by my last will and testament. You must be asking yourself why it is I left so much to you. The answer is simple. I know that you love Thandi. Because you love her, I know that I can trust you to see after her and Caleb once I'm gone. I leave you my fortune to ensure their happiness. Also, there is something that you should know. Although it is my belief that you already suspect the truth, Caleb is your son.

I knew it from the very first moment I laid eyes on him. However, I wanted him and Thandi so much, that it didn't matter. The two of them have brought so much happiness into my life. Only once before have I been so truly happy. Tom, it is my sincere hope that you will somehow relieve yourself of your present situation, so that you too can find the happiness you deserve. I wish you well, Tom. Please take care of yourself and your family.

Sincerely,
Victor

When she finished reading, Thandi looked up to Tom with tears running down her cheeks.

"There is much that we must discuss," Tom said.

"Yes… yes I suppose there is," Thandi said, smiling.

Epilogue

Two years later, Tom was amicably divorced and he and Thandi were expecting their second child. He had told Thandi his secret, and much to his surprise, she had not cared that they were siblings. Half-siblings, that is.

Besides, they had already had Caleb and the two were very much in love. And though life had been good for them, it had also come with its challenges, such as Tom's endless warring with Stafford in court.

Stafford had challenged the three wills and lost; but he promised Tom that he wasn't done fighting. He had sworn that he would fight him all the way up to the Supreme Court, if necessary. With three wills backing him, and three very competent, knowledgeable attorneys, Tom was not concerned.

The Old Newport Mill was up and running, and business was booming. For the first time in his life, Tom felt completely happy. Never would he have imagined that his life would take such a strange but wonderful turn.

But, even more wonderful was the day Thandi found Victor's mother. She was in town shopping with Corin and Henry when she saw her at the market. At first, she wasn't sure if the woman was in fact Lily. The woman was older, and although age had altered her appearance, she still resembled the young girl in the photo.

"Excuse me, Miss," Thandi said, walking up to her.

The woman turned around and met Thandi's gaze.

"Please, forgive my intrusion, but would your name happen to be Lily?" Thandi, asked.

"Yes, Ma'am," the woman replied curiously.

Thandi smiled. "Are you familiar with a family by the name of Richmond?" She asked.

Lily's face paled as if she had seen a ghost.

"Yes...yes, I am Ma'am," She stammered.

Thandi lit up inside. *I've found her! I found Victor's long lost mother!* She thought.

"Forgive my manners," Thandi said as she properly introduced herself, and asked the woman if they could talk.

244

With her Missus' permission, Lily went with her for a short stroll. After their talk, Thandi returned home and told Tom all about Lily.

Days later, unbeknownst to her, Tom set out to find her. With the name of her owner, it took little effort. After hearing Tom's offer, the owner was more than happy to part with his aging slave. And so, Lily became a part of their growing family and life went on happily. At least, for some time.

The End

ABOUT THE AUTHOR

Born in Columbus, Ga. and raised in Detroit Michigan, Angel Strong age 42, is an event planner by day and avid reader and writer by night. Unlike most girls who kept diaries in their youth, Angel wrote her thoughts into poems, lyrics, and short stories early on as an outlet to escape reality.

Encouraged by her ninth grade English teacher, at age fourteen Angel entered and won her first poetry contest, and at age sixteen she won a second place literary award in a short story competition.

Angel's passion for writing remained through adulthood and has resulted in several non-published works, sold lyrics, and the recently published historical romance novel, Thandi's Love.

Although she has spent her whole life writing, Thandi's Love is Angel's first published novel, and what she herself proclaims to be her 'Greatest work thus far'.

Angel currently resides in Michigan with her beloved six children, and their naughty bunny Luna-Belle.

AUTHORS NOTE

Dear reader,

I appreciate your interest and sincerely hope that you've enjoyed this story. Please take a few minutes to stop by www.amazon.com and let me know what you think of Thandi's Love. Your feedback and reviews would be greatly appreciated.

Sincerely,

Angel Strong